Legacy

12/2/16

Dear Claire,
 I'm so glad that you and Hannah have become such good friends. You are welcome in Lafayette anytime. Happy Reading

Stephanie

Legacy

Stephanie Fournet

© Copyright Stephanie Fournet 2015

ALL RIGHTS RESERVED. This book contains material protected under International and Federal Copyright Laws and Treaties. Any unauthorized reprint or use of this material is prohibited. No part of this book may be reproduced or transmitted in any form or by any means, electronic or mechanical, including photocopying, recording, or by any information storage and retrieval system without express written permission from the author. The characters (except where permitted) and events portrayed in this book are fictitious. Any similarity to real persons, living or dead, is coincidental and not intended by the author.

ISBN: 1503223396
ISBN 13: 9781503223394
Library of Congress Control Number: 2014921778
CreateSpace Independent Publishing Platform
North Charleston South Carolina

For John and Hannah
You both inspire me anew every day.

Table of Contents

Chapter 1	3
Chapter 2	10
Chapter 3	18
Chapter 4	33
Chapter 5	45
Chapter 6	53
Chapter 7	57
Chapter 8	63
Chapter 9	67
Chapter 10	73
Chapter 11	79
Chapter 12	85
Chapter 13	95
Chapter 14	103
Chapter 15	110
Chapter 16	119
Chapter 17	126
Chapter 18	131
Chapter 19	147
Chapter 20	159
Chapter 21	165
Chapter 22	175
Chapter 23	182
Chapter 24	190
Chapter 25	200
Chapter 26	209

Chapter 27	221
Chapter 28	233
Chapter 29	240
Chapter 30	246
Chapter 31	258
Chapter 32	264
Chapter 33	272
Chapter 34	280
Chapter 35	289
Epilogue	295
Acknowledgments	301
About the Author	303

February

Chapter 1

Corinne Granger felt about 100 years old.

It didn't matter that she had only been alive for two and a half decades; the last two and a half months had made her an old woman.

She taped up the last box of Michael's clothes—the ones she could bear to part with—and carried it out to the front porch. Mr. Roush, Michael's father, would pick them up in an hour and take them to Goodwill. He and Mrs. Roush had offered to help her pack up everything, but Corinne had refused. She really didn't want anyone inside the house. Before this morning, she hadn't gotten out of her pajamas in two days, and the two-bedroom rent house that she and Michael had shared for the last year and a half was a wasteland of unwashed dishes and empty take-out boxes.

Of course, the only reason they *were* empty and not yet attracting vermin was because of Buck. Michael's three-year-old black lab saw to it no morsel of pizza or drop of soy sauce remained on Corinne's dishes or delivery containers.

Buck followed her out to the front porch and sniffed the stack of boxes. He gave a short whine, and Corinne reached down automatically and caressed his left ear, rubbing the warm flap between her thumb and fingers. It was a gesture Michael used to do, and now she did it countless times a day—almost without noticing.

Corinne looked at the dog's soft, glossy head and allowed herself a sad smile. Without him, she might not even get out of bed on some days, but Buck—at the very least—had to be fed, and he had to be let out. The lab often stood expectantly by the coat rack near the front door where Michael kept his leash, but Corinne hadn't walked him since the last time Michael asked her to—three days before he died. And that was eight weeks ago.

The memory of Michael in the hospital bed flashed before her mind, and she closed her eyes and scrubbed them with her knuckles until she saw stars behind her lids.

"It's cold," she told Buck. "Let's go back inside."

He followed her in, as she knew he would, staying right at her hip. She closed the door behind them, looked around the small living room, and sighed. The place was a disaster. A disgusting disaster.

Perhaps she could pick up the trash. She bent down and collected a pizza box, a China One bag, and some soiled napkins. Corinne's back and hamstrings protested with the ache that had become part of her body's essence. She carried these items to the kitchen where she faced an overflowing trash can that smelled faintly sour. When had she last emptied it?

Her shoulders slumped at the prospect. That would have to wait. She waded back to the living room, found the remote in the couch cushions, and flopped down. Buck scooted in between her and the coffee table and leaned against her legs as she turned on the TV.

The DVR was full of shows she and Michael watched together. *Elementary. Agents of Shield. The Daily Show.* Corinne bit her lip against its trembling and found the Food Network instead.

Giada de Laurentiis was making pancetta and cinnamon waffles in her bright kitchen, explaining in her soothing way how the warmth of fresh ground cinnamon made all the difference. Corinne sunk back into the couch and gave her mind over. The morning had been emotionally and physically exhausting, and watching the innocuous mixing of batter was like a morphine drip.

In the moments when he wasn't awake, Corinne had been jealous of Michael's IV drugs. Why had no one thought to give her some? Was there any worse pain than witnessing the love of your life die a slow and agonizing death? One that was so senseless and unfair?

As Corinne watched Giada pour her velvety batter into the waffle iron, she thought about how the anger had energized her before the end. Her anger had been her strength, making her ready to fight Michael back to health after the accident, ready to drag him out of hell. To push him through months of physical therapy. To help him walk again. To do whatever it took.

She never got the chance.

And then—*after*—the anger that had fueled her converted into a soul-crushing grief so violent and all-consuming, Corinne believed it would have to bring him back. Of course, it didn't. It simply took her heart with him. And now, she was hollowed out. Shucked clean of her will, of her energy.

Corinne's eyelids felt heavy as Giada drizzled melted butter onto her golden brown waffles. It was easy to fall asleep. She never stayed asleep for long now, but the feeling of fatigue never left her, so she dozed off all the time.

And sometimes, Michael would be there...

She was in their bed, aware of the morning sun on her face and Michael kissing her ear.

"I'm going to work. I'll see you tonight, love," he whispered.

"Mmmmm. Why do you have to leave so early?" she muttered, refusing to open her eyes.

Michael laughed quietly, tickling her ear, and brushed his lips against her temple.

"Because I'm not the artist in this operation. Real job and all."

"Real jobs are stupid," she said, reaching for him.

"Yes, terribly silly," he said, letting her tug him into her arms. His clean, pressed shirt was cool against her neck, and he smelled like pine needles and cocoa. "You're so beautiful."

"Be late today," she tempted.

"Can't. Meeting." He pulled away, but gently, and tucked the covers around her again. "Bye, love."

The sound of the door rattling stirred her, but in the Neverland of her dream it was only Michael leaving for work.

But Michael's gone, she reminded herself.

And Corinne opened her eyes. It was always like this. An assault of truth waiting for her each time she awoke. If she could keep sleeping, would she be able to stay with him?

The sound repeated itself, and this time Corinne heard it for what it was: knocking. Michael's dad.

Shit.

Buck was already prancing by the door and whimpering with excitement. She pulled herself up from the couch and tried to comb her fingers through her dark hair as she made her way to the door. Her hair felt oily, and with her hands up at her head, she could smell the tang of her armpits.

"Damn you, Michael," she muttered for the hundredth time and unbolted the door.

Corinne tried to paste on a semblance of a smile as she swung the door open, but the smile caved in when her chin trembled. When she looked into Mr. Roush's sad eyes, she saw Michael's, and Corinne had to grip the doorjamb before her knees could give out.

It wasn't until she forced herself to look away that she saw that Wes Clarkson, Michael's best friend, stood on her porch as well.

"Hi…" she croaked past the lump in her throat. Both men took her in, and Corinne was keenly aware that she looked as though she could have stepped from a horror show. Mr. Roush's face registered pity. Corinne thought Wes seemed faintly grossed out.

"Hi, Corinne," Mr. Roush offered, patting her elbow by way of greeting. Wes said nothing.

"Is this all of it?" Michael's father asked, gesturing to the stack of boxes by the door. Corinne nodded, not daring to speak if it could be helped.

"Is there anything else you'd like us to take right now?" His voice softened, making him sound even more like Michael. It felt like a longsword had pierced her in the center of her chest and anchored her to the floor.

"No, Mr. Roush," she whispered, hoping that if they left, she wouldn't have an audience to watch her collapse.

"Please, Corinne,…it's Dan," he reminded her, gently.

"Dan…Right…No, I'm good," she lied.

"There's something else," Wes spoke up, stepping forward. "If you don't mind…"

Wes picked up the first box in his stupid, hairless Hulk arms, and Corinne remembered Michael frowning the first time she'd called his friend "Maximum Density."

"What?" she asked, feeling a little irritated that he had come along.

"I was wondering if it would be okay if I took his bike," Wes said, eyeing her evenly. For a second, Corinne hated him. He didn't look destroyed. He didn't even look hobbled like Michael's father. He looked like he always looked—like a meathead. Glossy faux hawk, such a dark brown it was almost black, gray Under Armor t-shirt clinging to his marbled torso, ever-present black gym shorts. In February.

"What's the matter? Yours isn't fast enough?" She spoke softly, trying to make it sound like a joke, but his brown eyes hardened, and Corinne suddenly remembered him weeping at the funeral. She shook her head and took a breath to apologize.

"Actually, it's not for me," he answered, raising a brow at her. "There's a tri guy I know who teaches high school history. His bike is a piece of crap, and I figured Michael would want someone to use his Pinarello, especially—you know—a teacher who'd never be able to afford one."

Corinne knew she deserved the punch in the stomach that seemed to come with his words. Of course, Michael would want that—something good to come from his death. He might even have chosen to donate the bike to this history teacher while he was still alive.

Corinne nodded.

"It's in the spare room. I can get it if you load these," she said, pointing to the boxes. She turned back inside, letting Buck out onto the porch and listening to the men greet the dog as she walked away.

She stopped in the doorway of the spare room and flicked on the overhead light. Corinne hadn't been in the space since Michael's office sent someone to collect his laptop more than a month ago. The room held a queen-sized bed for the rare times they'd had overnight guests, but it was also where Michael had kept his desk, his bike, and a weight bench.

The black and red Pinarello Dogma 2 stood in its stand, Michael's matching helmet on a shelf above, along with finisher's medals from the MS150, the Rouge Roubaix, and La Vuelta.

Corinne stared at the bike and considered the irony. She'd always been so afraid of Michael wiping out in a race and breaking his neck or being hit by a car on a training ride. She'd never thought to worry about a head-on collision with a drunk driver at 9 p.m. on a Thursday.

She crossed the room and picked up his helmet and was only vaguely surprised when she saw tears splash onto it. Memories erupted in her mind. The time they had camped at Lake Lincoln State Park so Michael could ride in the Mississippi Gran Prix. They'd sat by the fire with the other racers from Lafayette, but instead of trading stories about the road race, Michael had whispered the names of the stars in her ear. He later proved to her that sleeping naked in their two-person bag really was warmer than sleeping with clothes.

He had never tried to hide how much he loved her. He'd told her first—just weeks after they'd been together—and he didn't rush her to say it back; Michael had already figured out that declarations of any kind did not come naturally to her. But he had opened her. He had filled her. He had loved her more purely, more completely than anyone else. And she would never know that again.

She cradled the helmet to her chest and shook with sobs. Corinne had learned in the last two months that she might be able to keep from crying now and then, but once the dam broke, she was lost. There was no stopping it until she'd wrung herself out. Weeping was a full-body endeavor, a cardio workout that doubled her over and took everything.

Which is why she didn't hear the front door or the steps in the hallway.

"Aw, crap," Wes muttered behind her.

Corinne wheeled around to face him, shock and shame checking her sobs. She slashed a sleeve across her eyes and under her nose, instantly outraged at his intrusion.

"What are you doing?" She flung the words at him, wanting to launch the bike helmet at him instead.

Wes threw his hands up with exaggerated innocence. A look of caution in his eyes replaced something else. Was it...*regret?*

"I just came in to see if you needed help," he said, eyeing the bike. "I...didn't mean to....Are you alright?"

Corinne felt her eyes bug before she scowled.

"Uh,...*No?!?* Do I look alright?"

Wes folded his arms across his chest and set his jaw. The muscles in his face signaled his teeth clenching.

"Actually, you look like shit," he said, blankly.

Corinne startled at the stinging words. Not the truth in them—she knew she must have looked like shit—but the fact that someone would say them to her. Didn't she deserve to fall apart? What happened to her should be a free pass to be left alone without ridicule, without judgment.

"Well, we all know how important appearances are to you, Mr. Personal Trainer," she spat. "I wouldn't want to offend your aesthetic sensibility anymore, so, by all means, get the fucking bike and let yourself out."

She tore past him, but not before his shoulders sagged and a frown crimped his brow.

"Corinne, wait—"

"Always a pleasure, Wes," she said, stepping into her bedroom and slamming the door behind her. Corinne locked it for good measure, tossed the helmet to the floor, and flopped face down on the bed. She expected another onslaught of tears, but her anger at Michael's best friend seemed to keep them at bay.

"He's such an asshole, Michael," she spoke into her pillow. Not for the first time. Just the first time he couldn't contradict her.

She could hear Wes messing with the bike, and she hoped that he and Mr. Roush would simply go without seeking her out. Surely, they would put Buck back inside and just leave her in peace.

She curled onto her side, listening. The sound of clicking gears crept under the door, and it was so easy for her to imagine Michael at home, getting ready to go out for a ride.

The house had grown so quiet without him.

Corinne closed her eyes and let herself pretend just for a moment. Sleep would come again, and perhaps her dreams would be merciful.

Chapter 2

Corinne's bedroom door slammed, leaving Wes standing there like a dick.

He had fucked up this little mission about as much as he possibly could, and he stared at his best friend's bike, unsure what to do next.

Wes touched the black grips on the bike's handlebars, feeling the worn places where Michael's hands had left their mark.

"I'm letting you down, man," he murmured, frowning.

Given the options, leaving the bike wouldn't help anyone, so Wes lifted the feather-light Pinarello out of the stand and guided it from the room. He glanced at Corinne's door as he crept down the hall, grateful that he couldn't hear the telltale rush of sobs that had met him earlier.

When Mr. Dan had told him about his plans to collect Michael's clothes, Wes had thought it would be the right time to ask about the bike. Considering how much Corinne had bitched about Michael's racing, he figured she'd be okay with him taking it.

But seeing her clutching Michael's red and white helmet and crying made Wes feel like an asshole.

He walked the bike through the living room and let his eyes take in the sight. It was pretty obvious that Corinne was in bad shape. Guilt, thick and mealy in his gut, sickened him.

Outside, Mr. Dan had loaded the last of the boxes into the back of Mrs. Betsie's station wagon, and Wes wheeled the bike to his truck parked along side it.

"Need a hand?" Mr. Dan offered, eyeing the bike with sadness.

"No, sir. I've got it," he said, securing it on the mount behind his tailgate.

Mr. Dan rested his arms on the bed of the truck and watched.

"It's good to see you, Wes. You should come by the house," he said, not meeting the younger man's eyes. "Betsie would appreciate it."

"How is Mrs. Betsie?" Wes asked, wincing as another measure of guilt filled his stomach. Still, Michael hadn't asked him to look after his parents; he'd asked him to look after his girl.

Mr. Dan shrugged.

"How are any of us? She's managing, I guess," he said, clearing his throat. "Claire and the kids come by a lot. That helps."

Wes watched him struggle, but no words came to his aid to help his friend's father.

"We've invited Corinne to come for dinner a few times," Mr. Dan continued, glancing back at the house. "I guess she's not up for it."

That's an understatement, Wes thought.

"Still, we want you to know that both of you are welcome at the house. Anytime." Mr. Dan looked him in the eye then. "The two of you loved him so. You're just as much his family as we are. It doesn't make much sense for each of us to miss him alone."

Wes nodded, and both men went through the pantomime of looking at their shuffling feet, swallowing hard, and sniffing.

When he could, Wes spoke first.

"I think I'm going to hang here for a while," he said, nodding towards the house. "It looks like Corinne could use some help in there."

Mr. Dan nodded and smiled the sad smile he'd given out since they'd arrived.

"Good. I'm glad to hear that...Thank you."

He offered his hand to Wes, and they shook firmly.

"Tell Mrs. Betsie I said hello, and that I won't be a stranger," Wes said, resolving then to make it the truth. Spending an hour or two at Sunday dinner with the Roushes was a hell of a lot better than being with his own parents, and he owed Michael's family more than just an occasional Sunday dinner. He didn't want to count the number of times he'd ducked out at Michael's house as a kid just to get away from the battlefield of his own.

Mr. Dan got into his car, and Wes called Buck to him. The dog listened without hesitation, as usual, and it made Wes smile. Michael had done an awesome job training that dog. Wes remembered the time when Buck was just a few months old, and Michael had taught him to sit still while he asked Wes to place a treat on Buck's nose. The pup had been hyper-focused on that dog biscuit, but he didn't so much as blink until Michael gave him the word to flip the treat into his mouth.

"Come on, Buck. Let's go find you a treat."

Wes opened the door slowly and let Buck bound in. Corinne was not in the living room, so he stepped inside and quietly shut the door behind him. A glance in the hall told him that she was still in her bedroom, so he headed to the rear of the house toward the kitchen.

"Jesus," he hissed upon taking it in. Dirty dishes filled the sink, and the trash can overflowed in the corner. Buck was already waiting for him by the pantry, wagging, fully expecting the treat he'd been promised. Wes found a near-empty box of Milk Bones, and Buck scrambled into a sit, head high, ready for his snack.

Wes reached into the box and came up with the second to last biscuit.

"Wait for it," he said, remembering Michael's commands. Buck's frame seemed to stiffen as he stared at the treat, but it was as though his whole body vibrated with barely-contained energy.

Wes slowly lowered the treat until it met the dog's nose, and he balanced it there before removing his hand.

And then he waited. Just as Michael had.

"Take it!" The words had scarcely left his lips before Buck flipped up the treat and caught it in canine triumph.

"Good boy," Wes praised, petting Buck's head. "Good boy."

Wes straightened up and surveyed the kitchen again. The trash had to be emptied before anything else could be cleaned up. He smashed down the overflowing pile until he could tie off the top of the bag and then carried the trash out the front door and to the bin. He'd be sure to take the garbage up to the street so Corinne wouldn't have to do it later.

Back inside, he put an empty bag in the trash can and set about picking up. Napkins, paper plates, newspapers, and take out containers lined the counters and showed up here and there on the floor of the kitchen and the living room. But everywhere—*everywhere*—Wes found wadded up tissues. They were in the couch cushions and on the coffee table. They were on the kitchen counters and the windowsill. There was even one on the microwave.

His guilt was quickly becoming a living thing within him, and he feared it would soon learn English and tell him off.

Wes tossed the last tissue into the garbage and went to the sink. He plugged the drain, squirted Dawn all over the pile of dishes in the basin, and turned on the hot water.

Michael had been unconscious for two days after the accident. The doctors had not really expected him to live through the first night, even after the surgery to stop the internal bleeding. But he had. And although Wes had gone to the hospital every day, they only had two conversations entirely alone, and in the last one, Michael told Wes he didn't think he'd make it, and he asked his last favor.

"But she hates me," Wes countered.

"Not really," Michael rasped, attempting to talk past the pneumonia that had developed from his broken ribs, punctured lung, and the immobility from the compound fractures in both legs.

Wes had to sit close to the bed even to hear him clearly. Michael looked gray and waxy, and when he'd told Wes that he needed to plan for the worst, Wes wanted to cover his ears. But the look in Michael's eyes made him listen.

"She does," Wes protested. "She thinks I'm a shallow man whore."

Even in gruesome pain and facing death, Michael remained Michael, and a half-smile claimed his face.

"And you aren't?" he teased. Wes rolled his eyes. Did sleeping with a few of his clients make him a man whore? Only one of them was married.

"She thinks I'm selfish."

"Case in point," Michael said, trying to draw a long breath and wincing. "This isn't about you."

"She's never glad to see me," he pointed out. A look of disappointment crossed Michael's eyes, and Wes backtracked, grasping for things to say. "I mean...she's awesome, Mike, don't get me wrong. Corinne's smart...and feisty...and talented, and I can see that you're crazy about her, and all, but you've got to stick around because there's nothing Corinne's ever going to want from me."

"I *want* to stick around," Michael said, and with those words, Wes finally caught the desperate sadness his best friend felt about the prospect of losing his own life. "But if I can't...I need to know that you will look after her."

"Okay," Wes said, awestruck. "I promise."

"She hasn't had it easy," Michael confided. "And it's not like she has tons of friends."

What a surprise.

"I get it. Just get better so you can look after her yourself."

But Michael hadn't gotten better. Blunt abdominal trauma led to infection. Infection led to sepsis, and his internal organs began shutting down. Michael died four days after Wes agreed to watch out for Corinne.

And he'd done a crap job of it.

Still, it wasn't like she'd made it easy. At the funeral, they'd sat next to each other behind Michael's family—his parents, his sister Claire, and her husband Elton. Corinne had worn this little black hat with a veil as though she were above having people see her cry.

But she did cry. Quietly. Constantly. She'd held onto her sister Morgan at the cemetery, and when they'd lowered Michael's casket into the ground, Corinne's legs sort of buckled, and Wes reached over and grabbed her by the elbow to keep her up.

Through the veil, she'd cut him a murderous glare and yanked her arm from his grip. Wes had stepped back like he'd been burned and looked at Morgan in wide-eyed confusion. Corinne's sister just shook her head, resigned to Corinne's weirdness.

Bitchiness, Wes amended the memory in his mind as he rinsed the last glass.

He dried and put away all the dishes and wiped down the counters. He looked around the kitchen, wondering if Corinne had any food on hand. The pantry revealed a few cans of tuna, three packages of Top Ramen, and a can of green beans. The plastic container that held Buck's Iams looked like it would cover about three more days.

The fridge was grim.

A rust colored head of lettuce in a Ziplock bag sat next to a container of moldy and blackened finger sandwiches that Wes was pretty sure came from the funeral. The one carton of milk in the fridge was dated late December.

Wes dumped everything into the trash, leaving only condiments and Michael's Abita Ambers.

"I could sure use a drink with you, man," Wes mumbled as he headed outside with a second bag of trash.

Buck followed him this time and found a tennis ball in the yard as they brought the trash up to the street.

"Wanna fetch?"

Buck answered by jumping backwards in the direction of the back yard with the ball in his mouth.

"Let's go."

As they made their way to the gate, Buck bounded back and forth from the closed gate to Wes about four times, seeming to try to show him the way to the ball-throwing wonderland and simultaneously asking Wes why he was taking so long to get there. He laughed at the dogs antics and pulled the gate closed behind them.

Buck immediately ran for the steps off the back porch and dropped the ball. Wes could almost see Michael sitting there on the top step, drinking a beer after a ride.

"Oh, man," Wes muttered, bracing for the memories.

A 60-mile ride up past Grand Coteau. Nearly four hours on the bike. A Saturday afternoon in October. He and Michael were on their second beer, throwing the ball for Buck, when Corinne came out of her sunroom— the little space behind the kitchen that she'd converted to a studio—arms splattered with paint. She stepped onto the porch, smiling, telling Michael to light the pit for burgers and surprising Wes with an invitation to stay.

"I guess she wasn't always terrifying," Wes told the dog. Buck tilted his black head at Wes in seeming confusion before nudging the tennis ball closer to Wes's feet.

He threw the ball until Buck's pink tongue nearly stretched down to the dog's elbows, and then him pushed himself off the steps.

"C'mon. Let's go make sure you have some water in the kitchen."

Out of habit, Wes climbed the porch and headed to the sunroom door, but it surprised him when he found it unlocked. It really shouldn't have been unlocked. Michael's—Corinne's house was in the Saint Streets, at the end of St. Joseph near the old Lourdes Hospital. It wasn't a *bad* neighborhood, really—full of UL students and faculty—but it was only about a 15-minute walk across University Avenue to one of Lafayette's poorest and roughest neighborhoods. And there was always plenty of foot traffic.

She knows better, Wes thought, pushing his way into the sunroom.

"Holy shit."

At first, Wes thought someone had come in through the unlocked door and trashed the place. Tubes of paint, some sealed and some ruptured, covered the floor. Brushes of all sizes had been flung around the room. One of the larger easels lay sprawled on the floor, its canvas facedown on the ground beside it.

Buck cautiously stepped inside, sniffing the burst paint tubes that had dried in large globs, and Wes surveyed the scene for a moment. Other than the mess on the floor, the room looked as he remembered, canvases of finished pieces, mostly portraits, hung from one wall. Fresh canvases were stacked against the bench seats that lined the windows, and paintings that should have been ready to deliver to galleries or clients stood shoulder to shoulder by the door that led to the kitchen. But these—and all of the others—sat under a fine layer of dust.

Ignoring the voice that told him to leave it, Wes bent down and turned over the canvas that lay on the floor.

Corinne's style gravitated toward vivid colors, oil paintings larger than life in a palette that the natural world could never match. A midnight sky of purple, orange, green, and gold that could not be mistaken for anything other than a midnight sky. An oak tree with leaves of blues, greens, and yellows, trunks in brown, peach, and red.

But her portraits were her most striking works. Wes had seen dozens in the same style. Faces that took up the entire canvas with colors that seemed to capture the soul. Michael had told him that Corinne was earning a reputation for these and had even had some portraits commissioned.

Wes had feared for an instant that the face on the other side of the canvas would be Michael's, but it wasn't. He saw eyes flecked with black, gold, and turquoise, capturing the true hazel, and long brown hair lit with pink, azure, and yellow. A smile the color of lemons and cherries.

Corinne.

And she looked happier than he'd ever seen her.

But now it was marred by shoe prints, stray daubs of paint, and dirt from the floor. Wes stood up and tried to brush away the dirt and shoe marks. He didn't think much could be done about the paint mess, but if Corinne wanted to touch it up, he had no doubt that she could.

Thinking that he had time to try to set the studio back in order, Wes grabbed the overturned easel and was placing the ruined portrait on the stand when the kitchen door opened.

"Buck? Where are y—" Corinne's call caught when she saw him, and her wide eyes moved between him and the self-portrait in his hands.

"What the hell are you doing?!?"

"I...was just—"

"What are you still doing here?" Corinne screamed, taking a step toward him. And despite the fact that he towered over her by a solid ten inches, Wes stepped back. "Get the hell out of my house, you creep!"

"I'm just trying to help!" Wes yelled back, but he was already backing toward the door, eager to get away from the crazy.

"No one asked you!"

Wrong there, bitch!

But Wes wasn't about to argue with his best friend's psycho woman. He was out the back door and across the yard in about three seconds.

"What were you thinking, Mike?" he asked out loud.

But the only reply he got was the sound of the deadbolt sliding home and the clank of the chain locking behind it.

Chapter 3

Corinne stood staring at her smiling face, the one she had thrown to the ground and trod over the day Michael died.

He'd asked for it for Christmas, a self-portrait modeled on a picture he had taken on their trip to Austin only months before. He'd wanted it for his office, saying he'd be the only IT director in town with a Corinne Granger original.

She'd brought it to the hospital on Christmas Day, two days before he died. Michael had opened his eyes for a little while, and Corinne thought by the lift in their corners that he'd seen it, known what it meant.

Hours later, he'd awoken again to find her crying beside him.

"I'm sorry," he'd whispered, his last words to her.

Corinne turned her back to the portrait and left the sunroom. She hoped he *was* sorry because the smiling girl on the canvas had died with him.

She stepped into her clean kitchen and sighed. When she'd gotten up and couldn't find Buck, panic had pricked through her. She worried that perhaps Wes and Mr. Roush had left him outside in the front, and when she didn't see him there or on the street, she'd rushed to the back, hoping they'd put him in the yard. She hadn't even noticed the emptied trash or the clean sink.

What she least expected to find was Wes Clarkson holding the last painting she'd finished.

And, apparently, he had cleaned up her house. Or Mr. Roush had. Of course, if it had been Mr. Roush, why would Wes still be here? And wouldn't she have found Michael's dad instead?

Still, it was hard to believe Wes Clarkson doing *anything* that didn't gratify Wes Clarkson. The man had never done his *own* dishes when he ate at their house, much less anyone else's. Once, about a year ago, Corinne had gone into the spare room the day after Wes had crashed for the night after a bender with Michael—only to discover that he'd puked on her sheets and left it to stew all day.

The bastard had managed to take a shower before he left and use all the hot water, but wash the sheets? Not a chance.

Corinne fixed herself a bowl of ramen and carried it to the couch. Ina Garten was making Chicken with Wild Mushrooms in Napa Valley. And then Alton Brown made a lentil soup with cumin, coriander, and something called grains of paradise. Then Rachel Ray was about to make a 30-minute shepherd's pie when Buck gave a lone bark and trotted toward the door.

That was when Corinne heard a car door out front.

"God, no," Corinne pleaded, still curled up on the couch. One round of visitors had been quite enough for the day. Buck looked at her and back at the door, wagging. Clearly, he disagreed.

A knock sounded, and Buck's tail wagged even harder.

Maybe if I just sit still, they'll go away.

"Corinne?" Morgan called through the door. "Are you awake?"

Corinne contemplated feigning sleep and hoping her sister would give up and go home. It probably wouldn't take too long for her to slip into another nap anyway.

"Corinne? I'm coming in..."

To her surprise, she heard a key in the lock and only had an instant to wonder how Morgan had gotten her hands on it before the door opened. Her sister spotted Corinne on the couch and frowned.

"Were you asleep?" she asked, waddling in and closing the door behind her. Morgan placed a hand on her pregnant belly and waited for an answer.

"No."

Morgan raised a brow.

"Were you going to let me in?" she asked, irritation clear in her voice.

"I hadn't decided."

"Corinne! You were just going to leave me out there until I left? I'm six months pregnant!" Morgan complained. "I have to pee every five minutes. I'd never make it all the way back to Sugar Mill Pond."

I don't recall inviting you...

"Well, what are you doing here? And how is it that you have a copy of my key?"

Morgan looked uncomfortable and shook her head.

"I'll tell you in a minute. First, I need the bathroom." And she was gone.

"Fine," Corinne said to an empty room.

She pushed herself off the couch and picked up her soup bowl and spoon. In the kitchen she contemplated just setting the dishes in the sink, but since it was empty, she almost felt bad about undoing the work that Wes—or whoever—had done, so she turned on the hot water and scrubbed the dishes herself.

Morgan came in, heaving a sigh of relief.

"Thank God." She pulled out a chair from the dinette in the kitchen and sunk into it.

Corinne regarded her over her shoulder as she rinsed the spoon.

"How did you get the key?" she asked again.

Morgan dropped her eyes and pursed her lips.

"It's Michael's. You gave it to me to pick up his suit...remember?"

Corinne closed her eyes. That afternoon was a blur of hospital and funeral home and the living room at the Roush's. But she did remember now.

She took a deep, slow breath, wanting to move away from the memory, so she repeated her other question.

"And why are you here now?" she managed on the exhale.

Morgan was silent.

Corinne put the spoon with the bowl on the draining board and turned to face her sister.

"Don't get mad, okay?" Morgan pleaded, tucking her chin the way she did when she was nervous.

Corinne folded her arms across her chest and leaned back against the sink.

"Why would I get mad?"

Morgan rolled her eyes and pushed a honey-colored curl away from her face.

"Wes Clarkson messaged me on Facebook about an hour ago," she said, watching Corinne for a reaction. "He said you seemed a little... overwrought."

Corinne felt the sting of shame, but she threw her head back in mirthless laughter.

"*Overwrought* is not a word in Wes Clarkson's vocabulary. What did he really say?"

"Well, if you must know," Morgan said, giving an impatient shrug and digging her phone out of her purse. "He said... 'Thought you should know that your sister is a whack job. Just left her place. Total CF. I don't think she's showered in days.'"

It felt like a blow to her gut.

Actually, you look like shit.

Humiliation bowed her shoulders, leaving her unable to look at her sister. She never should have let him in. Hell, she *hadn't* let him in. She should have thrown him out as soon as he came in for the stupid bike.

"Corinne...?"

"He's such an asshole," she hissed. "He doesn't know what I'm going through."

Morgan was silent again. This time, Corinne's eyes shot up to hers in defiance.

"What? What are you not saying?"

"Nothing...Just that he lost his best friend, honey," Morgan stood up and made a move toward Corinne who held up her hand, insisting on distance.

Morgan sighed.

"All I'm saying is that he may not know *exactly* what you're going through, but he knows what it means to miss Michael."

"He doesn't know what *I'm* going through," Corinne stressed, rapping her fist against her chest, grateful for the anger that tightened her throat. "Neither do you."

"Fine. We don't know. But he's obviously worried about you, and, frankly, I am, too."

"Wes doesn't worry about *anyone* or *anything*," Corinne scoffed, choosing the easier target to attack.

"Let's forget about Wes," Morgan said, swiping her hand like she could brush him away. "Why don't you take a shower, and we'll go see Dad?"

Corinne blinked in shock.

"Dad?...Why?"

Morgan raised a self-congratulatory brow.

"Because he does know *exactly* what you're going through."

An hour later, Corinne had showered, dried her hair, and dressed in a pair of clean jeans and a sweater that Morgan had somehow found in her closet. The hot water and droning hair dryer had made her sleepy and ready for a nap again, but Morgan insisted on leaving, so Corinne found herself riding shotgun in her sister's Camry on their way to Emeritus, their father's retirement community.

Clement Granger had suffered two strokes before his 60th birthday. The first, six years ago, had left him with a slight limp on his right side and an almost undetectable slur. The second, three years after, had left him in a wheelchair at first, the paralysis claiming most of the function on his right side. For two years, he'd lived in the assisted living complex, but with continuous physical and speech therapy, he could use a walker now and had graduated to the "Senior Independent Living" section of the campus.

No one could argue that Emeritus wasn't the best facility in town, but Corinne still saw the place as a kind of end-of-life processing plant. Healthy old folks who didn't want to take care of their yards anymore—or whose kids didn't want to feel guilty about them cleaning out the gutters—got an apartment or patio home in Senior Independent Living where they could enjoy the exercise classes and bingo and still drive to the Grand to catch a movie. Inevitably, a fall or the slow and steady onset of Alzheimer's sent residents to Assisted Living, where they could count on being bathed and babysat. Next stop was Skilled Nursing with its catheter and colostomy care and Medicare-certified beds. Finally, there were the beautiful Hospice Rooms with fresh flower arrangements and never-ending morphine.

Corinne had once teased her father about how he'd bucked the system by moving back a level. His barely intelligible reply—her dad was still embarrassed by his speech—was that he'd always been a rebel.

"Have you been to see him lately?" Morgan asked as they pulled into the complex.

"No," Corinne responded, refusing to feel guilty for the filial lapse. She'd been too busy watching her life fall apart.

Morgan parked the car and turned toward her.

"When was the last time you left the house?" she asked, her brows coming together.

"I don't know!" Corinne snapped. In truth, she did know. She had gone to the store 10 days before because she was out of toilet paper and dog food, but she didn't think Morgan would be impressed with this accomplishment, so she kept it to herself.

The afternoon sun was waning as Morgan regarded her sister with a sad frown. Corinne couldn't take it, so she opened her car door.

"C'mon. We wouldn't want Dad to miss the 5 p.m. dinner gong," she said with sarcasm.

Corinne strode away from the car, leaving Morgan to struggle with her pregnant belly. As she rang her dad's doorbell, she realized it would be a race between the Venus of Willendorf and *Cocoon*, and she almost found herself laughing.

As it happened, Morgan won, making it to the door just before her father opened it, and this made Corinne sad somehow.

"Sorry we're late, Dad," Morgan said, crowding his walker to give him a kiss.

Late? Had he been expecting them? Corinne was beginning to feel as though she'd been played. First, Wes Clarkson's intrusion, now this?

"Hey, Corie," her father said. It didn't sound like *"Hey, Corie,"* of course. It might have been *"acorn"* or *"a gory"*, but Corinne knew what he meant.

"Hey, Dad," she said, stepping into the apartment and attempting to skirt his walker to take refuge in the living room.

Her father's good arm shot out and grabbed her by the elbow, and he pulled her to him with a strength she didn't realize he had. In an instant, she felt the warmth of his chest and the bracing of his arm around her as he pressed a kiss to the top of her head.

Without warning, tears pooled in her eyes and spilled over onto his shirt. She didn't want it. Didn't want to go down like this in front of them, but the softness of his roughness, the scrape of his stubble on her forehead, the scent of Irish Spring at his collar was so familiar that she felt about six years old again, and her defenses caved.

"I know...I know, my girl," he whispered as she came apart against him. For what seemed like hours, the only thing she heard was the squeak of her sobs and his steady breath.

Morgan had disappeared into the kitchen, and when Corinne could finally pull away and dry her eyes, she smelled coffee.

"I'll be right back. I need a minute," she whispered to her father, ducked into his bathroom, and closed the door behind her.

The tissues in his bathroom were cheap, thin and flimsy. In the last two months, Corinne had learned to appreciate the good stuff. Puffs Plus was her brand of choice. She could cry in it all day and not have a raw nose.

It was funny how grief changed one's priorities.

After going through about seven sub-par squares, Corinne faced herself in the mirror. The shower had been a good decision. If nothing else, her brown hair was full and shiny, falling past her shoulders in attractive ribbons. If one ignored the gray circles under her eyes, her blanched complexion, and the red rimmed, puffy eyelids, she'd almost look human.

Morgan said that her dad knew *exactly* how she felt, but Corinne had never thought of it that way—until her father's composure-shattering hug.

She'd only been three years old when it happened, an accident just as senseless, just as random as Michael's. Corinne and Morgan's mother Alice had slipped and hit her head in the bathtub, dying instantly.

While Corinne could remember the loss of her, a sore spot that pulsed with both fear and heartbreak when she probed it, memories of her mom were only flashes. Sitting in her lap on a windy fall day while nine-year-old Morgan turned cartwheels in the grass. The smell of fabric softener and chocolate chip cookies and lovely brown hair coiled in a bun. That was all. That and a lifetime of wishing for more.

Corinne didn't know if the love her parents had shared was as all-consuming as what she felt for Michael. But her father had never remarried, and he'd rarely dated while she was still at home. And—before the second stroke—he only spoke of their mother when she asked about her. Perhaps, like herself, Clement Granger knew he'd been given just one great love.

She stuffed her pockets with a few extra cheap tissues just in case and went back to the living room. Her father sat in his recliner while Morgan set down a tray at the coffee table. It was all very civilized and foreign, but Corinne was grateful to busy herself with the task of adding milk and sugar to a mug and stirring.

She was content with this preoccupation until she realized that both members of her family were watching her as if she were some kind of lab experiment. She froze, mid-stir.

"What?"

"Nothing," Morgan said, brightly, dipping her chin.

Her father took a sip from his cup.

"*What?*"

"We're worried about you." This was from her father, and he said it slowly and deliberately so that anyone could have understood him.

For the second time that day, Corinne felt about a hundred years old. The coffee cup seemed like a cinder block in her hands. She lowered it to her lap to keep from spilling. When this feeling hit her at home, she could just lie down on the couch or in her bed and fall asleep for a little while. And then she'd wake up and be able to fix herself something to eat or let Buck out or find something on television. Or cry.

The feeling—if it could name itself—was That-Which-Is-Too-Much-To-Bear. And it visited her day and night. Michael's absence seemed to be the perfect empty space for That-Which-Is-Too-Much-To-Bear to inhabit, and because it was too much to bear—by its very nature—Corinne was pulled down. Again and again.

At the moment, That-Which-Is-Too-Much-To-Bear greeted her in the form of her sister and her father. Corinne had survived 57 days without Michael in the world. The thought of surviving months, years, decades longer was too much to bear, so she didn't think that thought. The prospect of returning to her old life—attending art shows, meeting clients, painting portraits, and otherwise being productive was too much to bear, so she stayed at home—where she could at least survive and add one more day to the total of Days Survived Without Michael in the World.

And now, it seemed, Morgan and her father did not think that this survival—which took everything she had and then some—was good enough. This was That-Which-Is-Too-Much-To-Bear.

And even trying to explain all of this to them was too much. Corinne sucked in a long, slow breath.

"I'm doing the best that I can," she said, sounding exhausted even to her own ears.

Her father blinked, but Morgan eyed her skeptically.

"Are you trying, Corinne? You hardly leave the house. You sleep all the time. You don't bathe for days..."

Somewhere deep inside her a werewolf, an ogre, a leviathan of anger stirred in its slumber. When she spoke, it was through gritted teeth.

"I'm doing the best I can, goddamnit. This is me doing fucking amazing."

Morgan's eyes widened in alarm, and almost as quickly as it had marshaled, the anger dissipated, abandoning her. Because Michael was the only one. He was the only one who was never spooked by her anger. Her crankiness. Her moods. He was the only one who got her. Who could take her.

He could spar when she needed a partner, absorb when she needed a target, and hold tight when she needed an anchor. And from the start, he could read her in an instant and know which one she sought. He could psyche her up when she needed to be tough, like the time the manager at the Gallery Cologne tried to cheat her out of $300. He could take a licking—like the time she'd balled him out about loser friends who ruined bed sheets. He could close his arms around her while she wailed. Like the time she missed her period, spent a week worrying about what they would do, and then felt heartbroken when it finally came.

She had been loved by someone who truly fathomed and fit her. And now he was gone, and the loneliness that his absence created, the whole and utter loneliness, was That-Which-Is-Too-Much-To-Bear.

"Maybe you need to talk to somebody," Morgan whispered. Bravely, Corinne thought.

She gave a hollow laugh.

"There's nothing anyone could tell me that could make this less awful," she said, her voice shaking.

I won't cry now. I won't cry now. I won't cry now.

"Maybe you need to do the talking," Morgan said, softly.

Corinne glanced at her father and rolled her eyes.

"Yeah, 'cause we're all about that in this family."

He had the decency to look away, but Morgan put on her war face and went in for the kill.

"So, you're not painting. How are you going to keep paying your bills?"

She could have said it with less impatience, but she didn't, and Corinne felt as though she'd been kicked. Couldn't they see that she didn't have the capacity to deal with the business of living? All she could do was survive.

But once Morgan asked the question, Corinne had to acknowledge the problem. She really hadn't even thought about money since the accident. Most of her bills were being paid through automatic draft, but that would only last so long.

Michael had worked for Hawthorne Tools in IT for four years, and the founding president had personally ensured that Michael's salary would be paid through mid-January, when his official replacement would step in, but that date had come and gone more than a month ago. And while Michael and Corinne—especially Michael—had discussed marriage several times, they had never even thought about things like term life insurance or death benefits. The $25,000 policy that Michael had through work had only just covered his funeral expenses and medical co-pays.

They'd shared joint checking and savings accounts, but they'd travelled a lot, and they had believed that there were years ahead to build up a nest egg.

The money would run out in a few months.

Corinne ached to tip over and go to sleep right there on her father's couch. She figured that a heroine addiction would be pretty sweet right about now. If all she cared about was getting a fix, life would be so much simpler.

But drugs were definitely not her thing. She barely drank.

Maybe an Ambien prescription…

"If you need to, you could move in with me and Greg for a while," Morgan said, her voice going soft again, and Corinne realized that she had been silently staring at her coffee mug for a few long minutes.

"What?"

"We've talked about it. You could have the spare room upstairs until you're feeling more like yourself," Morgan said, smiling now. "It would actually be pretty nice to have an extra pair of hands when the baby comes."

Corinne blinked. Live with Morgan? And her brother-in-law? And her new niece or nephew? Would she ever have a moment's peace? Could she leave the house that she and Michael had shared?

"Of course, we couldn't take Buck," Morgan added, wide-eyed. "I mean the courtyard is way too small for him. And all that dog hair…"

"Hell, no." Corinne swore.

"But, Corinne—"

"Hell. No." She repeated, shaking her head with finality. "Buck and I stay together. In fact, we'll stay right where we are."

It was a relief to say it. A relief to know that there was something she wanted when nothing else mattered.

She chanced a look at her father, expecting him to urge her to be practical, and she was surprised to see the left side of his face turn up in a smile.

Morgan looked back and forth between them before crossing her arms over her belly.

"Well, how are you going to pay the rent?" she asked, clearly irritated again.

She didn't have an answer. She didn't even have the energy to contemplate an answer, but as far as Corinne was concerned, it didn't matter.

"I don't know," she said, heavily. "But I'll figure something out."

March

Chapter 4

"Is the saddle the right height?" Wes asked as Chad Case passed him on the Pinarello, taking the lead on Highway 89.

"It's perfect. This is the sweetest ride!" Chad called, gliding in front and grinning.

If it weren't for Case's green helmet, Wes could almost convince himself that he was drafting behind Michael again, and the weight that had been hanging around his neck for the last month seemed to lighten.

That's how long the Pinarello had been parked by the front door of his apartment, and every time he saw it—coming and going or just sitting in front of the TV with a beer after work—he could almost hear Michael's voice dogging him.

Look after her. Look after her. Look after her.

Maybe now that he'd finally been able to iron out a ride with Chad and put the bike in his hands, he'd get some peace.

The ride itself *was* peaceful. They had started out in Youngsville by Sugar Mill Pond, just outside of Lafayette, and they'd been on the road for more than an hour, riding into New Iberia on the lazy Sunday morning, passing Lake Peigneur. Traffic was minimal, and even though the late March air was chilly, Wes's body warmed with exertion, and he felt the rightness, the euphoria he chased every time he got on his bike.

As an athlete, he worshipped the holy trinity: the swim, the ride, the run. He'd finished his first Ironman in Panama City in November: 14 hours, 22 minutes and 16 seconds. His goal this year would be to break 14 hours, and the bike was definitely his strongest event.

In one regard, it demanded the most focus—if you took your eyes off the road, you were gambling big time—but given that, it also came the most naturally to him, and even with his eyes trained ahead, his mind could unreel.

It also gave him the most distance. From his parents. From his mistakes. From his grief.

He'd gone on more than a dozen long rides since Michael's death, and it was when he was on his bike that he felt like things really were ok. That Michael wasn't really gone so much as out of sight. It wasn't anything he'd dare say to anyone else, but on his bike, Wes could almost *feel* him. And it was comforting.

The feeling never lasted, of course.

He still found himself reaching for his phone to text Mike once or twice a day. Every time he saw a meme about leg day—Michael's *least* favorite day at the gym, Wes wanted to send it to him. Their all-time favorite had been the one with the guy from *Lord of the Rings*.

"One does not merely sit on the toilet after leg day."

Amen to that.

And there would be a fraction of a second when he'd feel laughter coming on as he thought of Michael's reaction to the latest joke—before reality set in, and he remembered.

It was lucky for him that in those moments he was usually at the gym. When his anger threatened to overboil, he would jump on the treadmill, or do 20 burpees, or bench press his max, or climb into the sparring ring with another trainer.

Wes couldn't count the number of times he wanted to find that living sack of shit—that third-strike-DUI fucking cocksucker and waste his ass. Just shred him. If it hadn't been for Mr. Dan intercepting him at the hospital after Michael flatlined, he might have done it.

The only thing he could tell himself now was that the fuck-hole who killed Michael was looking at 30 years for vehicular homicide, and going away to Angola would be a hell of a lot worse than the terminal beatdown Wes would dish out.

Wes shook off these thoughts as he and Chad crossed the Delcambre city limits and turned around on Highway 14 to head back the way they'd come. The next eight miles would be almost due north into a headwind, and as they angled back onto Highway 89, Wes and Chad downshifted and prepared to work.

With 40 miles done and just under two and a half hours on the bike, Chad and Wes pulled back into Sugar Mill Pond where they'd left their vehicles. They'd burned about 2,000 calories on the ride, and although Wes was starving, he didn't like to let himself dive face-first into a breakfast buffet—after a race, sure, but not a training ride. That would just lead to sleepiness, and, before he knew it, the day would be over. But he needed to eat *something*.

"Wanna grab a bite at Romacelli's?" he asked Chad after securing his Colnago to his truck's bike rack.

"Yeah, but it's on me. I can't thank you enough for hooking me up with that bike," Chad said, his eyes alight.

"You got it. Let's sit on the patio. I doubt they'd thank us for coming inside," Wes said, wiping his sweaty hands against his soaked shirt.

The hostess at Romacelli's seated them next to the lit fire bowl, and they sunk gladly into the plush red patio chairs.

Chad flipped through the menu and eyed Wes.

"So, what does the fitness guru order for lunch after a ride like that. The pesto chicken pizza's looking pretty good to me, but I have a feeling that's the wrong choice."

Wes huffed a laugh. Case was alright. He didn't let ego get in the way of learning. Chad was fairly new to cycling, but he'd been hooked from the start, and he was grateful for advice and constructive criticism. And he was genuine. Like Michael. Wes felt sure that his late best friend would have liked the guy.

"The pizza does sound great, but I'm going to get the seared tuna. It's good to have some protein after an intense ride," Wes said.

Chad nodded.

A text chimed on Wes's phone, and he stole a glance at it.

Feeling a little out of shape. Can you come by today for a "session?"

Mrs. Wallace.

Bethany.

Bethany Wallace with the raspberry birthmark high on her left thigh.

For a moment, Wes wondered where *Mr.* Wallace could be on a Sunday afternoon, but then he pushed the thought from his mind.

I don't need that, he told himself. Bethany was fun, but "sessions" with her never made him proud of himself.

Their server came to the table with two waters and took their orders. When he'd gone, Chad eyed Wes, seeming troubled.

"Look, I just want to say thank you, again. A bike like that costs almost as much as my car," he said, looking both awed and concerned.

Wes felt glad that the guy was grateful, but he didn't want it to get awkward.

"Man, it's cool. Michael definitely put some miles on it, so it's not like it'd be worth the sticker price," he said, hoping that would be the end of it.

"Still, I'd never be able to repay the kindness," Chad said. "But I want you to know that I'm giving my Denali to one of my students, a great athlete. He's a good kid who could use the escape."

Wes felt his chest expand.

"I'm really glad to hear that, man," Wes said, trying to keep control of his voice as his throat tightened. Michael would have been all about this—helping somebody who, in turn, helped somebody else. Pride, one that he felt he had to be sharing with Michael, filled his lungs. He'd have to tell Mr. Dan and Mrs. Betsie about this.

And Corinne.

It was a good enough reason as any to go look in on her, even if she'd probably just throw something at him. Their last encounter hadn't been much of a success.

At least her sister Morgan seemed thankful for his message. And if he could feel certain that Corinne's family was looking after things, he wouldn't need to worry so much about letting Michael down.

Just then a couple walked past their table. Wes looked up and felt a frisson. Morgan and Greg Bates stopped when they saw him.

"Oh, hey, Wes," Morgan said, waving to him. He knew he shouldn't have been surprised to see Corinne's sister; Morgan and her husband lived in the Sugar Mill Pond development, just around the corner from the restaurant.

"Hey, Morgan. Hi, Greg," he managed, trying to shake the eerie feeling that his conscience had summoned them.

Morgan looked much bigger than she had at the funeral, like she should be headed straight to the maternity ward, not walking into a restaurant. It was difficult not to gawk. The trainer in him estimated it would take 10 months for her to get herself back in shape. Five months if she worked with him.

"Uh…This is my buddy, Chad Case," Wes said, willing himself to look her in the eye—and not in the belly—as he gestured to her. "Greg and Morgan Bates…How are y'all doing?"

Morgan rolled her eyes.

"Still two months to go," she said, sighing and patting her belly. "And I can't stop eating. Right now, this little guy wants a big plate of Cajun Chicken Pasta."

Not too big a plate, I hope.

Wes considered asking about Corinne, but he didn't really want to invite a lengthy conversation. Besides, Chad didn't need to hear about Michael's mental girlfriend. As luck would have it, their server stepped outside bearing a tray with their meals.

"Well, enjoy your lunch," he offered, hoping they wouldn't linger. Wes couldn't stand when people hovered over his table at a restaurant. It stirred some primitive urge in him to protect his food, especially when he was as hungry as he felt after a bike ride.

To his relief, the Bates took their cue to leave and headed inside. But as soon as they disappeared behind the door, Morgan stuck her head out again.

"Wes, would you mind stopping by our table on your way out?" she asked, sotto voce, as if Chad couldn't hear her. "I'd love to have a word with you before you go."

Aww, Christ.

"Sure," Wes said, pasting on a smile. "No problem."

He couldn't very well say no.

"Thanks," she said, smiling, but he didn't miss the strain around her eyes. "See ya in a bit."

Great.

Wes picked up his fork. The sizzling pink slabs of seared tuna steak should have made his mouth water. It smelled amazing, but he knew he wouldn't enjoy it. Whatever Morgan wanted to tell him, it concerned Corinne, and it wasn't good. Which meant that he was failing. He was failing Corinne, and so he was failing Michael. He stabbed a cut of tuna and shoved it in his mouth, feeling like hell.

"Mmm...This is awesome," Chad said, enjoying a hearty bite of tuna. "So protein after every ride?"

Wes swallowed and tried to get over his pity party. Talking training with Case couldn't hurt.

"Yeah, and it should be within 30 minutes of your workout, or you could sacrifice muscle."

Chad's eyes widened.

"Really?"

And Wes allowed himself to set aside his gloom and discuss his favorite topics: training and nutrition.

⁓〇

After the check had been paid and Chad thanked him half a dozen more times for the bike, Wes stifled a sigh and entered the restaurant. He found Morgan and Greg Bates at a booth, and Morgan beckoned him over to join them.

"Please sit down," she motioned to the spot next to her, and Wes reluctantly took it. His mind raced ahead, sketching out a grim picture. If Corinne was no better, could she be worse? He could only assume that what he'd seen at her house was evidence of someone in deep depression. How much worse could she get? Would Corinne try to hurt herself? If she did, would he be able to live with it? Would Michael ever understand that the job he'd left him was just too big?

"Thanks for coming by," Morgan began, smiling nervously. "I think it's lucky that we ran into you today...I never thanked you for contacting me last month."

Her eyes narrowed at the memory, worry replacing her smile.

"It's no problem...How's Corinne doing?" Wes asked, bracing himself for the confirmation that he was an unworthy best friend. Why hadn't he gone back to see her the next day? Or the day after that?

Because she hates you, asshole.

"She's about the same," Morgan shrugged. "I'm worried about her."

The same? Not worse? Wes chanced to feel a measure of hope.

"Well, maybe she just needs time," he offered, saying the words for Morgan's sake as much as his own.

"Unfortunately, she doesn't have time," Greg chimed in, looking, Wes thought, like an overgrown Boy Scout, creaseless, rational, and polite to a fault. Only the tone of his words gave any hint of annoyance.

"What do you mean...?" Wes asked as he watched the husband and wife eye each other across the table, a silent argument passing between them.

"She has time," Morgan amended, still looking at her husband for a beat before bringing her eyes to him. "She just doesn't have money."

Wes blinked. Given what he'd expected, the thought of money seemed so...*mundane*.

"Money?"

"She hasn't sold a painting since...*before*," Morgan struggled, trying to be gentle with her words. "Before the accident. And she's not working on anything new."

This Wes could believe, remembering the state of her sunroom studio. But he found himself frowning. Wes never knew, of course, how much his best friend made, but he knew Michael had a good job. He always had money. *Always*. Didn't he and Corinne have any savings?

"That doesn't make much sense," Wes said, still frowning. "Michael was always flush. Corinne must have something to fall back on."

Morgan nodded, knowingly.

"They had put away a little—a few thousand—but we're talking about a household that ran on two incomes that now—at least for the time being—has none. Corinne is paying bills out of their savings—when she's paying anything, that is," Morgan said, rolling her eyes in exasperation. "I went by yesterday and found a cancellation notice for her utilities. She was about 24-hours away from losing power."

Wes winced. He didn't know what their rent was, but in their neighborhood he wouldn't be surprised if it was near $1200. That alone would wipe out her savings in just a few months, not to mention the rest of her expenses.

Aww, fuck.

Wes realized then, with a sickening certainty, that he was a giant ass. He'd just lost Corinne at least six months worth of rent. For nothing. Gone. Michael's Pinarello could have been sold—easily—for eight grand. At least. He palmed his forehead and scrubbed his hands through his hair.

It hadn't crossed his mind for an instant that Corinne would need the money. He hadn't thought about her at all. He'd just been so proud of himself for doing something noble, giving Michael's bike to someone who'd appreciate it. And he'd let Chad thank him—like it was *his to give*.

Shame broke over him like sweat. Could Michael see—from wherever he was—how badly he'd fucked up? Wes hoped not.

"What can I do?" he asked, unable to look at Corinne's sister. Did she know what he'd just done? Was that what this was about? He couldn't ask Chad to give it back. No way. And Wes knew that he couldn't just put up the money; he didn't have that kind of cash in his savings. Even if he sold his Colnago, he'd only be able to erase maybe half of this debt.

Morgan bit her lip. Wes thought that she looked nervous enough to be asking for $8,000. She knotted her fingers together at the edge of the table, winding up for the snap. Wes held his breath.

"What would you think about taking the dog?" she asked, doubtfully.

Wes blinked, blindsided.

"What?"

"I know, I know it's a lot to ask," she started, almost breathless. "But Corinne could come and live with us for a while, but we can't take that dog."

That dog? Buck was the furthest thing from *that dog* Wes could imagine. He was smart, obedient, easy, and just plain fun. How could Corinne want to give him up? Wes dropped his guilt for a healthy dose of indignation.

"Buck is the best dog in the world! Corinne doesn't want him?!?"

It was Morgan's turn to blink. Even to his own ears, he sounded a little defensive, harsh. Wes noticed that Boy Scout Greg sat up a little straighter, his eyes going flinty.

"Um...well,..." Morgan began, looking down at her hands. "She does actually. She wants to keep him, which means she needs a house with a yard—she says—but I thought that if you wanted him...maybe she'd see...that she doesn't *need* to keep him."

Wes understood in an instant that he'd been wrong about Morgan Bates. From the moment he'd seen her at Michael's funeral as she kept Corinne steady, Wes knew that he and Morgan belonged to a kind of silent partnership. He, by oath, and she, by blood, were charged with the task of taking care of Corinne Granger. He wasn't in it alone, and that was a relief! It was why he'd messaged her after leaving Corinne's with the bike. As Corinne's sister, Morgan would know—far better than he—what was best for her.

But what if she didn't?

Wes had no doubt that Corinne needed to keep Buck. It wasn't just that he was Michael's dog. It wasn't just for the company. It wasn't just that Buck could keep her safe. He pictured the train wreck of a house he'd seen just weeks before. Dishes on the floor, trash overflowing, a fridge filled with rotten food. Corinne couldn't take care of herself. But she could take care of Buck.

He hadn't seen any sign that she'd neglected to feed him or let him out. At least, the house didn't smell like dog piss, and there were treats and food in the pantry. If she was managing to take care of him, that was something. To take that away from her had to be a mistake. Without that sense if onus, would she even need to get out of bed—or stay alive?

"Maybe she does need to keep him," Wes offered, hoping Morgan would see his perspective.

Morgan rolled her eyes again.

"If she could come and stay with us, we could look after her, and after she felt better," Morgan said, brightening. "She could help me with the baby."

Wes drew a breath to tell her what a stupid, selfish plan that was, but he clamped his mouth shut instead. He was used to telling people what he thought—even his clients. Especially his clients. It was one of the things that made him so successful. They made progress because he was honest, sometimes brutally honest. But Wes stopped himself because he couldn't see how telling Morgan off would help Corinne. And he couldn't help but feel that Michael would have disapproved.

"Maybe…," he started, grasping for ideas. "Maybe she could take a roommate."

Wes heard Greg huff a suppressed laugh under his breath. Morgan raised a brow and eyed Wes skeptically.

"You have met my sister, right?" she asked with sarcasm.

Yes, and you're just as charming.

But she had him there. Wes *had* met Corinne. Plenty of times. The woman could make you feel like shit on a shoe just by looking at you. Michael had to have known what Wes thought about her—that Corinne was 99 percent bitch and the other 1 percent was bitch—but Wes never dared say it out loud. Michael would have knocked his teeth in—or shown him the door.

It was embarrassing how much the guy loved her.

He couldn't have been the only person who could live with her, could he?

"I never heard Michael complain," he countered, only a little chagrined that it took him several long seconds to respond.

Sadness softened Morgan's eyes, and for the instant before she looked down, he could see more of Corinne in her.

"Michael was a saint," she whispered.

"Michael was awesome," Wes said, the familiar lump filling his throat. He swallowed with a shake of his head and pressed on. "But he had his fair share of flaws and vices. Roush was no saint."

The human tendency to idealize the dead, to sanitize their memory, had always grated on Wes. Even the day he'd lost his best friend, Wes vowed to himself that he would remember Michael as he was. Anything else was disloyal. Remembering Michael—the real Michael, with his set-downs, and his sarcasm, and his insistence that he was always right—this was the only way to honor him. Forgetting half of what made him who he was? Well, that was just insulting.

"I just meant that he had a gift for handling my sister," Morgan said, giving him a bittersweet smile.

No argument there.

"So you won't take the dog?" Greg chimed in, clearly eager to reach a solution and put the matter behind him. Wes cut him a look and wished that they were standing face to face. He loved to step into a jerk's personal space, cross his arms over his chest, and let his biceps speak for him.

"I'll talk to her," he conceded. "If she wants me to take Buck, of course, I will."

But she won't.

"Thank you, Wes," Morgan sighed, smiling in obvious relief. "She'll see that it makes sense."

Except it doesn't.

Wes pushed himself from the table, the euphoria from his ride long gone. His legs felt heavy and clotted, and the prospect of going to Corinne's just depressed him.

"I'll be in touch," he promised, vaguely, nodding to both of them, and left the restaurant.

As he walked away, he raked his fingers through his hair again. He didn't know why he'd agreed to talk to her about the dog. It wouldn't change anything. Nothing he could do would make one bit of difference. Helping Corinne was just beyond him. If anything, he'd made her life worse. He'd practically robbed her of thousands of dollars without a second thought. With that track record, she'd be homeless before the end of the week.

His phone chimed as he climbed into his truck, and for a nanosecond, Wes wondered if it was Michael. He slammed the door of his truck and dropped his head to the steering wheel.

A thousand shocks a day.

That's what it seemed like—crashing against reality and forgetting about it just long enough to crash right into it again.

After a solid minute of listening to the pulse of his blood in his ears, Wes sat up and read the text.

Don't leave me hanging, big man.

Bethany Wallace loved to drag her manicured nails down his chest, turning him to gooseflesh. Wes pictured her taking his nipple between her teeth and smiling up at him. It *would* be great to stop thinking for a while. His thumb hovered over the keypad as he weighed his options.

On my way.

Chapter 5

Buck's sleek, black ears were the softest things in the world. Corinne stroked the dog's head as he snoozed in her lap. Sunlight from the window caught the waft of dander, motes rising up from the velvety ears and swirling in the shaft of waning light. She had watched the display for a good 20 minutes, ignoring Trisha Yearwood and her Rainy Day Food episode.

She was biding her time until the sun went down. On her last trip to the store—five days before—she'd made an interesting discovery in the medicine aisle: ZzzQuil. It didn't taste much better than Nyquil, but it did work, helping her sleep through the night and then some, and it didn't require a prescription or the need to *talk* to anyone.

Corinne had made a deal with herself. She could dose up as soon as the sun had fully set. Not official sunset time, which the Weather Channel app on her phone said was 7:18, but when she could no longer see any remnant of sunset in the sky. If she waited that long, then she could take the dosage cup and fill it all the way to the top, not just to the factory-imprinted line in the plastic.

In the store she'd debated about liquid over gel caps, but she decided that the liquid gave her more flexibility. And while it was tempting just to re-dose as soon as she woke up in the morning—and several times throughout the day—Corinne actually feared what might happen if she did. She noticed, too, that even after five days of indulging in her special nightcap, she still felt it necessary to lie down a few times a day, even if she only actually slept a couple of those times.

The downside was ZzzQuil seemed to keep her from dreaming—or remembering her dreams—which meant the illusion she clung to was evaporating. Michael invaded her dreams so much that it felt like he was willing himself to stay near her, that he was really only just beyond the veil of a temporal reality.

Dreamlessness made him seem more...*dead*.

After the second night without a dream, Corinne vowed that she would shelve the ZzzQuil so she could get him back. But near midnight, as sleep eluded her, hopelessness enveloped. Her dreams weren't portals to another place in the universe that held Michael and the life they shared intact; her dreams were chemical pulses in her brain, determined to stimulate her pleasure centers the best way they knew how and fulfill her deepest wish. Corinne had scrambled out of bed at the realization and downed a dose right then.

The clock on the cable box read 7:37. The light had softened further outside, and Corinne knew she only had about 15 or 20 minutes to go. In the meantime, she would feed Buck his dinner and escort him outside.

"C'mon, boy. Dinner time," she said, bracing herself as he jolted out of his rub-induced stupor, clawed himself upright, and darted to the kitchen. She moved much more slowly, rising from the couch and brushing the black dog hairs from the legs of her pink and gray plaid pajama pants.

Corinne had taken a gamble today and won. Since Morgan's kidnapping attempt four weeks before, she had started trying to shower every other day—or every third day if she were honest, and she tried to put on day clothes by 10 a.m. just in case her sister came by. Morgan seemed to be averaging about three visits a week, but there was no rhyme or reason to her pop-ins.

But today she just didn't feel like bothering. She felt bloated and raw, and Corinne guessed she was about to start her period. She couldn't be sure anymore because she couldn't bear to take her pill after Michael died. What was the point? She doubted she'd ever have sex again, and the little pink box with it's foil backing was just another reminder of how many days she'd lived without him and the life they'd never get to have. But ditching them meant that she no longer could keep track of when she'd start.

Corinne fed Buck and watched him gobble up every kernel in the time it took her to wash her hands, and then she led him through the sunroom to the backyard without even glancing at her paints. She sat on the back steps and watched Buck sniff around the yard.

She'd gotten her period about a week after Michael died, and it had hollowed her out. There had been a hope she had not even admitted to herself that he had left her with child, a hope that there remained something to live for, something of him.

Buck was mid-squat when the scraping sound of a car in the drive carried over the yard. The startled look of the defecating dog made Corinne laugh, and as Buck gave two quick grass-throwing kicks and ran back into the house, she couldn't wait to tell Morgan that she'd disturbed Buck's evening poop.

"She's kinda late today, isn't she?" Corinne didn't bother hurrying to the front door since Morgan had refused to relinquish Michael's key, using it at every opportunity. Instead, she sauntered to the living room and plopped down on the couch. At least the late hour meant Morgan couldn't be sure that Corinne had stayed in her pajamas all day.

A knock sounded, and Buck gave one short bark.

"What are you waiting for?" she yelled from the couch. "Just use the damn key like you always do."

"Corinne, it's Wes. I don't have a key. Can you let me in?"

Buck barked again at the masculine voice and scratched the door excitedly. Corinne just blinked.

What the hell does he *want?*

She pushed herself off the couch again and went to the door, unlocking the bolt but leaving the chain latched. Sure enough, there was Wes frowning through the gap in the doorway, his glossy faux hawk looking extra mussed. She couldn't help but think that he was a caricature, something you'd find in an anime cartoon. They stared at each other for a beat.

"Well, can I come in?" Wes asked, the indignation in his voice hard to miss.

"That depends. What do you want? More of Michael's stuff?" At her question Wes blanched, and the frown disappeared.

"No," he said, his voice changing. "I came to see you."

A hint of guilt needled her, so Corinne opened the door.

"Come in."

If her welcome left something to be desired, Buck made up for it with fervent wagging and pitiful whimpering.

"Hey, Buck," Wes said, stepping inside and bending down to greet the dog. "I see that propeller tail."

Propeller tail. How many times had Michael called his dog that? Buck's tail, indeed, whirled around in a happy, manic circle, and the dog stole the opportunity to lick Wes on the cheek. Buck had greeted Michael in just the same way so many times. Without her even realizing it, tears splashed over Corinne's lashes. She quickly brushed them with the sleeve of her gray pajama top, trying not to go over the edge. She would have to choose irritation and impatience if she didn't want devastation to win the day.

"If he pees from excitement, you're cleaning it up," she said, harshly.

Wes stood, still scratching Buck behind his ears.

"He won't pee. He's a good boy," he said, cooing to the dog. Corinne folded her arms over her chest and eyed Wes with disdain.

"Why are you here, Wes?"

Wes looked her in the eye and sighed.

"I saw your sister this morning," he said, grimly.

Shit.

Corinne wondered what Morgan had said about her. It could only be humiliating. Had she told him about the day she'd arrived to see Corinne eating melted ice cream and cereal because there was nothing left in the house?

"Well, you two have just become best buds," she sneered. "Facebook and Sunday brunch, is it?"

Wes ignored her and crossed to Michael's favorite chair, the mod, charcoal swivel, and sat down in it. Corinne found herself staring again in shock. Had anyone sat in that chair in the last three months?

Wes looked back at her while she remained by the door.

"I've made a mistake," he said.

"Just one?" she asked, moving back to the couch and flopping down as Wes scowled.

"I'm trying to tell you something difficult, Corinne," he droned. "Could you just hear me out?"

Buck jumped on the couch with her, and she instinctively reached for his ears.

"I'm listening," she conceded.

Wes leaned forward and rested his elbows on his knees, and she watched him draw a deep breath. His color had washed out again, and for the first time, she felt curious. What on earth could bother *Wes?* If the guy had a conscience, it was news to her.

"Morgan told me that you are having money trouble," he started.

Corinne ignored the flush of shame and set her jaw.

"I have money. And that's none of your business."

His eyes shot to hers, and the ire she saw in them surprised her.

"It is my business."

"No, it's not, Wes. My life is not your business—"

"It is when I owe you," he barked, his eyes aflame and nostrils flaring. He actually looked kind of scary all pissed off, but his words confused her.

"You don't owe me anything, W—"

"Yes," he cut in. "I do. I took Michael's bike without giving you anything for it, and I gave it away for nothing."

"So?" she asked, incredulous. "I didn't want the bike. It wasn't like I was going to use it."

Wes shook his head.

"No, I mean it's worth a lot of money. A lot, Corinne," he explained, surprising her with a stricken look. "I should have sold it for you. I could have gotten like $8,000 for it, but I didn't think it through...I owe you a lot of money."

Corinne frowned. She knew the bike was expensive, but it wasn't like it had been hers. It was Michael's, and he would have wanted to give it away to someone—just like Wes had done.

"You don't owe—"

"I can't pay it all back in one lump sum, but I think I can do it in installments, like $300 a month," he said, shrugging.

"What?" Corinne felt her eyebrows leap as she did the math. "You think I'm going to take money from you for the next two years?"

Frowning again, he reached into his back pocket and produced a check that was folded in half.

"I know it's a long time to pay you back, but I intend to do it," he said.

What the hell?

This was too much to deal with. The future was impossible to contemplate. Corinne could not imagine what her life would be like in two years, but she could only hope that it would be better than it was now, that she *somehow* would have managed to move on. The thought of cashing a check from Michael's best friend for the next 26 months was like a yoke around her neck. It would always call to mind his bike, his races, his body glistening with sweat after a ride, his hunger to be with her after each shower.

Corinne knew that she didn't want to forget any of this, but the assault of memories was sometimes enough to bring her to her knees. Why ask for more?

"No way," Corinne said, sitting forward and refusing the check. "I don't want that."

Wes's color had returned, but he looked tired. In fact, he looked like nothing more than a Wes Clarkson impersonation. The same stupid hair. Under Armour t-shirt. Shaved legs jutting out of knee-length Nike track shorts. But where was the swell and swagger? And the pity in his eyes made her want to scream.

"Corinne..." he said, softly. "You need the money. Morgan said you aren't working. What are you going to do?"

"Ok, that's it," she said, bouncing to her feet and startling Buck. "You need to back off. I can take care of myself, and for the record, the thought of *selling Michael's things* so I can pay the bills is *absolutely disgusting.*"

He narrowed his eyes, and she thought that she saw some of the Wes Clarkson smugness return.

Good, she thought. *Better than his pity.*

Wes stood and flicked the check onto her coffee table, a curl of derision in his lip.

"You know, Corinne," he said, pinning her with a ruthless look. "Michael always said you were one of a kind. All I can say is thank God for that."

Michael.

You're one of a kind, and you belong to me.

The memories pounced. Catching his breath on top of her, their hearts coming back from near-explosion after making love, Michael would say those words and kiss her face, her throat, her chest.

Hearing them now from Wes with so much disdain was a physical blow. There was no hiding. Her lungs emptied in a sob, and her body bowed. Corinne gripped her thighs, and a wail escaped her throat before she could summon words. When she could finally inhale again, she let loose.

"Leave now!" she shrieked, though she hardly needed to. Wes was already backing away from her, eyes rounded in horror. Buck slunk low by her feet, his ears pressed tight against his head.

"Corinne, I'm sor—"

"Don't ever come here again! *Ever!*"

"I didn't mean—"

"I never want to see you," she vowed, reaching the door first and yanking it open, grateful that her fury at last was trumping her decimation. "I don't even want to know you!"

Wes backed out of the doorway with hands raised as though she'd strike him. At another time, it might have been funny.

"I fucked up," he said, just before she slammed the door in his face.

She turned the bolt and slid home the chain with shaking fingers. She clamped her mouth shut as sweat broke on her brow. She felt like she could retch. Corinne hated herself for coming apart in front of him. For letting him see how much his words destroyed her.

But they had.

If anyone was one of a kind, it was Michael. Clearly, his life's mission had been to love the unlovable. If Corinne didn't prove that, Wes certainly did. Michael would have been so much better off if she had been the one in the car that night. The world was full of unlovable people.

But it was empty of Michael.

Fearing that Wes still stood just on the other side of the door, Corinne sprinted for the bedroom before she gave in to a bottomless keening. Tears scalded her face and hands, and it was an age before her weeping eased enough for her to top off the ZzzQuil cup and slam it home.

Corinne spent the next three days in bed, getting up only a few times a day to feed Buck, let him out, eat a banana, drink some water, and pee. She kept the ZzzQuil bottle by her bed and helped herself to a special dose three times a day.

Morgan came by on Tuesday, but Corinne managed to stash the illicit bottle and convincingly claim to be suffering from a stomach bug. Morgan wasted no time retreating to the germ-free sanctuary of her car, resorting, instead, to texting Corinne morning, noon, and night.

After feeding Buck, she finished off the liquid sleep aid at 6:12 on Wednesday night. In the back of her mind, she knew that a trip to the store would be necessary the following day, but in her seamless ZzzQuil cocoon, this did not trouble her. She just tucked herself under the covers and fell asleep again.

Knocking woke her sometime later. She wasn't sure, but Buck might have barked. Opening one eye and seeing that her alarm clock read 7:42, she reached around to the corners of the mattress to see if the dog was still nearby. He was not.

Another round of knocking.

In her OTC inebriation, Corinne deduced that it had to be Morgan, key or no key. A stranger would have sent Buck into paroxysms of barking, and as much as Corinne wanted to ignore the disturbance, she couldn't leave her pregnant sister out on the front porch in the dark.

Still navigating with one eye, Corinne staggered out of bed and made her way to the front door. Her heart raced in an effort to keep up with her sudden movement, a flush coming to her face. She placed her head on the cool doorframe as she unbolted the door, and she was glad for the crisp night air that met her cheeks.

Until she saw him.

Chapter 6

Nothing helped. Wes had done everything he could think of to push Corinne Granger and the restless guilt from his mind. He booked clients back-to-back; he ran a solid half-marathon after work on Tuesday, and he'd met Bethany Wallace that afternoon for one of her "sessions," but the look of devastation on Corinne's face still haunted him.

He'd gone two rounds with Bethany before she invited him to spend the night—Julian Wallace was out of town on business—and the thought of lying next to her in the darkness had threatened to choke him. Wes had made an excuse about a 5 a.m. appointment, but instead of going home, he'd driven to the Saint Streets. He had to apologize to Corinne before he went crazy.

Wes was prepared for her to slam the door in his face—or knee him in the balls, but he was not expecting the sight that met him.

Glassy eyed and flushed, she slumped against the door sill, looking ready to topple over. The apology that he had rehearsed on the drive from West Bayou Parkway to St. Joseph—along with any sense of self-preservation he might have had—evaporated completely.

"Corinne, are you high?"

A slow-motion scowl took her face.

"No...I took some...Benadryl...for my allergies, and I was asleep…" Her gaze sharpened on him then. "What the hell are you doing here, anyway?"

Wes inhaled, trying to marshal the right words again, but she looked worse than ever. Her long hair was stringy, oily, and her face was drawn.

Bitch-fiend or not, Corinne was more than pretty. The first time Wes met her—before his very presence made Corinne clench her teeth—he'd thought she was mind-blowing, and for about five minutes, he was almost jealous of Michael's good fortune.

But the person in front of him looked like a junkie. In fact, every time Wes had seen her since the day of Michael's death, Corinne looked worse than the time before. And he felt sure that he was—in part—responsible. He certainly hadn't helped.

Wes met her gaze and held it.

"I *need* to apologize," he stressed. He risked taking a step closer to the door, and he watched Corinne weigh the options in her mind. Slam the door or let him in.

She cursed under her breath and undid the chain lock. He didn't waste any time stepping over the threshold, figuring that the look of tired resignation she gave him would be the best welcome he could expect.

"I need to sit down," she said, turning from him and careening to the couch. She wore cut-off sweat pants and a drop-shoulder t-shirt, and as she flopped onto the cushions, his eye caught a sharply defined clavicle and more than a hint of her first and second anterior ribs. Wes sucked in a breath.

Corinne was not eating.

As a personal trainer, he'd seen his fair share of anorexics. Women who had lost so much muscle—and probably bone mass—and still wanted him to help them "trim down" some more. He would try to explain that he didn't take clients whose BMI's were lower than 17.5. They'd inevitably leave angry after arguing about having so much fat.

Corinne was a far cry from that, but something was not right. She had gone from being svelte to almost gaunt, and it seemed to have happened in a matter of days. He wondered how many meals she'd eaten since he last saw her.

He sat down in the gray chair across from her and tried again.

"Corinne, I'm so sorry I upset you the other day," he started. She wasn't looking at him, but inspecting her fingernails instead. Buck sat at his feet and licked Wes's knee, wagging in what seemed a slow, encouraging way. He pressed on. "I know what I said was...well, it was wrong and thoughtless, and I know that Michael would be pissed as hell at me for it."

Her eyes had shot up at the mention of Michael's name, and he could see a kind of fierce defiance in them before they filled, and then it was his turn to look away.

"Believe it or not, I just want to help you..." He rubbed the palms of his hands over his thighs, not taking his eyes away from the floor, and waited for her to respond.

"I never pegged you for having a guilty conscience," she said, finally. Wes looked up to see her still wearing an expression of defiance, and he girded himself for an insult. "Judging from the fact that you smell like Black Orchid and twat, I'd say that it still needs some cultivation, but I'm impressed that it exists at all."

It hit him like a slap. The truth and all that it implied. As usual, she saw right through him, and it galled him. It galled him that she was right! It was his anemic guilty conscience that sent him clawing at Bethany Wallace, and it was the same guilty conscience that drove him here. She was right, and he wanted to turn away from it.

Wes wanted to fire back, asking her to name when she'd last eaten and what. When she'd last bathed. He wanted to ask her who the hell went to bed at 7:30 at night? But he inhaled through his nostrils instead. Wes counted to ten and reminded himself that if he was going to help Corinne—really help her—he was going to have to learn to let her little jabs go. And, for once, he realized that he could do that.

"How much money do you have left, Corinne?" Wes loved that he sounded no-nonsense, like her words hadn't left him dissected, gut peeled open and legs akimbo. He sounded like it didn't even matter, and it worked.

"That's none of your damn business," she hissed, her mouth turning up in a sneer, but she couldn't hide the truth in her eyes, the uncertainty.

"It is," he almost whispered, feeling the tide of power turn, remarkably, in his favor. He could afford for his voice to sound gentle, soothing. An idea had come to him, and he looked around the living room as though seeing it for the first time.

"Who else is on your side, Corinne?" he asked, letting go of the forceful tones he no longer needed. "Your sister wants me to take Buck so you can move in with her..."

He watched the confirmation of fear shape her eyes. It was the last thing she wanted. Well, it was the last thing she wanted *so far*.

"Well, you can't have him, and I'm not taking your money," she said, crossing her arms over her chest, almost daring him, but her eyes betrayed her, darting to Buck in worry. Wes almost smiled then in admiration, in solidarity.

No one's going to take him from you, Corinne. Not if I can help it.

"My money's no longer on the table," Wes said, seeming to dismiss her words. "And from what I gather, no one else is coming forward to bankroll you, right? I mean, Morgan and Greg have a baby on the way, and if I remember correctly, Dad's on a fixed income..."

Her eyes shot back to him, suspicion narrowing them.

"What's your point?" she snapped. "Or are you just trying to rub it in?"

Wes smiled. He genuinely smiled. Because he could almost feel Michael smiling with him, letting him know that he was finally, *finally,* doing it right.

"I'm not rubbing it in," he said, easily. "I'm just making my case."

"Your case?" Corinne looked really confused. Confused Corinne was almost cute.

"Yeah, to move in with you."

Chapter 7

"You've got to be joking!"

It had taken a while—too long—for her ZzzQuil fog to clear after she'd opened the door, but when Corinne heard Wes's ridiculous suggestion, she snapped to attention.

"Nope. Totally serious," Wes said, but his smile confused her. He looked so pleased with himself, his smile threatened to squeeze his dark eyes closed. Still, it wasn't the smirk of someone ready to yell *Gotcha!* and burst out laughing. Wes was grinning like a gambler whose horse just won by a nose. And Corinne didn't like the unease she felt in its power.

"You are not moving in with me," she said with more force than conviction.

"Does the front bedroom have a full closet?" Wes asked, craning his neck towards the hallway as though he hadn't heard her.

"Wes. Listen to me. You are *not* moving in." But she could already see him drawing up the space in his mind, picturing himself in it. Worse still, *she* could picture him in it. Leaving sweaty clothes in the bathroom. Air boxing to hip-hop. Talking about carbo-loading and drafting and bonking. In her face. Every day.

No.

Wes got to his feet and headed for the hallway to explore, and Corinne shot off the couch, intercepting him.

"Stop!" she told him, raising her open palm between them. "You are not going any further." She hated the way her voice wavered, not in fear, but in weakness.

"It's just the one bathroom, right?" Wes asked, peering into the hallway with the hint of a frown. Then he shrugged. "I don't think that'll be too big of a problem. I mean, I'm at work by 5 a.m. three days a week, and I can always shower at the gym…"

Corinne wondered when she had become so powerless. Was it the moment Michael died or in the months since?

"WES CLARKSON, YOU ARE NOT MOVING IN WITH ME!" Corinne shouted in his face. Except for the slightest squinting around his eyes, Wes did not flinch, did not react at all. Then he turned his gaze back on her and smiled that infuriating smile.

"Corinne, how much money do you have?" He spoke softly, too softly following her outburst. It made her by contrast seem out of control. She felt herself scrambling to wrest some of it back. There was no way she'd be out-maneuvered by Wes Clarkson.

"I have enough," she lied. Without meaning to, she crossed her arms over her chest, realized too late that it made her look defensive, and dropped them again.

"How much, Corinne?" Wes's eyes pinned her in place, keeping her from looking away. She drew a silent breath and braced herself to stare him down. What was he hiding behind that smile? The smile was real, she knew, not a put on, but what did it mean?

Corinne let herself forget about mounting a defense and hiding her weaknesses and tried to see into his instead. His eyes were a dark brown—with absurdly feminine lashes, and up close, Corinne could see the typography of his irises, a craggy landscape of ebony and mocha. If she were painting them, they'd be caramel, purple, and black. With a hint of indigo because now she saw what lived behind the smile: a sadness so inky and deep that it threatened to soak up all of the other colors.

Corinne broke her gaze and found herself answering his question.

"I have about three thousand," she muttered, suddenly disoriented and half-forgetting the crux of the argument.

Wes startled her then by clapping his hands onto her shoulders, trapping her before him and forcing her to meet his eyes again.

"That won't even last you through June. Hear me out," he said. "I'll move in and cover rent and groceries—"

"Wes, I can't—"

He stopped her with a little shake at her shoulders.

"Listen! Rent and groceries for six months. You'll still pay utilities and all your other expenses, but for six months you can afford that."

She couldn't argue with that. She *could* afford utilities and other bills for six months and more.

"But—"

"And in six months, you might be painting again; you might be ready to move. Who knows?" He shook his head at the uncertainty and pressed on. "Whatever you decide, you won't be broke, and you won't be homeless...It'll buy you some time."

His hands were heavy on her shoulders, almost enough to make her knees give. She felt the tug of inevitability suck at her feet. What would she do if she refused him? She hadn't wanted to think about it, despite Morgan's hounding, but the problem wouldn't just go away.

"What about your apartment?" Her voice shook, and when she heard it, she realized that her whole body was trembling.

"The lease is up at the end of next month." Wes sounded matter-of-fact. Fully committed.

"What about all your furniture? It can't all fit in here with our things..." It was going to happen if she didn't shut it down right now. Was staying in the house that important? Was holding onto Buck?

"I can put some of it in storage," Wes said, shrugging, like he'd already considered the possibility.

Could she live with him? Wes? With the partying on Friday nights? The whoring around? The stupid, stupid arm shaving? He drove her crazy! And could she live with knowing that she was in his debt?

"Wes, it's too much. I can't allow you to do it."

Another little shake.

"Corinne, *I owe you $8,000*. It's not too much. It's just right."

"But, Wes—"

His hands became vices on her shoulders, and his voice dropped an octave.

"He was my *best friend*, Corinne," Wes grunted. "He. Was. My. Best. Friend."

Their eyes locked again, and it seemed that everything had become indigo. Any fight Corinne had left seeped right out of her.

"Fine," she sighed, sagging under the weight of his hands and just catching herself before she crumpled. Wes shifted his grip to the top of her arms and steered her back to the couch.

"We're going to kill each other," she muttered, grateful to sink down onto the cushions again. "You do realize that, right?"

To her surprise, Wes grabbed the afghan that was draped over the arm of the couch before flaring it open and laying it on her lap.

"Oh, I'm looking forward to it, Granger," he said. The stupid smile was back. "I'm looking forward to it."

April

Chapter 8

"I don't understand, Wesley. Why do you *need* to put that loveseat in the pool house? It won't go with anything in there!"

His mother was practically chasing him through the French doors. Wes didn't bother coming to a halt with the dolly. Gloria Clarkson didn't remember the conversation she'd had with her son the week before, and the fact that she'd probably remember this one was just his bad luck. Of course, at 1 p.m., she more than likely hadn't started drinking yet.

"Mom, I called you two weeks ago and asked if I could store a few things in the pool house for a little while, and you said yes, *remember?*" Wes made sure that the irony in his voice was hard to miss.

He heard her footsteps stop behind him, and he imagined his mother blanching. Under no circumstances was Gloria Clarkson an alcoholic, and forgetting whole conversations with one's son about furniture storage was something an alcoholic did.

"I was thinking of another chair...the tangerine one," she lied.

Wes rolled his eyes and unlocked the door to the pool house.

"Like I'd own a *tangerine* chair, Gloria," he muttered.

"What did you say, Wesley?" she asked, closing in on him. He turned to see her standing with her arms crossed over her sable poncho sweater that perfectly matched her sable boots. Black skinny jeans completed the ensemble, and Wes would have bet money that every pair of pants his mother wore came equipped with some kind of industrial strength tummy panel. No one could drink three Derby's a night and not have a booze gut.

Wes shuddered at the thought.

"I said it'll only be for a few months while I'm living with Corinne."

Wes's mother screwed up her mouth like she'd eaten a bad cocktail olive.

"The one with the blue hair?"

In spite of himself, Wes smiled. When Michael had first started seeing Corinne, she'd sported an electric blue streak at the nape of her neck. Wes had invited them to a pool party his parents hosted two summers ago, and he'd secretly relished scandalizing his mother and her friends.

"Her hair's not blue anymore, Mother, but yes. Corinne. Michael's girlfriend."

Gloria Clarkson fingered the spill of beads at her bosom and shook her head.

"Such a pity," she sighed, and Wes counted to three as he pushed the dolly over the pool house threshold. On three, she expressed her disapproval. "Still, I don't see why you're getting involved. The girl must have her own people..."

His mother droned on, and Wes kicked himself for coming at all. Couldn't he just have sprung for the bigger storage unit? Then he wouldn't have had to keep the overflow at his parents' house, and he wouldn't have to suffer this conversation with her. One, unfortunately, she'd revive later when she wanted something from him.

Wesley, if you hadn't meddled with that blue-haired girl, I could host a decent luau. So, be a dear and at least come to brunch on Sunday. The Rossis will be here, and you know how tiresome it can be for poor Sarah.

He could almost hear it, and hearing and decoding were one and the same.

Wesley, you asked me for a favor, so you are in my debt. Come to brunch on Sunday and flirt with Sarah Rossi so your father won't.

It was better not to be in her debt. He hadn't thought that a loveseat and two end tables would cost him too much, but he'd been wrong before.

"I mean, it's not like she's his widow," his mother added in a tone that he knew she thought charitable. "For heaven's sake, they weren't even engaged."

Wes was pushing open the furniture arrangement in the living area of the pool house to make room for his loveseat, and his mother actually stopped talking to watch him in irritation.

"Mom, my best friend's dying wish was for me to help his girlfriend," Wes said, fully aware that his words would change nothing. "Can I keep these things here for a few months so I don't have to rent another storage unit? Tell me now while I still have the moving van."

Gloria Clarkson rolled her eyes.

"Wesley, you're always so dramatic," she sighed, waving a hand at her disrupted tableau and turning toward the door. "So, I can count you in for next month?"

Aww, fuck. Here it comes.

"What's happening next month?" Wes asked, his intestines already shrinking.

His mother tsked and put her knuckles to her hips.

"Why did I even bother to send a save-the-date? You never read your mail," she bemoaned, rolling her eyes again. "James Hargett, one of the senior partners, is running for judge! We're hosting his announcement event. You *must* come, Wesley."

Showing up for brunch with the Rossis or the Belamies was one thing. His parents' closest "friends" were as fucked up as they were, so the "happy family" charade was not as high stakes with them. An event like this one—with a few hundred people—was like juggling knives.

While Wes's mother "was not an alcoholic," Wes's father, Harold Clarkson, "was not a drunk." Once, when they were both 16 and Wes had turned up at the Roush's front door at 10:30 on a Sunday night, Michael had asked him to explain the difference.

"An alcoholic is embarrassing," Wes had said, lying flat on Michael's bed and bouncing a tennis ball against the ceiling. "A drunk is mean."

Harold Clarkson was handy with a belt, but as a lawyer who represented all manner of filth, he knew better than to leave marks, even after an absurd number of scotch and sodas. But he knew how to cut someone open with his eyes and burn their entrails with his tongue. He could do this with or without a drink—as his history in the courtroom attested, but the more hydrated he was, the more bloodthirsty he became.

When he'd gotten old enough to think such things—11 or 12—Wes always marveled that his parents had so many friends. If he couldn't stand to be around them, how could anyone else? Still, at their cocktail parties, Wes's father was always at the center of a raucous and well-heeled circle. Men, young and old, surrounded him like bums around a trash can fire.

It wasn't until Wes was 19—and already working at Lafayette Fitness Club—that he understood. Weak men—no matter how rich or handsome—were attracted to power. The kind of power Harold Clarkson had didn't just come from money—though he had it—or his leonine handsomeness that would distinguish him even in old age; it came from a core of confidence that he could take from anyone what they held most dear. A fortune. A child. A life. Not that he *would* take it, but that he *could*.

Wes assumed that his father's associates were just as repelled by this power as they were drawn to it—if they understood it for what it was. But whether they did or not, they sensed, like Wes did, that when they were in its presence, the danger came from turning one's back on it.

A party for a partner who was running for a spot on the bench would spell trouble. Half of the guests would be members at the gym, and a fair number would be Wes's actual clients. Between keeping his mother from falling into the pool and dodging his father's questions about when he planned to give up "this faggoty personal trainer thing and go to law school," Wes thought he'd rather face a firing squad, but this—his mother had determined—would be the price of furniture storage.

Wes suppressed a sigh and accepted his fate.

"Sure...I'll be there."

Chapter 9

The last Sunday in April was Shove-In Day.

That was what Corinne was calling it instead of Move-In Day. It wasn't even 10 o'clock in the morning, and Corinne thought that if she started screaming now, she might never stop.

"That won't work," she said, stopping Wes and his friend Chad at the front door. "There's no way two queen-sized beds can fit in that room!"

Wes arched a brow at her as he steadied the bedframe he was holding.

"No shit. This one's staying; that one's not," he leveled, smugly.

"Wes, don't I get a say? It's my stuff—" He cut her off.

"Look, Corinne, more than half of my belongings are in storage, but I'm keeping my bed. Non-negotiable, which means that one goes." He pushed past her through the living room, and Chad gave her an apologetic shrug.

"Well, where's it going?" she demanded, hot on their heels. "I don't have anywhere to store it, and that bed actually belongs to me, you know."

Wes pivoted his end of the frame carefully into the hall.

"Mr. Dan and Mrs. Betsie said that we could move a few things into Michael's old room upstairs until you need them again," he said, disappearing down the hall and leaving her feeling a little chagrined for her attack.

Corinne didn't like feeling chagrined; she'd rather feel annoyed. She was being invaded, after all.

"Well, at least let me strip it before you start taking it apart," she murmured, squeezing past them and yanking the ice blue duvet off the bed. She removed the sheets seconds before Wes and Chad slid the mattress off and pushed it down the hall.

Corinne looked back at Michael's desk and his weight bench. This had been his space, just as the sunroom had been hers. She knew—with a kind of full-body certainty—that Michael would have approved of Wes moving in, but *she* wasn't ready to walk past the doorway and not be able to picture Michael bent over his laptop, working. Or Michael, gorgeous Michael, bench-pressing, shirtless and glistening.

Everything was being erased.

She stared at the room, at these *things*, and she felt her heart start racing. She didn't recognize her life anymore. She didn't recognize herself. Corinne leaned back against the wall to steady herself because now her legs shook underneath her as if the ground were vibrating. She clutched the bundle of bedding in her arms to hold onto *something*, but a murky fear—like she'd only felt in the hospital when doom had replaced hope—overtook her.

Corinne heard the men come back inside, talking, and she wished she could retreat to her room, but her body would not obey. Trembling and clutching was all she could do.

Michael, help me!

"...the box springs will be a bitch," Wes said, turning into the hallway. Out of the corner of her eye, she saw him stop short.

"Corinne...?"

She didn't want to look at him, but Corinne doubted that she could turn her head even if she tried, but Wes stepped in front of her and met her eyes with a puzzled look that shifted quickly to something else.

"Chad, could you give us a minute?" Wes spoke without taking his eyes off her.

"Oh...sure..." Corinne heard Chad turn from the hall and clear the living room in no time.

Inside, Corinne was dying. She had no idea that someone could endure such suffocating fear and stinging humiliation in the same instant. She could feel that her face had hardened into an ugly pre-cry mask and was frozen there.

"Corinne..." Wes spoke softly, as if he were addressing a child. "What's going on? What are you thinking?"

Corinne opened her mouth, but no sound came out, and then, from some ancient place in her mind, she remembered to draw air into her lungs. The gasp that followed was ear-splitting, like she'd never inhaled before.

"Breathe…" Wes told her, placing a hand on her arm. "And tell me."

"Idon'tthinkI'mreadyforthis!" she rasped on the exhale and swallowed another breath, greedily.

"Here, give me those." Wes took the sheets and bedspread from her and dropped them to the floor before grabbing her hands and stacking them on top of her head.

"Whatareyoudoing?"

"You're having a panic attack," Wes explained, calmly. "This will help you breathe."

"Howdoyouknow?" She wanted to sound challenging, but it came out squeaky.

Still, Wes raised a brow at her, but she caught the hint of a smile in his eyes.

"Human physiology," he said. "You should probably sit down. Any second now, the adrenaline's going to wear off, and you'll go all rubbery."

Corinne took another deep breath, and as if on cue, her knees started knocking. Wes walked her to Michael's desk chair, and she collapsed on it.

Wes sat on the box spring at her knees and watched her, silently.

"That's never happened before…" she managed, pulling her hands to her face and looking at him through her splayed fingers. Now that the terror was ebbing, she wanted to crawl in a hole.

"What set you off?" he asked, peering through her fingers with a scrutinizing frown.

Corinne hesitated.

"I…don't want you to move in," she stammered, feeling like a teen-aged stepchild.

Wes blinked, his face an unreadable mask.

"You don't want me to move in? Or you don't want me to move your stuff out?" he asked, pointedly.

This time she didn't hesitate; she blurted.

"I don't want you to move Michael's stuff."

The mask melted, starting with his eyes, and Wes's whole posture softened.

"Oh," he whispered, taking in the room around them. "Okay."

Corinne dropped her hands.

"Okay?"

Wes craned his neck to survey the space again and nodded.

"I just want my bed, Corinne. I can leave everything else the way it is...for as long as you need me to."

"*Really?*"

"Yeah, it's no big deal," he said, shrugging, and Corinne wondered if he was lying. "I stored a lot of my stuff. Most of the boxes are full of clothes and shit."

Corinne stared at him. This was not the Wes she knew, and it was weirding her out. She didn't like the idea of being in Wes Clarkson's debt or feeling like his charity case. She'd told him that the bike wasn't important to her, and she'd meant it, but it did help to remind herself that the dollar value involved negated any pity factor on his part.

But she didn't lie to herself. As much as she chafed against the idea of living with Michael's best friend—or living with *anyone*—she knew it was her best option at the moment. She still couldn't think about painting. The finished work that remained in the studio seemed to have been done by someone else; Corinne could hardly remember what it felt like to be inspired to touch brush to canvas. She didn't like to think about it, but there were moments when she wondered if she'd ever paint again.

Corinne shook her head to clear her thoughts.

"Thank you," she mumbled, finally.

Wes tilted his head and eyed her cautiously.

"What?" she demanded.

"Well, there is one other thing I'd like to bring inside..." Wes bit his lip, looking doubtful.

Good God, what is it?

A sex doll? A bong? His *Playboy* collection?

"Yeah...?" Corinne prompted, wincing.

Wes pressed his lips together and stared at her.

"What, Wes?"

Her worry doubled, tripled.

"Would you freak out...if I put my La-Z-Boy in the living room?"

Corinne let go the breath she was holding with a laugh.

"Go ahead...." She nodded. "Sure."

Wes smiled then, white teeth and dimples, a full expression that she hadn't seen since before.

"Dude, *awesome!*"

This she recognized. And while his juvenile jargon made her roll her eyes, Corinne was a little relieved. It would be worse if he seemed like a total stranger, wouldn't it?

As it turned out, there were several other things Wes wanted to keep that she wouldn't have even considered objecting to, but he asked her permission anyway. His XBox—which had been to the house on *several* occasions—found a permanent home under the TV. His own TV and stereo actually fit on Michael's bookshelf in his bedroom, and Corinne had no problem making space on the kitchen counter for his pint-sized *Capresso* machine, which was actually smaller than her coffee pot—even with the steamer arm extended.

"I've gotta have the caffeine jolt before a ride," Wes explained, but then quickly added, wide-eyed, "But I swear, Corinne, it's super quiet! It won't wake you up, I promise."

Corinne felt herself smiling.

"And it makes cappuccinos and lattes?" she asked.

"Yeah, I'll show you later. It's pretty easy."

The last thing to come in, of course, was his bike.

"If you want, you can keep that in the sunroom," she offered with a shrug. "It's not like I've been using it, and it might make you feel a little less cramped in your room."

Wes's friend Chad had just left, and Wes was easing his Colnago through the front door when she spoke. He stopped and regarded her with a raised brow.

"You sure?" he asked, again seeming doubtful.

"Yeah, I'm sure."

"Thanks, Corinne." Wes aimed his bike towards the back of the house, and Buck followed him, clearly hoping that a trip to the backyard was in store.

The task of moving him in and getting him unpacked had taken just a few hours, but for Corinne, it was more physical activity than she'd had in months, and now that the work was done, she felt exhaustion settle over her.

She went to her room and closed the door behind her. Corinne stood there with her hand pressed to the wood. She felt the difference, closing the door in a house that no longer held just herself, that was no longer hers and Michael's. She lived with someone else now, and she felt a little dizzy at the change. It was almost like the sensation of falling—an unexpected dipping—the way reality bobbed like a cork and sent out little waves of shock.

Michael was gone, and this was Corinne moving on.

She wanted to pull away from the thought, so she turned from the door and retreated to her bed, their bed. Tears welled in her eyes because she didn't want to move on. If she couldn't go backwards and touch the days when Michael was still alive—which to her still seemed so near that he was almost within reach (really, it was only 122 days, the blooming season of a creme myrtle, the lifespan of a red blood cell, a guarantee on a new mattress)—then at least she didn't want to move forward.

Corinne didn't have a choice, but if she did, she would hibernate indefinitely. Curl up in bed and let the world spin on like in a time-lapsed video where she was the rock or the lake or the mountain, and the skies strobed from day to night, clouds chasing moons, chasing dawns.

Chapter 10

Wes was half-starved after spending the middle of the day moving in, and his nerves were raw from walking on eggshells around Corinne. After he had set his bike up and found that she had closed the door to her bedroom, the tension across his shoulders eased, and he allowed himself to hunt around the kitchen for some lunch.

The prospects were grim. Although he'd brought over what remained in his fridge and pantry, Wes had skipped his usual grocery run in preparation for the move, and now he was left with stale bread, canned tuna, and some mayo and mustard. He fixed himself an edible sandwich, finished off his lunch with a Clif bar, and dug out his phone to make a grocery list—which he figured would be pretty long since Corinne had next to nothing.

Twenty minutes later, his roommate had still not emerged, so Wes scribbled a note on the back of a Chinese takeout menu, telling her he'd be back in an hour, and he taped it to her door sill.

His trip to Rouse's was epic. His shopping cart had never been so full, nor had the bill ever been so high, but he returned to the house almost two hours later with provisions like milk, cereal, and eggs, bread, sliced turkey breast, and greens, paper towels, trash bags, and dog food, and—best of all—potatoes, fresh asparagus, and ribeyes for dinner. He also tucked a six-pack of Abita Purple Haze in the fridge for good measure.

Wes wasn't expecting Corinne to be over-the-moon grateful about his haul, but he at least thought she'd to be awake to see it. When he got back to the house, everything was as he'd left it, the door to her bedroom still closed with the note still dangling from the frame.

It wasn't until after he'd come in from cleaning the barbecue pit and loading it with fresh coals that he started to worry. It was after 4:30, and there were still no signs of life. Even if she was just sleeping—and three and a half hours was a ridiculously long nap—Wes didn't think she'd had anything to eat since he'd arrived. He crept into the hall and listened outside her bedroom.

Nothing.

Extreme fatigue, Wes knew, was a symptom of depression. No one could blame Corinne for being depressed, but in his college exercise physiology and psychology classes, Wes had learned enough to know that depression could be caused by chemical imbalances or by life events, and that either cause could trigger a vicious cycle that trapped a person. Before Michael died, Wes would not have called Corinne depressed. Prickly, yes; depressed, no way. She was always feisty—and as vibrant as her paintings. She ranted; she did not brood. She analyzed; she didn't sulk.

If she was depressed in the wake of losing Michael—as Wes had no doubt she was—then that alone could make her want to sleep all the time, but her own inactivity deprived her brain of serotonin and endorphins, which would only worsen her depression.

But this was something Wes was equipped to handle. He leaned toward the door and knocked gently.

Nothing.

"Corinne...?" he called, softly.

Still nothing.

Wes knocked again, more firmly this time, and only silence answered him. Unbidden, an image of her terror-widened eyes came to him. She'd looked so lost that morning, like she was drowning in her fear. And just at the prospect of moving Michael's things. Wes again felt like he'd been punched in the sternum just thinking about it.

Could the panic attack have been enough to sap her of her strength and send her into such a deep sleep that she couldn't hear him? Or was it something else?

Another statistic from one of his health classes rose in his mind: *the leading cause of death for people 25-34 is suicide.*

Wes gripped the door handle and turned, knowing full well that Corinne would probably resent the intrusion. He pushed the door open, preparing himself for a beat down.

Corinne lay there—on top of the covers—in a fetal position, eyes gently closed and lips just parted. Her brown hair fanned across the pillow behind her, and for once she looked peaceful and content. As still as she was, Wes could clearly see that she had lost weight—and Corinne had never had much to spare. Her jeans gaped at the waist, and the curve of her hip was muted.

Still, quiet like this—not yelling at him or crying or freaking out—Corinne was beautiful. He allowed himself the acknowledgment that she was probably just as beautiful when she was yelling, crying, or freaking out, but that he was likely too pissed off or—truth be told—too scared of her to see it.

That was it, he realized. That was what Michael had that he didn't. Not only had Michael seen the beauty—which everyone saw—he hadn't been afraid of the crazy. He was immune, so he could totally handle her.

And, somehow, Michael had thought that Wes could totally handle her, too.

So far, so good. He could almost hear Michael saying it.

He had gotten her to agree to the roommate proposal, and he had talked her down from a panic attack. Yes, he had cost her $8,000, but he was digging himself out of that hole, and progress was being made.

Maybe he *could* handle her.

"Corinne..." he whispered.

Her face registered nothing, no fluttering eyes, no frowning. Wes reached over and lightly grabbed her shoulder and gave her the slightest nudge.

"Corinne," he spoke a little louder. Eyes still closed, Corinne rolled onto her back and flung her right arm onto the pillow above her head. A dreamy smile came to her lips.

With that one languid motion, she became someone else, a woman issuing an invitation to be kissed, to be touched.

But he was not the man she invited.

Talk about a rude awakening.

Wes stepped back at once. He understood instantly that he had trespassed, standing where he should not, seeing what she'd never have him see. He walked backward towards the door and had almost made his escape when Corinne opened her eyes.

"Whoa!" she said, sitting up in bed, bleary, but becoming fully alert. "What are you doing in here?"

To his relief, Corinne didn't seem furious, as he should have expected. Just confused.

"I...um...I was checking on you," he stammered, lamely. "It's been hours...and I knocked and called your name a few times."

Corinne scrubbed her face with the palms of her hands, waking herself up. She spoke through them.

"Ok, House Rule #1: Do not wake me up unless there's a fire," she said. "Ok?"

In spite of himself, Wes smiled. He couldn't really see himself following this rule, especially if she planned to take three-hour naps on a regular basis, but he agreed anyway.

"Ok," he said, nodding. "Anything else?"

Corinne swung her feet over the edge of the bed and planted them on the floor before interlacing her fingers and stretching her hands above her head. The motion pulled her t-shirt tight against her breasts, and Wes quickly looked at his feet.

"Yeah," she said. "I don't think we should be in each other's rooms."

Wes stepped back again until he was standing fully in the doorway.

"Ok, so House Rule #2: I stay out of your room. You stay out of mine," he affirmed.

Corinne crossed the room and made to leave, but Wes stood in her way.

"What are you doing? I have to pee," she announced, eyeing him skeptically.

"Well, just hold on," he said. "I have a few rules of my own."

Corinne gave him a pointed look and crossed her arms, cocking her hip.

"Oh, you do?"

"Yeah. House Rule #3: All residents in this house—including Buck—get a minimum of 30 minutes of exercise six days a week."

Corinne's eyes bugged.

"What?!? Hell, no."

"Why not?" Wes asked, calmly.

"That has nothing to do with rooming together."

Wes crossed his own arms.

"I disagree. Exercise improves mood, and health, and appetite, and sleep. It'll help us get along better."

"That's just ridiculous," Corinne sneered, shaking her head.

Wes wanted to sneer back, but he kept his tone even.

"Well, so is sleeping away a perfectly good Sunday afternoon. We can have house rules, or we can have anarchy. Take your pick."

She glared at him, and he could see that he was winning. Was this one of the ways that Michael had managed her? Ultimatums? He realized that besting a woman like Corinne could be quite an ego-builder, and he suppressed a smile.

"Does yoga count?" she asked.

"Of course."

"What about walking?"

"Definitely."

She deliberated for another minute.

"Fine. Now, let me pass."

Wes held up a hand.

"Hang on, now. You got two rules. I get one more," he said, sounding reasonable, but knowing that he was pressing his luck.

"What?" Corinne cocked one eyebrow, humorlessly.

"House Rule #4: We eat three square meals a day."

Corinne rolled her eyes.

"I see what you're doing."

"Get your shoes on. We're going for a walk," he told her. "I'm going preheat the oven. We're having steak and potatoes tonight."

Surprise overtook Corinne's face.

"We are?"

This time he couldn't stop the smile.

"Shoes on, C."

Wes turned to head for the kitchen, but he didn't miss it.

"Shoes on, C," she mimicked in a nasally voice, but as soon as he slid the potatoes into the oven, she stood in the kitchen doorway wearing her sneakers.

Chapter 11

Buck was ecstatic. He jumped with so much excitement that Wes couldn't snap on his leash until he ordered him to sit twice.

Corinne checked her watch as they stepped outside: 5:11. Sunset time was 7:36. She still had more than two hours before she could re-dose.

Technically, this wasn't really true since she had already taken almost a capful of ZzzQuil when she'd gone into her room, but she would definitely need another dose to be able to sleep tonight after such a long nap. Corinne was glad now that she'd stashed the bottle in her bedside table; Wes certainly would have seen it when he woke her.

It had been so strange to wake up and find someone in her room. What surprised her most, though, was that it hadn't scared her. Or even pissed her off, really. It was sort of...*nice* that someone else was in the house.

With Buck pulling ahead, they crossed through the yard and turned left on St. Joseph.

"Settle down, boy," Wes told the dog. After he'd lifted a leg along the half fence that edged the front yard, Buck seemed to relax enough to stop pulling, but he sniffed the ground excitedly as they walked.

"It's been a while since I took him," Corinne admitted, coming up beside Wes.

"I can tell," he glanced down at her, but he smiled.

It was only when they stood side by side like this that Corinne remembered how tall Wes was, 6'2" to her 5'4". Michael had topped out at 5'11", but to Corinne, he'd always seemed larger than life. No man seemed taller, and certainly not Wes, whom Corinne had always thought of as younger, too. In fact, Wes was older by two months.

"What?" Wes asked, narrowing his eyes at her. She was still craning her head, studying him.

"You had a birthday recently," she said.

Wes looked surprised, but he nodded.

"Yeah, last month. Why?"

Corinne shook her head.

"I was just thinking about Michael's birthday, and I knew yours was earlier," she said, watching the road in front of them now. "I knew it was March. I just didn't know the date."

"The 20th. When's yours?"

"June 17th." She and Michael had gone on their first date the week before her birthday. It would be two years this summer. Corinne doubted that Wes knew this, but she didn't feel like telling him, so she said nothing, and they walked the rest of the block in silence.

Spring was half over, Corinne realized. The azalea bushes on her street had bloomed. Those were her favorites, and she had not even noticed them beginning to open in the previous weeks. Now, their spent petals were another bittersweet reminder that life goes on.

Corinne sighed at the thought, and Wes glanced down at her again.

"What?" he asked, again.

She shook her head.

"Michael," she said, simply. She had pulled on a sweater before they left, and she was glad for it now, jamming her hands into the pockets and letting her nails dig into her palms to keep the tears from starting.

"Yeah, I know," Wes offered.

Corinne inhaled deeply through her nose.

"Look, I might need to make up another rule," she said on the exhale.

They stopped at the corner of Ray Avenue to let a car pass, and Wes faced her.

"Which is?" he asked.

Corinne started walking again so that she wouldn't have to look directly at him.

"Michael is the only thing we have in common, but I *can't* talk about him all the time. I'll lose it," she said, quickly, wanting to get past the admission of all of her pain. That alone was risky territory. They passed a mailbox that was covered in Carolina jasmine, and she let herself drink in the rich yellow, focusing on the color instead of her feelings.

"He's not the *only* thing we have in common," Wes offered. "There's Buck..."

Corinne laughed at that, and Buck, hearing his name, tilted his head back to eye them appreciatively.

"And there's the fact that we now both exercise six days a week..." Wes added, smiling.

Corinne rolled her eyes.

"And there's steak. Don't forget the steak."

"Who could forget steak?" Corinne allowed.

Buck paused to sniff the base a eucalyptus tree with interest and then marked it himself.

"No, I get it," Wes said, giving her a grim kind of smile. "I know you never really understood how Mike and I were friends."

Corinne felt her eyes bug, and her face flamed.

"That's not what I meant at all," she insisted, honestly. "I mean it just might be hard for us to be..."

"Friends?" He'd raised an eyebrow and looked amused now, his dark eyes dancing in the late afternoon light. She couldn't help but see the humor, the cosmic irony in it, and she laughed a tired laugh.

"You have to admit it. Michael had...very singular taste in friends," she said, lightly, smiling even, but the truth of it, the rare beauty of it stuck in her like an arrow.

"You mean it's weird for a guy to be best friends with a narcissistic jock who parties like a rock star and in love with a badass, genius painter who doesn't have time for that shit?" Wes meant for it to be funny—and it would have been—if she still thought of herself that way.

Corinne tried to keep smiling, but the muscles in her face just wouldn't hold. They just slipped into something like a wince. Wes watched the whole thing, and his eyes went from playful to cautious until she turned away.

"What?" Wes asked, softly. He stopped walking, so Corinne had to stop, too. She thought about ignoring his question and continuing on, but she didn't think she had the strength to play it off. Maybe being honest would take the least out of her.

"I'm not that person anymore," she said, looking back up at him, ready to see the truth confirmed on his face. Instead, she saw confusion.

"What do you mean?" he asked, frowning.

Corinne frowned back.

"I'm not the person Michael fell in love with. I'm not 'badass' anymore," she said, gesturing back in the direction of the house. "I can't even move furniture without having a breakdown, and I'm certainly not a painter. I can't picture *wanting* to paint."

There it was, the admission that she had lost everything when she lost Michael, even herself. The only thing that kept her from crying over it again was Wes's bewildered expression. Maybe she'd gone too deep for a personal trainer and short-circuited him.

"Trust me, Corinne, you're still badass," he said, finally, looking at her without a trace of duplicity. "And you'll paint again...When you're ready. You've just taken a hit."

She watched him for a long moment. If he pitied her, he did a good job of hiding it, and, either way, Corinne was grateful.

They crossed Howard Street, and Corinne felt weary of being the focus of so much attention.

"What about you? Won't having me as a roommate interfere with your rock-star lifestyle?" she teased.

"Um...I'll manage." A hint of wariness hardened Wes's eyes, and Corinne remembered too late that Michael had once told her Wes's rule about girls. He never brought them home. Hook-ups always happened at the girl's place, not his, so he could leave when he wanted to.

"That's because he's a pig," Corinne had told Michael.

Whether or not Wes thought that Corinne knew this rule, it hardly seemed fair to judge him about it now. Or even bring it up. Who was she to look down her nose at the way anyone else led his life? Glass houses and all that. There was a reason she had become a total basket case. Maybe Wes had his own reasons for his actions.

And maybe—just like her—he wished like hell things were different.

When they reached Souvenir Gate, they turned left and headed back down on St. Patrick. A couple in running attire sat on the steps of a house to Corinne's left. It was clear that they'd just finished a run. Both dripped with sweat, and the young woman rested her heels on the lowest step while she stretched her hamstrings by reaching for her toes. The man, who looked a little older, grabbed the tail of her long braid and gave it a playful tug, making the woman laugh.

Corinne watched them hungrily. Happiness was such a fragile creature. The couple in front of her might have years ahead to make each other happy. Corinne hoped that they did. But the life that stretched out before her seemed very long indeed to watch other people be happy.

At that moment, the young woman must have felt Corinne's eyes on her because she looked up and waved. Corinne waved back, a little abashed at being caught staring, and turned away again.

Buck had settled down considerably as they made their way back, but when they rounded Juliette and turned back onto St. Joseph, he started pulling again, eager now to be home.

"I think someone's ready for his dinner," Corinne said.

"Yeah, and Buck's hungry, too," Wes deadpanned.

Corinne laughed.

"You're funny," she offered.

"Yeah, I am," Wes said, mounting the steps to the front porch and eyeing her like she was the last person on earth to figure this out.

And maybe she was. Michael had told her this several times, but she hadn't seen it. Corinne remembered thinking that Wes was juvenile for scraping off the "sham" on Michael's bottle of Axe Dual 2-in-1 Shampoo & Conditioner in their shower.

Well, it *was* juvenile, but it made Michael laugh for a month.

"The steaks will be ready in less than an hour," Wes said, stepping inside the house ahead of her. "Don't even think about disappearing in your room. If you fall asleep again, I'm giving yours to Buck."

Corinne halted in the doorway and raised an eyebrow. She was half-tempted to head to her room without a word, but she thought better of it. After everything he'd done for her in the last couple of days, that would be worse than ungrateful.

Still he couldn't just boss her around. That wouldn't do.

"So, do I have leave, Your Grace, to go take a shower?" she asked with no small amount of sarcasm.

Wes turned and eyed her over his shoulder with a wicked grin.

"Granted."

Chapter 12

Wes congratulated himself as he rinsed the asparagus. He'd gotten Corinne out of the house for a few minutes of fresh air; he was about to ensure that she ate a real meal, and she was currently showering.

This last point was difficult to push from his mind. The rush of water from the bathroom carried through the small house, distracting him while he worked. As he chopped off the white ends of the asparagus stalks, he'd hear the irregular thrumming of water on the tub floor, and he imagined—without meaning to—the spill of water over Corinne's hair and down her shoulders.

The third time this happened, Wes grabbed his phone, connected it to the speakers at the little work station in the living room that held Corinne's Mac, and tapped his music library. "On To The Next" by Jay Z flooded the house, decimating any other sounds. Wes helped himself to a beer and stepped in time to the base that shook the windows as he brushed olive oil over the asparagus.

He'd just sprinkled the ribeyes with Tony Chachere's when Corinne appeared in the kitchen doorway in yoga pants and a t-shirt, toweling her hair, eyes wide.

"You've got to be fucking kidding me!" she shouted over the music. She sounded pissed, but Wes thought she might have been fighting a smile.

"What?!?" Wes mimed a shrug, unable to help himself, and he took a sip of his Abita to hide his amusement.

Corinne narrowed her eyes at him in what he knew was a mock scowl, and she turned on her heel and headed out of the kitchen. He thought she'd just storm back to her room, but when the opening notes of Eminem's "The Monster" cut out and were replaced by Arctic Monkeys' "Fluorescent Adolescent" at the same deafening volume, he laughed to himself and carried the tray of asparagus outside.

Night had fallen, and the air was chilly. The floodlights off the sunroom gave the grill more than enough light, and Wes could see that the coals were ready. He could still hear the music from inside the house, so loud it could have been a party, and the smell of grill smoke and the taste of beer gave him a head rush of memories that nearly blew him away.

Michael.

"It's almost like you are here," Wes said aloud. Too late, he scanned the yard to make sure no one could hear him, but he was alone, and the feeling—the pull of talking to Michael—was too strong to resist. It was like drafting behind a semi instead of riding against a headwind. No work at all. Just flow. He told Michael about his first day as Corinne's roommate.

"I'm looking after her," he said to the night air. "But I sure wish you were here to do it instead."

After he'd turned the veggies a time or two, he pushed them to the edge of the grill and went back in the house to grab the steaks. Corinne's music was still playing—M83 sang about waiting in a car—but she had turned the volume down to a conversational level, and Wes could hear the blow dryer coming from the bathroom.

It shut off just as he headed back outside.

"Steaks will be done in like eight minutes, C," he called on his way out.

"Ok!" She called back.

When he came back inside, Wes was surprised to find the small kitchen table set with two places, a potato on each plate. Corinne had even put out butter and sliced lemon.

"Awesome," he said, carrying in the sizzling steaks and steaming asparagus.

Corinne gave a half laugh.

"Least I could do," she muttered, standing behind him as he served both their plates. "There's no way I can eat all that."

The steak alone took up most of her plate. With the potato and asparagus, it *was* pretty full. Wes shrugged at her.

"So we'll have leftovers. Want a beer?"

"Sure...," Corinne still stood awkwardly, staring at the table with the hint of a frown. Wes guessed that the scene was too domestic, too intimate for comfort.

"Is it too weird?" he asked, opening and Abita for her and handing it over. She took it without looking at him, but she didn't answer right away.

"No,...It's just been a while since I ate a real meal...You know...at a table...with someone else," she looked at him then, and he could see her defenses wall up. "I know that sounds pretty pathetic."

Wes shook his head.

"It sounds familiar," he said. It was suddenly important to him that she not see him as a threat. He was guilty of judging how she'd managed to get by after losing Michael, and maybe she couldn't forget that. He wished she could. "I've lived by myself for the last three years, and I can probably count on one hand the number of meals I ate at a table when I was in my apartment. Most of the time, I just sat in front of the TV."

She looked at him then, and Wes could still see the suspicion, the absence of trust. And he wanted to change that.

"C'mon, sit down before it gets cold."

Corinne sat, and he followed, cutting open his steaming potato and adding some butter and salt. He felt Corinne's eyes on him, and he looked up to find her staring.

"What?"

Wes thought that he saw the color rise on Corinne's cheeks.

"This looks delicious...Thank you," she said, looking humbled and awkward. It was better than her seeming suspicious or defensive, but he still didn't want her to thank him. He was *supposed* to be taking care of her.

"Don't get ahead of yourself. It might taste like crap," he joked. But when Wes squeezed lemon juice onto the ribeye and cut into the pink and tender brow, he knew it would be perfect.

"Wow," Corinne said through a mouthful.

"Mmm," he replied, losing himself to the rapture of it. Wes knew he was hungry, but Corinne seemed to wake up to her appetite. She was refined and mannered, but Wes saw the strain in the muscles of her neck and in her wrists as she wielded knife and fork. The almost wild look in her eyes. The girl was half-starving.

"Ohmygodthisissogood," she muttered moments later.

Wes was torn between patting himself on the back and punching himself in the head. Sure, he was succeeding, but why had it taken him so long to see what she'd needed? Michael had been gone for four whole months.

"So. Good." Corinne looked up from her plate, half-amazed. "I had no idea you were such a good cook."

Wes allowed himself a wry grin. Her surprised smile was pretty cute.

"My talents are pretty much limited to the grill," he said, regretting that he'd never offered to cook for her and Michael. "You're an awesome cook, though. Your pineapple upside down cake is like crack."

The smile she wore faltered, and Wes cursed himself. Thanksgiving was the last time he'd had that cake. Corinne had brought it to the Roush's, and after Mrs. Betsie's turkey and cornbread dressing and all the trimmings, he and Michael had glutted themselves on huge, golden slabs of paradise.

Corinne was picturing this, too, he could see, and she'd already warned him that their conversations could not consist of trips down Memory Lane. Wes scrambled to think of something else to say.

"You look like you're slowing down there," he said, pointing to her plate. She had hollowed out her potato and eaten almost half of her ribeye and most of the asparagus.

"Yeah, I'm done," she said, assessing her plate. "I couldn't eat another bite. I haven't had such a big meal in a long time."

Wes knew this was an understatement.

"If you put away the leftovers, I'll start on the dishes," he offered.

"Sure," she said, but she didn't meet his eyes. "Just excuse me for a second."

Corinne pushed herself up from the table, and Wes worried that his slip had triggered another crying spell, but she was gone and back in less than a minute. Corinne re-entered the kitchen wiping her mouth with the back of her hand.

He found himself on instant alert. What the hell had she done? He hadn't heard her close herself into the bathroom, so she couldn't have made herself throw up or anything like that.

Wes stopped the drain and filled the sink with hot water and suds while watching Corinne out of the corner of his eye. He knew that he might have been making something out of nothing, but it didn't *feel* like nothing.

They cleaned the kitchen without a word, and Wes started to wonder what the rest of the evening would look like. Left to herself, Corinne would probably retreat to her bedroom, and he wanted to try to break her of that habit.

"Have you seen the second season of *House of Cards* yet?" he asked, hoping it would spark her interest.

Corinne shook her head.

"Nope."

No spark.

"Would you like to watch the first episode with me?" Wes asked, watching her closely and half-expecting her to turn him down flat.

Corinne raised and dropped a shoulder.

"Sure," she said, but the energy and color she'd had during their walk and most of their dinner had dimmed.

At least she isn't going off to her room.

After they shut off the lights in the kitchen, Corinne curled up on the couch, and Buck joined her. Wes had to fight the smile at the picture they made, and he plunked himself down into his recliner and grabbed the remote.

He selected the Netflix episode and hit play, and Wes felt a frisson.
I live here now.

Wes was surprised by how okay he felt. He'd always been comfortable in Michael's home, even if he never felt the warmest welcome from Corinne, but he didn't think that hanging out with her in the living room would feel so...*normal*.

It was a relief that she hadn't fought him at every turn. He'd been surprised when she'd agreed to his set of rules after outlining hers, and he hadn't expected her to be so compliant about his suggestions to walk, to eat, even to watch TV.

Wes let the manipulations of Senator Underwood draw him in, but when Kevin Spacey pushed the reporter in front of the train, Wes glanced at Corinne to check her reaction.

Nothing.

She was slumped against the armrest of the couch, sound asleep.

What the fuck?

It wasn't even 9:00, and she'd slept all afternoon.

Wes turned off the TV and stood up. Buck picked his head up off his paws and watched him eagerly.

"C'mon, boy," Wes whispered and led the dog to the door. Buck ran out into the night and lifted his leg on a camellia bush in the yard before darting back in.

Wes locked up the front door, crossed the house, and made sure the back door was secured. He went back into the living room and studied Corinne. She hardly looked comfortable, but he had to assume that House Rule #1 didn't just apply to waking her up in her bedroom, so he left her alone and got himself ready for bed.

The weirdness factor presented itself when he tried to adjust to his new room. He looked around the space. It wasn't that his stuff and Michael's stuff were mixed together. That wasn't it at all. He and Michael had shared a dorm together freshman and sophomore year at UL; staying in a room with Michael's stuff was no big deal. And it wasn't just that it was his first night *living* there. Sure, it didn't quite *feel* real yet, but there was still something else that unsettled him.

Wes had a 5 a.m. client in the morning, so he made himself get into bed. He turned off his light, clicked on the TV, and aimlessly flipped through the channels. He'd left the lamp on in the living room so Corinne wouldn't wake up in the dark and freak out. When he turned off the TV a few minutes later, the soft light fell across the foot of his bed.

The house was so quiet, he could hear Corinne's breath.

He was still awake, lying on his back minutes later when the rhythm of her breathing changed, and he heard her stir. The light went off then, and he heard Corinne walk into the bathroom and close the door.

Water ran, the toilet flushed, water ran again, and then the door opened and the light clicked off.

And then nothing.

The house was entirely dark. Corinne must have been just standing in the hall, listening. Listening for him as he was listening for her.

His cock jumped at the thought.

Oh, hell, no, he told himself, flipping onto his side, angling away from the door. Wes took one of his spare pillows and pulled it over his head. If Corinne stood in the hallway for another hour or went into her room, he didn't know because he couldn't hear anything through the pillow.

He'd never lived with a woman before, he reminded himself. The presence of a female roommate—no matter who she was—was bound to...take him by surprise. It was no big deal.

Right?

May

Chapter 13

"Corinne? Wake up...Wake up, Corinne," Wes had her by the shoulder and was shaking her rudely.

Why is he breaking House Rule #1? He's only been here three weeks? Has he forgotten already?

Corinne could tell that the lamp by her bed was on even before she opened her eyes. When she finally blinked awake, she found Wes standing over her, shirtless, glaring angrily and holding his phone.

"What the hell are you on, Corinne? I've been trying to wake you for like five minutes. Morgan's in labor," he said, shoving his phone in her face. "You weren't answering, so she called me."

Oh, shit!

Corinne tried to push herself into a sitting position, but she felt like her head weighed 100 pounds.

"Crap. What time is it?" she croaked, reaching for her phone. 2:12 a.m. Six missed calls.

Shit.

Corinne hit Morgan's number, and Greg answered on the first ring.

"Jesus, Corinne. Where the hell have you been?" her brother-in-law scolded.

"I'm sorry, Greg. I was asleep. I must have left my ringer off," she lied. Wes raised an eyebrow at her and crossed his arms over his bare chest. "Where are you? How's Morgan?"

"We're getting in the car and leaving for the hospital. Her contractions are about two minutes apart," Greg said, sounding breathless and a little panicked. "Morgan wants you and her dad there. Can you pick him up?"

"Um...I guess so..." she hedged. Corinne thought she heard moans in the background.

Morgan!

"We'll be at Women's," Greg said. "Call when you get there."

And he hung up.

"Shit," Corinne muttered, staring at her phone.

"Call your dad and get dressed," Wes barked. "I'll take you."

Corinne frowned up at him.

"I can take myself. Go back to bed, Wes."

Wes shook his head, scowling.

"You are in no condition to drive. You'd probably fall asleep at the wheel and plow into somebody."

Corinne gasped at the suggestion, and Wes's eyes lost some of their rancor.

"Sorry," he mumbled. "I didn't mean that."

Corinne bit her lip and blinked at him.

"I'm sorry they woke you. You seem really upset."

Wes's brows rose.

"That's not why I'm upset, C." He scrubbed a hand over his face and dragged it through his hair. "Look, just call your dad and get dressed."

Corinne figured it was best not to argue anymore, even if she knew she could drive safely. The idea that she could ever hurt someone the way Michael had been hurt was too much for her. She shook the thought from her mind and called her father.

Ten minutes later, she found Wes in the living room, dressed and carrying a duffle bag. She gave him a questioning look, but he just stuck his hand out.

"Where are your keys?"

She dug in her purse and handed them over, feeling like a child.

They didn't speak the entire drive to Emeritus. Corinne sat awkwardly in the passenger seat of her little-used Mazda 3 and dreaded what was ahead. Morgan had asked her to attend the birth, and Corinne had agreed, absently, but now that it was upon her, she didn't really know if she could go through with it. It would be too intense, and Corinne didn't think she could handle intense right now.

She leaned back against the seat and closed her eyes for just a moment, but suddenly they were outside her father's apartment. It surprised her that her dad waited by his front door, leaning against his walker.

"Good morning, Mr. Granger," Wes greeted him with a pasted on smile as he got out of the car. Corinne followed, unsure how Wes would explain his presence.

Corinne's father mumbled a greeting, but he eyed Corinne with a question she couldn't misinterpret.

"Wes gave me a ride be—"

"Because I didn't want her to drive across town alone at this hour," Wes declared, offering her father his left hand to shake, matching her dad's good arm.

Half her father's face lifted in surprise, followed by a smile.

"Thank you, Wes," he managed.

Before Corinne knew what was going on, Wes had settled her father into the back seat of the car and tucked his walker into the trunk. As Wes started the car, her father leaned forward, squeezed her shoulder, and gave her an approving look.

What the hell just happened?

There was only one intersection separating Emeritus from Women's & Children's Hospital, so Corinne had no time to ponder the question. She did breathe a small sigh of relief that Morgan and Greg had picked this hospital over General where Michael had spent his last days.

Still, the smell was the same, and it hit her as she stepped through the automatic doors. A shudder ran through her, and she crossed her arms around herself. An instant later, Wes placed a hand between her shoulder blades.

When she glanced up at him in surprise, she saw the same haunted look in his eyes that she must have worn.

"That fucking smell," he whispered.

They found Morgan's birthing suite on the second floor, and Wes stopped outside the door.

"I'm going to find the waiting room," he said. Corinne checked her watch. It was almost 3 a.m.

"Wait, don't you have work in a couple of hours? You should head back," she said, frowning. "Greg can take us home later."

Wes just shook his head and gave her an enigmatic smile.

"I've got it covered," he said before heading down the hall.

Corinne watched him go and then followed her father into Morgan's room where she found her sister sitting on a giant exercise ball, panting. Greg sat in a chair in front of her, bracing her up.

Whoa.

Morgan's eyes were closed, but her brow crimped, and her light brown hair crowded her face in damp curls.

"I need more ice chips…" she begged. "More ice chips, please, Greg."

"Of course," he promised before waving Corinne over and whispering. "She's transitioning. The nurse said she's at six centimeters. Come sit with her while I get more ice. Remind her to breathe."

Greg stood, still cradling Morgan's head and shoulders, and when Corinne made no move to take his place, he glared at her.

"Sit!" her brother-in-law hissed, so she sat, and before she knew it, Morgan was slumped against her, her legs and the stability ball tucked between Corinne's knees. Morgan's skin was hot and flushed, and when the next contraction came, Corinne thought her sister would pull her out of the chair.

"Breathe, Morgan," her father said, as clearly as he could. Somehow, he had appeared by Corinne's side in a chair identical to hers, and he helped to brace Morgan's weight with his left arm.

"Oh, Daddy…" Morgan whimpered, still not even opening her eyes.

"Shhh. Doing great, Morgan," he cooed.

Corinne watched her sister with a mixture of fear and awe. She'd heard Morgan talk all along about going natural, but she'd always doubted her sister's commitment to it when the going got tough.

Well, the going seemed to be getting pretty tough, and Morgan wasn't crying out for drugs.

Corinne swallowed. On the next contraction, she reminded Morgan to breathe.

Three hours later, Corinne held Clementine Granger Bates in her arms.

She didn't know what to feel. Her niece was the color of a peach and softer than any earthly thing could ever be. Corinne was enraptured with her.

And still with every breath-taking moment—from the one when she'd actually seen the baby's head crown to the one when the little life she was holding locked eyes with her and *saw her*, Corinne couldn't silence the voice.

Michael will never get this. We'll never have this.

"Don't cry *on* her, Cory," Morgan scolded, gently, reaching for the baby.

"Ah! I'm sorry," Corinne sniffed, handing Clementine over and wiping her eyes.

Greg was snapping pictures, which he'd been doing almost non-stop since he and Corinne had bathed the baby—under the watchful eye of one of the nursery staff. Corinne's father stood at the edge of Morgan's bed where he'd positioned his walker; he was radiant with pride, but there was a hint of sadness in his eyes.

Corinne realized without warning that he was missing their mother, that Alice Granger should have been there beside him to welcome their first grandchild. At least little Clementine wouldn't know the difference, she'd never know what it felt like to lose her. If she was lucky, maybe she'd make it through life only losing loved ones to old age.

Corinne looked around the room and frowned.

"Where's Wes?" she blurted.

"Oh, he left a while ago," Greg said behind the camera. He looked up and pointed toward the door. "He asked that you bring home his bag, and he left your car keys."

Corinne saw the duffle bag that had been dumped in the chair by the door. When had that happened?

Corinne eyed her brother-in-law.

"Well,...How did he leave? Did he get a ride?" she asked, mystified.

"No, he ran to work," Greg said, casually, raising the camera to his eye again, seeing only his little family.

"He *ran* to *work?*" Corinne gaped.

"Yeah, that's what he said."

"When was this?" She couldn't believe what she was hearing. Had that been his plan? Wes had said he had it worked out. Did he just plan to take off on foot in the dark of night?

"It was when I went out for ice chips. Right after you showed up."

Corinne went to the door and grabbed her keys and the duffle. The bag was completely empty. Whatever had been in it, Wes had taken with him. The guy had planned to run to work.

Because of her.

Corinne bit her lip. She knew it probably wasn't that big a deal for Wes to run across town, but the fact that he'd insisted on driving her—of getting up hours early to drive her—and running the four or five miles back to the health club more than awed her.

It also made her a little worried. The roads from Women's & Children's Hospital to LFC were major thoroughfares with speed limits of 50 mph.

Corinne found her purse and pulled out her phone.

Monday, May 19 8:20 a.m.
You ok? I can't believe you ran to the gym.

Corinne stared at the screen, waiting for him to reply. She let her breath go once her phone chimed.

Monday, May 19 8:22 a.m.
All good. No worries. Baby?

Corinne smiled in relief.

Monday, May 19 8:23 a.m.
Clementine Granger Bates. 8 lbs, 4 oz. Mom and baby are just fine.

Monday, May 19 8:23 a.m.
Awesome. See u @ home.

"Oh, I think she's hungry," Morgan announced. Corinne looked up from her phone to see Baby Clementine rooting eagerly at Morgan's hospital gown. When her sister made to lift it to suckle the newborn, Corinne took her cue to leave.

"C'mon, Dad. I think we should leave this little family unit to themselves for a while."

Her father muttered his agreement, but he shuffled to the head of Morgan's bed to kiss his daughter and granddaughter and once again slap his son-in-law on the back.

Corinne rolled her eyes at his obvious pride, but her face ached with the smile it gave her.

The trip back to Emeritus was short, but more than once, Clement Granger uttered—clearly—the same words.

"A new life...a new life..."

When they reached his apartment, Corinne retrieved her father's walker from the trunk and walked him to his door.

"One day, Cory," she thought she heard him say.

Corinne pressed her lips together because it would do no good to tell him that he was wrong; besides, she probably wouldn't be able to get through it without breaking down. And that wouldn't help anyone.

Instead, Corinne kissed her father goodbye, promising that they would be the first to visit the little family at home once they were discharged the following day.

The sun was shining, and the car had soaked up the heat. As Corinne headed home, the warmth drove the last of the adrenaline from her. The birth had been thrilling, but exhaustion gathered around her like a cloak.

Buck went berserk as soon as she came through the door, alerting her with jumps and twirls that his breakfast was hours late.

"Sorry, baby," she cooed, following him to the pantry and serving him a heaping scoop of food. Corinne opened the fridge and stared inside. She was too tired to eat, but she was incredibly thirsty.

Wes had chilled cans of coconut water, and the label of the coconut with a straw sticking out of it was too tempting to pass up. She grabbed one and opened the tab, and the cold, mildly sweet liquid was heaven. It didn't satisfy Wes's rule for one of her three squares a day, but she told herself she'd eat something later.

Corinne carried her drink to the couch and plopped down. *The Today Show* was still on, and even though the A-list hosts had already passed the baton to Tamron Hall and Natalie Moralis, the chatter about spring fashion and pet spas was better than silence.

In a moment, it didn't matter what was on because Corinne's muscles seemed to soak into the cushions, and her eyelids melted closed. Her last cogent thought was that she needed to thank Wes for his morning heroics.

Perhaps a pineapple upside down cake.

Chapter 14

Wes adjusted his Camelbak and waited for the crosswalk signal at Johnston and South College. The pack carried his keys and wallet, the sweaty t-shirt he'd run to work in that morning, and something for Corinne. After obsessing about her all day at the gym, he'd come up with a plan.

She had scared him half to death.

When the call from Morgan had woken him, he'd knocked and called Corinne's name outside her door for what seemed like forever. Before barging in, he'd even wondered if she'd left the house in the middle of the night. Which was crazy because Corinne *never* left the house.

Wes had crossed the room in the darkness, but when he touched her shoulder to rouse her and she didn't respond, he'd snapped the light on in confusion. Confusion quickly morphed to panic when she wouldn't wake up, and he half expected to see an empty bottle of pills on the pillow beside her.

Of course, there had been none, but clearly, Corinne was taking something. Too much of something, to be exact.

The crosswalk lit up for him, and he broke into a run again. The distance from the house to the health club was only a little more than three miles, but Wes was ready to be home. It was only just past 11, and he'd finished a six-hour shift at the gym. He had the afternoon and the evening to try to confront Corinne, but Wes knew that he had to be careful about it.

He reached the house, unlocked the door, and immediately slowed his movements when he saw Corinne asleep on the couch. Buck was curled by her feet, and the dog raised his head and thumped his tail sleepily.

Not much of a guardian, Buck.

As quietly as he could, Wes shut the door behind him and stepped closer. As usual, Corinne was lying on her right side, tucked in the fetal position; she didn't stir at all when he came through the door.

Wes sighed. He couldn't keep an eye on her every minute of the day, but he was beginning to wish that he could. In the last three weeks, they'd walked Buck every evening and eaten dinner together. Either he cooked, or they ordered in. Whatever it was, they would talk over the meal, slowly finding the safe topics.

The gym was always good for a story, be it funny or ridiculous, like the young guys who choose to go into the cold plunge in just their Under Armour briefs, moose-knuckling their way into the water in front of the unsuspecting golden girls of swim aerobics—and coming out mouse-knuckling ten minutes later. And then there were the entitled mothers who thought that club membership meant after-school care for their lawless brats. No shortage of material for stories.

Unlike before, Corinne now laughed at his anecdotes. And unless he was imagining it, she was glad to see him when he came in from work. Sometimes, he knew the moment he stepped through the door that she'd been crying, maybe for a long time, but instead of being furious with him for invading her privacy—like she had the day he took the Pinarello—she looked relieved.

And he was always glad to see *her*.

Wes realized this after their fourth day as roommates. That morning at the gym, one of the ladies he'd worked with for about five months told him that she had just reached her 50 lb. weight loss goal, and with words of gratitude and a few tears, she had given Wes a $50 gift card to Ruth's Chris Steakhouse. On his way home that day, all he could picture was telling Corinne.

And even now, conked out on the couch after driving him insane that morning, she was still the person he wanted to see.

Don't be a creep, Wes told himself, turning away from her and walking into the hall. In his room, he dumped the pack on his bed and stood in his doorway. Corinne's bedroom was directly across the hall from his, and she'd left the door open. Wes tiptoed back into the hall again and studied her.

She was obviously sleeping soundly. If he didn't take the chance now, he might have to wait another day or more.

He felt torn about violating her space, but what had happened during the night could not happen again. Whatever she was doing was dangerous. Corinne might not understand, but Michael surely would. Anyone else would.

Wes crept across the hall and into Corinne's room. The obvious place to look—the only place, really—were her bedside table drawers. Wes stood in front of them and worked his jaw.

Bedside tables were forbidden zones. TMI deathtraps. What if he found a dildo in there? Would he ever be able to look Corinne in the eye again?

Without meaning to, he pictured Corinne...*doing that*. And all the blood in his body headed south.

"What the fuck is wrong with you?" he whispered, scrubbing his face with his hands to clear his thoughts. He took three deep breaths and slid the top drawer open just a couple of inches. A plastic bottle with a purple label tipped into view.

Not wanting to see anything else, Wes shut his eyes, opened the drawer a little wider, and reached for the bottle.

ZzzQuil?

The half-empty container looked just like NyQuil, except it was purple instead of green. Wes read the label: *Diphenhydramine HCl 50 mg in each 30 ml dose*. He pulled the dosage cup off the lid and eyed it. A faint blue stain crept all the way to the top, past the 30 ml line.

Corinne had been overdosing—no doubt—on purpose.

Before he could get caught in her room, Wes shut the drawer and smuggled the bottle into his bedroom. He dug out his phone and read about ZzzQuil overdose.

Flushed skin. Drowsiness. Dilated pupils. Confusion.

Wes had seen these in Corinne on more than one occasion. The rest of the symptoms—like rapid heart rate and low blood pressure—he couldn't detect by looking at her, but he would have bet money that she'd experienced them.

He kept reading. The one bright spot was that the OTC sleep aid was not habit-forming. Corinne's continued abuse of it was a choice, not an addiction. She wanted to sleep. Maybe even day and night.

Wes winced at the thought. He no longer felt like he wasn't living up to Michael's expectations. Helping with her living expenses, feeding her, getting her out of the house and moving; these things he knew would have satisfied his best friend. But knowing that he was doing the job wasn't enough.

He didn't want Corinne to hurt anymore. And he definitely didn't want her to hurt herself.

She was trying to go numb. He understood that. He'd done his fair share of self-medicating in his life. Enough to know that it didn't make anything better in the long run. Sleeping all of the time would only stall Corinne and keep her from her life. Without this liquid escape, Corinne would have to work out her grief.

But Wes intended to be there with her while she did.

He took the bottle with him, and he set out through the house again, moving as quietly as possible. When he got to the sunroom, it took him a while before he found what he was searching for, but once he was armed with everything he needed, he went back to the living room to wait.

And he didn't have to wait long. As soon as he sat down in his recliner, Corinne turned over on the couch and stretched. Her eyes were still closed, but the hem of her t-shirt rode up, and Wes caught a glimpse of her taut abdomen before he made himself turn away. When he looked back, Corinne was squinting at him in confusion.

"When did you get back?" she asked, her voice still thick with sleep.

"Just a few minutes ago," Wes answered, bracing himself. She had not seen the array of items on the coffee table in front of her, and once she did, Wes knew that she would go ballistic.

"Mmm...Thank you for helping me this morning." Corinne scooted herself up on the couch and reached her arms over her head, grabbing each elbow and rocking side to side. In front of him, her body elongated deliciously.

There was nowhere to look.

The pale olive underside of her arms. The rise of her breasts. The curve of her waist.

"I...um...you're welcome," Wes muttered, dragging his eyes down to the safety of her feet, but even they were bare, fine-boned, beautiful. He pinched the bridge of his nose to clear his focus and forced himself to look Corinne in the eye. "But we need to talk."

She was still blinking the sleep from her eyes, but she frowned her pretty frown and held his gaze for a moment before her eyes shifted to the coffee table and took in the bottle, the sketch pad, and the card.

"What the hell..." Corinne's features steeled, all remnants of sleep gone. She pinned him with her stare. "You went through my stuff, Wes?"

The accusation he could take; it was the look of hurt in her eyes that lanced through him, but he wasn't going to let this be about him. She was in too much trouble.

"Corinne, I know what you've been doing."

He watched her blink at the certainty in his voice. Wes knew just by watching her that she would deny it. The Corinne he knew—then and now—didn't show weakness, not without first putting up a fight.

"You don't know shit," she leveled, a hardness in her eyes almost masking the doubt she felt.

Secretly, he didn't mind the fight. He was grateful that this much of her remained.

"I know you're having a hard time," Wes said, not taking his eyes off her.

"Shut up! You had no right to go into my room!" Corinne sat up completely now, feet on the floor, ready to do battle.

"I was worried about you...I *am* worried about you," he said, honestly.

She gave him a dirty look and crossed her arms over her chest.

"Because I take a sleep aid now and then? It's over-the-counter, Wes," her tone was superior, defensive. She wanted to make him feel stupid, which had once been something she excelled at, but those days were over.

"It's not 'now and then.' It's every day. Probably twice a day," Wes said, pinning her with his eyes even as his voiced stayed calm.

"Such *bullshit*," she hissed, scowling at him. He watched her. Closely. Everything in her expression was a bluff. Everything formed a wall.

He had no doubt that he'd break through.

"What's this about? Are you regretting moving in?" she accused. "Is that where this is coming from?"

Wes's eyes bugged. Nothing could be further from the truth.

"Hell, no," he said with force, feeling anger for the first time. "This isn't about me. I *know* what you are doing, Corinne, and it scares me."

She blinked at him then, clearly surprised. He was a little surprised, himself—surprised that he'd said it out loud.

Corinne recovered first.

"Look, it's sweet that you're worried about me, but you've got the wrong idea," she shrugged, giving him a pitying smile.

She's good, Wes thought. *But I'm better*.

"If I've got the wrong idea, then you won't care if I pour the rest of this down the sink." He was out of his chair and grabbing the bottle before Corinne could react.

"Wait!" she said, jumping from the couch, but Wes was already heading for the kitchen. No matter how she'd taken the confrontation, the ZzzQuil was going down the drain, but Wes would have preferred to have her buy-in.

"Wait!" she shrieked again, blocking him at the kitchen sink. "Give that back!"

"I can't do that," he said, simply, holding the bottle away from her in his right hand as she came at him from the left.

"But it's mine," Corinne whined, and then she surprised him by lunging in front of him and making a grab for the bottle. He only managed to kept it from her reach by lifting it over his head. And Wes nearly dropped it when her thighs pressed into his left hip as she made for another go.

It would have been funny, Wes thought, if it wasn't so messed up.

The contact with her body rattled him, and he pushed her away.

"Corinne! Stop." The edge in his voice left no room for opposition. "This ends now."

He watched as her eyebrows bunched, and she seemed to shrink in front of him.

"But I really can't sleep without it," Corinne said, looking terrified. "I've tried. I swear, Wes, I've tried...Please...just give it back."

Ouch.

The pleading look in her eyes made him feel like an ogre, and something in her voice pulled at the muscles in his chest. A part of him wanted to give in, but he knew he couldn't.

"C, I can't let you do this," he said, meeting her eyes, hoping she saw that he wasn't trying to hurt her. Just the opposite. "I know you just want to sleep. I get it, but this isn't good for you. It isn't helping."

"No, you don't understand." Her voice had lost almost all volume. The panic in her eyes made him want to reach out for her. "I won't be able to sleep *at all*. I've tried. I don't remember my dreams when I take it, and I tried to stop because I wasn't dreaming about Michael anymore, and then I just couldn't sleep at all...I'll lose it if I can't sleep, Wes. It's too much."

Corinne's pupils were like saucers, and her lips had blanched. Wes dropped the bottle in the sink and grabbed her just as her knees failed.

"I've got you," he promised.

Chapter 15

Somehow, she was back on the couch, and Wes was sitting next to her. Corinne could remember a sinking feeling, a sponginess in her legs and then Wes's arms, but the rest was just a racing heartbeat and a cold sweat.

"You're okay," he whispered, and it was then that she felt his hands moving up and down her sleeves.

She was shivering. And Wes's hands were warm.

As soon as that thought registered, she scooted away, hugging herself. Wes dropped his hands immediately and sat a little further back, but he didn't take his eyes off her. Corinne could only look at her knees. How could she face him when he knew all her secrets? He had to think she was the most pathetic creature on earth.

What if he tells Morgan and Dad?

This new horror forced her to look up.

"Are you going to tell anyone?" she blurted. She hated how juvenile she sounded. How weak. But Wes just frowned—not unkindly—and shook his head.

"No, I'm not going to tell anyone."

Corinne closed her eyes and let herself sigh. At least she would be spared further humiliation. Everything sucked. Everything. But Corinne knew that things could always suck worse.

"Thank you," she forced herself to say.

"I won't tell anyone..." Wes repeated, but something in his voice made her look up again. "But things need to change."

He spoke with absolute conviction. When had that happened? Corinne regarded him, the cast of his eyes, the line of his jaw. When had he become so...*mature?* He had never struck her as someone with authority. And other than his vanity, she'd never understood the personal training thing. But now she did. Wes knew how to tell people what to do, and she could believe that they'd listen. That they'd *want* to listen.

"I know," she allowed.

She knew things needed to change. Corinne figured that if she wanted to, she could just go out and buy another bottle of ZzzQuil, hide it somewhere clever—in a box of tampons in the bathroom—and keep dosing all of the time, but she couldn't fool herself; that was no way to live. It was almost a relief that Wes had caught her.

But how would she get to sleep?

And how would she face all of the hours in between?

This time, she sighed a deeper, more bottomless sigh.

"Talk to me," Wes said, still eyeing her relentlessly.

"I'm never going to sleep," she declared. "I'm going to lie awake for the rest of my life and probably go nuts in the process."

Wes cracked a smile, but his brown eyes were shadowed with sadness.

"Tonight's gonna be rough," he conceded with a nod. "But after tomorrow, it'll get better."

Corinne raised a brow at him.

"How do you know?" she challenged.

He raised a brow to mimic her, but he couldn't keep a straight face.

"Because you are going to be too worn out."

The grin Wes wore was downright evil, and Corinne bit her lip.

"What's that supposed to mean?"

Wes reached across the coffee table and picked up a plastic card.

"I don't have to be at the health club until 8:00 tomorrow. And you're coming with me." He said it with the same authority he'd asserted a moment before. "You'll go to the 8 a.m. yoga class, and then at 9:30, you have a personal training appointment with me. Here's your membership card."

He handed her the card bearing the fitness club logo, her name, and a membership ID number.

"What the hell—"

"After that, you'll chill by the pool with your sketchpad." Wes thrust the 9 x 12 spiral bound pad into her hands. "And, just so you know, I'm not taking you home until there's new stuff in it, so you'd better use your time wisely. I'll join you for lunch, and later you can check out the sauna and the hot tub and all of that. I don't get off until 4, but that's enough to keep you pretty busy."

Corinne blinked at him.

"You'll probably want to pack a bag with your swimsuit and a change of clothes," he said, nodding. "Oh, and I didn't know what pencils you'd want to take, so you should pack some of those, too."

Corinne looked from him to the sketchpad to the membership card.

"Wes, I can't afford a membership," she said, flatly.

Wes shook his head, dismissing her concern.

"I put you on my account. I get a discount. It's all good," he said, smiling.

Corinne held her expression as still as possible. A part of her wanted to smile back. She was lucky that anyone thought about her enough to plan a whole day for her. But then again, he was pretty much telling her what to do, and the other part of her was a little pissed off. Since when did she let anyone tell her what to do?

Since Wes decided to move in, she realized.

Still, his plan was better than any she had, and while the prospect of spending the whole day trapped at the health club kind of terrified her, she was also curious to see how it would feel to be out of the house that long. Corinne promised herself that she could always decide to hate it and refuse to go back.

She took a deep breath to settle her nerves.

"Okay, I guess."

Wes kept it in check, but she could see that her assent made him happy. The muscles in his cheeks fought against an all-out smile, but his brown eyes grew boyish, the light in them turning all the way up.

This time she did smile back. His delight in his triumph was just a little contagious, and at the same time, the fact that it was in an effort to help her challenged her understanding of Wes Clarkson. Was this a side that Michael had known all along? A willful, even stubborn Good

Samaritan? Bossy as hell? Had he come to Michael's aid like this in the years they'd been friends?

Corinne hoped so because she'd seen the reverse on more than one occasion.

"Enough about tomorrow," Wes said, gracefully moving the attention from her issues. "Tell me about today. About your new niece."

So she did. She told him about Clementine's arrival in the world and how amazing and terrifying it was to hold her and bathe her, how Granddad Clement was fit to burst with pride.

They talked over sandwiches for lunch, and when Wes excused himself later, saying that the lawn needed mowing and he wouldn't have a free afternoon for a while, Corinne followed suit, joining him outside to pull weeds from the neglected front beds. Once or twice when she'd straighten up to shove a handful of weeds into a lawn bag, she found Wes's eyes on her. From his expression, she didn't feel leered at or self-conscious; she felt watched over.

They walked Buck that evening and ordered Chinese for dinner.

"*House of Cards* marathon," Wes suggested, sitting down next to her on the couch and opening the container of Kung Pao Chicken. "I'll stay up with you until you get tired."

Corinne gave him a sheepish smile. It was sweet and surprising, but she knew she wouldn't sleep for a while. If at all.

"Thanks, but you don't have to do that." She helped herself to the fried rice and one of the egg rolls. "I'm probably not going to be able to sleep, but I'll take the *House of Cards* marathon."

"I'll stay," Wes said, almost inaudibly, passing the Kung Pao container to Corinne, but not meeting her eyes.

It was humbling, Corinne thought, only half paying attention to Kevin Spacey's scheming. Wes was forcing her to redraw her definition of him. All afternoon, she had shied away from the unpleasant realization that she had long ago dismissed Wes Clarkson as something less than a fully-realized adult, one encompassing depth and complexity. She was guilty of labeling him. Mocking him. She had—aloud to Michael many times—called him names: *Overgrown Frat Boy, Arrested Development, Maximum Density.*

Corinne watched him out of the corner of her eye and wanted to cover her head in shame. He had moved in with her so she could stay in this house. He had stocked her fridge and pantry with food that *he* cooked for *her*. He had made her take care of her body. He'd tried, anyway.

He'd woken her up during the night after she'd taken enough diphenhydramine to stagger a horse, and he'd driven her across town so that she could be there for the birth of her niece.

That thought pricked her. Had it not been for Wes, she probably would have slept through the whole thing. She thought about little Clementine and swallowed against the bitter lump in her throat.

What had she done to deserve any of it?

And now, Wes had made it his mission to bring her back to the world. To get out of the house. Exercise. Draw?

The last possibility sent a chill of fear through her. What if she couldn't?

Corinne glanced at Wes again. She watched, amused, as he took a bite of egg roll and hummed to himself. Wes *loved* to eat. Corinne suspected that it was because all of his exercising left him perpetually hungry. Of course, running to and from work that day probably had something to do with it.

He had done that for her, too. With a resolving nod to herself, Corinne decided that she would give the sketchbook her best shot in the morning. If Wes could do all that he'd done for her in the last month— even in the last day—she could face some charcoal and paper.

After they finished one episode of *House of Cards*, Corinne cleared the dishes, ignoring Wes's protests. When she got back to the living room, Wes had changed into the cotton t-shirt and shorts she'd noticed him wearing on Saturday mornings. Those had been the only days she'd woken up in time to find him still at the house, still in his pajamas.

"You look tired," she acknowledged, knowing that he'd been up since 2 a.m. "You can go to bed, you know. It's a lost cause."

Wes shook his head.

"I'm good."

They settled onto the couch and started the next episode before Wes grabbed her right foot and pulled it into his lap. When she tensed and made to pull away, he gripped tighter.

"Try to relax," he said, giving her a half-smile. "Nothing weird, I swear."

Corinne glared at him for a whole second until he squeezed her foot in his hands and started to massage.

"Holy hell!" she gasped as pure ecstasy flooded through the sole of her foot. Wes chuckled and used his thumbs to mold her arch and heel. Corinne fell against the arm of the couch and sighed.

"Jesus Christ..." She closed her eyes and felt his fingers find all of the bones that fanned out to her toes, tracing each one with exquisite pressure. Her muscles unspooled. Even Corinne's jaw relaxed under his touch.

"Why?...Why are you doing this?" she managed to ask, succumbing to a kind of delirium she could not remember ever experiencing.

Wes watched her, smiling, clearly pleased with himself.

"Because you need it," he said, simply.

She began to protest.

"But you don't even—" But just then, he began rolling her toes between his fingers, and she melted even more. Corinne closed her eyes against the tears that had suddenly formed.

Her body had not felt such pleasure in months. She had not been touched like this in months.

Stop it, she scolded herself, not wanting to break down in front of him yet again. Corinne swallowed her tears and mastered her voice.

"But you don't even like me," she finished.

Wes's hands stilled, and she kept her eyes closed, fearing that she'd forced him to agree with her.

"Corinne,...look at me," Wes whispered.

She slowly opened her eyes. Wes still smiled at her, but his eyes had narrowed in confusion.

"Aren't we friends now?" he asked her, gently. Then he shrugged. "I've never given a foot rub to someone I didn't like."

At this, she laughed, and if it was possible, she relaxed even more. Wes surrendered her right foot and reached for her left.

"Oh heavenly day…" she murmured.

"Stop talking," he mock scolded. "And could you rewind it? I just missed that whole scene."

Corinne was completely limp by the time Wes finished with her left foot.

"Thank you," she whispered, kind of in awe.

"Mmm Hmm. And after my next marathon, you'll do mine, right?" he teased. "I warn you, though, the post-race funk is pret-ty bad!"

Corinne's feet were still in his lap, and she playfully kicked at his knee, making him laugh.

"Yeah…Sure…" she deadpanned.

He grabbed a foot and squeezed.

"Stop talking! You're ruining the show!" he hissed, trying to scowl at her, but his smile killed the effect.

Corinne tried to concentrate on the plot, but the events of the day made it a challenge. It was clear to her that she really didn't know very much about Wes Clarkson.

By the end of the third episode, Corinne looked up to find that Wes had tipped over and was sleeping with his head on the opposite armrest. Knowing how stubborn he was, Corinne decided against waking him and trying to send him to bed again, so she curled against the armrest behind her and turned the volume down as the opening trumpets played.

When the feds busted poor Lucas Goodwin, Wes rolled onto his back and stretched his legs across the cushions against hers.

Corinne held her breath.

Lean and warm, his legs pressed into her skin. His own skin was as smooth as hers. He'd finally explained that shaving his arms and legs helped him to get in and out of a wetsuit during a triathlon without plucking himself. Corinne had to admit that his hairlessness didn't seem so stupid anymore.

Positioned head to toe as they were, Corinne could feel the heavy muscle of his right thigh against her right foot and the cording of his calf on her knee. Every inch of him was warm.

It felt nice.

Despite her certainty that she'd lie awake the whole night, Corinne slept like that until morning. She awoke with the sun in her eyes as something brushed her thigh. Looking down, she saw Wes's legs tangled with hers and his hand on her knee. His eyes were still closed, but with her stirring, they blinked open, and Corinne saw the mixture of surprise and confusion as he took her in.

Then his gaze fell between them, and Wes's eyes rounded in alarm. Corinne followed his look and caught the unmistakable shape that stretched his cotton shorts just as Wes leapt off the couch.

"Shit, I'm late," Wes muttered as he sped to the bathroom.

Too stunned to reply, Corinne stared at the bathroom door he'd closed behind him. It wasn't the morning wood that shocked her; it was Wes's obvious embarrassment. The man made more boner jokes than a seventh grade boy. At least, he had with Michael. Had this changed about him, too? Or was it her? Did she embarrass him?

She shook the thought from her mind and got up to feed Buck. Wes had been right about running late. It was 7:19, and she still needed to pack her things for the gym.

At the health club, Wes had just enough time to point her toward the yoga studio before meeting his next client, promising to be back for her when her class ended. The studio was full, but Corinne was able to find a spot for her mat close to the back. Although she'd taken her fair share of yoga classes, she'd never been to Wes' club, and she had to admit that it was by far the nicest health club she'd ever seen. Not posh or intimidating, but aesthetic, well lit, and roomy.

The instructor was a tall, wiry man in his early 40s whom Corinne liked immediately. His voice was compassionate, but not hokey, and as the group sat in lotus and the wind chime soundtrack played, he instructed them to focus on their breath and dedicate the class to something important.

Corinne immediately thought about Michael.

But then the instructor added more.

"Dedicate the class to something that you know you need—not want, but need—that you have not let yourself attain," Simon, the yoga instructor intoned. "It may be peace; it may be patience; it may be healing."

What about all three? Corinne wanted to ask aloud, but instead, she chose healing. If she had healing, she reasoned, she would also have peace, and if she had healing, she probably wouldn't need so much patience.

And when Simon told them to close their eyes and envision what their dedicated practice would honor, Michael was there. He simply was there. But he wasn't Michael, her lover, in his biking shorts or wrapped in a towel. He wasn't dream Michael, teasing her with memories from their life. He was Michael, the love: the love that she knew transcended pain, outlasted loss. And in her mind's eye, he drew closer to her with a radiance that she could both see and feel, and the feeling was like a warming that would fill her center. It would stop the pain.

"Now open your eyes," Simon instructed. "And slowly, slowly come to standing at the front of your mats."

The moment was over too soon. Corinne was not at all surprised to find her lashes wet with tears, but she didn't feel the need to slam shut her eyes and recapture the sensation. In fact, the feeling of that energy still held, and so she focused on it through each sun salutation, each warrior, each downward-facing dog.

The hour passed in an instant, and as she lay on her mat in shavasana, Corinne felt suffused with ease. It was better than ZzzQuil by about a million times. She had no doubt that she would come back tomorrow.

Chapter 16

Arms spread out at her sides, Corinne lay on the mat closest to the door and draped one bent leg over the other. Watching from the glass panel next to the entrance, Wes swallowed, thinking that those were the same legs that had been tangled with his only hours before.

He backed away from the door before anyone noticed him ogling. Before Corinne noticed. The class would be over any minute, and he definitely didn't want Corinne to see him staring at her—especially after waking up next to her with a stiffy. If she could have read his mind, she'd have known that it wasn't just an innocent, REM-sleep boner. Not for the first time—he had to admit—Corinne had been the subject of his dream. His fingers were travelling up her thigh when he'd awoken.

It was one thing to lust after your chick roommate, but it was something else when she was your best friend's girl.

I'm such an asshole.

They hadn't even been living together for a whole month, and Wes was already in trouble. The night on the couch had made that clear, even though it had been coming on for weeks. Catching himself looking at her, always eager to be with her, thinking up ways to make her smile. This was not what Michael had in mind when he'd asked his best friend to watch over her.

The thing that addled him was that he'd known Corinne for almost *two years*. He'd known her and—truth be told—resented her for most of that time. Because she clearly hadn't liked him. And other than thinking that she was Michael's hot, but bitchy girlfriend, she'd never crossed his mind.

But now, that opinion seemed like it belonged to another life, and so did Corinne's disdain. She was someone else entirely now. And he knew that it wasn't just because losing Michael had changed her. He sensed that he'd just never seen everything, and living with her guaranteed that he did. She could still be feisty as hell, but she was also vulnerable, grateful, and easy to be with. He *liked* being with her. He liked *her*.

But that was as far as it could go. She didn't need to know that she had taken up residence in his mind just as much as he'd taken up residence in her house. She didn't need to know, and he wouldn't act on it. And with any luck—like every other crush he'd had—the feeling would dissipate eventually.

This seemed like a sound plan until Corinne walked out of the studio. Tears were streaming down her face, but she was smiling.

"Why are you crying?" he asked, approaching her in confusion. His confusion only mounted when she crashed into his arms and hugged him tightly.

"That was...amazing!" She sobbed against his chest. "Thank you! Thank you so much!"

In spite of himself, Wes closed his arms around her, breathing her in as time seemed to halt. In the span of about two seconds, he learned all number of things: 1) Her hair, which was as soft as it looked, smelled like honeysuckles; 2) The places where his body met hers—arms, chest, thighs—hummed with an electric current; 3) Her gratitude was like an achievement unlocked; 4) He wanted to keep holding her.

She pulled back, wiping her eyes, and he released her at once.

"I'm sorry," she said, shaking her head, but still smiling. "That was just really powerful…I had no idea…"

"Must have been some class," Wes said, trying to recover from her embrace—and the loss of it.

Corinne nodded, breathing deeply and trying to compose herself.

"Yeah…" she sighed. "I think I need a minute."

"How about some breakfast? We both had to get out of the house pretty fast this morning."

"Sure," she said, nodding again. "Lead the way."

It took everything in his power not to take her by the hand, but Wes managed to lead her to the snack bar without touching her. Corinne wore her hair in a high ponytail, making her look vibrant and carefree. With her arms bare in her purple tank top and her charcoal yoga pants hugging her hips and thighs, Wes had to force his gaze away from her.

"What's 'Bullet-Proof Coffee'?" she asked, staring up at the wall menu.

"It's awesome in a cup," Wes declared. "High quality coffee made with either butter or coconut oil. It boosts performance, revs up your metabolism, and keeps you full. Some say it kicks up your immune system and is full of antioxidants, but I don't really know about that. Wanna try it?"

Corinne raised her eyebrows at his enthusiasm.

"And how many cups have *you* had today?"

She was teasing him, and Wes had to concentrate on not letting her see how much he enjoyed it. If she had been any other girl, he would have tickled her at the waist with a pinch and then caught her by the wrist as she jumped away. She'd be in his arms again before she knew what happened.

But she wasn't any other girl. She was Corinne. Michael's Corinne. So he ignored her taunt and asked her again.

"Coffee or no?"

"Please. With coconut oil."

Louis Elway stood at the register waiting to take their order, and Wes fought the urge to step in front of Corinne and shield her from his sight. Wes had partied with Elway—100 percent manslut—more than once, and taking in the way the guy devoured Corinne with his eyes, Wes instantly regretted every encounter. The one that now made him shudder involved a hot tub and a girl named Hallie they'd met at NiteTown.

"Well, well, well, Clarkson, who's *this?*" Elway crooned, tossing his sandy blond hair out of his eyes with a whip of his head.

Wes bristled at Elway's leering, but he should have known that Corinne would be immune to the pretty boy charm.

"*Eww,*" she muttered. It was quiet, so quiet he was sure she'd meant only him to hear. A grin stole his mouth, and he had to pretend to study the menu before facing Elway again, but beneath his amusement and relief at her response was a buzz of unease.

"She's off-limits, Elway," Wes began, eyeing his co-worker with a keep-your-mouth-shut expression. "Let's have two tall Coconut Bullets and two baked sweet potatoes, no butter."

"*Off-limits?*" Elway echoed in mock-disbelief, raking Corinne up and down with his gaze. "You mean you don't want to sh—"

"Elway! I mean it, man. Lay off," Wes snarled, sliding his membership card across the counter and giving Elway a murderous stare.

"Touchy! Touchy!" Elway teased, enjoying Wes's suffering, but he must have sensed how close he was skating to mortal danger because he swiped the card and gave Wes their ticket without another word.

The unease Wes had felt a moment before ballooned into dread. He was aware of Corinne stepping in by his side as he moved down the counter, but he was afraid to look at her. How much had she inferred from Elway's remark? If she found Elway repugnant and sleazy, how was he any better?

The fact that she already knew about many of his less-than honorable moments made him cringe now. It occurred to him that he would have liked to make many of the truths in his past untrue.

"You okay?" Corinne had moved around to face him. Her expression was one of confused curiosity.

Wes didn't want to lie to her, but he didn't want to tell her the truth, either.

"Yeah, I guess. Elway just rubs me the wrong way."

"Really?" she asked, feigning surprise. "He seems like such a prince!"

Wes knew that she was going for humor, so he tried to smile, but her comment only made him feel worse. He'd known for years that he couldn't be like Michael Roush, but he was just now realizing that he didn't want to be like Louis Elway. The only problem with that was history. A lot of history.

When their order was ready, Wes grabbed their plates, and Corinne carried their coffees. They found a table in the dining area and sat across from each other. Corinne eyed her coffee, which was whipped to a light brown, and took a sip.

"Wow...That's different," she said, sipping again. "Mmm. I like it. Very full-bodied."

Wes took a sip of his, glad that she enjoyed it.

"Yeah, it's good. And you can feel it at work," he said, balling up his fist. "It gives you...you know...mojo."

"*Mojo?*" Corinne asked, arching a brow. Her look was so playful and light, Wes had to laugh. She was such a mystery, a puzzle of contradictions that one could spend ages trying to riddle out. She was funny; she was somber. She was terrifying; she was afraid. She was open; she was closed.

She was lost, but she made him feel found.

"And I have to say," she continued, unaware that he'd lost the thread of the conversation. "I've never had sweet potatoes for breakfast. What's up with that?"

Wes tried to contain his smile. Fitness and nutrition were his passions, and when she asked him questions like that, he could show Corinne how much he knew—that his job wasn't just about making people look good—as she'd once accused—it was about making people feel good. Feel good and live well. And if she would let him, he'd help her to feel better, too.

"The sweet potato is a perfect food," he said, slicing into his and watching the steam rise up. "It's low on the glycemic index, so it's a great carb. It's full of protein and fiber and packed with vitamins and minerals. If you were stranded on a deserted island with only a life-time supply of sweet potatoes, you'd survive just fine."

She'd listened intently to his dietetic lesson, all the while wearing an intrigued smile. He allowed himself to wonder what it meant but willed himself not to ask.

"I'm impressed," she said, cutting open her potato. "That's quite a resume for a humble little root vegetable."

Wes shrugged.

"Lots of great things have humble beginnings," he offered, thinking of his own past and allowing that it wasn't so much humble as notorious. Was there a health food that had notorious beginnings? Something in nature that started out toxic but then turned out to be wholesome, good? He'd have to look.

His musings about toxic roots reminded him of his parents' party that was coming up. He hadn't asked Corinne to go with him—he doubted she'd accept anyway—but he didn't like the idea of leaving her alone on a Saturday night. If she came with him, at least that would be one less thing he had to worry about.

"There's something I want to ask you," he started in, though he thought that the matter was hopeless. "What do you think about political fundraisers?"

Corinne's eyes bugged.

"Uh...I...don't?" she stammered in confusion.

Wes, you idiot.

"I mean...would you be opposed to going to one? Next Saturday?" He tried again, thinking that if he made it sound more like a favor for him, she might be more willing. "My parents are hosting for one of my dad's partners who's running for judge—James Hargett—and I need to be there. I was hoping you might want to come with me."

She blinked at him, a cautious look overtaking her eyes.

"They're pretty boring, but there's always good food, and there will be a band," he floundered. "I'd be grateful if you could do me a solid and come."

Wes watched her shoulders rise and fall with the deep breath she took. She was either thinking it over or preparing to give him hell.

"I don't know..." she said, finally, frowning. "I don't know if I'm ready for that. It was a big deal just for me to come here today."

Wes knew this was true. He winced at the thought that he might be pressuring her with too much, too soon, and his motives for asking her weren't entirely altruistic. Yes, he'd be able to keep an eye on her and make sure she was okay for the night instead of sitting at home by herself, but he'd also be able to be with *her*, and it bothered him how much that desire inspired his request.

"I get it. Just think about it," he encouraged with a shrug. "And if you want to just give it a try, we can go for a little while, and I can take you home as soon as you are ready."

Corinne nodded.

"I'll think about it."

After finishing their breakfast, Wes took Corinne to the cross-training room on the second floor.

"When was the last time you worked out with weights?" he asked.

Corinne huffed a laugh.

"Like...freshman year?"

Whoa.

"Well," Wes said, handing her a 20 lb. kettlebell. "I did say that you'd be tired tonight."

And sore.

He grabbed a 35 lb. bell for himself, and he demonstrated how to do lunge walks. Then, side by side, they traversed the room, switching hands at each turn. At the end of the third lap, Corinne was gritting her teeth.

"Jesus," she hissed.

It was the same routine he did with all of his female clients on the first day, but it was the first time that a client's distress ever bothered him. It was that way with Corinne, he was learning. Her suffering made his chest tighten.

"Just one more round," he soothed, saying it for himself as much as for her. When they reached the end of the row, Wes took the kettlebell from her hands, which shook.

"Good job," he said, trying to regroup as he set down both weights and led her to the med balls. He gave her a 10-pounder and showed her how to spread her stance and hammer it into the wall above her head.

"Core strength and tricep toning," he told her. "Twenty-five times."

At 17, she paused to curse him.

"I hate you," she growled.

Ouch.

Wes laughed, hoping that she was joking.

"Wait until tomorrow."

Chapter 17

Corinne's arms shook as she tried to peel her sports bra over her head. It felt like her whole body was shredded. With what little energy she had left, she pulled her bag from her locker and dug out her bikini, cover up, and flip-flops.

Once she'd changed, she grabbed her sketchpad and charcoal case, stuffed her bag back into her locker, and went in search of the pool. It was hard to miss. The double-Olympic sized pool was skirted with dozens of mostly empty lounge chairs and dotted with enormous canvas umbrellas.

Corinne chose a chair in the sun, slipped off her cover-up, and stretched herself out. The May breeze was cool, but the sun was almost directly overhead, so she didn't feel chilly. She pulled on her sunglasses and took in her surroundings.

Aside from the lifeguard some 20 yards away, there was a lone swimmer doing laps several lanes from her, an older woman lounging under one of the umbrellas with a book, and a man and a woman face down on their fully reclined chairs, sunning themselves. The only sound was the rhythmic slap of the swimmer's strokes as he glided through the water. She watched him for a moment, witnessing how the water and the midday sun came to life over his skin, magnifying each other. The translucence and the motion could both be captured with oils, she knew, but she didn't think it would translate as well in a sketch.

Not wanting to think about the sunbathing couple and their story, Corinne hid behind her sunglasses and turned her attention to the woman reading. She was a series of curves and shadows. Even under the umbrella, she wore a gorgeous, teal floppy hat, and her swimsuit—one of those baby-doll-dress styles—was scalloped at the hem and shoulders. Her breasts and belly were generous and grandmotherly, but still somehow sensual. Her plump arms tapered into beautiful, well-manicured hands, nails painted a pale pink as though the woman could not wait for summer. Her toes echoed the color.

And while Corinne couldn't hope to catch any of the pink with her charcoals—the woman begged to be painted in watercolors—her shape made the decision easy. Corinne had doubted whether or not she'd be able to live up to the sketching assignment that Wes had set for her, but she was determined to at least try. She didn't let herself think about it too much—how long she'd gone without her art, why she had lost it in the first place. She just opened her sketchpad to a clean page, chose a three-inch piece of charcoal, and started with the hat. Corinne's only hope was that her subject wouldn't get up to leave anytime soon.

Twenty minutes later, the woman rose, collected her things, and left the pool, but it didn't matter. By that point, Corinne was filling in shadows, darkening patches of fabric to show texture, smudging the edges of the woman's toe pads to try to capture the buffed look of her skin.

It was only just after noon when Corinne cocked her head and regarded the effort. It wasn't her best work, surely, but it was an exercise, a test, and she had passed. She took a deep breath and let out a comfortable sigh. She had proof—both for herself and for Wes—that the day had been a success. The heaviness in her muscles promised that she would sleep, and the poolside sketch had shown Corinne that her art had not totally abandoned her. She remembered, too, the sense of healing love that had come with the yoga lesson.

Corinne flipped to a fresh page in her sketchpad and started drawing from memory. It wasn't difficult: the wave of his hair, the way that light there was both reflected and absorbed; the arch of his brow and the depth of his eyes. She spent time on the mouth and the interplay of stern cheek muscles behind the bow of his lips, the striking philtrum above them and the strong chin below.

She had been at it at least an hour when a shadow passed over her, but she was so intent on what she was doing that she didn't look up.

"My God. That's *me!*"

Wes stood over her with his mouth hanging open. The look of confident intensity that stared up at her from the page was far from the one of humbled awe that hovered over her. Somehow sensing the disconnect, Wes closed his mouth and sunk onto the edge of the lounge chair next to her.

Except for giving her quick, disbelieving glances, Wes couldn't seem to take his eyes off the sketch.

"Corinne,...that's *amazing!*" he stressed in hushed tones, still lost in the drawing. "I didn't think…"

He trailed off.

"You didn't think what?" Corinne asked, curious. Wes's eyes left the page and found hers, but they were impossible to read.

"Nothing," he said, shaking his head. "It's just really good."

"You didn't think I could do it?" she asked, shrinking inside at the thought and hating herself for it. Wes's eyes rounded in horror, and his hand shot to her elbow.

"No! Of course not," he insisted, shaking his head. He seemed to wrestle with himself over his next words. "I didn't think…you saw me."

Corinne felt her eyes widen in surprise. The statement revealed so much and spawned so many questions. She looked at the sketch again. It was Wes, through and through, she realized, but it was the man who sat beside her now, not the one who'd been her beloved's best friend only months before. If she had to describe the man in the sketch, she would have said that he was vigilant, determined, adept. And handsome.

Had it ever occurred to her to sketch a portrait of Wes Clarkson before Michael's death, it would have been a very different thing entirely, and she understood now how unfair she had been because the picture she'd carried of him in her mind would have only been a caricature, overemphasizing his flaws and minimizing things she could no longer deny he possessed. Loyalty. Good humor. Vulnerability. Michael had recognized all of these traits in his friend, and had tried to share them with her from the start. Why had it taken the greatest tragedy of her life to see this?

What else in her life was she missing? What was she missing about her sister? Her father? Herself?

And did they—like Wes—feel that she wasn't *seeing* them?

"Wes, I'm sorry," she said, lamely, forcing herself to look into his eyes, which in the sun took on the color of a creek bed—only with so much more depth. "I was very wrong. I've treated you badly most of the time that I've known you."

Wes chuckled, the bronze of his cheeks blushing slightly.

"I can think of a few times when I deserved it," he said, shrugging.

Corinne shook her head, wanting him to understand what she was only just now understanding herself.

"No, I never really gave you a chance. I was snobbish and judgmental—stupidly. I thought that because I didn't recognize your values that you didn't have any...I couldn't have been more wrong." The smile he wore faded, and a frown creased his brow. Shame and regret threatened to choke her. "You've been so good to me through all of this, and I don't deserve it."

"Ok, now, stop," Wes said, taking her hands in his and squeezing them. His touch felt like forgiveness. "You absolutely deserve it. I'm just glad you don't hate me."

It was her turn to laugh, and she squeezed back at his hands.

"How could I hate you?" Corinne remembered a time when this might have been true, but it seemed foreign to her now. Wes Clarkson was now solidly her friend. He might even be her best friend if she deserved such a thing.

"Um, you told me you hated me just this morning," he teased, making her laugh again. He hadn't let go of her hands, and she was aware of the fact that she didn't want him to. It felt too nice.

"That was just my muscles talking," she dismissed, lightly. "You were just trying to make me stronger."

Wes's eyes warmed at these words, and Corinne was glad that she'd spoken them. He was trying to make her stronger in every way possible, and she had the presence of mind now to be grateful for it. She had to do something in return.

"So, you really want me to go to this thing next Saturday?" she asked, watching him carefully. His eyes widened in hope before he pressed his lips together cautiously.

"Only if you're up for it," he said, now watching her closely. But it was clear to her that he wanted her to go with him and that she should. It would be the first time she'd be at a large gathering since the funeral, and it might be really hard, especially if she had to talk about Michael, but knowing that Wes would be with her made it seem doable. The fact that he wanted her to go suddenly mattered more than her fears.

"Okay," she agreed.

Just as Wes promised, Corinne's body was exhausted by the end of the day. After a dinner of spaghetti and salad—which Corinne and Wes prepared together—Corinne kept herself awake while Wes channel surfed, but at 9:30, she said goodnight. When she climbed into bed, sleep came immediately.

And so did her dreams.

It was happening again.

Night. The hospital. Fear. Mrs. Betsie, crying. Corinne had seen it all before. She knew what was going to happen. What had already happened.

Michael.

"There's been a mistake," Mr. Dan told her. "Michael wasn't alone in the car."

"What?" Corinne asked, confused, knowing that Michael was already gone. Had been gone for so long.

"Wes was with him, too," Mr. Dan said, sadly.

"But...he couldn't..." she tried to argue.

"He's gone, too, Corinne. I'm sorry."

"That's impossible! I just saw him!" she cried.

"I'm sorry..."

Panic closed in on her like a demon.

"No! Wes! Wes!"

Chapter 18

Wes shot up in bed, his heart racing.
What the fuck?

The house was quiet, but something had woken him.

"No!...No!" Corinne wailed from her room.

Wes got his feet and raced into the hall, ready to beat whoever was hurting her.

"Wes!" she cried just before he burst through the door, spurring a round of barking from Buck.

"Corinne!" he yelled, searching blindly for the light switch. Wes expected to be tackled or shot as Buck barked again, but the light that flooded the room revealed no rapist or serial killer. Just a terrified Corinne blinking now against the glare. A distressed Buck sniffed Wes and whined.

"What wa-was someone in here?" Wes asked, panting and still searching the room, the floor, the closet.

Corinne sat up in bed. She was trembling violently, and she looked stunned, focusing on him in confusion.

"Oh, thank God," she whimpered and buried her face in her hands. Every nerve in his body was on high alert, set to commit justifiable homicide.

"What happened?" Wes asked. His pulse pounded in his throat; he'd never been so scared in his life.

Corinne drew her knees up and seemed to hide behind them.

"Wes...oh shit...I'm so sorry," she groaned. "It was a dream...a nightmare."

"What?" he asked, relief coursing through him in a rush so that he let himself stumble to the foot of her bed to catch his breath.

"Holy shit," he panted. "You scared the hell out of me."

She looked up at him, finally, agony written all over her face.

"I'm so sorry," she said, clearly mortified. "I feel so stupid!"

Wes closed the distance between them, sat on the edge of her bed, and took her in his arms.

"No, it's okay," he said, shaking his head. "I thought someone was hurting you."

He pulled her tighter against him, and it was then that he realized how tightly she clung to *him*. She was still shaking uncontrollably.

"Hey, are you okay?" he asked, softly, drawing back to look at her.

She nodded against his chest, but she still gripped him fiercely.

Now that he could see that she was safe, his heartbeat leveled off, and he let himself draw a deep breath. But it was clear to see that the crisis wasn't over for Corinne. The dream still had its claws in her.

"Was it about Michael?" he asked, softly.

Corinne went still against him.

"I don't want to talk about it," she said, finally.

Wes just nodded. Corinne never showed weakness if she could help it, and she must have thought talking about a bad dream made her look weak. She was too tough for that. It was something he had to admit he admired about her.

Still, he thought, rubbing a hand up and down her back, *she doesn't have to be tough all the time. I can do it now and then.*

Holding her like this made him feel…capable. Like he could protect her against anything. He sure as hell *wanted* to protect her against anything.

And he wanted to keep holding her.

Corinne must have read his mind because the instant that thought filled his head, she sat up straight and pulled away, clutching at herself instead of clutching him.

"I'm so sorry," she stammered, frowning. "You've had a shitty night's sleep three nights in a row, and it's all my fault."

Wes looked at the clock by her bedside. It was 1:43 a.m. He was wide awake now, but he wanted to tell her that she was wrong. Sleeping with her on the couch the night before had been pretty great.

He stood up instead.

"You'll be ok?" he asked, gently.

Corinne nodded, but she couldn't seem to meet his eyes for more than a second. It bugged him that she was embarrassed. The episode had scared him because he thought someone was attacking her, but whatever haunted Corinne in that nightmare had made her call his name, and he wished he could tell her that he'd always come running.

Always.

He stepped back into her doorway and put a finger on the light switch.

"Corinne,...like I told you last night, we're friends now. If you need something, just tell me," he said, willing her to understand that he'd do anything for her. That he wanted to. "That's why I'm here."

He flipped the light off.

"Goodnight, Wes," she whispered from the dark.

"Goodnight, C."

Wes returned to his room and climbed back into bed, but he'd left the doors open between them in case she fell back into her nightmare.

He stared at the shadowed ceiling above him, listening to the darkness. Sleep was a long way off, and between him and oblivion was a riot of feelings. The fear had been unprecedented. Even now, the memory of it made him shiver. The thought of someone in Corinne's room, forcing—

Never!

Wes jerked away from the thoughts. The images. But there was one thing he knew for sure; he would kill anyone who tried. In the moments when she'd cried out, he could have broken down the door—broken it to splinters—to get to her.

And then she was in his arms, safe, and he'd never known such relief! All he'd wanted was to hold on.

It had felt *so* good. Wes realized that it was the second time in 24 hours that he'd been allowed to take her in his arms. He drew in a slow breath through his nose and felt the sensation in his chest like a clenched fist. This was more than a crush. Even now, the urge to go back to her took everything he had to master.

She's not yours, he told himself. *You can never have her.*

He shut his eyes and stifled a groan in the darkness.

"*Wes?*"

Wes's eyes shot open. The whisper came from his open doorway.

"Corinne?" he whispered back.

Silence.

Wes propped up on his elbows and squinted. He could just make out her shape in the entrance.

"What is it?" he asked, this time more loudly.

"Did I wake you again?" Corinne's voice sounded small and frightened. He sat up fully in bed.

"No, you didn't wake me," he promised. "What do you need?"

He heard her step into the room.

"Would it be...Can I..." she struggled. Wes heard her take a deep breath and let it go. "Can I sleep in here tonight?"

Wes swallowed and forced his voice to come out even.

"Yes,...of course," he managed, throwing back the covers and wondering if he were dreaming.

Don't touch her, you asshole.

"Thank you," she said, crossing the room and finding his bed. "I'm sorry, Wes. I'm just still freaked out."

"I get it. It's okay," he said, holding his breath as he felt the mattress dip beneath her. Wes tucked his hands behind his head to keep from reaching for her, but she pressed in next to him, the signature of her heat meeting his skin, and she laid a hand on his chest before quickly drawing it away.

Did she want to touch him? For comfort? Wes rolled on his side to face her and found her hand. Was she still shaking?

"Corinne? Talk to me," he urged, squeezing her hand. He wished he knew how to help her. "Tell me about the dream."

He felt her shake her head.

"I can't," she gasped. He knew her well enough to hear that she was fighting a sob. "I know it's wrong...but I really wish you hadn't poured that bottle down the drain."

The closed fist in his chest punched him in the heart.

"Oh, C, you don't mean that. Come here." Wes opened his arms, and despite his ache to pull her into them, he wanted it to be her choice to move into his embrace. And she did. She crashed into him.

He knew that she was panicked, tortured by something that she couldn't even talk about, and that she needed to be held, to be soothed. He knew that this was the only reason she was in his arms, in his bed. But for a moment—just for a moment—he let himself imagine that she felt what he did.

It was a cruel trick to play on himself because she didn't, and she wouldn't, and this feeling like he'd finally found out what he was supposed to do with his life wasn't really his to keep.

"I don't know what I'd do without you, Wes," she whispered against his chest. She didn't sound quite as upset now. Lying with him was helping. But Wes didn't fool himself. He knew the physiology. Humans were social animals who could be soothed with an embrace. Chest to chest, oxytocin increased, cortisol decreased, blood pressure dropped.

As clinical as it sounded, it still felt pretty damn good, and he was lucky to be the one comforting her.

Wes allowed himself to press his lips against her forehead in a chaste kiss.

"Try to get some sleep, C."

She nodded, already seeming to be on the edge of slumber. And even after she did drift off, her breathing deep and unhurried, Wes held her, drank her in, and cursed his stupid heart.

"Is this alright?"

Corinne stepped into the living room in a jade green dress that nearly made Wes swallow his tongue. He saw the dress—with its sheer layers floating over solid fabric—but mostly, he saw skin. The inches above her knees before the hem flared around them. The bare back and shoulders that only the spill of her hair covered. And most maddeningly, the vertical cutaway between her breasts where pale skin announced the absence of a bra.

"How does it stay on?" he asked, stupidly.

Corinne rolled her eyes, turned her back to him, and swept up her hair.

"It's a halter top, silly," she said, showing him the band of fabric that clasped behind her neck. Her movement stirred the air with her honeysuckle scent, and Wes cleared his throat and clenched his fists to resist touching the plane of her back. They'd slept in his bed ten nights in a row—just slept—and Wes thought that his sanity might be at risk. But it meant that he got to hold her and Corinne got to sleep without drugs, so what was a little insanity?

"So? Will it work?" she asked again.

Oh, it'll work, Wes thought. *On killing me.*

"You look great," he managed.

She turned toward him, smiling. She looked better than great. She was stunning.

"So do you," she said, appreciatively, taking in his new gray suit. "Two buttons. A sharp lapel. Very *GQ*."

He'd bought the suit the day after she'd accepted his invitation because he didn't want to take her out in the one he'd worn to Michael's funeral. Wes was glad now that he had. He'd have to look his best if he was going to stand by her side all night.

"It feels good to dress up, but I'm nervous," she said, turning back toward her room. "I'll just be a sec."

Wes watched her go with a pang. He wanted her to have a good time, but he also knew that there were so many factors about the evening that would be out of his control. Especially his parents. The night could turn out to be great—a way for Corinne to return to society without too much attention on her—or it could twist into disaster.

Wes tried to unknot his shoulders at the thought. He stepped into the kitchen and eyed what remained of Michael's makeshift bar on top of the fridge. Besides simple syrup, a couple of shot glasses, and a shaker, there was a bottle of Crown, some Cuervo Gold, Triple Sec, and a bottle of Kettle One.

Michael's shot of choice was tequila, so instead Wes pulled down the Kettle One and the Triple Sec. He grabbed a lime from the fridge and washed it.

"C, I'm making a kamikaze," he called across the house. "You want one?"

"God, yes!"

Wes took down the shaker and the shot glasses and got to work. Moments later, Corinne entered carrying a gold clutch that matched her shoes, and Wes handed her the shot.

She took it with shaking hands, and they eyed each other.

"You look just as nervous as I feel," she said, frowning. "Why are *you* nervous?"

"Why are you nervous?" he countered.

"I asked you first," she said, raising a brow at him. Wes debated what he should say and decided to be honest.

"I want you to have a good time and be okay..." he started. "But I'm worried about my parents."

Corinne's hazel eyes narrowed in confusion.

"Why?"

Wes eyed the brimming shot glass in one hand and ran his fingers through his hair with another.

"They can be...a horror show sometimes."

Her expression didn't change, and Wes began to regret saying anything.

"I've met them a couple of times. They seemed pretty normal," she said, shrugging.

Wes laughed, mirthlessly.

"They're anything but normal, but sometimes they can keep it together."

Wes thought about the two times Corinne had encountered his parents. The first time was at the pool party almost two years ago. Michael knew well enough how to read the Clarksons, and he'd made introductions before Gloria could get sauced and before Harold could get ugly. Then Michael and Corinne had pretty much stayed in the pool with the younger crowd for the rest of the afternoon. As for the second time—at Michael's funeral—Corinne couldn't be expected to notice how his mother teetered at the gravesite or hear the hissed argument between his parents on their way back to the car.

He pushed thoughts of his mother and father from his mind.

"Now you. What are you nervous about?"

Corinne bit her lip and looked up at him.

"Losing my shit in front of everybody," she said in a near whisper. "Crying. Or worse—freezing or panicking like you've seen me do more than once."

After almost two weeks of going with him to the gym, Corinne looked so much healthier. He knew it was the time in the sun and the use of her body that showed most, but she'd sketched every day, and she'd gone to her sister's to see the new baby a few times, and these things lifted her up as well. Still, crying spells happened almost daily. Wes knew it was normal and that it was a sign that she was dealing with her grief, and he agreed there was a chance that she would break down at the party.

"I'll be there with you," he promised. "And if you need to leave or just get away for a few minutes, say the word."

"What word should I say?" Wes could tell by the look in her eyes that she wanted to sound light and funny, but that she needed a real answer—one she could use in front of other people—to make her feel safe.

"Ask me about Buck. If I fed him or let him out or whatever. And I'll know." It was the perfect code word. Buck was someone they shared but who'd belonged to Michael, and Buck was also a protector and friend. Invoking him would communicate both the distress and the promise of security.

Corinne's eyes welled, but she managed to smile and nod.

"Will do," she said.

She was being so strong. Wes looked at her and felt so proud of the steps she had taken in just a few short days. He raised his shot glass to her.

"To facing our fears," he said.

Corinne rolled her eyes and released a breath.

"Kamikazes, indeed," she said, clinking her shot glass against his.

Wes threw back his shot and watched Corinne's face screw up as she did the same. He laughed and shook his head; Corinne had never been much of a drinker.

"Ready?" he asked.

"As I'll ever be," she sighed.

⁓○

Shelly Drive was choked with the parked cars of Lafayette's influential and elite. As soon as they'd turned onto the riverfront road, Corinne had stilled beside him, her eyes going wide.

"That's a lot of people," she whispered.

Wes reached across the seat of his truck and grabbed her hand.

"The more, the better," he said, trying to reassure her. "We'll just blend in."

She nodded nervously.

"Okay."

Wes parked his truck several houses from his parents', and he jogged around the cab to help her down. He took hold of her hand again, and when she squeezed back, half of his tension evaporated. Wes promised himself that he wouldn't let go until she did.

"I forgot how big this place is," Corinne said as they turned up the walk toward the sprawling, two-story stucco.

"Yep," Wes agreed, grimly.

"And you're an only child?" she asked.

"Yeah. One son. Six bedrooms and a pool house with two more," he said, shrugging. "I never understood that math."

Of course, he did understand why his parents never had more children. It may have been the most humanitarian decision of their lives.

Wes pushed open the heavy oak door, and the din of conversation and laughter rolled over them. Corinne tensed, and he squeezed her hand in response.

"C'mon. You got this," he said, leading her into the marbled foyer. The great room at the center of the house was full of people, many he recognized, but some he didn't. Wes smiled and waved to a few but kept making steady progress toward the back of the house, knowing that the outdoors would be the least oppressive place for Corinne. "I just want to let my mother know we are here, and then we can get a drink and find somewhere to sit outside."

Corinne nodded. As he expected, Wes found Gloria Clarkson just outside the French doors, holding her black Ego-T e-cigarette in one hand and her ever-present Derby in another, talking with a group of women who couldn't have resembled her more.

"Hello, mother," Wes said, pressing a dry kiss to her cheek and inadvertently smelling the sting of bourbon and the cloying, brown-sugar scent of vaping. "You remember Corinne, don't you?"

If Wes's mother was picturing the disrupted furniture arrangement in her pool house, she didn't show it.

"Corinne!" she sang, leaning in and giving Corinne and airy embrace. "Marjorie, Delia, this is Wes's friend Corinne...Corinne..."

"Granger," Wes supplied, feeling his collar heat with embarrassment, but Corinne only smiled politely and shook hands with the other ladies.

"Corinne Granger? Not the portrait artist?" the one standing closest to his mother asked.

Corinne's eyes widened in surprise.

"Yes, actually, that's me," she said, looking a little mystified.

"I'm Marjorie Jamison. You did a series of portraits for my sister, Allison Knight."

"Oh, yes, of her children," Corinne confirmed, smiling genuinely this time. Wes let out a little sigh of relief that the recognition didn't seem to bother her.

"Gloria, are you a patron?" Marjorie asked, turning her fawning attention back on his mother, who was completely thrown by this news.

"I...uh...no...not yet...," she stammered, cutting Wes an accusatory glance as though he'd been hiding Corinne's talent from her.

"Oh, you must commission her! She's incredible! You should see those portraits," Marjorie praised.

The last thing Wes wanted was for Corinne to have to work for his mother.

"She's pretty busy at the moment," Wes said, feigning disappointment. Corinne squeezed his hand, and Wes wasn't sure if she was admonishing his lie or thanking him for it. He didn't care. Working for Gloria Clarkson wouldn't do her any favors.

But his mother seemed undeterred.

"When do you think you might be ready to take on new commissions?" Gloria asked, pinning Corinne with her gaze. Wes felt his teeth set on edge. His mother wasn't asking because she was any great art connoisseur; it was because of her friend's reaction to Corinne. Corinne was a commodity. Something trendy and expensive. Something that showed her status. The fact that she didn't know five minutes ago that Corinne Granger had a following didn't matter at all.

Wes felt a growl of annoyance building in his throat, but Corinne spoke up before he could lay down the boundaries.

"I think it will be several months, but I can certainly call you, Mrs. Clarkson," she said, vaguely.

"Oh, please, call me Gloria, of course!" Wes's mother tittered. "Wesley, you must remind this darling girl to contact me when she has an opening."

Wes clenched his jaw.

"Of course," he lied. It would be best now to just walk away. "Now, if you'll excuse us, I promised Corinne a drink. Lovely party, mother."

He pulled Corinne behind him and headed directly towards one of the bars that had been set up near the pool house entrance.

"I'm sorry about that," he muttered over his shoulder.

"I survived," Corinne replied.

He glanced back and took her in. She didn't look any worse off for the encounter, but he wanted to make sure.

"You're really okay?"

Corinne shrugged.

"Yeah, I mean I'm glad you covered for me, but it was nice to be reminded that there's still interest in my work."

Wes felt his eyes bug.

"Of course, there is. Your work is great," he stressed. "And you'll be ready one day to do commissions again...Just not for her."

Corinne glanced back in his mother's direction just as Gloria Clarkson threw back her head in faked amusement at her friends' gossip. It was hard stop his lip from curling in disdain.

"Would it really be that bad if I did?" she asked.

Wes felt his expression harden.

"Not that I'm going to," she quickly added, taking in his disapproval.

"You don't need to spend any more time with her," he said, hating the thought of Corinne coming to the house without him.

"Why not?" she asked gently after a moment. There was a look in her eyes that Wes didn't recognize. It wasn't mere curiosity; she seemed like she *needed* to hear the answer. Wes was pulled in by the look, and he was answering almost before he knew it.

"She drinks. A lot," he said, keeping his voice low, but Corinne listened intently, taking in every word. She had a pained look in her eyes. "I used to think she drank because of him. His temper. His women. But now I think she stays with him so she can keep drinking. Like who could blame her...you know?"

He shook his head and rolled his eyes.

"Nothing about her is real," he said, shooting a look at his mother. He watched her take a gulp of her Derby and check how much was left in the glass. Gloria never emptied a glass; she always kept her drinks at least half full. Once her Derby dipped below half, she'd have a bartender top it off or trade it in for a fresh one. Gloria Clarkson hadn't *finished* a drink in 20 years.

"You'd never be able to paint a portrait of her," Wes said, bringing his eyes back to Corinne. "Well, that's not so. You'd paint one that told the truth, and she'd have to sue you."

He gave her a grim smile, but Corinne couldn't seem to match it. He should have stopped, but something made him keep going.

"And the whole time you were here, she'd be sure to tell you everything wrong about yourself, saying it as if she were doing you a favor. And God help you if you didn't respond with gratitude," Wes swallowed and shook his head. "And then there's my father…"

Wes could feel his own scowl. Corinne, by contrast, looked troubled.

"I don't want you anywhere near that," Wes muttered. Corinne bit her lip and frowned.

"Funny. I was going to say those words to you," she said, softly.

Wes's breath caught in surprise and a slow smile conquered his scowl. For a moment, he couldn't think of how to respond, but he became aware that he still held her hand in his.

"Let's get that drink," he said, finally. "What would you like?"

She shrugged and followed him to one of the outdoor bars.

"Whatever," she said, seeming to relax and returning his smile.

"One Abita Purple Haze and one cosmo, please."

As they waited in silence, Wes squeezed the hand in his and ran his thumb over her knuckles. He told himself that he wanted to soothe her—and he did want to—but he also had to admit that touching her—that being allowed to touch her—soothed him with a rush all its own.

The bartender handed over their drinks, and they walked idly through the yard.

"So..." Corinne started, a question shaping the word, a keen look coming into her eyes. "You still drink...even after growing up in an alcoholic home...Does that ever worry you?"

Wes felt his mouth kick up in a smile. He loved that she didn't shy away from intense questions. And his answer had just as much to do with her as it did with anyone else.

"I think I tried to become a drunk for a while," he admitted, the smile turning a little chagrined. "I never apologized for messing up those sheets in your spare room."

"Oh Lord," Corinne said, rolling her eyes. "I was so pissed at you for that."

"I'm sorry....I know. Michael made sure I knew," Wes admitted, wincing at the memory of Michael ripping him a new asshole. "He told me that if I was trying to become a drunk like my parents, I needed to get better at hiding it. He said I'd never fit in with them if I didn't fake it."

Wes's mouth tasted the bitterness of the memory, but he was grateful to his best friend for finally holding him accountable. At least someone did.

"What surprised me, though, was that Mike had been watching me get wasted for a good eight or nine years before that lecture," Wes said, meeting Corinne's eyes. "He never told me how much it bothered him until my behavior affected you."

Corinne's eyes went wide with a kind of wonder, and she squeezed his hand.

"Yeah, I still drink," he said, holding up his Abita. "But I haven't been drunk since...I don't really want to."

A radiant smile stole over Corinne's face, and Wes felt a rising sense of pride.

"Well, I never thought I'd say this," she said, shrugging. "But I'm glad you puked on my sheets, Wes."

Wes threw his head back in laughter, and Corinne joined him.

They carried their drinks down the slope of the lawn near where the bandstand and dance floor had been set up. Wooden folding chairs and tables had been laid out in little clusters at conversational distances around the dance floor, and Wes chose a table that was set further apart from the rest. Corinne let go of his hand when she sat, and although Wes wanted to reach for it again once he was settled beside her, he restrained himself.

"This is nice," Corinne said, nodding toward the band that, at the moment, was playing a cover of Passenger's "Patient Love." The last rays of the sunset had painted the Vermilion River a color that resembled its name, and there was just enough of a breeze to keep away the mosquitoes.

Corinne was smiling now, relaxed and enjoying the evening, finally, and Wes breathed a sigh of relief.

"Yeah, it is." The tension of interacting with his mother and trying to explain his parents was forgotten. Wes realized that he couldn't remember the last time he'd felt so at ease at his childhood home, and he smiled.

"What are you smiling about?" Corinne teased, smiling herself.

Wes shook his head. How could he explain to her that her presence had turned a place he usually hated into one where he could relax?

He was able to enjoy the music, the beer, the sunset, and Corinne's smile for another 30 seconds before he saw Bethany Wallace crossing the lawn, headed straight for them.

"Aww, fuck," he muttered before he could stop himself. Any peace he had felt evaporated in an instant.

"What's wrong?" Corinne whispered, eyeing him anxiously. He met her look and never knew worse regret. He said the only thing he could.

"I'm sorry."

Corinne looked up and registered Bethany closing in on them. Wes saw the moment that Corinne understood everything, her face hardening. He was a pig, and she would always think of him as a pig. No matter what he did for her, he couldn't redeem himself.

"Hello, Wes," Bethany said, ignoring Corinne and tossing her auburn curls over her shoulder. She fondled the plunging neckline of her black wrap dress and sipped her martini.

"Hi..." Looking at her sickened him. Bethany and Corinne weren't even the same species. Of course, if Bethany was the lower life form, so was he. That thought only disgusted him more.

"It's been a while since we last...*worked out*," Bethany said, laying eyes on Corinne this time and stressing the words just for her.

Tormenting him was one thing, but insulting or offending Corinne was something else.

"Yeah, I'm done with private lessons," he said, firmly. "I only see clients at the club."

Both women reacted to this statement with surprise, Bethany's face an ugly scowl and Corinne's a look of unguarded curiosity.

Bethany recovered first, rolling her eyes.

"I know you better than that, Wes. You can't stay away for very long," she teased, absently stroking the expanse of cleavage that her dress revealed, reminding him, no doubt, of how much time he'd spent in the general vicinity. With shame, he remembered the night that Corinne accused him of smelling like this woman. What had she said?

Like Black Orchid and twat.

The memory stung like a slap. Why was it that he had to own each and every one of his sins in front of Corinne? He hadn't been with Bethany since—nor with any woman, and he wished there were some way to say as much.

"Come on, Wes. When are you going to come by and put me through the paces again?" Bethany sighed, impatiently.

His collar was on fire, his disgrace burning and smothering him at the same time.

"I told you," he choked through gritted teeth. "I'm done with that."

To his shock, Corinne reached out a hand to him.

"Would you like to dance?"

Chapter 19

The band was playing Spandau Ballet's "True" when Corinne clasped her fingers behind Wes's neck and felt his hands settle at her waist. Wes and Corinne were among the youngest at the party, and the throwback brought dozens of couples to the dance floor.

It didn't matter, as long as they could escape the company of that vile woman. Wes's discomfort as she approached had been palpable, but Corinne had not been prepared for the flare of jealousy that ignited in her at the woman's presence.

What does that *mean?*

She allowed herself to glance up at Wes who was looking down at her with undisguised awe.

"What?" she asked.

Wes frowned and seemed to weigh his words.

"You're not gonna...call me a dick or a man-skank or anything like that?"

"No..." Corinne responded, hearing the irritation in her voice. "Do you *want* me to?"

She pushed back to step out of his arms, but he pulled her into him, holding her tighter, and shook his head.

"No. I don't."

She let him keep her close for a few seconds before gently putting inches between them again, but the sensation of his body pressed against hers stayed with her.

"I don't want to be that person anymore," she said, trying to reclaim the flux of their conversation. "The kind of person who judges others that way and treats them like shit."

The expression of awe gave way to one of hesitant relief.

"Corinne..."

Wes closed his eyes for a second and gave just the slightest shake of his head. She felt her arms rise up on his shoulders as he took a deep breath, and when he glanced down at her again, a pulse of tension seemed to leave his body. Corinne couldn't help but think that he looked unbelievably vulnerable, so deep were the depths of his eyes. Had anyone ever protected those depths?

He'd steadied her through two panic attacks and an awful nightmare; he'd shepherded her across town in the dead of night; he'd held her when sleeplessness threatened. With Wes, she was always protected. Here, in the circle of his arms, she was safe.

But who looked out for him?

Corinne sighed and then breathed him in. He smelled clean and warm, like cedar and cinnamon. It was a scent familiar to her, she realized, but here on the dance floor it took on something new, an added layer of life. Above her hands, still clasped behind his neck, she could feel the tickle of his hair. When she lifted two of her finger to touch its softness, Wes closed his eyes again and stilled, and an unmistakable look of suffering crossed his features.

And in that instant, Corinne understood.

For one perfect moment, she saw everything. She saw how beautiful he was. So beautiful that it hurt to look at him, and the only balm was to look more. She saw how she could open him with her touch. How he longed for it. She saw that he found her beautiful, too. That he ached to show her this without words. That their lips were only inches apart.

But when the moment closed in on them, Corinne shrunk back. She let go of him, and Wes opened his eyes just as she pulled away.

"I think I need...some water," she panted.

"Corinne?" he asked, frowning. "Are you okay?"

Corinne clutched herself so that he couldn't reach for her hand. She fled the dance floor and headed for the safety of their wooden chairs, sinking down as she started to tremble, but by then Wes was there, hovering over her.

"Could you please get me some water?" Her voice shook, and she couldn't make herself look him in the eye.

"Yeah...I'll be right back."

Night had fully set, and she was grateful for the shadows that hid her. Her mind roiled with beastly fears, an infested sea, and she dared not look beneath the surface. Still, each one showed its ugly face to her in the moonlight.

What would Michael think of her, swooning in the arms of his best friend? If she loved him as much as she thought she did, how could she even notice another man? Who was she to do this? It was too soon. It was wrong.

And what about Wes? He was the rope that slowly pulled her up from the well of hell; if she allowed them to cross that line, what would happen after? Surely, he would cut and run. And where would that leave her?

Alone. All alone.

There was another fear, too. One that seemed to saturate all the others in its own blackness, one that she pulled away from it was so unbearable.

Friendship. They couldn't have anything more than that. She had let her guard down too much, and now she needed some distance. Anything else risked her own annihilation.

Using a breathing exercise she had practiced in yoga that week, Corinne tried to calm herself, and it helped a little, but she dreaded Wes's return because she had no idea what she would say to him.

Except when he walked up to her, carrying a glass of ice water, she didn't feel dread anymore; she felt relief. Because she wasn't alone. He was there, and he made her feel better—like he always did.

Wes handed her the glass with a concerned frown, and she was sure he'd question her, but when she took the water, he sat next to her without a word. She sipped. Her breathing had calmed, and she was no longer shaking.

"I'm sorry," she whispered.

"What for?"

Corinne looked at him to see if he was being ironic. He wasn't, and she cocked her head in surprise.

"For freaking out."

Wes studied her silently. She watched him take another deep breath, and he leaned forward with his hands on his knees as though he were bracing himself for something.

"I'm sorry for freaking you out," he said, quietly. He looked sincere, as if he truly believed he was at fault.

"You didn't do anything wrong," Corinne said and meant it. "It was me."

He watched her, looking unconvinced, but he must have decided not to press the issue because he shook his head again.

"Are you okay now?" he asked. "We can go if you need to."

Corinne shook her head this time. Sitting there with him was all she wanted to do. She couldn't deny that she was attracted to him, and it was probably true that he felt the same, but none of that changed the fact that he was the person who made her feel safest. Knowing that she was attracted to him didn't suddenly make her want to run away. In fact, knowledge was power, and if she understood herself—had prescience of the possibility for disaster—she could gird herself against it.

"No, I think I'm okay. Let's just hang here for a little while."

This statement seemed both to surprise Wes and set him at ease. His shoulders relaxed, and he sat back in his chair.

"You hungry?" he asked, looking hopeful. "I could fix us a couple of plates. You could stay right here."

Corinne smiled. She wasn't that hungry, but, of course, *he* was hungry. When wasn't he hungry?

"Sure. That sounds good. Thanks."

Wes pushed himself up from the chair.

"You want another cosmo?" Wes asked, echoing her smile.

Corinne shook her head again.

"Nah, just a plate. Thanks."

He was about to turn and leave when a woman in the cluster of guests in front of them broke away and ran towards them through the shadows.

"Corinne!" she cried, sounding surprised and happy.

Corinne stood and found herself in the embrace of an old friend.

"Heather!" she squealed, hugging back.

Heather Lamarche and Corinne Granger had been stressed out art students together at UL freshman year. They'd often kept each other company afterhours in the studio space in Fletcher Hall, toiling to finish their latest assignments.

When Heather later switched to industrial design, they'd still meet for lunches and dinner dates when they could, but after Corinne's honey blonde friend got a graduate fellowship at Ohio State, they'd lost touch.

But Heather had been home for the holidays when Corinne lost Michael.

"I never thanked you for coming to Michael's funeral," Corinne said, mustering her courage to say the words. At the service, she'd been in such a haze of grief, she had barely spoken to her old friend, and she couldn't bring herself to get in touch with her afterwards. "And I'm sorry I never returned any of your calls or texts...I just couldn't..."

"Oh, please stop," Heather said, looking pained. "How are you doing now? You look great!"

Corinne felt herself blush, humbled by her friend's ready forgiveness.

"I'm...getting better," she hedged. "It's been hard."

Then she caught sight of Wes still standing by her side, a questioning look in his eyes, and she reached for his arm.

"Heather, I'd like you to meet my friend Wes Clarkson...He's pretty much the reason I'm still in one piece," she said, honestly, meeting his gaze for a moment and hoping he knew she meant it. "Wes, this is Heather Lamarche. We were in art school together."

Heather and Wes shook hands, smiling warmly at each other.

"Clarkson?" Heather asked. "Is this your house?"

Wes was quick to shake his head.

"No, it's my parents' house," he answered. The pinched look that came to his eyes was almost imperceptible, but Corinne caught it. "My father works with James Hargett, the guest of honor. I really don't know the man."

Heather smiled and shrugged.

"Me either. I've lived out-of-state too long to keep up with local politics. My sister is friends with his daughter," she explained. "I'm just tagging along tonight."

"Are you still in Ohio?" Corinne asked. "Have you finished school?"

Wes placed a hand over hers and squeezed it.

"I'll let you guys catch up while I get us some food," he said, excusing himself.

She watched him walk back to the house while she talked to Heather. He looked back at her once, she noticed, just checking in.

"I just finished with my MFA," Heather was saying, drawing her attention back. "I have a few job offers, but I wanted to come back home for a little while before I settled on something."

Corinne smiled, hoping to hide her envy. In a way, both of their lives were starting over, only Heather was looking forward to a fresh start while Corinne was trying to pick up the pieces.

"I'm glad you've made a stop home so I could make amends," Corinne said.

"Nonsense," Heather sighed, rolling her eyes. "Of course, if you want to make it up to me, let's go out for a Girls Night like we used to while I'm still in town."

Corinne bit her lip. The thought was more than a little scary.

"What? Did I say something wrong?" Heather asked, eyes wide.

"No, it's alright," Corinne said, trying to shake off her nerves. "I'm just really getting back to a life that might just be considered normal. Of course, we should go out."

Heather studied her.

"Are you sure? I don't want to push you."

"I'm sure," Corinne answered, nodding. Only she didn't sound very convincing.

"I tell you what," Heather said, gently. "I should be in town through June at least. If you are ready to go out before I get back to the real world, call me, and we'll make plans. If not, I'll check on you again when I come home for Christmas."

"Deal," Corinne agreed.

Over her shoulder, Corinne spotted Heather's friends waving manically.

"I think your party wants to you back," she said, pointing. Heather's eyes followed, and she gave a wry grin.

"Yeah, I think I'm the official purse-holder for all of the photo opps," she said. "I'd better go."

Heather grabbed Corinne in a hug again, and she gladly squeezed back.

"It was great to see you," she said. "I'll call. I promise."

"Good," Heather said, winking.

Corinne sat back down in her wooden chair to wait for Wes. The thought of mingling until he returned terrified her. She hoped that he would come back soon; she felt unmoored without him, which didn't make her proud.

To keep herself from looking around desperately for Wes, Corinne watched the scene before her—the band, the couples dancing, the twinkling lights suspended over the lawn—and she let herself think about color.

The night sky could be captured in indigos, grays, and yellows. The dancers would be all black against a checkered floor of lime green and purple. The band begged to be painted light blue and gold.

She was picturing the lead singer of the band in hot pink when someone approached from behind.

"I see my son has left you all alone."

Corinne jumped at the voice and turned to see Harold Clarkson standing over her shoulder.

"H-he's getting me something to eat," she said in a rush, craning around in her seat.

At this, Mr. Clarkson's mouth formed a smile that did not reach his eyes, and he strode around until he stood in front of her. He carried a tumbler half-filled with amber liquor and ice, and he swirled it leisurely.

"Are you having a good time?" he asked, peering down at her. Corinne saw the resemblance between father and son, the same coloring, the same bone structure, but Mr. Clarkson had nothing of the genial, warm look in the eyes that Wes had, nor the fullness in the mouth that was always ready with a smile. Indeed, Harold Clarkson was thin-lipped.

"Yes...thank you for inviting me," Corinne said, taking a sip of her water to combat the dryness in her mouth his arrival seemed to inspire. She glanced toward the house, hoping to see Wes on his way back, but she only saw strangers.

"He might be some time," Mr. Clarkson said with a cold smile. "Last I saw, he was in the company of a few young ladies...Clients, I suspect." He was watching Corinne so closely that she tried not to show any reaction to this information, not that she was alarmed. Of course, Wes would get waylaid talking to people he knew at his parents' party. She could survive for five minutes without him.

Surviving five minutes with his father, on the other hand...

"Suppose we get to know each other a little better in his absence," Wes's father purred, setting down his drink and offering her his hand. "May I have this dance?"

He wasn't really asking, Corinne understood. She was certain he had given her no opportunity to refuse, but she tried to demure anyway.

"I think I should wait here for Wes—"

"Come, come, Miss Granger. It'll only be a few minutes," he declared. "I insist." This time, Corinne knew that he would not let the matter go, so she rose slowly and allowed him to take her by the hand. His was cool and dry, and he held hers with an almost imperceptible touch.

On the dance floor, he fitted his left hand at her waist and held her right aloft, leading her with precision. She felt, at once, like a marionette, and it was clear to her that Harold Clarkson probably had that effect on most people, regardless of whether or not he was dancing.

"I'm glad we are having this opportunity to speak, Miss Granger," he said.

Corinne couldn't agree. In fact, she had no idea how to respond. "Oh?"

"Yes," he said, moving her through a turn that made her watch her footing. "I'm trying to understand the nature of my son's relationship with you...It's very strange."

Corinne frowned.

"We're friends," Corinne said, hearing a defensive edge creep into her voice. "What's strange about that?"

Mr. Clarkson pressed his lips together in a look of skepticism.

"Hmm...I don't know about that. I know he was friends with Michael—allow me to re-extend my condolences," he said with a stiff nod. "But it's challenging to picture my son being friends with someone such as yourself."

Corinne felt a slap of indignation. *What the hell?*

"I don't know what you mean by—"

"Don't be offended, Miss Granger; I meant no insult," he said, smiling with a look of delight now. "You seem too refined and accomplished to be someone who would...*associate* with him. My son's a good boy, I suppose—"

"He's a good *man,*" Corinne interjected, her indignation quickly turning to offense. How could this be Wes's father? How could he talk about his son like this?

Mr. Clarkson gave a little laugh of condescension.

"Forgive me. I see him as a boy because I'm still waiting for him to grow up and do what he was meant to do," he said.

Corinne was about to ask him what he'd meant when, over his shoulder, she caught sight of Wes crossing the lawn carrying two plates. He spotted her empty chair, and she couldn't mistake the look of concern that took his face. He started scanning the crowd, and Corinne willed him to see her before Mr. Clarkson turned her again.

Their eyes met, but the instant Wes registered that she was dancing with his father, his look became murderous.

Oh, shit. What have I done?

Wes set the plates down at an empty table and stalked toward them, but as he was about to reach the dance floor and cause God-knows-what kind of scene with his father, Corinne managed to wave him off, giving him the "ok" sign. Wes stopped in his tracks, his seething only just under control, when Mr. Clarkson turned her again, and her back was to him.

"Aah, I see he's noticed that you've left your post," Mr. Clarkson teased, sounding very pleased with himself.

"Yes, he's a *gentleman*," Corinne said, stressing the last word.

He gave another amused chuckle and shook his head.

"He's a rake, like his father," the man said, and the fingers at her waist came alive with the smallest touch. But it was *there*. Corinne nearly froze. "But perhaps you see in him what he might become."

She locked eyes with the older man. Even though he both intimidated and repulsed her, his injustices against Wes made her bold.

"I assure you, I see him as he is. It is a shame you don't," she said, proud that her voice did not betray her nerves.

"Well…I can see why he's so taken with you," Wes's father said, sizing her up. "You might be just the person to spur him to go to law school."

"Law school?" It was Corinne's turn to laugh. She couldn't help it. "In the time I've known Wes he's never, *never*, talked about wanting to go to law school!"

Harold Clarkson's thin lips seemed to thin even more.

"I'll be damned if he wastes his life working at some health club," he said with venom.

After five minutes in his company, Corinne shouldn't have been shocked, but she was. She stepped out of his hold and planted her feet.

"Wes helps people to build a better life for themselves," she said, proudly, and with no little heat. "He's wasting nothing."

Mr. Clarkson rolled his eyes.

"He'll never amount to anything if he sticks to that," he said, a sneer curling his upper lip.

"I may never amount to anything, Dad, but I'm cutting in," Wes said, suddenly beside her, grabbing her hand.

Corinne should have regretted his arrival, his overhearing the hurtful words, except she was so glad to see him, so glad to be able to leave his father's company with him.

"Wesley, stop acting like a child," his father scolded, but Wes didn't even look at him as he pulled Corinne away. His eyes never left hers.

"I'm sorry about that," Wes said to her. "He's an asshole."

"It's okay," she said, shaking her head. Silently, she agreed with him, but she doubted it would make Wes feel any better to say it aloud.

"You were getting upset," he said, for an instant brushing his thumb over the furrow of her brow where she still held a frown. "I couldn't hold off."

It seemed as though his touch sunk into her, easing much more than her frown. She wanted to close her eyes and relax into the feeling, but a new understanding tugged at her.

Wes had grown up with Harold Clarkson as his father, all of his life hearing the sort of things she'd just heard. She pictured Wes as a brown-eyed little boy growing up in this cold house—alone—with the people she'd met tonight, and her heart seized. How had he survived? How had he made it to adulthood with any sanity—much less confidence and compassion?

Before she could master the urge, Corinne reached for his face and stroked her thumb across his cheek. Her eyes sought his, and what she found in their dark pools was unguarded and raw. There was pain there, yes, the acknowledgment of pain, but there was a startling fusion of fear and trust.

Words would betray them, so Corinne said nothing, but she hoped he understood what she did not say.

You are beautiful. You are precious. You are not alone.

It would be so easy to tip forward and press her lips to his. And, God, didn't he deserve it? Her cheeks flushed at the thought, but she knew it was true. He did deserve to be shown that someone saw him for who he was.

Her lips parted, but before she could reach up to him, his mouth was on hers, hungry and desperate. His warm lips crushed against her own with such fervor that she understood at once how hard he'd been restraining himself. Wes's arms were wrapped low around her back, drawing her up to him, and she felt herself grow long and fluid in his embrace. She answered him touch for touch. The hand that had stroked his face now held his cheek, anchoring him to her; the other clung to the back of his neck.

A rush of heat swept down her chest when she opened her mouth to his tongue, welcoming his with her own. She felt his groan vibrate in her own throat, and there was no thought, only sense. He was strange;

he was familiar. He was rough; he was gentle. It felt wonderful, and it hurt. Because the past and the present were locked in battle, and they wrenched her with merciless hands.

She broke the kiss, but pressed her forehead against his. They both fought for breath.

"God, Wes, what are we doing?" she whispered, closing her eyes.

Corinne felt him loosen his hold, and fear coursed through her.

"I'm so sorry," he answered.

She opened her eyes to see his stricken look, and she shook her head at him.

"I don't want you to be sorry," she said. "I'm just confused."

He nodded, clearly miserable, and at that moment the blare of the music and the crush of the crowd made themselves known again, and humiliation climbed on the heap of her emotions as she took in all of the eyes that had watched them.

"Can we go home?" she asked, praying he'd say yes.

Chapter 20

Wes blamed his father.

Before he'd seen Corinne in that asshole's arms, he had been thinking clearly. He'd kept himself under control—mostly. Dancing with Corinne had been like taking a heroine bath, but at least he hadn't tried anything.

But seeing Harold Clarkson touching her made him want to smash something. Preferably his father's skull. When Corinne had waved him off, he hadn't taken his eyes off them for a second. If his father had laid a hand on the bare skin of her back or brushed his lips to her ear or pinched her bottom—things he'd seen the man do to countless girls over the years—Wes might have killed him.

And maybe Harold knew it. Because he hadn't tried anything like that. He'd just pissed off Corinne. And if Wes had overheard right, she was angry over something the man had said about *him*. It had sounded like Corinne was in the middle of defending *him* when he'd interrupted. And Wes wasn't prepared for that.

He'd pulled her away from his father, and everything began to give.

No one had ever defended him against his father. No one. Either no one had bothered to—like his mother—or no one had been strong enough. Not even Michael. Michael had given him the refuge of his home and his friendship; he'd told him again and again that what his father said about him was bullshit, but even Michael called Harold Clarkson "sir" and always treated him with respect. *Faggot. Piece of shit. Pussy.* Michael had heard the man call his son these names more than once, and he'd always clamped his mouth shut.

But not Corinne. And as he'd held her again and looked at her, it was as though a landslide had started inside him. It felt like everyone he'd ever known his whole life had told him "no," and she said "yes."

Wes was lost the moment she touched his face.

He'd claimed her sweet mouth before giving any thought to stopping or asking her permission. He knew as soon as his lips touched hers that he wanted to die kissing her. How could someone so fierce and strong be so tiny in his arms? How could someone so small fit against him so well? How would he ever stop kissing her?

But the moment she'd drawn back, he knew exactly how. Because he wasn't Michael, and he shouldn't be kissing her in the first place.

Now, they drove home in near silence. She'd already told him twice to stop apologizing, but he didn't know how they were going to move on from it.

And there were things he couldn't reconcile. She had pulled away, but before that, there was no denying that she'd kissed back. The muscles in his stomach clenched at the thought and then clenched again as he remembered how it felt when she drew him down to her.

But Wes couldn't hold Corinne accountable for that. She'd said that she was confused, and he had no doubt that she was. It was unfair of him even to touch her. She missed Michael so much, and she was only just now coming back to the land of the living. Hell, she'd probably been picturing Michael the whole time.

Wes scrubbed a hand through his hair to erase the sting of that thought, and as if to betray the tumult inside him, his stomach growled—a sound absurdly loud and epic—filling the silence of the car.

Corinne raised a brow at him with a hint of a smile.

"Are you going to starve before we get home?" she asked.

Only if I'm lucky, Wes thought, wishing he could fall into a hole.

"You haven't eaten either," he pointed out. Talking about food was better than nothing.

"Nah, I'm good," she said, giving him a one-shoulder shrug.

"Nope." Wes shook his head. "Three squares a day."

This was better. This he could do. Just focus on taking care of her.

"It's ok. I don't need anything." It was almost undetectable, but there was an edge in her voice, a hint of her usual stubbornness. If she wanted to put up a fight about this, he was ready. They had already passed Ground Patti and Izzo's on Johnston Street, and he merged into the turning lane to make a left onto St. Mary.

"We're going to Olde Tyme," he said, flatly. "If I get you a shrimp poboy, will you eat it?"

Wes was met with eye rolling.

"Do I have a choice?" she huffed.

"Sure," he said, sweeping his hand out toward the horizon as if to illustrate her wealth of choices. "You can have shrimp, or oyster, or ham and cheese, or roast beef, or anything else, but you're getting something."

Corinne narrowed her eyes at him as though she could vaporize him with her stare. Wes matched her look with one of stone, glad that he could hide how much he loved her fighting spirit.

"Fine. Shrimp...no ketchup."

His stone cracked then, and he had to bite down on his smile and concentrate on driving. He'd given away pretty much everything with that kiss. How he was crazy about her. How she had become the reason behind everything he did. It wouldn't do to keep showing her something she didn't want to see. If she got totally weirded out, she wouldn't want to live with him anymore, and that thought brought an iceberg up into his chest.

His mind rebelled at the loss. Of course, he'd go if she wanted him to go, but no more walks at the end of the day? No more driving her to the gym in the morning? No more sitting across the kitchen table, telling her stories and hoping she'd laugh? What had he done with himself before he lived with Corinne? Whatever it was, it sucked compared to being with her.

He was pretty sure she wouldn't be sleeping in his bed after that kiss, and losing that was enough. So he swore to himself that he'd keep his cool.

"PJ's and *Orphan Black*," she announced as they entered the house. Wes tried to catch her expression, but she darted through the living room too quickly. Were they okay? Was she pretending that everything was fine, or was she relying on their take-out habit of food and Netflix to keep them from having to face each other across the kitchen table?

Wes carried the white paper sack bearing poboys and fries to the kitchen, an intrigued Buck following at his heels.

"We got something in common, little buddy," he muttered to the dog. "We both want something we can't have."

He tucked the take-out bag far back on the counter, safely out of reach, but Buck still sat with a ridiculously hopeful expression.

"Yeah, me too."

Wes went to his room to trade his suit for drawstring shorts and a t-shirt, and when he returned, he found Corinne in the kitchen, pouring drinks. The pink and gray plaid pajama pants and pink tank covered more than the maddening jade green dress had, but somehow, she seemed even more irresistible. Wes congratulated himself on pretending not to notice.

"Water for the triathlete," she said, handing him a glass. "And Coke Zero for the artist."

Wes rolled his eyes.

"The artist needs water, too, but since this meal is already a nutritional nightmare, the personal trainer will let it slide."

She ignored him and proceeded to pour her glass.

"Are you still riding tomorrow?" she asked, not looking at him.

"Yeah, I have a brick." He was planning a three to four-hour bike ride and a two-hour run. He'd be gone until after noon. Was she asking because she was glad to be rid of him for a while?

"Why do they call it a brick?" she asked, grabbing the poboy bag from the counter and leading the way to the living room.

"Bike. Run. Ick," he said, following. "By the end you're ready to puke."

Corinne took her usual spot on the far right side of the couch.

"Mmm, sounds *great*," she teased, unpacking the sandwiches at the coffee table.

Wes considered keeping a little distance between them and sitting in his recliner, but when she set the poboys side-by-side, he gave up and sat next to her. He nearly groaned when Corinne flipped her hair behind her shoulders because he knew what it was to touch both her hair and her shoulders. Her back. Her waist. Her mouth.

His tongue had been in her mouth less than an hour before. How could she be asking him questions about training like nothing happened? How could he answer using the word "puke"? How could he answer at all when all he wanted to do was push her back against the couch cushions, cover her with his body, and kiss and taste every inch of her?

You stupid prick.

He forced himself to get a grip. So what if that was what he wanted? Clearly, Corinne didn't. She probably hadn't wanted it the first time, and there wouldn't be a second time.

Resolved to think about anything else, Wes picked up half of his poboy and took a giant bite.

And mayo erupted down his chin.

"Awwffuck," he muttered around the mouthful.

"Oh, shit," Corinne said, attempting to hide her laughter. "You have mayonnaise all over your face!"

"No, *really?*" he asked, not even bothering to stem the sarcasm as he stood and aimed for the kitchen in search of napkins.

Corinne followed, still laughing.

"I'm sorry," she said, overcome with hysterics and clearly not sorry. In spite of himself, he felt a blush stinging his cheeks as he wiped the glob from his face.

There definitely wouldn't be a second time.

"I'm sorry," she repeated, eyes tearing with glee. He was roasting with embarrassment, but it was almost worth it to see her laughing like that.

"Yeah, *sure* you are."

"Here," she said, taking the napkin and stepping toward him. "You missed a spot." She reached up and dabbed at the corner of his mouth.

For the third time that day, she stood before him, touching him, and the humor left her eyes as she studied his mouth, and he could have sworn that her pupils grew.

Did that just happen?

But before he could tilt her chin up to be sure, a savage, rustling sound reached them from the living room, and Corinne turned toward it.

"Buck! No!" she yelled, chasing after him.

Wes caught sight of the lab tearing toward Corinne's bedroom with half a shrimp poboy in his mouth.

"Well, I'll be damned…"

Chapter 21

Sunday morning was the first in nearly two weeks that Corinne didn't start off with a yoga class—simply because there wasn't one. But when she'd awoken to an empty house—how Wes could get his bike out so soundlessly, Corinne would never know—she decided that she'd rather be at the gym than home alone. It was bad enough sleeping alone for the first time in almost two weeks, but after the kiss, Corinne thought that climbing into bed together would have been a bad idea.

And now her body definitely needed a distraction.

Though yoga was her favorite activity by far, on Thursday afternoon—instead of torturing her with circuit training—Wes had introduced her to the lap pool. Corinne was a decent swimmer, and the water never scared her, but she had expected that swimming laps would be about as fun as writing lines.

But as happened far too often, Wes had proved her wrong. Once she pinned her hair up, dunked her swim cap the way he'd shown her, and doused herself as she tugged it on, Corinne slipped into an empty lane and pulled on her new short fins, excited to practice again the series of drills that Wes had covered with her three days before.

Swimming laps wasn't boring; it was cleansing. There were so many things to concentrate on that—almost like yoga—her mind went quiet. As Wes had shown her, tilting her head down lifted her core up in the water, reducing drag. Swiveling onto one shoulder between strokes allowed her to glide efficiently, like the hull of a ship. Her kicks were to be powerful bursts, not the choppy flutters she'd always practiced. Arms and hands stayed close to her midline during strokes, maximizing power and stability.

And since she could feel the effect of each of these adjustments, Corinne knew moment by moment when she was doing it right and when she'd botched it. There was no room to think about anything else—just her body and the way it moved through the water—and before she knew it, an hour was gone.

She was glad for the reprieve. Since she'd awoken and long, long before she fell asleep the night before, she'd thought about Wes. And Michael. And what had happened. And what hadn't.

Corinne had cried—of course, she had cried—when she crawled into bed that night, into her and Michael's bed—because Michael was no longer the last man she'd kissed.

But as she climbed out of the pool and toweled herself off, she came back to this coil of thought, letting the truth of it shock through her again.

Now, the last man she'd kissed was alive.

And if the last man she'd kissed was alive, then Life might not be quite finished with her yet, which was a thought that gave her a curious whirring somewhere between her lungs and her heart.

It felt...*strange* to think about moving on. Five months ago, taking a vow of chastity seemed like her only course. She was Michael's, forever and ever. Amen. And even if she hadn't died when he did, she expected that life without him would be a half-life at best. Corinne had assumed that she would never welcome the chance to be intimate with someone else, but she had also felt sure that no one would try.

One kiss had shredded those assumptions.

What the night had taught her was that she wanted more than a half-life. Even without Michael. And even as this lesson stoked her with a kind of pride at her own ability to endure, it also made her feel terribly sad and more than a little disloyal. Didn't Michael deserve better? Didn't his memory warrant more devotion? And, she thought with a stab of pain, was moving on a sign that she was forgetting him?

Never, she thought, gritting her teeth.

And none of this even touched the source of all of this upheaval. *Wes.*

Chills broke out over her damp skin as she wrapped the towel around herself and headed for the locker room. The Sunday morning quiet at the health club had left the sauna blessedly empty, and Corinne took advantage of her solitude, stretching out on the baking wood planks.

The heat began to soak into her, and without her having to even reach for the thought of him, Wes filled her mind. If she were being honest with herself, lying in his arms every night had been more than just comforting. It had been blissful. And she was happy to keep it that way and not question how her feelings for him might be changing. But now, all she could think about was the ardent look in his eyes the moment before he'd kissed her. The way he had pulled her into him and held her so tightly as though she were his very life. The anguished lines around his mouth when she said she was confused. Corinne felt each of these moments again—more carefully and slowly now that she had time and distance to explore the memories. She felt each plunging rush, imagining what he felt.

She closed her eyes and sighed. Imagining what Wes felt changed everything.

It took away her shame and her disquiet. It filled her with awe, with heat. What *did* he feel? When had he started looking at her like that? What made him want to hold her the way he had? She wanted to respond in kind. Her wish was that she could slip into his dreams. Touch him, lie on top of him, kiss him a thousand times. Tell him how beautiful he was, what a good heart he had.

A dream. It could only happen there where she could be free from judgment. His. Her own. She would never be able to look him in the eye afterward. It had been hard enough driving home last night, pretending that everything was normal when her body was tuned in to every ripple of tension that rolled off him, every sigh of regret.

And in a dream world, there wouldn't be this fear that announced itself every time she thought about Wes that way. A fear that had darker depths than she had the courage to plumb.

A dream? Yes. In reality? No. The bottom line was that she was enough of a mess without taking him down with her, Corinne told herself. Wes deserved so much better than the wreckage of her life.

Yes, she was confused about how she felt. In truth, she felt too many things—guilt, desire, and fear among them—but one thing was clear: she only wanted Wes to be happy, to find someone with a whole heart to love him, someone strong who could show him that the tally of who he was came out to 1000 times more than the man his father thought he was, and he needed someone affectionate who could pour herself into all of the wells that his mother had left dry.

Even if Corinne wanted him and cared about him, she wasn't right for him; her heart wasn't whole; she wasn't strong, and she sure as hell wasn't affectionate.

The heat from the sauna had soaked through and now threatened to drain her. She rose from the bench, wrapped up in her towel, and stepped out onto the cool tiles of the locker room. She plodded back to her locker and started searching for her shower bag when she had to stop to let another woman pass.

"Corinne...Corinne Granger?"

She turned at her name and found herself staring at a tall, blonde woman in her late thirties who looked vaguely familiar. Her blue geo print knit dress and Rebecca Minkoff booties whispered style and sophistication, but it was her handmade jewelry that made her name fall into place.

"Ann Kergan," Corinne said, smiling, relieved that she wasn't left at a loss. The two had met at Gallery Cologne during an Art Walk event over the summer. Ann was showing a line of jewelry called "Evangeline," and Corinne was displaying a series of portraits.

"How are you?" Corinne asked.

The woman gave her a smile, but Corinne could see it was cautious. Somehow, Ann Kergan knew that Corinne had dropped off the face of the earth.

"I'm doing great," Ann said, tentatively. "How are you? It's good to see you again."

Corinne took this for the kindness that it was, and she shrugged.

"I'm okay," she said, honestly. She was still a mess, but she was making progress.

Ann's face changed to one of genuine feeling.

"I was very sorry to hear about your boyfriend," she offered. "I remember meeting him at Cologne when you were setting up. He was very sweet to help me carry in my cases."

At her words, the memory rushed in, details of a summer morning downtown that she had forgotten. After setting up her displays that day, she and Michael had gone to The French Press for brunch and Bloody Marys. Shows were always busy and stressful for her, and even though Michael worked all week, he never objected to helping her get ready for the Second Saturday Art Walk. He had a way of making light of the work and her frazzled moods, and before she knew it, they had the afternoon free.

Corinne closed her eyes for a moment and sent up a prayer.

I hope I said Thank you *enough*.

"Thank you," she said, aloud. To Ann for her condolences. To the returned memory. To Michael.

"Are you still with Cologne?" she asked, ready to move on from the subject before the memories became too much.

Ann rolled her eyes.

"God, no. Vincent is a thief!" she declared with venom. "He's never coming anywhere near my work again."

Corinne gave a rueful laugh.

"You, too? It's amazing he hasn't been arrested or sued," she said.

"Or blackballed," Ann said, and they both laughed. "Actually, Corinne, I think it's lucky that I ran into you. I'm setting up my own gallery—it's nothing as big as Vincent's, but I'd love to give you some space for the grand opening."

"Oh...I don't know...I haven't really been working since..." she let her voice trail off.

"I understand," Ann said, softly. "But the opening isn't until July 5, and even if you don't want to show anything, what about working for me for a few weeks to help me get set up? I could really use another set of hands and another pair of eyes."

The offer surprised her. It might be nice to have a job to do, but Corinne doubted that she was ready for anything full-time.

"Maybe," she hedged. "But it would have to be part-time...I'm still dealing with a lot."

"Of course! Of course, I'd take you part-time. Full-time. Whatever you want!" Ann readily agreed, looking excited. "Here, let me get your number. Maybe we could meet sometime this week. I'll show you the place and take you to lunch to hash everything out."

Had Corinne just accepted a job? She felt a thrill of nerves.

"Well—"

Ann's eyes widened with worry.

"I swear, I'm not trying to railroad you," she said in a rush. "If you decide it isn't for you, no big deal. I will totally understand."

Corinne regarded her. All she was really agreeing to was lunch. She could take her time contemplating the actual job offer.

"Okay," she said, giving Ann her phone number.

"Great! I'll be in touch," Ann said, moving to the opposite bank of lockers. "I'll let you enjoy the rest of your Sunday. It was good seeing you."

Corinne smiled, sensing that the woman meant it.

"Same here."

Corinne grabbed her shower bag and a couple of fresh towels and headed for the showers. What if she tried to paint something before her lunch with Ann? So far, she'd only been sketching—and she'd been pleased with her efforts, but maybe it was time to try again with brush and canvas.

She chose a shower stall, drew the curtain closed, and peeled off her swimsuit. If she *could* produce something, that would be an important step in getting her life back. Even if it was too early, taking the job would help her to establish her independence again. And maybe give Wes his freedom. If she could take care of herself, he could move on—and find that someone who could be all of the things for him that she couldn't be.

Corinne didn't like the prick of jealousy this thought carried, but she knew it wasn't fair to hold him back or keep him with her for longer than necessary. Still, she would miss him. So much. Corinne could not imagine that she would see Wes very often after he moved out. It wasn't like they'd hung out together before he'd moved in.

Of course, they hadn't been friends before. They were now, but wasn't that just a result of the circumstances? It was hard to picture Wes calling her to grab a pizza once he was back in his own place.

No, she would be letting him go, but it had to happen. It would hurt, but she would live. And it would be better to give them some distance before she became any more confused.

For the second time that morning she felt the bittersweet knowledge that she was getting stronger, picking up the pieces. Able to go it alone.

Yippee, she thought, sourly.

June

Chapter 22

Wes's first client on Thursday mornings was Mr. Grover Clabeaux. Mr. Grover was 83, and he'd been the shit back in the day, earning the IFBB's Mr. America title in 1958. He still came to the gym three days a week, mixing his strength training with water aerobics, the stationary bike, and walking on the indoor track. At Lafayette Fitness Club, he was something of a living legend, one of the oldest members and a favorite of the owner.

But these weren't the only reasons Wes escorted him from the weight complex to the indoor pool every week; the man was a character. Mr. Grover smiled and said hello to everyone, and he lit up whenever they stopped to talk to him for a minute or two. Walking with Mr. Grover was a slow process, but between greetings, the man dispensed all kinds of advice that made Wes laugh. He laughed, but he listened, too.

Never date a girl who smokes, Mr. Grover had said the first time he'd met the man. *Her kisses will taste like an ashtray.*

This was six years ago in Wes's early days at the club, and he'd learned that Mr. Grover was right sophomore year—the hard way. Since then, it'd been only non-smokers for him.

Clearly, by the taste of her, Corinne had never even seen a cigarette, Wes thought idly as he held the natatorium door for his elderly client.

"Thank you, son," Mr. Grover said, shuffling in. "Can't be late for my date."

Wes grinned at the joke. The 10 a.m. water aerobics class was almost all women over 60. Sometimes, Mr. Grover was the only man in the pool, and he loved every minute of it, but what he loved most was that Mrs. Clabeaux was always in the water waiting for him.

Mr. Grover stopped by the benches to remove his shoes, and Mrs. Clabeaux, sporting her flowered swim cap, waved to her husband and gave him a radiant smile.

Wes had never thought of it this way before, but standing there watching, he realized that Mr. Grover was an incredibly lucky man. Luckier than he'd likely ever be. Luckier than Michael had been. The man had enjoyed years—decades—of being welcomed with that glittering smile. Michael had been given such a smile, but not the years, and Wes could live to be 100, and he doubted anyone would ever be that happy to see him. At least not the woman he wanted.

"The way to a woman's heart," Mr. Grover said, seeming to read Wes's mind. "Is to let her know that she's it for you. The Alpha and the Omega. If she understands that—and you mean it and you live like you mean it, mind you—she'll be yours 'til the end of time."

Wes never questioned Mr. Grover's little sermons, but this didn't make sense to him, given his current situation.

"I can't imagine it's all that simple," Wes muttered, unable to keep his doubts to himself.

"Of course, it's that simple," the old man said, raising a finger for emphasis and looking Wes straight in the eye. "If you *mean* it and you *live* like you mean it."

Wes had no doubt that he meant it and, now, after rooming with Corinne and imagining how life could be if she were his, he guessed that living like he meant it would be as easy as breathing, but he felt certain—as though there were a brick in the pit of his stomach—that how *he* felt didn't matter at all.

"What if she's in love with someone else?" Wes asked as quietly as he could manage and still be heard. It was embarrassing, standing next to the pool that was quickly filling with old women, asking an octogenarian for dating advice.

But Mr. Grover's eyes lit up and, if possible, his ever-present smile pulled a little higher.

"Have you told her that she's your Alpha and Omega?" he asked, lifting an eyebrow.

This is ridiculous, Wes thought, regretting his question.

Legacy

"No, sir," he mumbled. But Corinne had become exactly that in a matter of months.

"Well...what are you waiting for?" the old man rasped, eyeing Wes as though he were an idiot.

Wes shook his head, ready to retract his question and move onto his next client.

"It's complicated," he answered, shaking his head. And then, unable to stop himself, "He'll always be the better man."

"Hogwash!" Mr. Grover bellowed, startling Wes. "The problem with your generation is that you've got no grit. You think that just because something is simple, it's got to be easy. It sounds like you've given up before you've even tried. Well, *that's not living like you mean it, son!*"

Wes stood frozen, paralyzed, and half of the women bobbing on their foam noodles were now in audience. Marla, the instructor walked in at *your generation*, and she eyed Wes with mild alarm.

Aww, fuck.

"You're right, sir," he stammered, already stepping back toward the exit, desperate to flee. "Thank you very much. Enjoy your class."

"Don't be afraid of a little competition!" Mr. Grover exclaimed, beaming. "Do you think I got Ester without a fight? Heck, no! The other fellows were lined up for miles!"

Titters and squeals. Now *all* of the women in the pool, plus Marla, were his amused audience.

Wes knew he looked horrified, but he tried to manage a respectful nod before sprinting out the exit. In his haste to escape, he burst through the double doors.

And nearly plowed into Michael's mom.

"Oh, God—"

"Wes, my goodness!" Mrs. Betsie gasped, clutching him by the arms to steady herself.

"I'm so sorry, Mrs. Betsie!" he said, cursing himself and feeling his red face flush another shade darker. "I shouldn't have been in such a hurry."

She chuckled and gave each arm a squeeze.

"You wouldn't be you if you weren't in such a hurry, Wes, dear," she said. Mrs. Betsie smiled for him, but he could see that her eyes looked tired, that the sadness that now lived at their edges would probably always be there. "I'm glad to run into you, though. Even if I might have been knocked down."

She released his arm and adjusted the swim bag on her shoulder.

Wes blinked.

"Are you going to water aerobics?" he asked, stupidly. Of course, she was. The woman was wearing beaded flip-flops and a fuchsia cover-up and carrying a mesh bag with a beach towel. How close had she come to witnessing the scene with Mr. Grover? Would she have known that Corinne was the woman in question? Would she be hurt if she did?

"Yes, I just started coming," she said, giving him a misty smile. "Michael always wanted me to exercise and take better care of myself...I feel better when I do."

Wes felt like a heel. Of course, Mrs. Betsie would be hurt. She didn't need him to fall for Corinne any more than Corinne did. Too bad he couldn't really help himself.

"How's Corinne?" she asked, when he'd just stood there in abashed silence.

Wes managed a smile.

"She's doing a little better," he told her honestly. She was actually doing a lot better. "She got a job last week at a new gallery downtown."

The corners of Mrs. Betsie's eyes lifted.

"Did she? Oh, that's wonderful," she said with a hushed awe. "Dan and I were getting so worried. You're such a good boy for helping her, Wes."

Kill me now, he prayed.

"It's nothing, Mrs. Betsie," he muttered, frowning.

"Well, it's not *nothing*, Wes. Dan told me how she looked the day you went over back in January. And I stopped by there a few weeks later, but she wouldn't come to the door, even though I'm sure she was home," Mrs. Betsie said, the worrisome memory clouding her eyes. "We were afraid we might lose her, too. You very well may have saved her life, Wes."

"Mrs. Betsie, please," Wes said, shaking his head. Her words were jarring him on too many levels. He couldn't stand her gratitude when he knew she'd be sickened if she learned of his feelings for Corinne, but he also didn't want to think about how bad off Corinne had been, how close he'd come to not helping her, what he would have done if she'd hurt herself.

"Alright, I see I'm embarrassing you," she teased, misunderstanding his agony. "If she's doing better, do you think the two of you might like to come to dinner on Sunday? It would be so wonderful..."

Her wistful look had returned, and Wes knew he couldn't refuse, even if he'd have to wear blinders to keep from ogling Corinne the whole time.

"I'll talk to Corinne and see if she's up for it," Wes agreed. "Thank you."

"No, dear, thank *you*," she said, her eyes filling. "Seeing you is like having a little piece of Michael back. We need it."

She reached for him, and Wes had to clench his teeth against his shame as he hugged her.

Because he'd been working with Mr. Grover, Wes hadn't seen Corinne following her morning yoga class, and he knew she was leaving right after to go meet her new boss at the gallery. After the embarrassing scene by the pool and the tortuous encounter with Michael's mom, Wes would have thought that he might be able to put her out of his mind for a little while, but, if anything, he wanted to see her or talk to her even more. It was pathetic, Wes knew, but for the first time in his life, he had it bad.

Even worse was how he felt about the job. He was happy for her, of course. Happy that she was ready to take on something that excited her and happy that she'd been given the opportunity. But beneath that, in the shadow of his mind, an itch of a thought kept at him.

She won't need you for long. Once she's really back on her feet, you'll have no reason to stay.

If the possibility that she would kick him out had worried him after the kiss, the certainty that he'd have to leave once she was strong enough haunted him now.

Look, asshole, he asked himself, *would you rather her weak and helpless or strong and happy?*

The answer was easy. Strong and happy. A thousand times over. Even if it meant he was out of her house.

But he didn't think he could handle being out of her life.

Wes reached for his phone on his way back to the second floor weight room.

Thursday, June 12 10:02 a.m.
How's work? Just ran into Mrs. Betsie. She wants us to come to dinner on Sunday. Want to?

Wes watched his phone for a response, but when he saw his next client leaning against the weight room wall, eyeing him impatiently, he put it away.

An hour later, he checked it again.

Thursday, June 12 10:44 a.m.
I don't know...might be hard. How'd she look?

Wes sighed. He knew it would be hard, and he didn't want to put Corinne through any more pain than she already had.

Thursday, June 12 10:58 a.m.
She looked okay. I can tell her you're not up for it yet.

Thursday, June 12 11:00 a.m.
No, don't. I can deal. Mrs. Betsie and Mr. Dan deserve better.

Pride lifted Wes's chest. There she was, his strong girl.

Michael's strong girl, he corrected himself. *Fuck it. OUR strong girl.* He wondered, absently, what Michael would think of that.

Thursday, June 12 11:01 a.m.
Whatever you say.

Thursday, June 12 11:02 a.m.
I say I can handle it as long as you are there.

Wes stared at his phone as a rush rose in his blood. Did she have any idea that he was hers to command?

Thursday, June 12 11:02 a.m.
I'm there.

Chapter 23

For a week and a half, Corinne had worked at The Green Door Gallery from 10 a.m. to 6 p.m., and she loved every minute of it.

Ann was the best boss in the world. There was a lot of work to be done, but Corinne was given license to contribute to the exhibit design and the gallery's decor, helping her boss to prep the wall space, arrange the lighting, and eventually make plans for each exhibit that would be featured for the grand opening.

The gallery was a small, rectangular space that provided about 600 square feet of area. Ann had hoped to showcase six artists in that arrangement, but Corinne convinced her to stick to only five, giving each enough room to highlight their best pieces and invite conversation clusters throughout the space.

Corinne had told Ann that she wasn't ready to be a featured artist, but her boss said that she still wanted her to have two or three pieces to display anyway. Corinne had, indeed, returned to her studio and opened her paints again. After two hours at it, her first canvas ended up in the garbage, and her second was poised for the same fate when Wes had come home from work on Thursday afternoon and stopped her from doing irreparable damage to it.

It wasn't a portrait or a landscape, but an abstract piece, a kind of synesthesia. She'd started by taking the 3x6 canvas oriented long ways on her easel, bisecting it down the middle with a kohl line, and filling in the left side in the darkest black acrylic. That part had been easy, of course, even though she wanted the brush strokes of the black to reveal intensity and strife.

The right side she'd thought to make white at first, but the white was too pristine, too full of light. She'd mixed a light gray that was just a hint darker than white and covered it just so, but this, too, seemed too simple to capture the background of what she'd planned. She had mixed and covered, mixed and covered until she was ready to lose her mind.

Thankfully, Wes had come home and found her struggling.

"I need contrast," she explained cryptically, never comfortable discussing a work in progress. "But not a stark contrast."

He stood there glistening in gym clothes after running home, nursing an Abita Purple Haze, and Corinne forgot the painting for a moment. She found herself wondering what it would feel like to run her fingers over the sinews of his forearms.

"A contrast?...Or a transition?" he had asked, frowning at her mess.

A transition, Corinne had realized. *Of course.*

She had immediately used the tip of her palette knife to score a faint line down the middle of the "white" side, and she proceeded to mix a darker gray.

After Saturday morning yoga, Corinne returned to her studio and the painting in question. Now the canvas—a kind of off-centered triptych of black, dark gray, and light gray that faded to the pristine white only at the very edge—was ready for the next step. More black, but this time mixed with scarlet, indigo, moss, violet.

She had envisioned dahlia-like explosions of these evil colors menacing the black stretch of canvas. The shapes overlapped each other, suggesting chaos and suffering. Corinne sat on her wooden stool and lost herself to the palette and brush.

She heard Wes come in after 2 o'clock. Her right shoulder and the back of her neck seared, but phase two wasn't finished yet.

"C?" he called from the living room.

Corinne smiled at the nickname. When Wes had first moved in, she had found it odd and irksome. No one had ever called her that.

But now she liked it because *Wes* did.

"Back here!" she answered.

She rolled her neck as he came in and found herself smiling again. He clearly had showered and changed after his last client, and his faux hawk was still damp.

"Wow..." he murmured, taking in the painting. "It looks totally different....Are those...dark bursts going to cover the whole thing?"

They weren't; she had something else in mind, but Corinne was superstitious about explaining her plan.

"You'll just have to wait and see," she said, circling her shoulder a few times before turning back to her work. She had almost reached the edge of the black background where she would stop for the day to let the grim colors dry.

"It's so cool," Wes mumbled, his words touched with awe. "Mind if I watch?"

"Not at all, but I'm almost done for now."

Wes found a camping chair near the back door and propped it open just behind her right side. She never took her eyes off the canvas, but the air in her studio changed. Corinne felt—quite surely—that Wes wasn't just watching her paint. He was watching *her*.

And it didn't make her nervous. In fact, it made her...*soften*. She steadied herself on her stool and concentrated on her brushwork.

But she was so *aware* of him.

Corinne could hear his breath and almost feel his eyes on her like a touch. Her belly warmed, as she felt, unmistakably, desire fill the small room. She knew that if she turned quickly to note the look in Wes's eyes that she would read longing in them.

And she was envious.

Because she wanted the chance—without limits—to watch *him*. In the two weeks since their kiss, they had both been so careful *not* to let their looks linger on each other. She knew it wasn't just her because she occasionally would catch Wes looking away if she glanced up while they watched TV. And he had caught her doing the same.

Corinne swapped out her filbert brush for a spotter and began tracing shadows, suppressing a sigh. She had so much resolve about how things should be between them—when Wes wasn't around. But when they were together, she forgot nearly all of that.

Instead, she wanted to explore him.

And it wasn't just a physical impulse. Yes, she wanted to explore his body with hers, to touch, to taste, to witness. But she wanted to explore him inside as well, to ask him a thousand questions she simply could not risk asking as merely his roommate, his friend.

When had he stopped hating her? What was he thinking now as he watched her paint? Did he feel this energy between them?

Or am I just crazy? she asked herself.

The shadows looked better, but her neck and shoulder were screaming, and she rolled them again.

"Take a break," Wes said, suddenly standing behind her. His hand landed on her right shoulder, squeezing her. "May I?"

"*Oh my God,*" she mumbled, slumping forward as warm relief halted the searing. He squeezed again and worked his thumb into her neck muscles.

"Is that a yes?" he asked, but she could hear the smile in his voice.

"Yes..." she managed. At that, his left hand came to her left shoulder, and he took over.

Delirium. Corinne turned to mush as he kneaded and rubbed. As his thumbs circled into her flesh, chills sped down her arms, and her eyes half closed. In the back of her mind, she worried that she might actually start drooling. For the second time, she was at the mercy of his expert hands, her body surrendering to him.

"It's the stool's fault," Wes said, softly, continuing his ministrations.

"Hmmm...?" Corinne only just managed to respond. Wes kept massaging in the same slow, deep rhythm.

"It's too low," he explained, gently. "Or your canvas is too high. You have to raise your arm too much, and the result is this pain and stiffness."

Vaguely, Corinne knew that what he said made sense, but she didn't care. All she cared about was how good his touch felt.

Touch.

Corinne was starved for it. In the weeks since they'd last slept in the same bed, she'd hungered to be touched again like that, gently, lovingly. It was different from being kissed. It wasn't exhilarating and confusing. It didn't ignite her and fill her with guilt. This was being nurtured, soothed. As Wes massaged her, her muscles relaxed, and her defenses did, too.

She didn't want her life to be over. And she didn't want to be alone. And here was Wes, beautiful and kind, showing her every day, every moment, that she wasn't alone.

But on the heels of this thought, fear arrived.

Holy shit!

Corinne sat up straight.

"Thanks, I'm good," she said, standing up and refusing to look at Wes.

"Y-you sure?" he asked, clearly thrown by her jolt. She busied herself by picking up her brushes, knives, and palette.

"Yeah, I'm done for today...I'm just going to go wash these outside."

She made for the back door, expecting Wes to stay behind, but he followed her and hovered on the top step as she turned on the faucet. Corinne glanced at him leaning in the doorway, watching her.

He looked good.

I've got to get out of here.

Corinne scrubbed the brush she held with extra vigor, forcing herself to focus on the task.

"So, what do you want to do tonight? I was thinking maybe we could go see a movie..." Corinne could hear the edge in his voice. Was he tense? She glanced up again. The corners of his eyes looked pinched. He *was* tense. "Maybe *Spiderman?*...Or something else...I think *Transcendence* is still playing. Johnny Depp..."

Corinne bit her lip. She couldn't sit next to him in a darkened theater for two hours, and she couldn't explain why she couldn't.

She had to come up with an excuse.

"Actually...I...um...am going out with Heather tonight," she lied, grasping for the one girlfriend who'd made an effort to keep in touch with her over the last six months.

"Heather?...Lamarche?" Wes asked, blinking in surprise. Of course, he was surprised. Other than the gallery, the gym, and Morgan's, she never went anywhere without him.

But that needed to change.

"Yeah...a girls' night," she said, finding the conviction as she spoke, but returning to the clean-up task so he wouldn't see through her. "She mentioned wanting us to get together when we ran into each other at the party. And I survived that...plus starting my new job...I think I'm ready for a night out."

When he didn't say anything in response, Corinne looked up again, fearing that he might doubt that she was ready for anything as normal as a night out, but what she saw in his eyes wasn't doubt. Was it *hurt?*

"That sounds good," Wes said, finally. "Maybe Chad wants to hang out tonight."

Corinne breathed a sigh of relief. She definitely needed to get some distance. Both of them needed it. She finished cleaning her tools and headed back into the house, aiming for her room, where she could text Heather in private and try to turn her lie into the truth.

"Yes! Drinks and dancing!" Heather squealed on the phone.

Corinne had to swallow her gasp. She'd made her bed; now she had to lie in it.

"O..kay...Where and when?"

"Pamplona on Jefferson," Heather said without hesitation. "Let's say...8:30? Then clubbing?"

"Sure…"

But Pamplona was the perfect choice, Corinne realized when the hostess seated her. She'd only been there a few times, and never with Michael. The white sangria was just as good as she remembered. As Corinne waited for Heather at the trendy tapas restaurant, she sipped eagerly, wanting to kill her case of nerves. The prospect of talking to someone other than Wes gave her the jitters, but Heather made it easy for her from the start.

"So tell me about this new job!" Heather sang, giving her a warm hug when she came in.

"It couldn't be better," Corinne answered, truthfully. She told Heather about Ann and her concept for The Green Door, and they split an order of the Catalan spinach, the ceviche, and the Castilian mushrooms. After another sangria and a dessert of chocolate truffles, Corinne was about as relaxed as she was going to get.

They'd covered all of the safe topics (work, Baby Clementine, her father, and yoga), and Corinne was grateful that Heather seemed to understand that this was necessary. They never mentioned Michael. They never mentioned Wes.

By the time they left Pamplona to walk down to City Bar, Corinne had a comfortable buzz and was looking forward to the obliteration that only deafening dance music could provide.

She'd left the house because she couldn't stop thinking about Wes. His hands on her body. *His* body. When they entered the crush of the club, with its aurora of smoke and laser lights, Corinne wondered if she just needed a night of raw carnality to keep her from obsessing about him.

Maybe that was it. She had lived like a nun for six months. She was only human, after all. If she didn't find Wes attractive, something would be wrong with her. Because he *was* attractive. Shockingly so.

But he was also Michael's best friend. And her roommate. And—for a while, anyway—her lifeline. What she was feeling for him wasn't just sexual starvation, but she *couldn't* go there. Her heart raced like a trapped rabbit's at the very thought.

But a stranger…? Someone who meant nothing to her? That might help to clear her head.

One night. No one would need to know.

The club was packed, and the dance floor was pulsing. Surely, if she was just looking for a one-night stand, she'd be able to find it here.

"Let's do a shot before we start dancing!" Heather shouted over the crowd. Corinne nodded in agreement, thinking that she'd need a little more liquid courage before setting her man-plan in motion.

"What kind?" Heather asked, pulling her to the bar. Corinne shrugged.

"I have no idea. Not a kamikaze. Something sweeter?" She thought of Wes, and wondered what he would think of her intentions for the evening.

"Melon or berry?" Heather asked.

"Berry," Corinne said. She didn't have to think about it; she knew he probably wouldn't approve.

Good thing he doesn't need to know.

She'd go home with somebody, satisfy the hunger that had been dogging her for weeks, now, and then be able to live with Wes without so much sexual tension.

Heather ordered, and a moment later the bartender set down two purple shots in front of them. Corinne studied hers, frowning.

"What is this?" she asked, having to yell over the music.

"It's a Purple Hooter!" Heather yelled back, making Corinne laugh. "Vodka, black raspberry liqueur, and lime juice. Come on! Let's take a selfie before we shoot!"

Corinne held up her drink and crowded in next to Heather, still smiling, before the flash blinded her.

"Now drink!" Heather yelled, and she tipped back her shot. It *was* sweeter than the kamikaze, but the vodka still burned her throat, and Heather laughed at the face she made.

"I wish I'd taken a picture of *that*!" she said, typing on her phone. "Okay, there, I tagged you."

Corinne rolled her eyes. She hadn't been on Facebook since a few days after Michael's funeral. The condolence messages had been too much. Corinne didn't have that many friends—on Facebook or off—but after Michael's death, everyone she ever met and certainly every one of Michael's friends—and he had a ton—wanted to pay their respects. She hadn't been able to handle it, so she stopped logging on.

"Want another one?" Heather asked, blue eyes gleaming. "We'll take a taxi home."

"Sure," she said, thinking that she wouldn't need a cab if she was able to find the right guy. But to approach the right guy, she'd need more alcohol. "Let's try the melon one this time."

Chapter 24

Burgers and beers had seemed like a great idea while Corinne was getting ready for her night out, but Wes pushed the remnants of his Big Pete and fries away from him, feeling ill.

It hadn't been the burger. It was the photo Wes had just seen on Facebook that made his stomach churn. Corinne and her friend Heather were doing shots at City Bar. At first, Wes had smiled to see the humor in her eyes, but then he noticed something in the background. Two blurry figures watched the women, and one of them looked disturbingly like the one-and-only Louis Elway.

"Wanna go to City Bar?" Wes asked Chad, waving the server over with their bill.

"Why? Is that where Corinne is?" Chad asked, his mouth kicking up in a grin.

Wes blinked.

"What makes you say that?"

Chad raised his brow.

"You've only been talking about her all night," Chad said, eyeing Wes with a mixture of mock disgust and real sympathy. "You've got it bad."

Wes suppressed a sigh. If he couldn't keep his feelings from Chad, he certainly couldn't keep them from Corinne, which was probably why she'd practically bolted out of the studio when he lost his head and started rubbing her shoulders. Any day now, she'd ask him to move out because he just couldn't keep it under control, and he was freaking her out.

"Yeah, I get it. It's a problem," he said, shaking his head.

This seemed to surprise Chad.

"Why is that a problem?"

"Because she's not ready for that, and even if she were, I'm so not her type," he said, handing over two twenties to their server and standing.

"Then why are we going to City Bar?" Chad asked, sounding doubtful, but getting to his feet.

"So I can keep an eye on her. *Duh?*"

Chad only smirked.

"*Sure.* Whatever you say."

City Bar was packed. Wes had only had two beers with dinner, and that was not enough to make the strobe lighting and Little Mix's "Move" any more appealing, but he shouldered through the crowd as Chad headed to the bar.

The dance floor was a sea of bodies. At first Wes didn't see any sign of Corinne or Elway, and he didn't know if he should be nervous or relieved. But he soon spotted her friend Heather, who was taller, and he realized that she was dancing opposite Corinne.

Who was backing up on some guy.

He didn't expect the jealousy that hit him like a blow to the gut. Because it was more than jealousy; it was pure ache. Her bare arm reached back as she stroked this guy's hair—dark hair that fell to his collar—and the bastard had his chin hooked over her shoulder. In that sleeveless purple blouse Wes had seen her in earlier, his eye had been drawn to the ruffles that gathered at her cleavage, and he knew that this asshole could see right down her shirt.

The man's hands splayed over Corinne's flat tummy, and her hips ground against his crotch to the rhythm of the music.

Wes had come here because he'd been afraid that Elway—or someone like him—would get her wasted or ruffie her drink or breathe on her. He hadn't been prepared for the half-lidded look of ecstasy she wore as she danced with this douche.

It hurt like a bitch!

Half of him wanted to tear through the crowd, peel that guy off her, and beat the shit out of him. The other half wanted to fall at her feet.

So he just stood there—watching—until Chad tapped him on the shoulder and handed him a beer.

One look and Wes knew that his buddy had taken in the scene, but he counted himself lucky that Chad had the grace not to say anything until Wes managed to get half of the draft down.

"You know what you said earlier about her not being ready?" Chad yelled in his ear over "Sofi Needs a Ladder."

Wes nodded, bitterly.

"Well, I think she's ready, man." Chad nodded toward the dance floor. When Wes just glared at him, Chad shook his head. "Dude, you'll never know if she's into you if you don't make a move."

Wes hadn't mentioned the kiss. And they lived together. If she'd wanted him to dance with her the way douche-boy was dancing with her, all she had to do was ask.

"I *have* made a move," Wes admitted. "She told me she was confused."

Wes saw the wince that Chad couldn't quite keep from his face.

Yeah, exactly, Wes thought, rolling his eyes.

"If I try again, I could ruin everything," he added, draining the rest of his beer. "All I can do right now is look after her."

Which is all I'm supposed to do.

"Well, don't look now, but I think you might be called to duty, Boy Scout," Chad said, nodding to the dance floor.

Wes followed his gaze and found Corinne. Instead of dancing on the guy, she was slumped against him. The half-lidded look he'd seen on her face before wasn't ecstasy; it was intoxication. The d-bag was trying to steady her, and Heather was nowhere to be seen.

Wes shot through the crowd and shoved the dude out of the way, grabbing Corinne.

"Hey, watch it, asshole!" the guy yelled. "She's with me!"

"Corinne? You ok?" he asked, pulling her into his arms just as she stumbled, crashing against his chest. He thought she probably weighed as much as a flower.

"I'm taking her home, man. Back off!" D-bag yelled, shoving Wes in the shoulder. Wes tucked her into the crook of one arm and pushed the guy away.

"You aren't taking her anywhere, Chester," Wes seethed, ready to kick ass if he had to. Adrenaline ratcheted up his heart rate and rippled through his muscles.

"Wes?...What are you doing here?" Corinne murmured into his shirt. He'd never seen Corinne drunk, and he decided that he didn't like it at all. She was far too vulnerable.

"Yeah, what *are* you doing here? She doesn't want you around, so fuck off!" the guy sneered.

Corinne's hand fisted into his shirt.

"Yes, I do," she slurred.

She does?

Wes's already racing heart kicked up even faster.

"Come on, let's get you home," Wes whispered down to her.

Corinne nodded. He started to guide her toward the exit, still pressed against him, when she stopped.

"Wait! We can't leave Heather," she mumbled, not even raising her head. "She went to the bathroom."

"I'll get her," Chad said, and Wes realized that he'd been at his back the whole time, ready to help if needed. The guy was quickly becoming a damn good friend.

"Thanks, man," Wes said, nodding, and he continued toward the doors. Corinne was sweating, and he was ready for her to either pass out or puke; he couldn't get her outside fast enough.

"Better..." she sighed when the night air hit them. "So hot in there." The June night was far from cool, but at least there was a breeze and the promise of a thunderstorm.

"Are you ok? Do you feel sick?" Wes asked, still steadying her. If he let go, she would probably topple forward.

"Mm okay," she said, but Wes was glad that his truck was just across the street. He'd drive with the window down just in case.

Chad came out then with Heather, who looked worried.

"Corinne? Are you okay? I'm so sorry!" she said, rushing to her friend.

"Mmm hmm..." Corinne answered with a lazy smile.

"How much did she drink?" Wes asked, thinking that Heather just seemed a little buzzed.

"We had drinks at the restaurant, and we did just a few shots at the bar," Heather said, biting her lip.

"Mmm...mmm. Five," Corinne mumbled, her eyes closed. "Three with you. Two with...Chester." She giggled then and looked up at Wes. "*Chester*...You're so funny, Wes."

He should have thought it was funny, but all he could think about was what "Chester" could have done if he hadn't shown up.

"That was dangerous, Corinne, and really stupid."

Her only response was to nuzzle further into his chest, which now ached at the thought of her being hurt. Lightning flashed to the west, and a slow thunderclap rolled toward them a moment later.

"Chad, can you make sure Heather gets home safe?" he asked, looking back at them.

Chad and Heather's eyes met, and Wes saw Chad's light up.

"I'd be glad to," he answered, extending his hand to Heather, who took it, looking equally pleased.

Wes told them goodnight, but Corinne didn't seem to notice their departure or the coming storm, so he set off with her across the street and helped her up into his truck.

"Did you hear me, Corinne? What you did tonight was stupid and dangerous," Wes scolded as he buckled her in. "That guy could have taken advantage of you."

"Mmm...I wanted him to," she whispered, never opening her eyes.

What the hell?!?

"You wanted him to?!" Wes yelled in shock.

That made her open her eyes halfway, but she held a finger over her lips and frowned at him.

"Shhh...Don't shout, Wes," she slurred.

Wes didn't know which burned hotter inside of him, his anger at her stupidity or his jealousy at her rejection.

"You *wanted* him to take advantage of you?" he asked again, not willing to believe her.

"Yes," she said, waving him away. "I wanted to have sex with him..."

She paused then to yawn, and Wes slammed the truck door and stalked to the driver's side as rain began to dampen the streets. He got in and yanked on his seatbelt.

"I wanted to have sex with him..." she said again, and it didn't hurt any less the second time, even as she patted his arm absently. "So I would stop wanting you."

Wes froze. For a good ten seconds, the only sound in the truck was the tap dance of raindrops on the roof of the cab.

"You wanted *me?*" he heard himself ask.

Corinne nodded and gave him a sleepy smile, still patting his arm.

"Why?" he whispered, afraid that anything more would bring her to her senses and she'd stop talking.

"Because you're sweet and good to me and sexy," she said, looking at him innocently, as if he should know all of this already. "And I can't stop thinking about you..."

Whoa.

The point in his chest that had ached so acutely a moment before now flooded with warmth, and in spite of himself, his cock stirred.

Stand down, soldier.

He caught the hand that was still patting his arm and squeezed it.

But then Corinne looked up at him, and her eyes filled with tears.

"But Michael...and I'm—" she bit down on her trembling lip and shook her head. "I shouldn't feel this way...It's not fair to you...You deserve someone who isn't such a mess!"

Wes's lungs had stopped working. Out of all of the reasons he thought she wouldn't want to be with him, this one had never crossed his mind. She wanted him, and she didn't think it was enough.

She was wrong.

Wes unlatched his seatbelt, moved across the seat, and took her in his arms.

"It's okay," he whispered, cupping her face and brushing away her tears with his thumbs.

He told himself that he couldn't kiss her now—not when there was a chance that she wouldn't remember, not when she was so vulnerable—but when she rose up and pressed her lips to his—gently, softly—he closed his eyes and let himself drown.

Her kiss was like a lost land—a place he'd remembered and had longed to return to his whole life. When her tongue swept across his lips, his whole body shivered, and Corinne again gripped the front of his shirt and pulled him to her. He moaned at her desire, and his tongue followed the path of hers into her precious mouth.

Wes Clarkson had never been in love in his life. Until now. He'd never allowed it. Never wanted it. Never come close. And it surprised him how something so foreign to him was so easy to recognize. This was love. Clearly. Undeniably. It had been with him for weeks, of course, but kissing her now gave it permission to draw breath and live.

"I've *been* wanting to do that…" Corinne whispered against his mouth.

"*You?* C, you have no idea."

Wes smiled and kissed her again. But then he reeled himself in. This wasn't okay. She wasn't in any condition to make decisions about them or to even talk things out. And there was a lot to talk about. That would have to wait until tomorrow.

He tucked her against him and started the truck. When he looked down at her a moment later, she was out.

Wes drove them home in the rain, half-elated, half-terrified. Corinne had never given voice to her feelings—confused as they were—and he couldn't predict what would come in the morning after she'd had a good night's sleep. And in all fairness, he'd never told her how he felt, either. Here, he was lost. The words—those three words—had never left his lips, and even though he wanted Corinne to know that he loved her, he was scared shitless.

Once he pulled into the drive, Wes scooped Corinne up and carried her to the door. She flinched against the rainfall and buried her face into him, but she didn't wake. Buck whimpered and jumped up on his hind legs when Wes came in still holding Corinne.

"Down, boy. She's okay," he said, kicking the door closed behind him. The dog followed them into her bedroom, but when Wes tried to lay her down on her bed, Corinne stirred.

"Have to pee and brush my teeth…" she said, reaching out to grab a hold of her bedside table, and missing it by a good six inches.

"Here," Wes said, pulling her up slowly and keeping an arm around her as they walked to the bathroom. He made sure she was holding onto the counter before he stepped back.

"Get out," she slurred, resting her hip against the counter and reaching for her fly. Wes huffed a laugh and took a step back toward the door, but when she listed toward the tub, he shot forward again.

"Let me help," he said, gripping her waist. Corinne shook her head wildly, throwing the rest of her body off balance until he steadied her.

"Mm not peeing in front of you."

"So kissing's fine, but not peeing?" he asked, unable to keep a straight face.

Corinne smiled, her eyes closed, and she nodded.

"Fine. Just let me help with your jeans," he promised, unbuttoning her fly and sliding down the zipper. He told himself not to think about what he was doing since she was beyond hammered, but he got hard again anyway.

"Grab hold of the counter," he told her as he backed out of the bathroom and pulled the door closed behind him. He went to the kitchen to get her a glass of water and two Advil, knowing that without it, she'd feel worse tomorrow.

When he heard the toilet flush and he thought he'd registered the sounds of the tap running, Wes gently pushed the door open to find Corinne standing at the sink in her blouse and panties, brushing her teeth.

The sight of her legs, lean and bare, made his breath catch, and the flesh that peeked out of her pink lace panties drove him nuts.

"You're beautiful," he said now because he could. He couldn't yet tell her that he loved her, but this he couldn't keep from saying. "So beautiful."

"I'b brushing my teef," she laughed through a mouthful of toothpaste, making Wes laugh, too.

"Yeah, and it's pretty damn sexy," Wes said, crossing to her. He wanted—how badly he wanted—to touch her, but he wouldn't let himself. Instead, he stood next to her and brushed his own teeth. When she bent over to rinse her mouth out, he simply steadied her elbow, and she let him escort her back to bed.

He made her take the medicine and drink the water, but as soon as he got her tucked in, Corinne grabbed her head and screwed her eyes shut.

"The room is spinning," she moaned.

"Bend your knee," Wes said, reaching under the covers, taking her right ankle in his hand, and planting her foot flat on the mattress. "That'll help."

"Better," Corinne nodded, laying her arm across her brow but opening her eyes to look up at him. "Would you stay with me, Wes?"

He hesitated for only a moment. Lying down with her again would be an exercise in torture, but wasn't he a glutton for punishment? He knew without a doubt that he would control himself. He walked around the foot of her bed, peeled off his shirt, and kicked out of his shoes. The question was, just how much self-torture was he willing to bear? Take the easy way out and lie on top of the covers? Or slip under them and pull Corinne's body against his?

Wes swallowed.

What if she never lets you get this close again?

The thought scared him. He hoped that wouldn't happen, but he couldn't be sure. Wes lifted up the blanket and slid in next to her. She immediately rolled into his embrace, making him smile. He bit back a moan as he welcomed her warmth and softness, her honeysuckle sweetness. Did anything feel as good as touching her?

But she pulled away and rolled on her back, frowning.

"More spinning..." she groaned.

"It's okay," he whispered, sliding his arm underneath her neck to prop her up, and she rested her head on his shoulder. "It'll stop soon."

She nodded, eyes closed.

"Thank you, Wes," she murmured, reaching up blindly and stroking his face. He kissed her fingers as they passed his lips, unable to stop himself.

He held her and watched her close her eyes. The lamp still burned next to her, so he reached over and turned it off.

"Mmm...thank you, Wes..." she whispered again. "So good to me... You saved me..."

Her words clutched his heart.

Where would she be right now if he hadn't chased after her tonight? Wes shuddered at the thought and pulled her tighter against him. And even if she hadn't gotten herself completely wasted, he would have lost his mind if she hadn't come home. Worry and jealousy would have eaten him alive.

Nothing in his life had prepared him for this. *Nothing*. He'd never had cause to worry about someone before. He'd lost Michael, the only person he cared about enough to fear losing, but he'd never worried about him a day in his life.

With Corinne, he worried about everything. If she was eating enough. If he'd locked the door before he left her sleeping in bed. If she would hurt herself again. If she would ever heal. If she would leave him.

He thought of Michael and how much he'd loved Corinne.

How did you do it, man?

At once, he was back in that god-awful hospital room, seeing the look in his best friend's eyes when he asked Wes to take care of Corinne. Those eyes had been desperate. Michael had known what it meant to love Corinne and to want to protect her.

And since he couldn't do it himself, he'd given her to Wes.

"Oh my God," Wes whispered into the darkness, understanding for the first time what a gift he'd been given.

Corinne had said that Wes had saved her. But he hadn't. Not really. That was Michael. By giving her to him, Michael had saved them both.

Chapter 25

Corinne bobbed on a swirling, green sea. She stood at the stern of a sailboat, clutching the railing, and watched the waves reach for her. They made her seasick.

"What are you afraid of? You'll feel better if you just jump in," Michael said, beside her.

Her eyes flew open to the glare of day, and Corinne flung herself from the bed and sprinted for the bathroom.

"Corinne?" Wes called from the kitchen, and she had the sense to slam the bathroom door closed before yanking up the toilet seat and retching.

Five minutes later, she was hollowed out with her throat on fire, shaking from head to toe, but she felt 100 times better.

"Corinne," Wes said, clearly standing just on the other side of the door. "May I come in?"

"H-hell no!" she stammered, pushing herself up from the bathroom floor, wishing that humiliation was fatal.

"I just want to help you," he said, but she could hear the laughter in his voice. He was *laughing* at her. There was no rock bottom, Corinne realized, no end to the degradation she could suffer in front of him.

"Go. Away."

"C, do you think I'm surprised that you're sick after last night?" Wes asked, pointedly.

Last night.

What exactly had happened last night?

Corinne could remember Heather. And Pamplona. And City Bar. And shots. And dancing.

And Wes?

Corinne caught her wide-eyed reflection in the mirror.

"Oh, shit," she whispered to herself.

Wes had come for her, but everything after that was a blur.

"Is this door even locked?" Wes asked, trying the handle. When it gave and he began to push the door open, Corinne shot forward and crashed into it, pushing him back.

"What the fuck, Corinne!" Wes yelled, but by then she had safely turned the lock. Something about keeping him out stirred a memory.

Wes unzipped my pants, Corinne remembered with a shock.

"What happened last night?" she choked out, hearing the panic in her voice.

Silence.

"Wesley Clarkson, *what happened last night?*" she demanded.

Corinne swore that she heard him sigh.

"Open the door, and we'll talk about it," Wes said, sounding tired.

Oh God, what did I do?

"Never mind. I don't want to know," she said, half wishing it was true and half hoping he'd fall for her bluff.

"Corinne...just open the door, baby..."

Baby?

The word was like a touch. An unexpected caress. It testified to much more than she remembered. Her blood froze.

Corinne looked at herself again in the mirror. She'd clearly slept in her clothes...at least *some* of her clothes. Her jeans, she now saw, where wadded up on the floor of the bathroom on top of her shoes. But she still had on her panties, bra, and blouse. She hoped that had to be an encouraging sign. If she'd slept with Wes, surely she wouldn't have woken up with her bra.

If I'd slept with Wes, I'd want to remember something.

And then she remembered him reaching over her to turn out the light.

She cursed again and sunk down onto the edge of the tub.

"Relax, Corinne," Wes said through the door. "Nothing happened."

Nothing?

Corinne made herself take a deep breath. Apparently, Wes had been in bed with her, but was that all? A year ago, she would have bet her life against it. But they had spent nearly two weeks just snuggling. It wasn't so hard to believe now.

Corinne knew that Wes wouldn't lie to her. And she also felt, deep down, that Wes wouldn't have taken advantage of her. He wouldn't hurt her.

She felt herself relax in that certainty. Wes would never hurt her. She had nothing to fear from him. But what about herself? She had gotten drunk last night with the intention of finding a one night stand. How much of a fool had she made of herself?

"Corinne...? We should talk," Wes said, as if reading her mind.

Maybe she really didn't want to know. Whatever it was, she needed to fortify herself first. She was a mess, and she needed to feel more put-together before facing him.

"Gimme a minute. I need a shower," she said.

There was a pause before he responded.

"Okay, but it's nearly 11, and we're supposed to be at the Roush's for noon."

"Oh, shit."

Corinne had completely forgotten their plans for Sunday dinner.

"C? You ok?" Wes asked. "Do you want me to call Mrs. Betsie and cancel?"

She still had the shakes, and the turmoil of the morning had overshadowed the fact that her head ached wickedly, but now that she was calming down, that pain made itself abundantly known. She didn't feel great, but that was her own fault. Cancelling on Mrs. Betsie and Mr. Dan would only make her feel worse.

"No, no," she said. "We'll go. I'll get it together."

"Can I get you something?" Wes asked. "Coffee or something?"

In spite of herself, Corinne smiled.

"Coffee would be great."

"You got it," Wes said, sounding relieved.

No, Wes wouldn't hurt her. He might laugh at her. He might push her. But he'd never hurt her.

"Wes?" she called.

"Yeah...?"

"Thank you."

She wasn't just thanking him for the coffee, but she couldn't expect him to know that.

"You're welcome," he said, softly.

Corinne heard him walk away, and she forced herself to stand. She brushed her teeth twice to annihilate the vile taste in her mouth before stepping into the scalding shower.

There was too much to think about. Wondering about the previous night only made her stomach clench in dread. Wes said that nothing had happened, but then why would he say that they needed to talk? Corinne hoped that it was just to fill in the blanks, but she doubted it was that simple.

She pushed those uncomfortable thoughts aside and considered Sunday dinner. The Roushes had made a point of inviting her for weeks after Michael died, and she'd gone the first two Sundays, afternoons that had really just felt like an extension of his funeral. But it had been so acutely painful to be there without him, even though she knew his family claimed her as one of their own. Seeing their suffering hadn't helped her any, so she stopped going and retreated into herself.

Corinne waited for that feeling of devastation to settle on her, but today it didn't come. There was grief, yes. She missed Michael. She would always miss Michael, but she felt ready to see his family again, and that readiness, that sense of strength was a relief.

Corinne turned off the shower, wrung out her hair, and dried herself. She wrapped her hair in a towel turban and put on her robe. She needed to get something in her stomach before it turned against her again.

When she stepped into the living room on her way to the kitchen, she met Wes coming out of it carrying a latte and a plate of buttered toast.

"Sit," he said, nodding to the couch.

"Oh, bless you," she sighed, knowing that if her stomach could handle nothing else, coffee and toast would be okay. She took her usual spot, but instead of sitting next to her like he so often did, Wes chose his recliner.

He waited for her to take a bite of toast and a sip of coffee before speaking.

"Are you ready to talk about last night?" he asked, an inscrutable look in his eyes. Corinne couldn't tell if he was pissed or disappointed or just bored with her drama. She couldn't say that she blamed him. Being her babysitter had to get old.

"I don't know. I'm scared," she said, honestly. "Maybe you could just answer some questions for me."

Wes's eyes softened.

"Fire away."

She started with something she hoped was fairly safe.

"How did you know where I was?" she asked, frowning. "Did Heather call you to come get me?"

Wes shook his head, looking a little abashed.

"No...Facebook."

Corinne rolled her eyes. *Of course*. But that didn't explain *why* he'd come.

"So...were you just coming to party with us? Or were you checking up on me?"

Corinne thought she saw his eyes wince at the implication.

"Actually...I didn't like the look of the crowd in the picture Heather posted," Wes said, cryptically.

"What does that mean?"

Now it was Wes's turn to roll his eyes.

"I thought I saw that creep Louis Elway in Heather's picture, and I didn't want him anywhere near you."

The vehemence in his voice left her a little stunned. A fiercely protective look had come into his eyes as he spoke, and Corinne felt it in her stomach like a touch.

"When Chad and I got there," he went on. "I didn't see Elway, but you were dancing with some guy, and it was clear you'd had too much to drink."

Now the look that he wore was one of strain, like he'd been worried for her. She took a sip of her coffee to hide her embarrassment. She had remembered the guy. Sean? Seth? And she also remembered the way she'd allowed herself to move with him. It had felt exciting at the time, but knowing that Wes had seen it now made her feel surprisingly guilty. She wanted to steer the conversation away from that memory.

"So, you took me home?" When she tried to picture getting from the bar back to the house, nothing rose up in her mind.

Wes nodded. Was there something he wasn't saying? Had she puked in his truck? Surely, he wouldn't miss the chance to tease her about something like that. But Wes looked like he was far from teasing her. Instead, he watched her closely.

"Okay, so how did I lose my pants?" she asked, wanting to know the answer and not wanting to know at the same time.

One side of Wes's mouth kicked up in a smile at that. It was the first time she'd seen him smile all morning, she realized, and she welcomed it.

"I just helped you get them undone," Wes said, holding up his hands in innocence. "The rest was all you."

A blush splashed onto her cheeks.

"I didn't pee in front of you, did I?" she asked, horrified. This made Wes laugh.

"No, C, you were adamant that I leave the room, which took some doing since I was sure you'd wipe out on the bathroom floor."

Corinne palmed her face in chagrin. At least she hadn't dropped her pants in front of him. She peered through her fingers and checked the clock on the DVR. 11:27. She still needed to dry her hair and get dressed, so the rest of the Q&A would have to wait until later.

"I need to get ready," she said, trying to overcome her mortification. "But I just want to know one more thing…"

"Yeah?" Wes asked, a hopeful look coming to his eyes.

"Why did you spend the night in my bed?" she asked, managing to speak only just above a whisper.

Wes's brow rose, but she could see this wasn't what he'd hoped she'd say. He almost looked…disappointed.

"Because you asked me to," he answered, softly.

She'd asked him to?

Corinne blushed to the roots of her hair, but was this really a surprise? Of course, she'd asked him to. She'd gone out to get away from the temptation of him. Without the inhibitions that came with sobriety, she would have asked for what she wanted. To be close to him. To lie in his arms again.

It was wrong of her to ask, but he'd given in anyway. She didn't know what to say to him.

"I'm sorry I was such a handful last night," she said, sincerely. "Thank you for taking care of me."

Wes shook off her apology.

"All that matters is that you are safe," he told her, but his eyes said something else. There was more.

"I'm guessing there's more we need to talk about," she said, biting her lip.

Wes shrugged.

"It can wait. We'll talk when we get back home."

Corinne knew that Wes seemed unusually quiet on the drive to the Roush's, but it took only a few minutes to reach the tree-shaded midtown neighborhood, so Corinne didn't try to make chitchat. She did, however, brace herself for the cascade of memories when Wes pulled in front of the two-story brick home with its garden wall of confederate jasmine.

At the sound of her blown out breath, Wes turned to her.

"You ok, C?"

She looked away from the house and back at him. She was a lot more okay with him by her side than if she'd come by herself.

"Yeah," she said, nodding. "I'm glad you're here."

"Always."

Wes reached for her hand, and she gladly squeezed his in return. An essence of the night before came back to her. Wes holding her against him. There wasn't much that she could remember, but that feeling she did. That feeling of safety and care. The feeling of being exactly where she wanted to be.

"You're pretty wonderful," she blurted. "Do you know that?"

Wes's eyes lit up and their corners creased with his smile. If she painted his irises now, they'd be gold.

"I don't know about that," he shrugged off her compliment, but she could tell it pleased him, and she warmed at the thought. "I just want you to be okay."

Corinne squeezed his hand again.

"I think I'll be okay," she said, feeling confident about it for the first time. "If Mrs. Betsie doesn't start crying, I won't start crying."

Wes kept his smile, but she saw the hint of sadness that touched his eyes, too. To move them on from it, she opened her car door.

"C'mon."

They went through the wooden gate into what Michael had called The Secret Garden. In the years after Michael and Claire moved out, Mrs. Betsie and Mr. Dan had cultivated every square inch of their corner lot. Raised bed gardens, beehives, and even a small chicken coop made their home a mini farm in the middle of the city.

Before Corinne and Wes had time to admire the corn stalks and blueberry bushes, the porch door opened, and Mrs. Betsie stepped out, drying her hands on her apron.

"Look, Dan, they're here!" she called over her shoulder.

The love in her eyes completely conquered Corinne's resolve, and her lashes were wet before she found herself in the woman's soft embrace.

"It's *so good* to see you, honey," she cooed in her ear, emotion only just catching in her voice. "It's been too long!"

Corinne buried her face into Mrs. Betsie's neck and let the sob break from her.

"I'm sorry, Mrs. Betsie," she wept. "I should have come sooner."

She pulled back and tried to dry her eyes, but Mrs. Betsie stepped in and employed her apron on both of their faces, making her laugh.

"You're here now," she said, wiping her glasses dry and setting them back on her nose. "That's all that matters...Wes, angel, come here!"

Corinne bit her lip against any more tears as she watched Wes bear hug Mrs. Betsie. When he let her go with damp eyes and a clenched jaw, Corinne found herself almost overcome with the urge to hold him.

She allowed herself to lay a hand on his back when Mrs. Betsie released him to lead them inside. When Wes looked down at her, their eyes locked, and something charged passed between them. Something pretty damn potent.

Corinne found herself hesitant to look away.

"Claire and Elton are running late. Abby decided to cut Thomas's hair herself, so they had to stop at Super Cuts to get it evened out," Mrs. Betsie chattered.

Wes broke the gaze first to respond to Michael's mother, and Corinne was glad that he did. She wasn't at all sure that she could form a coherent sentence. Wes's behavior all morning now made sense to her. His serious scrutiny when they'd talked, his look of disappointment, his quiet demeanor in the car. Something vital had changed between them last night. Wes had been the first to know it, and he was waiting for her to catch up.

She bit her lip and felt her stomach clench. The definitely needed to talk more later.

Chapter 26

As much as Wes loved the Roushes, he couldn't wait for the afternoon to be over so he could take Corinne back home and pick up where they'd left off.

He didn't really have a plan, but he was ready to lay everything on the table. Neither one of them needed to pretend anymore. Why deny what they felt for each other? By her own admission, she had feelings for him, but she didn't think she had enough to offer. There might have been more that upset her—more that held her back—but they could work through it together.

Wes wanted the chance to explain that he'd never want her to feel like she had to let Michael go in her heart to be enough for him. Even if he'd once thought that he could never measure up to Michael Roush, Wes's newfound gratitude for his friend somehow erased that hangup. Michael knew what it meant to love Corinne, and he'd tapped Wes for the job, a job he could have given to another loved one. Another man. But he hadn't. Wes couldn't help but feel now that Michael had judged that he was worthy—or at least would be worthy in time.

That time had come.

Wes was ready to begin. He didn't aim to carry Corinne home over his shoulder and throw her down on his bed—although the thought sent his blood thrumming through his veins like a raging river. He would take it slow. Court her. Make her comfortable with the idea of seeing them as more than roommates. More than friends. And then, yes, she would be in his bed.

These were the thoughts that coursed through his mind as Claire and Elton's kids played on the carpet at his feet, two-year-old Thomas sporting his own fresh faux-hawk after his four-year-old sister Abby had done a number on his mushroom cap.

"Don't tell Claire," Elton said, leaning over to Wes while they half-watched France humiliate Honduras in the World Cup. "But I'm kinda glad Abby went after him with those scissors. That bowl-cut looked too girly."

Wes hadn't seen the little man in a few months, but, of course, he thought high-and-tight was the best way to go.

"You won't get an argument from me," Wes agreed, running a hand over his own hawk.

Elton looked over his shoulder toward the kitchen where Corinne, Claire, and Mrs. Betsie were putting the finishing touches on lunch. Mrs. Betsie had sent Mr. Dan outside to pick a few tomatoes for the salad.

"How's Corinne doing?" Elton asked, his voice hushed.

Wes nodded.

"She's good," he said, meaning it. "She's come a long way."

"Betsie told Claire that she's working again," he said, grinning.

"Yeah, at a gallery downtown," Wes confirmed, proudly. "And she's started painting again, too."

Elton smacked him on the shoulder.

"Dan and Betsie say that you are the one to thank for that. They were pretty worried about her," he said. "Way to go, man. I know that it's not always smooth sailing with Corinne."

The rush of pride he'd let himself feel took a step back. Elton was a decent guy, but Wes wasn't about to listen to someone bad-mouth Corinne.

"Smooth sailing is for pussies. Corinne's awesome," Wes leveled, laying down the law. "Michael knew it, and I know it."

Elton's eyes bugged, but a smile lit his face.

"Whoa, man. I didn't mean any offense. Of course, she's awesome," he offered, quickly. But he must have read the possessive look in Wes's eyes because his smile ratcheted up even more. "Good for you, Wes."

Mr. Dan came back in, bearing a bowl of tomatoes, and Mrs. Betsie called to them from the kitchen.

"Boys? Could you please set the table? Dinner's almost ready."

Legacy

Sunday dinner at the Roush's, as usual, was a feast. Steamed and buttered corn, tomato and cucumber salad—all fresh from the garden—French bread and, Wes's absolute favorite—fried chicken. The Roushes always ate family style, passing the serving platters and bowls around the table, and when Corinne took the plate of chicken and only served herself one wing before passing it to him, Wes placed two thighs on his own plate and added another wing to hers. She raised a brow at him when he did this, and he raised one right back.

"Eat up, Granger," he mumbled under his breath. "House rules." If she thought he didn't remember that she'd only eaten a half piece of toast that morning, she was wrong.

When he passed the platter across the table to Claire, he saw that Michael's sister had caught the exchange and was eyeing him curiously.

"So, Corinne, when does your gallery open?" Claire asked.

Corinne laughed gently.

"Well, it's not *my* gallery. It's Ann Kergan's—she's an amazing jewelry artist. It'll open on the night of July 5th," she explained. "Tsunami's is catering. You should all come." Corinne gave them a smile and passed Wes the basket of French bread, taking, he noted appreciatively, a generous piece for herself.

Wes took a bite of chicken—crispy, salty, and mouth-watering.

"Mmmmmm," he moaned.

Next to him, Corinne stifled a giggle.

"Can we hope to see some of your work displayed?" Mr. Dan asked from the head of the table.

Wes saw Corinne's blush, and he reached for her hand under the table and gave it a squeeze.

"Actually, there will be two or three pieces of mine on display near some of Ann's work, but it'll be behind the register," she explained, shrugging. "Just a signature of sorts."

"But it's a step," Mr. Dan said, warmly, smiling down at Corinne. "I'm very proud of you…Michael would be, too."

It was the first time anyone at the table had actually said his name, and Corinne's hand clamped down on his own so tightly he thought his heart might burst for her. He squeezed back, promising to stay by her, to be the one she could hold onto.

"Thank you, Mr. Dan," she managed, but Wes could hear the struggle in her voice to keep from crying.

Mr. Dan cleared his throat, and it was evident that everyone was struggling to swallow. Elton, thank God, came to the rescue.

"When's your next race, Wes?" he asked.

Wes actually felt Corinne relax beside him, relieved to no longer be the subject of attention. He gladly took up the mantle, ready to talk triathlons for the rest of the meal if she needed.

"I have a Half Ironman in New Roads next month," Wes said.

Elton gave a low whistle.

"In this heat? You could be in for a brutal event."

Wes didn't miss the concerned look Corinne gave him at this, but he launched into the stats about temperature, elevation for the bike ride, the location of the route. Elton and the others asked him questions, and then Claire and Mrs. Betsie talked about a trip the family had taken to False River in New Roads years before.

In the middle of their reminiscence, a phone in Thomas's diaper bag chimed, and Claire reached behind her and grabbed it blindly. She checked the screen and slid it to her husband.

"Yours," she said.

Elton read the message and scowled.

"Crap. I have to go into the office."

"*Again?*" Claire whined.

"I'm on call, Claire," Elton defended, pushing himself from the table and clearing his place.

"At least you had time to finish your dinner," Mrs. Betsie said, always the peacemaker.

"Anything less would be a crime, Mrs. Betsie," Wes said, smiling at her. "That meal rocked."

Michael's mom's face lit up, just as he hoped it would.

"Thank you, dear."

Elton returned from the kitchen and thanked his mother-in-law. The diaper bag chimed again, and he reached in, looking exasperated.

"Yours," he said, handing Claire the phone.

Claire read the message, and her eyes immediately shot to Corinne and then to him. She didn't look happy.

What the hell?

"Pop-pop, can we go show Corinne and Wes the new chicks?" Abby asked her grandfather.

"Sure, kitten, as soon as we help Granny clean up the kitchen," Mr. Dan promised, rising from the table.

"You boys go on," Mrs. Betsie said. "The girls and I have got this."

Wes loved Mrs. Betsie, but she was traditional to a fault, and he wasn't about to shirk chores while Corinne did them.

"I'll help in here first," he said, stacking Corinne's almost empty plate on top of his own.

"But I want to see the chicks *now*," Abby whined.

Wes waited for someone to tell the child to be patient. Corinne spoke up instead.

"Go out with them, Wes. I'll be there in a few minutes."

Abby took this as the sign that everything was going her way.

"Yay! Chicks! Chicks! Chicks!" she chanted as she ran to the back door.

Wes arched a brow at Corinne.

"Thanks a lot," he murmured under his breath.

Outside, Wes and Mr. Dan followed Abby toward the mobile chicken coop where buff and black hens lazed in the shade of two pecan trees, their chicks clustered around them. At Abby's approach, all of the birds started a slow scurry toward the coop, a miniature red barn on a flat-bed trailer.

"Slow down, Abby. You'll scare 'em off," Mr. Dan called.

The two men watched the four-year-old halt in her tracks before taking slow-motion steps toward the confused birds.

"There's somebody who goes after what she wants," Mr. Dan said, keeping his eyes on the child.

Wes nodded, wondering how long Corinne would be stuck inside.

"By the looks of it," Mr. Dan continued. "You might know something about that."

Wes's eyes jerked to Mr. Dan's. The man turned to him and smiled.

"What, sir?"

"Don't 'what' me, son. You know exactly what I mean," he said, smirking now. "Two young people, both heartbroken, living together under the same roof. It's the best thing that could happen to both of you."

Wes felt his collar heat.

"Mr. Dan, I—"

"Michael would understand," he said, gently. "And Betsie and I would be delighted."

Wes swallowed.

"You're getting way ahead of yourself, Mr. Dan," Wes said, shaking his head.

"Maybe," the older man conceded. "But I see the way you look at her, and I just want you to know that we love you both. Nothing will bring Michael back, but that doesn't mean that something good can't come out of all of this pain."

He laid a hand on Wes's shoulder and gave it a fatherly squeeze. His own father had never touched him with anything close. Acceptance? Tenderness?

Hell, no.

"Michael was so lucky to have you and Mrs. Betsie," Wes said, forcing the words past the knot in his throat.

Mr. Dan looked him in the eye, unashamed to speak frankly to him. "You have us, too, Wes."

Damn. Wes thought the knot just might win. He turned his gaze to Abby, who'd managed to catch a chick at last and was cradling it to her with reverent affection.

"Not too tight, Abigail," Mr. Dan said.

They watched the child set the chick onto the grass and scramble after another one.

"I'm going to look in on Corinne. We need to be going soon," Wes said.

Wes headed back toward the house, ready to take Corinne home. He opened the door to raised voices, and what he heard hit him like a kick in the balls.

"I am *not* in love with him!" Corinne's voice, jagged with distress, stopped him in his tracks. "I *can't* love him!"

"Oh, really?" Claire said, her voice laced with sarcasm. "Then why did I just get a text from Mimi Andrus saying she saw the two of you *kissing* outside City Bar last night?"

Oh, shit!

He heard Corinne gasp, but he couldn't make himself move.

"Well? Is it true?" Claire demanded.

"I-I'm not sure…" Corinne stammered, sounding horrified.

"What do you mean, you're not sure? Are you fuck-buddies?"

"No! I wouldn't do that!" Corinne insisted.

Wes hated Claire's ugly words, the accusation in her voice, but what paralyzed him was Corinne's tone. She sounded disgusted at the very thought of being with him.

"Well, what *is* going on with the two of you?" Claire asked, bitterly. "I saw the way he was looking at you during dinner, and you liked it, Corinne. It hasn't even been six months since my brother died. Are you so eager to replace him?"

"God, no!" Corinne nearly wailed, pain sharp in her voice. "Look, I know that Wes might think he has feelings for me, but I haven't encouraged them."

Her voice broke then, and he heard her sobbing.

"Claire, how can you say these things," she cried. "Losing Michael almost killed me."

The sound of rapid footfalls on the stairs behind him brought Wes out of his agonizing trance.

"What on earth is going on?"

Mrs. Betsie, wide-eyed and carrying Thomas on her hip, searched Wes's eyes before stalking toward the kitchen.

"Claire Roush Benson, what the hell are you doing?!?" Mrs. Betsie sounded furious, but Wes couldn't listen to any more. He left the house through the front door and made his way to the truck.

He sat in the front seat, waiting for Corinne, knowing that after such an ugly scene, she'd be outside any second. Wes thanked God that their drive back to the house would only be mere minutes. A blackness like he'd never known fell over him and everything else. He needed to escape.

The front door opened, and Corinne emerged, running toward the truck. Her face was a mask of misery when she pulled the door open.

"Wes?...Oh my God, Wes, I'm so sorry!" Corinne sobbed, tears streaming down her face. "You must hate me!"

"No," he said, frowning at the ridiculous statement. "Of course, not."

I'm just a fucking idiot.

Corinne climbed into the truck and grabbed his arm. Her touch—something he craved but now knew he could never truly have—seared him, and he removed her hand from his arm and set it on her knee.

"Oh my God, I've wrecked everything!" she keened, eyes wide.

No, that was me.

"It's okay, Corinne," he managed. "It's not your fault."

Wes started the truck and pulled away from the Roush's, so ashamed of leaving Michael's parents' house in such a state of disgrace.

"There are some things I need to explain," Corinne said, speaking through stuttered breaths.

"No, you don't," Wes said, not looking at her but wanting to spare them both.

"Can we at least talk about this when we get home?" she hiccupped.

Wes shook his head.

"I need to go for a ride. We can talk later," he said, vaguely. A plan was already taking shape in his mind. He needed to iron out a few things before he could say anything to her.

She sighed with what sounded like relief.

"Okay, as long as we can work things out," she said, sounding hopeful.

෴

At the house, Corinne went straight to her room, and Wes went to his. He sat on the edge of his bed, held his head in his hands, and let the pain rip through him in one monstrous blow. Elbows on his knees and gritting his teeth, he suffocated a howl that would have taken the walls down.

He knew she didn't love him, but he'd let himself hope that attraction and trust would have given them enough of a start. That they could build on the chemistry and the already solid friendship the months together had brought them.

He *knew* she didn't love him. But hearing her say that she *couldn't* still tore him in two.

Wes made himself stand and change into his cycling clothes. He had to get out and clear his head, and he had some decisions to make. Ones that would still allow him to keep his promises to Corinne without intruding on her life anymore. And ones that might help him get over her.

July

Chapter 27

Wes had not been home in more than two weeks. At least not while Corinne was in the house.

She had come back from the gallery a couple of times to find that things of his had disappeared. The hamper in the bathroom had been emptied of his clothes, and his shaving kit was no longer on the counter. The mail would be sorted, and only items addressed to her remained.

Today, she had come home at 3:30, and his Capresso was no longer on the kitchen counter. She checked the pantry, and gone, too, were his Stinger Waffles, Clif Shot Bloks, and Nathan electrolyte tablets.

Her best guess was that he was staying with Chad.

She had texted him about twenty times, and for every four or five messages, she'd get a reply. Usually only a "yes" or "no" answer and only to questions that had nothing to do with the two of them or the awful afternoon at the Roush's.

Corinne couldn't blame him for leaving or for avoiding her. She hated herself.

Claire's accusations had split her open, ripping out the stitches that a few fragile months had sewn into her heart. And, worse, in the moments she'd stood in the Roush's kitchen and absorbed Claire's anger and sense of betrayal, she had allowed her own doubts about Wes—and what she felt for him—to consume her.

"It must be nice that you're already over Michael," Claire had said once they were alone. The words had shocked as hard as a bomb blast, and they had landed in the field of her guilt. Corinne wasn't *over* Michael. There was no such thing. But she *was* healing. Her options had been to heal or die, and Wes had shown her that she still had a life to live. Still, the

implication that she wasn't forever scarred, that she wouldn't always love Michael, was one that hurt deeply.

And then when Claire had accused her of being in love with Wes, she had denied it. Denied him. How could she love Wes when she still loved Michael? How could she ever love anyone again after losing Michael? There was no other option but to deny it.

And yet...

But that was crazy! Corinne had long since admitted to herself that she was attracted to Wes, that he was attracted to her, but she couldn't let herself love him. As much as she wanted him—and she *did* want him—Corinne could never allow it to happen.

But Claire had seen the attraction, seen it in Corinne's eyes and actions. Corinne had felt so exposed, so condemned when Claire had asked crudely if she and Wes were "fuck buddies." Because Corinne knew that she had come dangerously close to being just that. She had asked Wes into her bed that night and God knows what else. And in her shame at that self-knowledge, she had denied and denied again.

And Wes had heard everything. At least, according to Mrs. Betsie, he'd heard enough. Enough to be deeply hurt.

It made Corinne shudder every time she pictured his face as he'd waited for her outside the Roush's. The light in his eyes had almost completely shut down, his pupils mere pinpricks. His dark complexion had become a sickly olive, and the set of his jaw signaled pain.

She ached to think about how much she'd hurt him. Corinne had never been so sorry in her life.

Even though she knew she deserved to be alone, two weeks without him had been almost unbearable. She missed him keenly. And she realized that it wasn't just loneliness that ate at her. She didn't just miss having someone to have dinner with, or walk Buck with, or sit in front of the TV with at the end of the day.

She missed *Wes*.

She missed the way he hummed in pleasure at every meal; the way he riled Buck into a frenzy before their walks; the way he'd tuck a blanket over her legs when they curled up on the couch with a movie.

As much as Corinne wondered how he was doing and *what* he was doing, she couldn't bring herself to corner him at the gym. She'd switched to the 6 a.m. yoga classes so she could get to the gallery early, and every time she went to the health club, she hoped that she would run into him. But he clearly didn't want to see her, so she wasn't going to make it awkward by hounding him.

Buck broke through her haze of self-pity with a whine of impatience, ready to be let out and entertained now that she was back from work.

"Alright," she sighed, following him through the sunroom to the back yard. Buck's red Kong frisbee—one she'd seen him gnawing on that morning in the kitchen, now was outside on the top step, a sure sign that Wes had played with the dog on his visit.

Corinne felt a pang of envy.

"So, he'll spend time with *you*, I see," she said, sourly.

As if in answer Buck bounced on his hind legs and waited for her to pick up the toy. She sat down on the steps and threw the disk across the yard. Wes had probably sat in the exact same spot doing the exact same thing only hours before.

Selfishly, she imagined parking her car down the street out of sight and waiting for him to stop in one day. If she sprung herself on him, would he run away? Would he stay and talk? They'd never had the discussion he'd promised when they left the Roush's that afternoon. He'd gotten on his bike and left for hours, so long that she'd texted and called out of worry. Well after dark, when she was nearly beside herself, he'd sent her one terse message: *At Chad's. Don't wait up.* And she hadn't seen him since.

If he walked in right now, Corinne didn't think she could stop herself from tackling him to keep him from leaving again. The thought itself made her pulse spike. She needed a chance to apologize and explain why she'd been such a coward, but what she needed even more than that was just to see him. Just to touch him.

Unable to picture going another day without hearing from him, she pulled her phone from her pocket and sent him yet another text.

Tuesday, July 1: 3:47 p.m.
The gallery opening is Saturday. I hope you will still be my +1.

Corinne knew it was kind of low to remind him of an obligation he'd made before she had clearly hurt and disappointed him, but if he turned her down, at least she'd know how badly she'd screwed up. If he came, then maybe she'd be able to fix things.

She tucked her phone back in her pocket, thinking that if he responded at all, he'd take his sweet time doing it. She guessed that this was part of her punishment, and, again, she couldn't blame him.

But before she could even pull her hand away from her pocket, his response came.

Tuesday, July 1: 3:48 p.m.
I don't think so, C. I can't be around you right now.

Pain, swift and stunning, sliced through her like a dagger. She heard the breath leave her lungs and was grateful no one witnessed how her body sagged. Corinne stared at the screen and tried to calm herself before responding.

Tuesday, July 1: 3:50 p.m.
You make me sound like a disease. Is that what I am?

She needn't ask the question. The answer was obvious. She was toxic. A danger to others, better avoided or quarantined. She had to accept his sense of self-preservation.

Tuesday, July 1: 3:51 p.m.
God, Corinne, no. I just can't.

She'd already texted him saying that she was sorry countless times, but she couldn't stop herself from doing it again.

Tuesday, July 1: 3:52 p.m.
Wes, you can't know how sorry I am. We need to talk.

She waited, clutching her phone and praying that he'd give in. And even as much as she writhed with guilt again about what she'd done, it was a blessing just to hear from him.

Tuesday, July 1: 3:55 p.m.
I can't do this right now.

She texted right back.

Tuesday, July 1: 3:55 p.m.
Then when?

Corinne stared at her phone for five long minutes before accepting that he wasn't going to respond. It wasn't until Buck sniffed her face and licked her tears in whimpering distress that she realized she was crying.

꧁ ꧂

The night before the gallery opening, Corinne and Ann stayed at The Green Door until well after midnight, putting finishing touches on each exhibit and going over the floors and windows until they gleamed.

The space looked amazing.

Ann had asked her to design and build a movable partition that glided on hidden casters, and this panel served to bisect the gallery as well as provide the necessary wall space for two of the smaller exhibits. With one artist on the east wall of the gallery and another on the west, the long south end was the natural focal point for their best and biggest display by a local photographer whose black and whites were crisp, stunning, and larger than life.

At the north end of the gallery, near the entrance, Ann had repurposed an antique, painted pine counter that had once stood in a general store. This now served as their purchase counter, and the length would be enough to set out wine and hors d'oeuvres on one end and a display case of Ann's jewelry on the other.

Behind the counter and near the front windows was the five-foot expanse of wall Ann had insisted that Corinne claim for some of her paintings. She had chosen a few finished pieces that had sat untouched and nearly forgotten in her studio from the fall, but she'd also included the abstract piece she'd finished two weeks before and one other.

The last, the warmest and most captivating, was one that had seemed to paint itself. Corinne had debated about sharing the portrait with the public, but after she'd finished it two days before, it seemed to stare at her from the easel in her studio and demand to be shown. He wouldn't be there to see it anyway, so why not give in?

"It's striking," Ann had said upon first seeing it. "Those eyes command the whole room. Who is he?"

"That's my friend Wes," Corinne had told her, unable to look at her boss while she spoke, but glad that the potent effect of the portrait wasn't limited to herself.

"He's gorgeous, honey. He burns with life!"

"Yes...he does."

She had used her poolside sketch as a reference, but memories had put the heat into his eyes and the ache across the brow. Corinne would never have admitted it to anyone, but the portrait was really a crystallization of the look he wore right before Wes had kissed her that night on his parents' lawn.

It was a moment she had relived in her mind a thousand times.

Looking at the portrait, hung to its advantage beneath the spotlighting, its power seemed to magnify, and the longing that Corinne had born for three weeks ached within her.

She had left Wes alone after their last text exchange, wanting to give him the space he seemed to need, but it wasn't easy. Corinne thought about him constantly.

Even as she and Ann shut off the lights and locked up at a quarter to 1:00 in the morning, Wes was in her blood. It didn't help that The Green Door was on Jefferson Street, and she could almost hear the music thumping from City Bar one block over.

She and Ann had parked next to each other in the side lot, and they always walked out together when they put in time after dark.

"Get some rest, Corinne. I don't want to see you here tomorrow until at least after 3:00," her boss insisted.

"Yes, ma'am," she teased. If Ann mistook her silence and weariness for fatigue after the long night, Corinne wasn't going to disabuse her.

"You've done a terrific job, Corinne," Ann said, warmly. "I never could have pulled this off without you. You should be very proud."

Corinne gave her boss a genuine smile.

"I am proud, and you should be, too," she said. "It is going to rock so hard! I'm so grateful just to be a part of it."

The women said goodnight, and Corinne made the short drive home to her empty house.

In her dreams that night, Michael walked through the gallery and smiled at everything she'd done. He made the circuit from exhibit to exhibit and finally ended at the antique counter, staring at her paintings. He nodded at the two he'd seen before and then studied the abstract piece knowingly.

"This one's as much about him as it is about me," he said about the haunting starbursts that morphed into flowers across the ever-lightening canvas.

Corinne simply nodded, not needing words in her dream.

But then Michael stepped close to the portrait and stared into Wes's eyes.

"This one's not finished," Michael told her, frowning. "Why would you hang it up before it was finished?"

"It is finished," Corinne insisted, looking at it again and seeing Wes's intense gaze.

But Michael just smiled at her, infusing her with warmth and comfort, filling in the cavity of fear inside her with peace.

"So stubborn. You never did listen," Michael said, love shining in his eyes. "That's why I had to give you to him."

Corinne woke after 10 a.m. to Buck growling petulantly in her doorway.

"You are aware that it's Saturday, right?" she asked, peeling back the covers. Buck tilted his head at her words, hearing nothing that sounded like the promise of food.

The essence of the dream still clung to her as she fed Buck and let him out. The feeling of comfort was still there, even if the dream didn't make much sense.

But comfort was all she felt. Gone was the wish to dive back into her dream and seek him out again. That bitter sense of loss that used to torment her after she dreamed of Michael didn't grip her anymore and hadn't in some time.

She was free to look forward to her day, and this one filled her with an almost giddy sense of anticipation. The green door at The Green Door would open to guests at 6 p.m., and Ann expected that they would welcome at least 150 patrons that night.

Corinne had bought a new outfit for the occasion, a sleeveless column dress with black and white splicing. The round neckline was professional, but the short length still made her feel fashionable and feminine. Her nude platform pumps should be comfortable enough for a few hours, but Corinne planned to wear sandals in the gallery until just before they opened. She and Ann would both be wearing some of her boss's pieces, and Corinne could not wait to sport those.

After she made herself a veggie omelet and toast (which only made her think of Wes), Corinne showered and left for the salon. She had planned to get her hair and nails done, and as excited as she was about the opening, she was glad for the soothing distraction of having her hair shampooed, cut, and styled.

She and Ann texted each other all afternoon, making sure that each remembered all the last-minute details: ice for the bottled water, change for the cash drawer, the flower arrangements.

Bearing a bag from Taco Sisters (Ann had sent a desperate text saying she hadn't eaten all day) and carrying in her dress, shoes, and make-up bag, Corinne returned to The Green Door at 3:30 that afternoon, practically vibrating with excitement.

Wes's eyes, larger than life and a kaleidoscope of mocha, bronze, gold, and azure, seemed to track her from the portrait, evoking Michael's strange words. Every time she thought about Wes, her heart gave a little drop, plummeting as she remembered that he would not come tonight. *Why* he would not come.

I can't be around you right now.

She was grateful for the bustle of the afternoon as she and Ann arranged flowers and tweaked the lighting; otherwise, her longing to see Wes would have sacked her.

As soon as the staff from Tsunami set out their trays of avocado, Philadelphia, and lava rolls, Ann and Corinne took turns changing in the gallery's small bathroom. Even the tiny space testified to Ann's aesthetics, the apple green vessel sink commanding the eye and playing against the greens, blues, and browns in the glass tile backsplash.

At 5:30, Ann dumped the A/C's thermostat in advance of the first guests to combat the July evening's heat and humidity, and they greeted the first smiling visitors minutes later. The five featured artists—representing a range of ages and styles—arrived almost simultaneously, and Corinne and Ann lost themselves to the job at hand of making introductions, giving cursory tours, and pouring wine.

They sold their first piece—a watercolor by a local artist—at 6:20, about the time that Morgan, Greg, and Corinne's father arrived.

"You look beautiful!" Morgan sang while wrapping her in a hug. "I still can't fit into any of my old clothes!"

"Thank you all for coming," Corinne told them, moving to her father's embrace and then kissing her brother-in-law on the cheek. "Where's Clementine?"

Morgan rolled her eyes.

"Aren't we good enough?" she asked wryly. "Just kidding. She's at home with a sitter. This is our first night out, but we are on the clock. Gallery. Dinner. Home."

"I gave Clementine her first bottle this week," Greg boasted, proudly. "She should be good for a few hours, but we don't want to press our luck."

The new parents could have gone on like this all evening, but at that moment, Morgan spotted Wes's portrait.

"*Oh my!*" she gasped, walking away from Corinne and the others, clutching her heart with drama that only Morgan could achieve. "Corinne, what haven't you been telling me?"

Corinne colored. She'd told her sister nothing. Nothing about their earth-shattering kiss at the Clarkson's party, or her ill-fated night at City Bar, or Wes's departure. The portrait didn't reveal all of that, but it revealed enough.

"That's hardly the look of a roommate," Morgan muttered when Corinne drew up to her, her father and Greg following.

"I suppose not," she said, evasively.

Morgan cut her eyes at her sister, sizing her up.

"I guess you're not going to spill anything *now*, are you?" she asked, archly.

"You're damn right," Corinne mumbled.

Greg chuckled at this, but Corinne's father narrowed his eyes, catching, Corinne was sure, the mask she'd donned to hide the ache that had set in again.

The gallery door opened, more guests filed in, and Corinne took her chance to escape.

"Guys, please stay and enjoy some food and wine. I need to get back to work," she said, hoping to hide her relief.

Corinne handled two more sales, both of these for the rising star of a photographer whose work commanded the south wall. As soon as the second of these transactions was completed, Mrs. Betsie and Mr. Dan approached her, smiling.

Corinne was sure she'd paled. She didn't think she could face them after the way she'd left their kitchen weeks before, but they didn't give her long to berate herself.

"Corinne, you look so lovely!" Mrs. Betsie gushed. "And look at this place! You've done such a beautiful job."

"It's Ann's vision," she demured. "I'm lucky to be a part of it. I couldn't have dreamed of a better job."

Legacy

"It's good to see your work on display, too," Mr. Dan said, nodding to the space behind the counter. Corinne was glad that neither of them commented on the portrait, but it was clear that both studied it intently.

Somehow, Corinne found a little courage, wanting to put that Sunday behind them.

"I'm so sorry for the way I left things the other day," she said, genuinely. "There are so many things about that afternoon I regret."

Mrs. Betsie's brows drew together in a disapproving frown, and she shook her head.

"You, my dear, have nothing to be sorry about," she said, sternly. "Claire should be the one asking forgiveness."

Mr. Dan seemed a little more diplomatic.

"She's grieving. Just like all of us," he said. "I don't excuse the way she behaved, but, Corinne, please try not to take it personally—although it was very personal."

Michael's father looked both sad and ashamed.

"I think she may understand how wrong she was, but she has her pride, too," he said, shrugging. "Still, I wouldn't be too surprised if she calls you soon with an apology of her own."

As far as Corinne was concerned, she was the worst offender, denying Wes at every turn. She'd gladly forgive Claire if Wes could find his way to forgiving her.

"I understand," she said, simply. "None of this has been easy."

But that wasn't really true. Some things had been surprisingly easy, like Wes making her feel safe. Getting her to take better care of herself. Making her want him.

She shook these thoughts from her mind.

"Let me get you both a glass of wine, and then I'll show you the exhibits."

By 7:30, the small gallery was bursting with people. Corinne spotted a few of her own patrons and made a point to greet them personally, and many of the guests she recognized as members of the arts community, artists as well as avid supporters.

After opening several more bottles of wine, Corinne decided to take the empties to the bin outside behind the back of the gallery. It was hot and sticky outside, and the brief errand had her sweating. She came back in and was about to duck into the restroom to freshen up when she saw him.

Wes had come in with Heather and Chad, and all three were staring at his portrait.

He looked so beautiful.

The glossy, ebony flame of his hair. The muscularity of his neck and shoulders, not quite hidden by the cut of his dress shirt. The dark curling of his eyelashes that didn't once blink as he beheld himself.

Corinne watched him in profile, and she let herself feel the throes of longing and regret. But before she'd had her fill, he turned, his gaze landing on her with precision, as if he'd felt her there the whole time.

His expression was unreadable, and she nearly quailed, wondering if she'd be better off chasing after a customer. But she'd waited too long to see him, so she put one foot in front of the other until he was just an arm's reach away.

"You came," she said, lamely. Corinne swallowed and tried again. "I'm so glad you came."

Chapter 28

H is plan was a total failure.

Three weeks away from Corinne had done absolutely nothing to mute Wes's feelings for her. One look was all he needed to make this clear. He still wanted her. He still needed her. He was still so fucking in love with her it threatened to eat him whole.

Chad had talked him into going to the gallery opening, saying that it couldn't make his mood any worse. Wes knew that he'd been an ass the three weeks Chad had let him room with him—for free. His friend deserved better. When Wes had agreed to go, he decided that he wouldn't be a killjoy the whole time, especially since Heather and Chad were going together.

The last thing he expected, though, was to come face to face with a painting that told the whole world how he felt. When he first laid eyes on it, he couldn't look away. It captured everything he felt about Corinne. His aching desire. His utter despair. The man in the portrait lived in heaven and hell, looking at everything he wanted in life, never being able to have it.

But the painting meant that this was how she saw him—irrevocably hung up on her.

"I know Wes might think he has feelings for me, but I haven't encouraged them."

The words still burned him from the inside out. One look at that painting, and it was clear he'd never needed any encouragement. He had jumped in with both feet.

It was fucking embarrassing.

Wes had used Chad's prodding as an excuse because, of course, he'd wanted to come. He wanted to see her. And he wanted to congratulate her on the work she'd done—both at the gallery and within her own life. Getting back to work had been a huge step for her, one that he understood better than anyone, and he wanted her to know how proud he was.

And she'd asked him.

When she'd texted to see if he was still going, he'd told her no. Corinne had thought he was upset, and she kept apologizing for what she'd said at Mrs. Betsie and Mr. Dan's house.

He needed her to understand that he wasn't angry about that.

"I am not in love with him!...I can't love him!"

As much as it hurt to hear her say it—with so much vehemence—he couldn't and wouldn't blame her for how she felt. He understood perfectly. She was attracted to him—as she'd confessed in his truck that night—but she couldn't act on it because it wasn't enough. Corinne had said it wasn't enough for him, but who was she kidding? It wasn't enough for her. *He* wasn't enough.

Hearing her talk about him when she thought he wasn't listening had cleared up any question. His feelings were a problem. His presence was a problem.

So he had left. Staying with Chad for free meant that he could keep his promise to Corinne and continue paying her rent for three more months. And then they could go their separate ways. Wes didn't think he could conjure a thought that disgusted him more, but it was the best he could give her.

He continued to stare at the picture of his own passion as these thoughts ran through his mind—until he felt her.

There was no other way to describe it. The gallery was packed with people, and the drone of conversation buzzed at an almost uncomfortable level. But he became aware that she was watching him, and he turned at once.

God, she's so beautiful.

So many things he treasured about her were clear in just one look. The strength that carried her announced itself in the set of her shoulders. The vulnerability that softened her peered out of her eyes. The brilliance that was her art surrounded her and set her apart in this space she had helped to create.

The urge to go to her was stronger than the desire to draw breath, but Wes didn't want to be the man in the painting, obsessed and in pursuit. He held himself still for the impossible seconds it took her to cross to him.

"You came," she said, sounding surprised and looking somehow relieved. "I'm so glad you came."

Her hazel eyes glittered under the gallery lighting. Had they always been this big?

"I wanted to," he admitted. "You've worked so hard on this...It's pretty amazing."

A smile that he felt all the way down to his navel lit her face at his praise, and seeing it made every ounce of agony he'd have now or later absolutely worth it. Now that she was in front of him, all he could think about was how much he'd missed her. It was a relief—a huge relief—just to see her again.

"How have you been?" she asked, carefully, a slight frown crimping her brow.

"Okay," he shrugged, not wanting to touch on how miserable he was. Wes blurted the first thing that came to mind. "I've been training a lot...I have a half next weekend."

"Oh, yeah," Corinne nodded, her frown deepening. "Where is it again?"

"New Roads," he said, watching her carefully. "Case and I are going to drive up together."

"Oh," she said, seeming to force a smile. "Well, good luck."

"Thanks," he said, awkwardly. Corinne had never been into racing. Even if she'd gone to some of Michael's, at best, she had tolerated it. He steered their talk back to the gallery. "This place looks awesome, Corinne."

Her frown disappeared.

"Can I show you around?" she asked, and the look of tentative hope she gave him almost broke his heart. Of course, she could show him around. He'd have to pull himself away sometime tonight—sooner than he wanted—but now he'd go wherever she led him.

"Please," he said, letting go of his heartbreak and allowing himself to feel happy for her.

To his surprise, she held out her hand to him, and he took it without hesitation. It shouldn't have surprised him. They'd held hands a few times. Still, her touch made his stomach quiver. The sensation blotted out everything else as she guided him through the crowd.

"The exhibits are wonderful, and we'll get to those," she said leaning into him and dropping her voice to a whisper. "But I want to show you some of things that I did."

She steered him to a partition in the middle of the gallery that featured almost a dozen small watercolors.

"You see that wall?" she asked, smiling. "I built that."

"You built it?" he echoed, beaming, studying the sleek panel that seemed to float above the ground. "That's frickin' cool!"

"Yeah, I drew up a design, and I built it myself," she said, clearly proud and almost surprised by it. "It's mobile. You can roll it around."

Wes knew that it was just one of the many things she'd done to make the gallery a success, and the fact that she wanted to share her pride with him set him apart from everyone else there.

"You're so damn talented," he told her, truthfully.

She pointed up to a series of lights on the ceiling.

"I installed those, too," she said, beaming. "Can you picture me up on a ladder like a handyman?"

Wes could picture it vividly, and the thought of her falling or electrocuting herself took a year off his life.

She told him about all of the artists, pointing them out across the gallery, but she didn't make any introductions. Wes noticed that several eyes tracked from the portrait on the front wall to him and back. He'd even caught people whispering with knowing looks. He should have felt exposed. In a way, he *did* feel exposed, but he also felt blameless.

Yes, that's me on the wall. Yes, I really can't help myself.

As they made the circuit around the gallery, Corinne still held his hand. She tugged him toward the back door and looked at him shyly.

"Could we step outside and just talk for a minute?" she asked.

Wes hesitated. He didn't know what good could come of it, and he didn't want things to turn awkward between them when they'd come safely this far.

"Please..." she added, an anguished look coming to her eyes.

He didn't want to go, fearing that she'd actually put into words what he already knew—that she thought they were better off as friends. But he nodded anyway.

Wes followed her out the heavy steel door and into the sudden quiet of the July night. After the flood of voices inside, the song of cicadas and the murmur of traffic on Jefferson Street was almost soothing. Corinne closed the gallery door behind them, and they stood alone in the back lot.

He was aware that his hand entwined with hers felt clammy and knew it would only grow more so in the blanket of humidity that the night provided. He looked down at their hands because it was easier than waiting for what she had to say.

"I've really missed you," she said, softly.

At first, the words startled him, as unexpected as they were. He'd missed her unbelievably, but Wes had not considered that she'd been missing *him*.

But, of course, it made sense. For three months, he'd been her safety net. Her security blanket. Her friend. Just because their feelings for each other didn't match didn't mean that she felt *nothing* for him. Of course, she cared about him in that friend way. In the grand scheme of things, that made him almost lucky. The woman he loved at least knew he existed.

He looked at her then, reminding himself to make the most of the time he had with her. To savor it. To allow himself to store up some memories.

"I've missed you, too," he admitted, though it couldn't be much of a surprise to her.

But she did look a little more relieved. Still, he saw that the anguished look, one that tucked a hint of worry between her brows, hadn't vanished.

"Does that mean you'll come home, then?" Corinne asked in a rush before biting the corner of her lip.

Aww, fuck.

"I-I can't, Corinne," he stammered. He loved her—so much—but they couldn't go back to the way things were. Not now. The tension for both of them would be so awful, especially knowing how she saw him. Wes refused to cling to her, cling to hope.

But at his words, her frown deepened, and her mouth shrunk.

"Are you...Are you doing this to punish me, Wes?" she asked, trembling now, looking chilled even in the summer heat.

"What? God, no!" He gripped her elbow and gave her arm a little shake. "Why in the hell would I want to punish you?"

"Because I hurt you," Corinne's shoulders sagged as she said this, and to his horror, Wes thought she looked like she would cry. "I hurt and denied you. Wes, how could I have done that? I'm so disgusted with myself."

"Stop," he whispered, moving his hands to her shoulders. "I'm not punishing you, baby. *You* are."

Corinne eyed him doubtfully and ground her lip between her teeth, but she at least seemed to keep any tears at bay. He didn't want her crying tonight. Tonight was about her success. Her progress.

"You think I'm angry with you," he said, softly. "But I'm not...It's okay."

She shook her head.

"It's not o—"

"Shh. I say it's okay," he insisted, gripping her shoulders again.

She shook her head a second time, frowning down at her feet. Then she brought her eyes to meet his.

"Do you know what you mean to me, Wes?" she asked, her eyes as big as river stones.

Wes's mouth kicked up in a smile in spite of himself. When she said his name and looked at him like that, he could almost trick himself into hoping. He raised his hand and caressed her cheek with the back of his fingers.

She was so beautiful, so alive and complex that he felt more alive just being with her. Building a life with Corinne would be—

"Do you...?" she demanded, searching his eyes.

He pushed his fantasy aside and gave her his answer.

"That night...*that* night," he said, tilting his head in the direction of City Bar just down the street. "You told me that I saved you."

Relief took her face, and she brought her palm to his cheek.

"You did," she said. "You did."

And before he knew what she was about, Corinne had closed the distance between them. She was kissing him. Again. Again, he could taste, and touch, and savor everything he wanted. Her kiss was a drug, beckoning him to dive in, headlong, threatening to shred the last of his self-control.

No.

It killed him. It decimated him. But Wes closed his fingers around those shoulders and pushed her away.

"I can't, Corinne," he gasped. "I can't go down this road again."

Chapter 29

It hurt. Corinne didn't bother denying that it hurt when he rejected her. And she might have been upset—if she didn't think she deserved it. But she had it coming. Corinne had behaved as though he didn't matter to her.

When he did. Maybe he mattered more than anything.

Wes didn't trust her not to hurt him. He didn't know that three weeks without him had taught her a great many things. About him. About herself.

So when he pushed her away, Corinne didn't hold it against him—even though it hurt. So badly. Instead, she cleared her throat and stared at their feet until she could summon enough dignity to look him in the eye again.

"I should probably get back inside," she said, evenly.

Wes nodded, but he looked miserable. She might have deserved to suffer, but he certainly did not, especially now that he seemed pained for hurting her.

"It's my big night, after all," she said, forcing a smile and brushing her fingers along his forearm to reassure him.

A measure of relief came to his eyes, and he turned to pull the door open for them.

"Next time I'm at the gym, maybe we could have lunch," she ventured, watching his reaction.

When he wanted to be, Wes was a master of the poker face. His guarded look left her no hint about what he thought—except the certainty that he didn't want her to know what was going on in his head.

"Maybe so," he said, simply.

This didn't sound very encouraging, but she wasn't about to call him on it. Instead, she slipped inside and tried to reassume the sense of confidence that the gallery always gave her.

As soon as they stepped back inside, Ann eyed her desperately from behind the counter. It was time to sell some art.

"I've got to go," she said, quickly to Wes. "Stop avoiding my texts and calls, okay?"

Wes gave a rueful laugh.

"Okay," he agreed.

It wasn't much, but maybe they could move on from here. Still, she didn't want to leave his side. She would have been happier to stay by him all night and try to convince him to come home. Instead, she let herself squeeze his hand again.

"Thanks for coming," Corinne said, and then she pulled away and darted to the counter to help her boss.

For the next two hours, Corinne didn't stop. She greeted, toured, poured, sold, and, finally, cleaned up. But the whole time, a nagging anxiety tore at her. A little after 11 p.m., Ann hugged her with tearful pride, and both women walked out to their cars.

Corinne checked her phone as she started the Mazda and found a text from Wes. Seeing his name on the screen was enough to make her heartbeat step up.

Saturday, July 5 9:42 p.m.
Stopped by the house to feed Buck and let him out. Figured you'd be a while getting back tonight.

His words made her smile, and she texted right back.

Saturday, July 5 11:14 p.m.
Thank you so much! Just leaving Green Door now. Glad Buck is good to go.

The nagging made her stomach tighten, refusing to be ignored now that she was alone. Corinne heard the phone chime as she drove, but she resisted the urge to check it until she got home.

Saturday, July 5 11:16 p.m.
Be careful going home. Lots of crazies downtown. Text when you get in.

This one made her breath catch. He still worried about her. He still cared about her, and he didn't seem to be keeping his distance anymore. Corinne hoped all of these things were true, and she quickly responded.

Saturday, July 5 11:29 p.m.
Home safe.
It was great to see you tonight. Thank you.

She was kicking off her shoes and unzipping her dress when another text sounded.

Saturday, July 5 11:34 p.m.
Glad I came. Good to see you, too. So proud of you.

Corinne's hand flew to her heart at this.

"Oh, my," she whispered to herself. Another message followed right behind it.

Saturday, July 5 11:34 p.m.
Michael would be, too.

She thought it was sweet for him to say it, and she knew that it was true, but Corinne was keenly aware of the realization that—tonight—it was Wes's good opinion that mattered most to her. She didn't see how she could tell him that, but Corinne now wished she could.

Before she could text back, her phone chimed again.

Saturday, July 5 11:35 p.m.
Gotta ride tomorrow. Night, C.

An unpleasant and all-too-familiar feeling knotted in her stomach. It warred with the nagging feeling, edging past it in her mind, and she texted back.

Saturday, July 5 11:36 p.m.
Please be safe! Goodnight, Wes.

Corinne changed into her pajamas, let Buck out one last time, and went to the bathroom to brush her teeth. She eyed herself in the bathroom mirror and sighed. The house without Wes felt so empty. After she let the dog back in, locked up, and crawled into bed, she stared at the ceiling in the darkness.

She should have been exhausted. The day had been full and rewarding, and her body should have been tired, but her eyes didn't want to close.

What if? She wondered.

What if they had not gone to the Roush's that day? And Claire had not pounced on her? And Corinne had not said the things she said…?

Would he be just down the hall?…Would he be closer?

He'd slept in her bed that night. Because she'd asked him to. The scraps of memories teased her. Sleeping in Wes's arms always felt so good.

Corinne wanted to do it again. She wanted to do other things, too.

She wanted to see him tomorrow after his ride, and she wanted to eat dinner with him, and she wanted to walk Buck with him. And it wasn't because the house was empty. And it wasn't because she was lonely. And it wasn't because she was sad.

She wanted to kiss him again. She wanted to feel the skin under his shirt over his abs. She wanted to lie beneath him.

But she was afraid.

As Corinne lay alone in bed, she let herself feel the band of fear that cinched around her middle. It had been closing in on her for weeks, and to keep it at bay, she had lied to herself. And she had lied to Wes. Because lying was easier than facing it.

If you love him, you will lose him.

This was the language that the fear spoke. And Corinne believed that it spoke the truth. How could she not believe it? It had been truth her whole life. She'd loved her mother. Before anything else, she could remember the love and the loss that seemed to be the very genesis of her life. The unspoken lesson of her childhood was irrefutable: what you love the most and need the most will be taken from you.

And then the love that eclipsed everything, the love that finally seemed to be the answer had found her.

Michael.

When they'd met, she couldn't push him away. He wouldn't go. And so she'd let her guard down and loved him with everything she had. He'd made her believe that the hole in her heart that she could only fill with art or anger wasn't meant to be a hole at all. It was the place where her love started, where there was and had always been so much more to give.

Then he'd gone and died on her.

And now her stupid heart was asking her to love again. It scared the piss out of her.

If she were honest with herself, her heart had asked her to love weeks ago, and the answer had been and was still yes. She loved Wes. She loved his passion for life, how he lived in his body with so much intensity. How he ate with such joy, worked with real conviction. She loved how he cared for the people in his life. He'd made sure that Chad—someone who needed and deserved it—got Michael's bike; he visited the Roushes, as devoted to them as their own son had been; he'd upended his own life to watch out for her. She loved how he hadn't given up on her in the beginning when she'd tried to push him away, too.

Corinne loved how he played with Buck, and joked with her, and sang along to awful hip hop music. She loved how he ran his hands through his hair when he was agitated, the way the house smelled after he shaved.

She loved the way he looked at her.

Corinne loved Wes Clarkson, and she'd allowed him to believe that she didn't. Denying it hadn't made anything better. It didn't make her love him less; in fact, it made her love him more, miss him more.

Legacy

It didn't matter that she hadn't meant to fall in love with him. Six months ago, she didn't think loving anyone else was possible, but now, looking back on their time together, it was impossible to think that she could have avoided it. Wes was wonderful.

Corinne had denied how she felt not because she didn't love Wes, not because she couldn't love Wes, but because she couldn't face losing him, too. The way she'd lost Michael. The way she'd lost her mother.

Losing her mother had maimed her, teaching her to guard against closeness, prompting her to push people away. Losing Michael had almost killed her. If she let herself love Wes, and she lost him, too…

But lying in her bed, staring up at the ceiling, Corinne saw the irony. By denying how she felt, she'd lost him anyway.

She had to fix things—if Wes would let her.

Corinne sat up against the pillows, switched on the bedside lamp, and started making plans.

Chapter 30

Wes and Chad shouldered their bikes up the stairs to Chad's second-floor apartment on Sunday, drenched, exhausted, and starving. The 25-mile training ride in 85 degree heat had kicked their asses, and sweat still streamed into Wes's eyes. He wiped it away so he could focus on the plastic rectangle on Chad's doorstep.

"What's that?" he panted, pointing as they reached the landing.

"Don't know." Chad set his bike down and bent over with a grunt. He picked up the container and handed it to Wes. "It's for you. There's a note."

But by then Wes could already see the unmistakable golden promise through the Rubbermaid plastic.

"Pineapple upside-down cake!" he gasped, taking the dish from Chad and reading his name in Corinne's pretty script across the card. He cracked the lid and immediately inhaled the heavenly brown sugar and butter syrup that soaked the top of the fluffy, golden cake.

"Dude, you are sharing that," Chad declared, making a grab for the container. Wes jerked it safely out of his friend's reach.

"Hands off, Case," he barked. "Get the hell inside."

Chad scowled.

"Asshole, I let you live here for free," he grumbled, but he unlocked the door anyway, carrying the Pinarello carefully through.

"I didn't say I wouldn't share," Wes leveled, following him. "But, bitch, you don't get to touch this cake."

"Fine. I'll get some plates."

Wes eyed his friend with disbelief.

"Hold on there, ace. This is Corinne's pineapple upside down cake," he explained with indignation. "You don't just dive into it in a post-ride binge. We've gotta eat something to take the edge of first so we can savor it. Make us some turkey sandwiches while I read my note."

"Remind me again how long you are staying?" Chad griped, but he set his bike in its stand in the living room and made his way to the kitchen.

Wes put up his own bike before sitting on the couch and plucking the note from the plastic lid.

"You'd better not be putting your sweaty ass on my sofa," Chad called from the kitchen.

Wes shot up and winced at the ass-shaped wet spot he'd left on the microsuede. Wes knew that they both had a case of the hangries after the killer bike ride, but he didn't want to piss off Chad for real.

He set the cake on the coffee table and tore open the envelope. The surprise of the dessert in light of his mind-boggling hunger had almost overshadowed the fact that Corinne had brought it. That she'd been on Chad's doorstep that morning. He'd thought about her for 25 miles, arguing with himself over his decision to push her away rather than face more heartache.

And she was thinking about me, he realized with wonder.

He held her note carefully as he unfolded it, mindful now of the racing of his heart.

Wes,

I've been a jerk. And an idiot. And a chicken shit. I want to make it up to you.

Love,

Corinne

He laughed at her short, blunt sentences, but he shook his head. She was still trying to apologize, still believing he was upset with her. Wes knew she didn't understand why he had to stay away, but he wasn't going to put it all out there for her, either. Maybe that made *him* a chicken shit, but he couldn't see the point in explaining to Corinne that he couldn't live with her anymore because he was in love with her, and he never stood a chance.

He was too far gone to be able to live with her, especially if she kept surprising him with kisses the way she had at the gallery last night and in his truck weeks before. It was too damn hard when he knew she could never love him.

Still, he didn't want her out of his life completely. He couldn't stand that either.

He pulled his phone out of his armband and strode into Chad's spare room. Wes could hardly call it *his* room. Most of his stuff was still at Corinne's. And in storage. And at his parents' house.

Living like a fucking nomad, Wes told himself.

But nomads roamed without a home, and whenever Wes thought about home, Corinne filled his mind. He tapped her number and allowed himself to feel grateful for a reason to call her.

She picked up on the second ring.

"Hey, Wes," she answered, sounding happy to hear from him.

Wes couldn't help the smile as her voice tugged at him.

"You made me a cake," he said, still a little in awe that she'd done it.

"I did," she said, clearly pleased with herself.

"It wasn't necessary," Wes said.

The line went quiet for a moment.

"Oh, I think it was."

Wes could still hear the smile in her voice, but he imagined that it sobered some.

"Corinne,...I'm not mad at you," he tried to explain.

"I'm very glad to hear that, Wes," she answered. "But that's not why I made you a cake."

Wes frowned.

"Then why did you?" he couldn't help but ask.

"Because you like it," she said before he heard her draw in a breath. "And I like you."

The words felt good, like the brush of fingertips down his back.

But I love you, Wes thought with a pang.

"I like you, too," he managed.

She paused again.

"Can I make you dinner tomorrow night? At the house?" she asked, sounding hopeful—and a little meek.

His stomach fell.

"Corinne..." He didn't want to keep telling her no, but she threatened his composure. He didn't think he could be in the house with her where he'd last held her as she slept.

"What about lunch, then? At the club?" she stammered, in a rush. "Just lunch tomorrow."

Wes suppressed a sigh. She wasn't going to give it up. Wes knew this. As many times as she'd called him or texted him in the last three weeks, he knew she'd just keep at it. This was typical Corinne.

"Yes. Lunch tomorrow."

"Yay!" she sang.

She wanted to be friends, and he had to allow them some space and time to actually *be friends*, even though it was hard. But he didn't have to torture himself. He didn't have to go back to the house or hold her hand or let her kiss him.

Would you actually stop her from kissing you AGAIN? he asked himself. He shook off the question and decided it was time to say goodbye.

"Well, thanks for the cake, C," he said, hoping he didn't sound as low to her as he did to himself. "I'll meet you in the snack bar at noon."

"At noon, Wes," she echoed, sounding, he thought, a little low, too.

In spite of himself, Wes was waiting outside the snack bar at 11:55, less than a minute after he'd finished with his 11 a.m. client. He'd reverently devoured two pieces of Corinne's perfect pineapple upside down cake the day before, and Wes was convinced it tasted better than anything he'd ever eaten. He admitted to himself that this was probably because she'd made it for him alone, but that changed nothing.

And even though he knew it was foolish and hopeless, all night and all morning, his mind had returned to Corinne, knowing he'd see her again. So the fact that he was only five minutes early for their lunch date was something he regarded as a marginal victory. It was better than watching her finish her yoga class from outside the studio like a stalker.

When he saw her slender, petite frame—stunning in her fitted yoga attire—descend the stairs across from him, Wes silently promised that he wouldn't make a fool of himself, even though a part of him—a ridiculously demanding part of him—wanted to beg Corinne to give him a chance to make her happy.

I'd do anything.

He pushed the desperate thought from his mind. Wes tried to offer Corinne the kind of smile a friend would—not one from an obsessed loser—sure that he'd look like a douche either way.

But she just smiled back, maddening him even more when she stepped into his space and pressed a chaste kiss to his cheek. It *was* something a friend would do, but she brushed him with the signature of her heat and intoxicated him with her honeysuckle scent, and for a moment, he couldn't speak.

"How are you, Wes?" she asked, eyeing him carefully.

I'm in love with you.

I'm miserable.

I'm this close to throwing you over my shoulder and bolting for the door.

"I'm...good. You?" he managed.

"Hungry," she answered, smiling and leading him into the snack bar. "You gonna order for me today, coach?"

Wes gave a rueful grin. That had been their routine. They hadn't worked out together in almost a month, and he missed it. Maybe she did, too.

"Sure." When they made it to the front of the line, he ordered two turkey burgers with steamed broccoli while Corinne grabbed them each a vitamin water.

"Thanks for taking care of Buck the other night," she said. "With all of the stuff going on at the gallery, I didn't even realize how late I'd be."

"It's no problem," Wes said, shaking his head. "Anytime you need me to look in on him, I'm happy to do it."

Corinne's eyes met his, and she gave him a sad smile. He held his breath, ready for her to say something about moving back, but just then their order was called.

He grabbed their plates and carried them out into the dining area, finding a table near the racquet ball courts. Wes busied himself by dressing his burger with mustard and ketchup while Corinne pushed broccoli around on her plate.

This is going to be brutal.

The tension between them felt like a force field, holding them still and silent—and apart from each other.

"I took on a new commission," Corinne said, finally breaking the silence.

"You did?" Wes asked, relieved for something to talk about, but also surprised and pleased for her.

"Yeah, a guy at the gallery opening wants me to do a portrait of his wife," she said, looking wistful. "It was so sweet."

"Yeah, it's quite a gift to be painted by Corinne Granger," he said before he could help himself.

Corinne's brow crimped in worry.

"Oh, Wes," she sighed, heavily. "I really should have asked your permission before hanging that portrait. I'm sorry."

Wes felt his eye shoot open in surprise.

"What? Corinne, no," he said in a rush. "I wasn't being sarcastic. I mean it. Seeing that portrait was pretty powerful."

Corinne bit the corner of her lip—adorably, Wes thought.

"Really? If I'd thought you were coming, I would have at least given you a heads-up," she admitted. "To be honest, I didn't give it much thought. I just really liked the painting."

He didn't have a right to, but Wes felt proud.

"It's a good painting," he said, softly. "I'm glad you showed it... Really."

The worry left her face, and her hazel eyes shone with happiness. Wes felt his insides warm at her look.

If you let me, I'd give you everything.

"Well, I'm sure it's the reason I got that commission," she said, looking up at him through her lashes, trying to hide how proud it made her.

"Oh, really?" Wes teased, the tension he felt earlier now forgotten. Finally, he dug into his turkey burger.

"Yeah, really. I've had three offers on it," she said, soberly. "But I don't think I want to sell it."

The last words came out softly, and Wes looked up from his plate and locked eyes with her again. Was there something in them he hadn't seen before?

Wes was about to say her name, when the look on her face changed suddenly to one of alarm as she focused behind him.

"Well, well, well, if it isn't my slacker son and the artist who's out of his league."

Wes heard his father's voice drip down on them, and he saw Corinne's eyes narrow before he turned around.

Harold Clarkson carried a tennis racquet over his shoulder and bore a wicked smile. The sadistic mischief in the man's eyes made Wes get to his feet, instinctively shielding Corinne with his body. Wes knew that his father hadn't been drinking, but he recognized the blood-thirsty look in his eyes. It was clear that he'd had a bad morning—in court or in a settlement meeting, no doubt—and he'd come to the gym to best an opponent on the tennis courts and regain some face.

But finding Wes—especially finding Wes in front of an audience—was better than any tennis match. Wes could read all of this in his father's eyes in an instant, and adrenalin surged through his veins.

"Aren't you going to invite me to join you, Wesley?" his father asked, leering.

"No, I don't think so," Wes said, hearing the steel in his own voice. His father didn't come to the gym often, and whenever Wes spotted him, he usually headed in the opposite direction—if he was alone. Harold Clarkson had cornered him a couple of times with a client, which was always awful, but since his father rarely frequented the weight rooms or the cross training areas, Wes could almost forget about that risk.

Today, he and Corinne were sitting ducks, but Wes wasn't going to run.

"What's the matter?" his father teased. "Are you afraid that your girlfriend will drop you for a seasoned and successful man?"

"Corinne is a friend, Dad," Wes admitted. It pained him to say it, but he didn't want Corinne to think he'd allow his father to believe they were together.

Harold Clarkson smirked.

"As I recall, you had your tongue down her throat in my backyard not long ago," he gloated. "What happened? She figure out you weren't good enough?"

At once, Corinne was by his side.

"You're so wrong!" she insisted, eyeing Wes's father with hatred. "You're *so* wrong. *I* don't deserve *him*....and neither do you!"

Wes felt his eyes widen in shock as his father's face contorted with derision.

"Don't scowl, honey," the man told Corinne. "It distracts the eye from what little cleavage you have."

"You fucker," Wes growled as his hands fisted his father's crisp, white collar. "You so much as speak to her again, and I will fucking end you."

Wes saw his father's eyes bulge before the man could recover and level him with a menacing stare.

"Do you think I'm above having you arrested for assault?" the older man hissed, glaring at Wes with cold disdain.

"Wes..." Corinne whispered, laying a hand on his shoulder. "He's not worth it." People at the tables around them were turning to watch now as father and son were locked together, staring each other down.

But in that moment, Wes did not care. He was done cowering before Harold Clarkson.

"Do you think I'm above snapping your neck right here?" Wes asked, low enough so that only he, his father, and Corinne heard the words. He pressed his thumbs against his father's carotid arteries and felt the racing pulse. "You've bullied and tortured me my whole life, Dad. One way or the other, you are never coming near me or Corinne again."

Wes narrowed his eyes as he looked into his father's, wanting the man to see the dangerous depth of his conviction. It was as deep as his love for Corinne, a depth he hadn't known was there. He *could* kill his father right now. Maybe it should have scared him, but it didn't.

It was a relief. This was the end of all of that shit.

Harold Clarkson must have glimpsed something of the truth because he broke his gaze and jerked himself out of Wes's grasp, straightening his collar as his face flushed, but he could not meet his son's eyes.

"You always were a sorry excuse for a son," he muttered with disgust, but he slunk away. Faster than Wes would have expected.

As Wes watched him go, a peace unlike any he'd ever known settled over him. It was over. Harold Clarkson held no threat over him any longer. Perhaps he hadn't for years. Perhaps Wes had really been shut of him as soon as he entered manhood, but he hadn't known it.

But now, standing beside Corinne, he knew.

That part of his life—the part where he tip-toed around the disaster of his parents and hoped not to be sucked in—was over. His life, he now realized, was his own.

"Oh, Wes!" Corinne gasped, sounding shaken, her hand still clamped on his shoulder.

He turned to her and found her pale and trembling.

"It's alright," he said, calmly. "He can't hurt us."

Corinne hugged her elbows and bit her lip.

"But...what if he tries to get you fired?" she asked, frowning and clearly concerned.

Wes shook his head.

"He won't," he said with certainty. "But even if he did, it's our word against his. The man clearly insulted you. The bottom line is I'm not worried."

"You sure?" she asked. She stared at him, still frowning, but the strain around her eyes eased a little.

Wes gave her a gentle smile and sat down again, gesturing for her to do the same.

"I'm sure."

She took her seat, but she just stared at the remaining half of her turkey burger.

"Ugh. I don't think I can eat any more," she said, shaking her head. "How are you so calm?"

Wes picked up the rest of his burger and took a bite. He shrugged.

"Guy's an asshole," he mumbled through a mouthful. Wes swallowed before continuing. "He always has been. He's never going to change, but I think I just figured out that I don't have to live with it anymore...I'm free."

Legacy

This made Corinne smile a slow, beautiful smile that spread across her face and lit her eyes.

"I meant what I said." Corinne met his gaze across the table. "You deserve so much better."

It was something a friend would say. Wes was tempted to ask what she'd meant about her not deserving him, but he suspected it would only make him feel worse. The easiest thing to do now would be to make a joke.

"Tell me something I don't know," he said, forcing a smile.

"Remind me why we are doing this again?" Chad asked as they secured the bikes to the hitch on the back of Wes's truck.

It was 4:30 in the morning, and they had a 90-minute drive ahead of them before the Hellfire Half Ironman at False River.

"No guts. No glory," Wes said, moving to the cab of the truck and checking the rest of his gear one more time. "C'mon. Let's hit it."

Gun time wasn't until 7 o'clock, but they still had to check in and stash their stuff at each transition. It would be Chad's first half, and even though he was whining like a little girl, Wes knew that his friend was more nervous than anything else.

They jumped into the truck, and Chad tilted his seat back, looking to get comfortable.

"What do you think you're doing?" Wes asked, raising an indignant brow.

Chad shot him a glare.

"I'm going back to sleep. What does it look like?"

Wes shook his head and started the truck.

"Hell, no, bitch. You have to stay awake to make sure I stay awake," Wes said, only half-joking.

Chad leaned back and crossed his arms over his chest.

"Sucks to be you," he muttered, closing his eyes.

Wes narrowed his eyes at his foolish friend and suppressed a snicker. He waited the ten minutes until they merged onto I-49 and Chad was snoring softly beside him before he tapped his new Linkin Park album and cranked "Guilty All the Same" as loud as it could go without blowing the truck's speakers.

"WHAT THE FUCK!!!" Chad cursed, spazzing out next to him and sending Wes into a fit of laughter. Wes slapped Chad's hands away from the volume knob on his stereo three times before Chad gave up.

"Fine! Fine! Fine! I'll stay awake, you mother fucker!"

Wes just laughed and brought the volume down to a sane level.

"Asshole-piece-of-shit-cock-sucker," Chad spat, raising his seat back up. "I think I like you better when you're pouting over Corinne."

"Ow," Wes still laughed, but the blow struck home just the same. "Reach back there and get me a Clif bar and a boiled egg. And don't forget to drink up that water. It's going to be hot as piss today."

Wes ate his breakfast and drove, but Chad's words had summoned thoughts of Corinne, which—if Wes were honest with himself—were never far from his mind anyway. He hadn't seen her since their lunch on Monday, and—unlike the weeks before—she hadn't contacted him at all until last night, when she'd texted to wish him good luck at the race.

Wes figured that her comparative silence signaled that she was moving on, accepting his decision to distance himself and letting go.

It hurt like hell.

Wes tried to focus on the race ahead of him to distract himself from the ever-present ache.

At 4:30 in the morning, traffic was nonexistent, so they made the trip in good time. Wes had done the Hellfire the past two years, so he already knew where he wanted to park and where the transitions were. By the time the sun was coming up, they'd checked in, been inked with their numbers, and set up their bikes and gear.

Five minutes before gun time, Chad and Wes were in their wave group, treading water just off the dock with swim caps and goggles around their heads. It was 76 degrees, and the sun wasn't even over the tree line.

"This is going to suck," Chad hissed. "Why did I let you talk me into this."

Wes just grinned.

"If you don't DNF, you'll be one bad-ass triathlete. That's why," Wes reminded him.

One side of Chad's mouth lifted in a smile.

"I *am* pretty badass," he allowed with a shrug. "At least, Heather thinks so."

Wes rolled his eyes and would have given Chad a hard time about being hung up on Corinne's friend, but the sound of the National Anthem silenced him. In spite of himself, his heart rate sped up, and he stretched his neck and rolled his shoulders, trying to stay loose.

The gun sounded, and Wes, Chad, and a hundred other people launched themselves through the water. This was always the worst part: the lake churned up with hundreds of arms and legs thrashing and colliding, swimmers trying to break out of the pack and only managing to get kicked in the face while kicking someone else in the groin.

Wes lost Chad immediately, but a tri isn't a team sport. He wished his friend well, but he couldn't race his best if he spent time looking over his shoulder. Wes could only focus on stretching out his strokes and making it to the buoy and back across False River to the first transition point. His personal record for a half was 5:11:14. It would be hard to beat that in this heat, but he wasn't going to let himself wuss out just because it was July in south Louisiana.

By the time he pulled himself ashore and bolted for his bike and bag, he was three minutes ahead of his PR. It was early, but a good-sized crowd had already turned out to cheer on the athletes, and Wes felt grateful. Crowd support helped so much, especially as the day would wear on.

His hands shook with adrenalin as he pulled on his bike shoes and strapped on his helmet. After he walked his bike out of T-1, Wes straddled his Colnago, clipped in, and took off.

And he almost wiped out two feet later. Because there she was. Holding the most amazing hand-painted poster bearing his name, Corinne jumped up and down behind the barricade, cheering for him.

Chapter 31

It hadn't taken much to convince Heather to go with her to New Roads and surprise the guys. If Heather's wistful smile was any indication, she and Chad were getting along just fine.

The two women had worked on posters at Corinne's house Wednesday and Thursday night, and Corinne was proud of hers. They were really paintings on poster board, the first an aerial view of False River that she had based on images from Google Maps, but she had incorporated Wes's racing colors into the landscape.

After living with both Wes and Michael, Corinne knew that triathletes and cyclists took their attire seriously. Michael had worn black, red, and white, matching his Pinarello, and Wes was no exception. Corinne knew that he'd be dressed in a black and turquoise tri-suit to match his bike, and so the shoreline of her poster was predominantly those colors, with accents of white, red, and green to mimic the camps that dotted the water's edge. The lake itself was a riot of brown, sky blue, and white, and superimposed over the water was Wes's name in his racing colors.

She and Heather had found a spot along the barricades and watched across the lake as the athletes took to the water, the sound of the starting gun reaching them after the first wave jumped in. As swimmers crossed the water to the buoys and cut back to the landing where they waited, there was no way to tell which ones were Wes and Chad, even with Heather's binoculars. Everyone wore swim caps and goggles and splashed through the water with impressive speed. Corinne found herself grateful for the many kayaks that patrolled the lake, ready to rescue a struggling swimmer. But she tried to remind herself that Wes was a strong swimmer. She'd seen evidence of it firsthand.

The memory of them in the lap pool together stirred her breath, his naked chest just inches from her body as he showed her how to improve her stroke. It was better than worrying about his safety, so she held onto the memory until she finally spotted him climbing out of the water at the boat launch, running towards the bikes.

"Wes! Wes!" Corinne held the poster over her head and shouted his name. She knew that her voice was lost in the general roar of the crowd. Wes was a good 100 feet from her at one of the rows of bike racks, pulling on his shoes. The muscles in his arms and legs swelled with the effort of swimming more than a mile in open water, and Corinne found herself swallowing at the sight. He was gorgeous!

"Wes! Go, Wes!" she cheered, proudly, a smile splitting her face.

"Yay! Wes!" Heather cheered beside her before she spotted Chad coming out of the water. "Chad! Go, baby, go!"

Corinne watched Wes mount his bike and start to leave the transition area, and she screamed his name with everything she had, jumping up and down and flailing the poster, looking—she was sure—like a complete maniac.

But it worked. Wes's eyes locked with hers, and she saw the surprise and the wonder as he took her in.

"Go, Wes! Go!" she called, beaming in triumph that he'd seen her. Wes winked at her, and before she knew it, he was out of sight.

A moment later, Chad's shoes were on, and as he passed them, both women shouted his name, catching his attention.

"You rock!" Chad yelled, pumping his fist and smiling. "Heather, I love you!"

Heather gasped beside her, her eyes going wide.

"I LOVE YOU, CHAD CASE!" she shouted as he rode away. The double fist pump look-ma-no-hands testified that he'd heard her.

Corinne gaped at her friend who stood stunned, blinking in surprise.

"You didn't tell me it was so serious," Corinne intoned, a smile growing to match the one beginning on Heather's face.

Heather shrugged.

"I...didn't know...I mean," she struggled for words, but her face was aglow. "I thought it was just me."

Corinne shook her head in disbelief.

"So that was the first time either of you said it?" she asked, but she hardly needed to. It was written all over Heather's face. The surprise. The joy. The life-changing realization.

"Yeah, it was," Heather whispered, softly.

Corinne thought of Heather's job offers. She might leave any day now.

"So does that mean..." But she stopped herself.

Let her enjoy the moment.

But Heather's eyes found hers, and they looked completely calm and content.

"I'm not sure what it means, but whatever it is, it's good," she said with certainty.

Could it be that easy? Corinne wondered. Just shout "I love you!" and accept the uncertainty that came with giving your heart to someone else? It was what Michael had done with her—so easily, fearlessly. And while Corinne had given him her heart and soul, she had been so much more cautious about it.

But she loved Wes.

It had taken her long enough to realize it; so long that she had hurt him in the process, and now, if she was going to try to make it right, if she was going to set him straight, she would have to be just as obvious as Chad Case and Heather Lamarche. Just as candid. Just as vulnerable.

Baking cakes and having lunch wasn't quite enough.

"C'mon," Corinne said, heading back to Heather's car. "We should be able to spot them twice on the loop before the second transition."

Corinne had checked the route online days before. The bike leg would take the guys two laps around the oxbow lake, bringing them down Main Street each time. Heather and Corinne walked to Espresso, Etc. on Main, where they could get a street-side table in the shade, drink iced lattes, and have croissants while they waited for Wes and Chad to make their way around.

Legacy

It was already 80 degrees, and the humidity was like shower steam. Corinne could not imagine biking and running for hours in this heat. The swim would be ok, she thought. But would starting out on the ride soaking wet help to keep them cool or only serve to make them uncomfortable? It seemed miserable no matter what.

"Triathletes are crazy," she muttered, taking a sip of her coffee as she and Heather sat down.

Heather gave her a wicked smile.

"I think it is totally sexy!" she whispered, her eyes alight. "Chad is trying to talk me into getting a road bike. He's already got me running with him."

This surprised Corinne. Like herself, she'd never thought of Heather as the sporty type. Was this the euphoria of young love at work or something else?

"And you like it?" she asked, hearing her own skepticism.

Heather shrugged, but the smile didn't falter.

"Yeah, I mean, it's tough at first, but I've surprised myself with what I can do," she said with obvious pride. "We ran *three* miles the other morning! I've never done that in my life. It makes me feel...*strong*."

Corinne nodded. Weight training with Wes had made her feel stronger, too. Maybe they could get back to doing that...if her plan worked.

If anything changed after today.

Thirty minutes later, the sound of sirens announced the lead bike, so Corinne and Heather grabbed their next round of signs and stepped to the edge of the sidewalk. Spectators in little clusters spanned the length of Main Street as the first bike whizzed by.

Her second poster was a stylized image of a cyclist in turquoise and black streaking across the page, trailing colors behind him. On the road beneath him, she had stenciled, "Wes, if you can read this, pedal faster!"

It was something she'd hope he'd laugh at later because she was sure he'd pass it in a blur. Perhaps twenty cyclists had zoomed by them when she spotted Wes coming, and the sight of him so near the front of the pack set her screaming.

"Go, Wes! You're doing great!" she yelled, and this time his eyes found hers before he blew by. "One more loop, Wes! One more!"

And he was out of sight seconds later, but the look he had given her, the smile he had given her made her take a calming breath. She told herself not to read too much into it because the moment had lasted less than two seconds, but she thought he looked at her with hope.

Were they hoping for the same thing?

If she had her way, she'd find out soon enough, and that thought gave her a case of butterflies, so she tried to distract herself by watching the race, searching the cyclists for Chad.

The bike was Wes's strongest event, and he'd put some distance between himself and his friend. Heather and Corinne spotted Chad a good ten minutes later, more mid-pack, flying by in a mess of dozens of riders.

"You're still here?!?" he shouted to them, thrilled and surprised.

"Of course, baby!" Heather yelled as he passed, laughing at the look on his face.

"Stay there! I'll be back in an hour!" he shouted back, making them and the surrounding crowd break out in laughter.

Corinne spent the next 30 minutes debating with herself. Little by little, she was losing her nerve. Corinne wasn't at all sure if she should hold out her third poster or chuck it into the nearest trash can.

"What is wrong with you?" Heather asked, sucking down the last of her second iced latte. "You've been staring at that thing long enough to burn a hole in it."

Corinne looked up at her friend and back down at the poster she'd spread out on their table.

"Is it too much?" she asked, chewing the corner of her lip and trying to look at the sign with fresh eyes.

Swimmers, bikers, and runners—all mimicking the decal sticker that Wes sported on the back windshield of his truck—chased themselves around a dark pink cartoon heart. Beneath the image in the same black and turquoise were the words: "My heart belongs to a tri guy."

"It's too much. I should trash it," Corinne declared before Heather could answer, but she looked up to check her friend's reaction anyway.

She was met with a raised brow and a very stern expression.

"Don't you dare trash it!" Heather scolded, shaking her head with disapproval. "You have no idea. Do you?"

"About what?" Corinne asked.

Heather rolled her eyes.

"About Wes! About how he feels. What he feels." Heather splayed out her palms in disbelief. "The guy has got it bad for you, Corinne!"

It was Corinne's turn to roll her eyes.

"No, he doesn't," she dismissed, feeling a hint of her shame return.

"Uh, yeah, he does," Heather clucked. "And you know it because it's as clear as day in that painting of yours."

Corinne shook her head, afraid even to believe Heather.

"That moment in the painting was *before* I totally blew it. Wes can barely stand to be around me now," she lamented, making a grab for the poster. "And this is just going to make things more awkward."

Heather yanked the poster out of her grasp.

"Corinne, I've spent a lot more time around Wes in the last month than you have, and I'm here to tell you: that guy is so into you, he'd need a bulldozer to dig his way out," she said, glaring at Corinne. "You're showing him that poster, and it'll make his fucking day!"

"I don't know, Heather..." Corinne hedged, losing faith in her plans by the second. "Chad seemed a lot happier to see you than Wes did when he saw me."

"That's because he thinks you just see him as a friend," Heather said, exasperation tight in her voice. "Don't you think it's time you made it clear to him what he means?"

Corinne stared at the poster and tried to picture Wes before the day she'd hurt him. Since then, he'd been so guarded with her. She longed for a time when they could both let down their defenses. When nothing stood between them.

She'd have to give up her fears. All of them.

Heather stood up from their table.

"The lead bikers are coming," she said, looking past Corinne. "Better make up your mind."

Chapter 32

"Shit!"

Wes cursed as he watched half of his second Stinger Waffle crumble out of his left hand and fall out of sight. He didn't even really want the strawberry-flavored disc, but he was approaching his third hour in the race, and he needed to refuel again.

His biggest problem, though, was that he couldn't stay ahead of his thirst. Which was probably why the thought of the flat, sweet waffle made him slightly nauseous. He shoved what remained into his mouth and tried not to lose any ground as he chewed, the morsel seeming to swell and glom onto his tongue.

As best as he could tell, he was in 17th place. Counting was only possible on the one out-and-back stretch just past the center of town. After the police cruiser blew past him ahead of the lead bike, Wes thought he'd only ticked off 16, but missing one in the tangle of cyclists jockying for the top spots would have been easy. Wes knew one thing for sure: no one had passed him in the last hour, and he had gained on two more riders.

But all remnants of the morning cool had burned off, and the humidity had only seemed to magnify the 10 a.m. sun, already painting the blacktop on the shadeless stretches with a heat mirage.

He sucked out the last of his Powerade from the Xlab in front of him. It was lukewarm, but at least it carried some electrolytes. He was sweating ridiculously, probably losing liters of fluid an hour.

Wes knew that he needed to replace some salts, and he needed to stay hydrated or else he'd start cramping soon, but grabbing a bottle up ahead from one of the volunteers would slow him down.

He licked his lips, which were dry and salty, and he cursed again. Wes angled his bike closer to the line of spectators and volunteers with their arms outstretched, offering bottles.

"Gatorade! Gatorade!" one guy hawked. Wes eased his pace and snatched the offered bottle.

"Thanks," he muttered, picking up speed again. Filling his torpedo took only seconds, and he tried to pace himself between sips to rehydrate without making himself sick. The 13.1 run that awaited him was going to suck.

But Corinne awaited him, too.

Every time his mind drifted to that thought, he found a little burst of strength to push harder. It was what had moved him up at least 12 spots since the bike leg started. Seeing her as he left transition had completely baffled and pumped him.

What did it mean that she was here? Was it another act of friendship? Was she still trying to make amends? Or was it something more?

When he thought about the last possibility, Wes felt his stomach dip.

Don't get ahead of yourself, he thought. *Just ride.*

But how could he when he was riding toward her?

The roadside crowds started to grow again as the lead riders ahead of Wes returned to the center of the small town. In a few minutes Wes would pass the cafe where Corinne and Heather had surprised him the second time. The closer he got to the main drag, the nicer the camps that lined the lake were—until houses gave way to businesses, bait shops, and gas stations.

As soon as Wes saw Regions Bank on the left, he started scanning the curb on the right near Satterfield's where he'd seen the girls before.

And there she was.

Wes could feel his heart hammering at the thrill. His face split with a smile when their eyes met, and he forgot the misery of the heat and the fatigue in his body.

And maybe it was the heat. Or maybe it was the fatigue. Maybe one had to push the body to its limits to deepen the power of the mind. But whatever it was, in the instant when Wes found his eyes locked with the hazel wonders that were Corinne's, he knew without a doubt that he would love her for the rest of his life.

Even if it was a one-sided love.

There was no one else for him. Not before. Not after. Just Corinne. And he could accept that. Hell, he didn't *want* to love anyone else.

Wes pulled his gaze away to check his position seconds before he passed her, and he let himself glance back just as he did.

"Read the damn sign!" Heather shouted, pointing frantically at the poster Corinne held.

Wes frowned and tried to focus on it as it flashed by, but then they were behind him, and looking back would mean slowing down—or wiping out.

What had he seen? Something pink? And words?

"My heart...."

Two words. He'd caught the first two words. But those words had to be good, right? What about her heart? Anything that Corinne wanted to show him about that fierce little muscle that he longed to know—to claim—had to be good.

What would it feel like to lay his ear against her chest and hear its beating? To hold her against him and know that he cradled something so fragile and so strong. To surrender to the sound of the life that owned him.

Wes had to shove these thoughts from his mind, or he'd be tempted to DNF right there, cut back against the flow of riders and head straight for Corinne.

Instead, he carried his pace, followed the flag-waving volunteers, and turned onto North Carolina Street to head toward the second transition.

By the time Wes crossed the fourth mile marker on the half-marathon route, he had passed two runners splayed out on the road with leg cramps. He was making decent time for 90 percent humidity and 84 degrees, but seeing the agony etched on those defeated faces scared the crap out of him. He grabbed two cups at the next water station.

Still, if anything, he was sweating even more than he had on the bike, and he was losing ground. Runners—none he'd passed on the bike—caught and passed him. Running was certainly not his strong suit. Any chance he'd had of breaking or even matching his best time all came down to holding it together now to protect the strong ride he'd had.

At Mile 7, Wes followed the turn on the route and spotted Corinne directly in front of him. She and Heather stood beneath a cluster of oak trees at the edge of Douglas Park, talking, not yet seeing him, and this time, he did look at the sign she held, but it was different from the one before.

"Run, Wes!

Just don't run away!"

The words shouted at him above a cartoon. Unmistakable, the houses along St. Joseph stood in miniature as a cartoon Wes ran away from a cartoon Corinne, who chased him with arms outstretched.

The naked admission of the sign shocked him, humbled him.

His breath nearly left his lungs when he looked up and saw her watching him, saw the raw, defenseless look in her eyes. What was it costing her to stand there and hold that sign?

Whatever it was, he'd pay it back a thousand times over.

He closed the distance between them, and Corinne launched herself into his arms, stretching up on tiptoe and offering him her mouth. Wes took it, hungrily, sealing his lips against hers. He felt her come alive against him, grabbing the neck of his soaked tri-suit, pulling him closer, and unleashing little cries from her throat. Wes felt like every race in his life had been a quest for this. This moment.

And it was over much too quickly.

"Save it for later!" Heather shouted at them, gripping him by the arm. "People are passing you!"

Corinne pulled back from him then, and he saw that her lashes were wet, but the heat in her eyes nearly scorched him.

"Go," she said, never breaking her gaze when she tilted her head in the direction of the finish. But his feet wouldn't move, and it wasn't just because his legs were locking up.

Corinne's hand still on his chest gave him a little shove, but she smiled.

"Go!" she said, again, this time with a chastising lift in her brow. "I'll meet you at the finish line."

"You damn well better," Wes said, pulling away, only half-believing what had just happened. He stepped back onto the road, but he didn't want to take his eyes off her. When she shooed him away with a regretful smile, Wes picked up his stride again.

If his legs could have groaned, they would have. Loudly. The 20-second stop had been a cruel joke played on his muscles, and they protested now at his demand to keep running. His calves felt like tree branches, wooden and ready to snap. The flesh an inch above his knees seemed to simmer. His muscles weren't cramping yet, but he was dangerously close. He knew instinctively that pointing his toes too much as he kicked back in his stride would be enough to send his calves straight to hell.

He had dealt with muscle cramps in the early days of this triathlon training, and they were almost unavoidable on a full Ironman, but he'd never had them on a half. But this was his third Hellfire, and he couldn't remember the first two being so miserably hot.

And he certainly couldn't remember wanting to finish so badly.

At the next water station, Wes gulped blue Powerade and took the offered to-go size packet of salt. He tore open the little square and shook the crystals on his tongue, and it was like giving the base of his brain a salt-flavored orgasm.

Wes shut his eyes for a moment and let the rush course through him, making his lungs expand and his stride loosen up just enough so that he believed he could finish the last four miles.

I'll finish, and Corinne will be there, he knew.

And then they would talk. Talking had been long overdue. And after they talked, would they be able to move on from there? Would there be something more than pain and regret and longing between them?

Wes thought of Michael and the sense of rightness he'd woken up with on that Sunday morning now more than a month ago. He'd believed then—with almost an eerie sense of reverence—that things between him and Corinne were meant to be. It had only taken a few hours for that faith to be shot to hell.

Would that happen again?

Wes searched his memory for every conversation he and Michael ever had about Corinne.

In truth, she hadn't come up all that much, which in hindsight had to be a good thing. In those days, Wes had dismissed her as bitchy and aloof. If he hadn't, if he'd seen her for who she was—complex, passionate, brave, and so, so beautiful—wouldn't he have fallen for her even then?

If he had been the man he was now, yes. Of course.

But he hadn't become that man until after Michael's death. Until he started to know Corinne. He hadn't been someone who looked beyond himself until he'd had to look after someone else. He hadn't been someone who could stand up to his asshole father until the man's abuse threatened Corinne. He hadn't known real happiness until Corinne's happiness mattered more than anything.

And that thought tapped a memory.

An evening. Another run. His best friend beside him.

It was late October, and the days were shorter, cooler. Wes had been tapering for Panama City, and he'd invited Michael to do an easy 5k through the Saint Streets after Michael got home from work.

Corinne had not been happy to see him, Wes recalled, complaining that she had made a gumbo that was nearly ready, and it would be an hour before Michael was back and showered and they could eat.

At the time, Wes had silently wondered why it was such a big deal. Couldn't she eat without him if she was hungry? But Wes watched—mildly disgusted—as Michael snuck up behind Corinne as she stood at the stove and wrapped his arms around her middle, nuzzling her neck.

It was an intimate gesture, one that had embarrassed Wes to watch, so he'd stepped into the living room, grabbed one of Buck's toys, and instigated a game of canine tug-of-war. Moments later, Michael had returned, smiling a conspirator's smile, but instead of heading to the door, he'd detoured toward the bathroom. The sound of the tub filling had confused the hell out of Wes. It must have surprised Corinne, too, because she stepped out of the kitchen with a look of amused curiosity.

Wes had almost left when he heard the door shut against muffled laughter, but minutes later, Michael emerged alone, grinning, clearly still reliving the scene he'd just left.

"C'mon. Let's go," he'd said.

But Wes had remained rooted to the floor wearing his best *what-the-fuck?* expression.

Michael had rolled his eyes and laughed, leading them outside. When he'd locked the door behind them, he shrugged his shoulders.

"Sometimes, she doesn't know how to let herself be happy," he'd said, simply. "It's easier just to show her the way."

What little morning cloud cover the day offered had now burned away, and Wes crossed the marker for Mile 10. But all he could think about were Michael's words. He hadn't remembered them before today, but they were all too true.

Sometimes Corinne didn't let herself be happy. Sometimes Wes didn't either. Wouldn't it be easier if they just showed each other the way?

When he reached Mile 12, his agony gave way to a heady sense of euphoria. He hoped it was the salt and electrolytes and not heat stroke messing with his head, but he didn't let himself question it. He had about ten minutes left until he reached the finish, and if he was getting a second wind, he'd ride it into the ground.

Ten minutes later, Wes heard Corinne call his name as he approached the finish. He was sprinting, which may not have been a good idea, but nothing else mattered but getting to her. He crossed the treaded finish line sensors—his finishing time 5:10:45—and someone congratulated him and draped a medal over his head. Then a foil blanket landed around his shoulders.

And then a tiny figure collided with his, her arms circling around his ribs, and the sound of his name filling his ears.

"Wes. Thank God you're okay!" she panted, squeezing him, her cheek pressed against his chest. "Some of the runners have collapsed from the heat. You are okay, aren't you?"

She tipped her chin up, and Wes saw the fear that rimmed her eyes. He squeezed back.

"Never better," he said, smiling. It wasn't entirely true. His body felt butchered, bled dry. "But I need to walk or I'll lock up. And I need some calories."

Corinne untangled herself from him and took his hand, suddenly in charge.

"C'mon. There's bagels and bananas and drinks over here." She pulled him in the right direction and loaded him down with sustenance. Corinne cracked open one of the water bottles for him, and after he'd drained half of it, she peeled off a piece of bagel and pressed it to his lips.

"Eat," she said, never taking her eyes off him. Wes opened his mouth and obeyed, stunned silent. Corinne tore off another piece and fed it to him, frowning up at him with a kind of rapt concentration. A feeling that he'd known just once soaked through his belly, up his spine, into his chest.

The last time he'd felt it, he'd just watched her square off with his asshole father, defending Wes against the man's insults. And here was the same amazement, the same surprised sense of awe, of relief.

With the simple gesture of filling his mouth, Corinne threatened to buckle his knees. It was the sexiest fucking thing. She was taking care of *him*. When was the last time someone had done that? The way she did now? With such single-minded focus?

Never.

He felt a little ridiculous at this realization and how, with the third bite she offered him, chills spilled down his neck. Wes shut his eyes and swallowed it passed the growing lump in his throat.

What the hell is wrong with me? I'm not a little boy.

But this feeling? His love (and was this Corinne loving him back?) made him feel just as vulnerable as any helpless child.

He reached for her hips and pulled her against him, unable to keep still and just feel. If she couldn't love him back, how would he recover?

"Please come home with me," she whispered then, turning his heart over in his chest.

Chapter 33

As clearly as she could tell, Wes was starving.

After she'd plied him with two bagels, one banana, a bottle of water and a bottle of Gatorade, they'd watched Chad finish his race and collapse in Heather's arms, both looking wildly happy and a little insane. It hadn't taken long for them to agree that Corinne would drive Wes back in his truck while Chad rode with Heather.

The foursome stopped at Satterfield's for burgers, sitting on the balcony on the second floor overlooking the lake. Wes watched jet skiers on the water, and Corinne watched him. He'd agreed to come home with her, but did that mean he'd be home to stay? She couldn't wait until they were alone to find out.

He and Chad had changed out of their tri-suits at the park, and now he wore the red and white race t-shirt, a clean pair of shorts, and his finisher's medal. It made her smile. That and the salt crystals along his hairline and down his neck were the only evidence of what he'd put himself through that morning.

And, of course, his frightening appetite.

Wes had ordered two burgers, a plate of fries, and a lemonade, and he moaned his pleasure at every bite. This, naturally, made Corinne smile, too. Watching the race had been more nerve-wracking than she'd expected, especially when triathletes started being packed up in ambulances because of heat exhaustion.

Knowing Wes meant that she had no doubt that he would run himself into the ground before he'd give up on anything, and this had scared the hell out of her as the day wore on, fearing that he'd collapse on the road with heat stroke. But he looked okay now, plowing through his second burger, muttering about how good it was.

He looked up with a mouthful and caught her staring. Corinne watched his cheeks color at her smile, and he reached under the table to find her hand and squeeze it. It felt so good just to be with him. He couldn't imagine how much she'd missed him.

I love you, she wanted to tell him. *And I'm so sorry I hurt you.*

"If I never see this lake again, that'll be alright with me," Chad grumbled, eyeing the water with disgust. "I think I got kicked about 12 times. Once in the nads."

Chad seemed to shudder at the memory.

"You'll be back next year," Wes teased, narrowing his eyes. "Just wait. We both will."

Corinne swallowed a groan. Then she would be here, too.

If Wes wanted her in his life.

And she had enjoyed herself. Watching him had been thrilling—when she wasn't terrified. Corinne reminded herself that she had already accepted the way of the world. There were no guarantees that her heart wouldn't be broken again. There were no guarantees that a terrible accident wouldn't take someone else she loved. But loving Wes—and how could she not?—was worth the risk.

"You slowing down?" he asked her, breaking into her heavy thoughts and pointing to her half-eaten burger.

Corinne nodded.

"Yeah, you want it?"

Wes shook his head.

"Nah, but get a box. Maybe later," he said, giving her a boyish smile.

Corinne laughed, the sensation a lightness bubbling up from her chest. Wes was so good at making her laugh. She hadn't really let herself enjoy it before.

Now she wanted to enjoy everything.

"C'mon, C. Let's get out of here," Wes said, after their server had brought over a to-go box and the check. His tone was light, but Corinne saw a hint of tension around his eyes.

Was he dreading their drive back to Lafayette? An hour and a half together in his truck? Corinne certainly wasn't dreading it, but a ripple of nerves coursed through her anyway.

Would he hear what she had to say? Would it make any difference? Did he really still have feelings for her, as Heather believed?

Corinne hoped, fiercely, that he did, but she had been the one to kiss *him* on the race route, not the other way around.

Both Chad and Wes got up slowly from the table, gritting their teeth and hissing as they started to walk again.

"Dude," Chad groaned, hobbling slowly. "No one would look at us right now and think 'those guys are athletes.'"

Corinne and Heather laughed, and Wes smirked.

"Just wait until we have to go down those stairs," he muttered. "Going down is a hell of a lot harder than climbing up."

Their descent on the stairs would have been almost funny if it hadn't looked so painful. Both men took them sideways, gripping the banister and swearing under their breath.

"Just leave me here, Heather," Chad whimpered halfway down. "Save yourself."

Heather threw her head back, laughing, but she draped Chad's free arm around her neck and helped him down.

"Need a hand," Corinne asked, offering her right to Wes. Without a word, he gripped it with surprising force, the strain of each step vibrating through his body.

"Thank Christ," Wes grunted when they finally reached the bottom. He handed Corinne the keys to his truck and limped around to the passenger side. "Case, either stop at the club and do the cold plunge or take an Epsom salt bath when you get home."

"Fuck the cold plunge," Chad called, as Heather opened her car door for him, and Chad wailed pitifully as he sunk down into the passenger seat.

"Epsom salts!" Wes called back, and Corinne heard him stifle a groan as he climbed up into the cab. He flopped against the seatback, eyes closed, and wiped away the sheen of sweat that had misted his face on the short journey from their table to his truck.

"You okay?" Corinne asked after climbing in next to him and starting the engine.

Wes opened his eyes and found hers. His already tanned skin had bronzed even darker after six hours in the sun. He was impossibly beautiful, but he looked exhausted.

He gave Corinne a tired smile.

"It could be worse," he teased.

Corinne had prepared in her mind everything she wanted to tell him, but as she looked at the man across from her, the man who had saved her, the man she loved, all she wanted to do was take care of him.

"Why don't you try to take a nap?" she offered, reaching over and brushing his damp hair away from his forehead.

Something softened around Wes's eyes, and he grabbed her hand and pressed it to his lips.

"Maybe that's a good idea," he said, watching her carefully. "If it's okay with you."

Corinne nodded, but she hedged her bets.

"As long as you don't bolt as soon as we get to the house," she said.

Still holding her hand, Wes lowered the back of his seat, intertwined his fingers with hers, and rested their joined hands across his stomach.

"I'm not going anywhere."

The muscles in Corinne's abdomen danced, and she pulled onto the highway one-handed.

Wes still slept as Corinne merged onto I-49 in Opelousas. They would be home in half an hour. And they didn't need to hurry. She didn't need to hurry. Because Wes wouldn't take off as soon as they got there.

Of course, she wasn't entirely sure what would happen. Only what she wanted to happen.

Corinne glanced over at him asleep next to her. He'd released her hand just a few minutes after dozing off, but she'd kept it tucked into the crook of his arm, her thumb running slowly over the terrain of muscle in his forearm.

She longed to touch every inch of him.

It was both strange and comforting now to think of him as Michael's best friend. It was as though they had been reborn into the same tribe. Neither of them was the same person they'd been when they'd met each other two years before, yet somehow, the people they were now had been shaped for each other, by each other.

If he still wanted her, if he could forgive her...

Wes stirred then beside her and reached for the hand that rested on his arm.

"You doing okay?" he asked, his eyes opening just a peek.

"Yeah, I'm good," she said, giving him a smile before putting her eyes back on the road. "And you? Are you feeling okay?"

Wes blew out a breath then and raised the back of his seat until he was sitting up next to her again.

"I'll live," he teased. Then he looked at her, and as Corinne's eyes flicked back and forth from the road in front of her and Wes's gaze, his smile tempered to something thoughtful.

"Thank you," Wes said.

Corinne stared ahead, suddenly shy.

"For what?"

Wes didn't hesitate.

"For driving. For coming out there and cheering me on. For all of those posters," Wes said, his voice dropping. "No one's ever done anything like that for me."

Corinne felt his hand tighten around hers, communicating something that words could not. Something about fear and hope and promise.

Were they fearing and hoping and promising the same things?

Interstate 49 melted into Highway 90, and Corinne turned right onto Willow. They'd be home in mere minutes, so she held herself back from asking. She could wait before diving in.

Five minutes later, they pulled up at the house and heard Buck barking at them from the back yard where Corinne had left him that morning.

"Someone's going to be glad to see you," she said, hopping out of the truck as Wes edged himself out with a disturbing slowness, a grimace claiming his face.

Legacy

"I just hope he doesn't knock me down," Wes gritted out through his teeth.

"I promise, I won't let him," Corinne vowed, reaching into the back seat for Wes's gear bag before he could do it.

"Hey, I could have gotten that," he said, hobbling behind her toward the front porch.

Corinne rolled her eyes at him.

"Sure you could, champ," she teased.

Buck's excited barks grew more demanding as she unlocked the door, so Corinne dropped the gear bag in the living room and sprinted to the back.

The black lab whined and scratched as she opened the screen door to her sunroom, and he would have torn past her if she hadn't commanded him to sit. Buck obeyed, begrudgingly, his coat twitching over his back with a barely contained energy.

"Easy," she soothed. "Heel."

Together, they walked through the house to find Wes closing and locking the front door. As soon as Buck saw Wes, he broke away from Corinne, but he seemed to sense that he couldn't be rough with his friend today. That didn't stop the lab from whimpering, wagging fiercely, and licking Wes's legs.

"Hey, boy," Wes cooed, petting the dog's gleaming coat. "I'm glad to see you, too."

Corinne smiled at the pair. Wes staggered to his recliner and collapsed in it. Buck took the opportunity to perch his front paws on Wes's thighs, eliciting a whimper, before the dog started licking his face.

"Ok, now you really need a bath," Corinne said, laughing. "I've got some Epsom salts in the bathroom closet. How about I draw one for you?"

Wes scrubbed Buck's head affectionately, pulling the dog's muzzle away from his face.

"In a minute. I need to drink about a gallon of water and use my foam roller first."

"I'll get them," Corinne offered, only just stopping herself from telling him how good it was to have him in the house. She didn't want to scare him away or make him think she had assumed he was back for good.

In his room she found the textured foam roller that looked like something out of Minecraft, and she went to the kitchen and filled a glass of ice water before bringing both to him. Wes eyed the roller with dread, but he accepted the glass gratefully.

"Thank you," he whispered, looking up at her with heat in his brown eyes. He drained the glass in one long pull, and Corinne watched the muscles of his throat as he drank. Watching him made her feel a little drugged, slack-limbed and slow.

She took a deep breath to pull herself together.

"If you're going to be a minute, I'll go take a quick shower," she said, already stepping away. "You're not the only one who's been outside all day."

Wes smiled and eyed her appreciatively.

"Yeah, your cheeks and your nose are a little pink," he said around his smile. "It's a good look on you."

Corinne felt her cheeks blush even more, and the muscles above her navel warmed.

"I'll just be a minute."

"Take your time," Wes said, pushing himself to his feet with an agonizing hiss. He grabbed the foam roller. "This isn't going to be pretty."

In the bathroom, Corinne stripped off her clothes while the shower warmed. She desperately wanted to be clean in case…In case. But she pushed that thought from her mind because there was the chance, too, that Wes might not stay after all. And he might stay only to once again be her roommate. Nothing was certain. Her hands shook as she raced through her shower routine, scrubbing her hair with extra force and shaving with an almost masochistic haste.

Once she was done and wrapped up in a towel turban and her robe, Corinne found the salts and filled the tub for Wes, her heart beating with so much insistent speed that there was no way she could forget her nerves.

The closer she drew to laying herself bare, the more terrified she became.

Corinne opened the bathroom door and found Wes standing on the other side.

"I don't think anyone's drawn a bath for me in 20 years," he said. Corinne thought that he was trying to appear amused, but she saw something else beneath the look. A kind of confused innocence. She held herself back, but that look made her want to touch his face. It was unguarded, so open and fragile. So beautiful. She wanted to promise to protect that part of him for the rest of her life.

"I think it's time someone did," she told him, wrapping the ties of her robe around her hands to keep from reaching for him. Her words meant more than the sum of their parts, but she needed to wait a little longer before she could say as much. Corinne could see the way Wes's sore muscles seemed to cinch him in with an ache that was visible. He needed to sink down into the warm water and relax.

And she needed to try to keep her mind off the image of him doing just that.

Chapter 34

Wes stretched out his legs in Corinne's cast iron tub. He'd soaked for a good 15 minutes, and the tightness that had clamped along his back and down his legs was finally easing. He'd scrubbed the salt and sweat from his body and out of his hair, and as the bath water cooled, Wes was keenly aware of the quiet of the house.

What was Corinne doing?

Had she dressed? Or was she still wrapped in that white robe that tortured him with the glimpse of skin below her throat, the bareness of her legs, the possibility of nothing on underneath.

God almighty.

Wes stood, and water ran down his thighs. He ignored the sensation and the ache of his erection and wrapped himself in a towel. He felt more put together than he had at the finish—when his emotions threatened to get the better of him—but only just.

As he stepped into some drawstring shorts and shrugged on a T-shirt, Wes tried to tell himself that he was ready for whatever happened next. The way he saw it, there were three possible outcomes. 1) Corinne wanted him to move back and live as roommates as they had before. 2) Corinne wanted him to kiss and caress and curl up against at night, but she wasn't ready for anything more. 3) Corinne wanted him the way he wanted her.

He knew that the third option was the least likely because how could she? How could she want him the way he wanted her? He loved her. He loved Corinne with his body. With his breath. With his fear. With his shame. He loved her with his soul. With his suffering. With his joy.

He couldn't expect that from her. He wouldn't. Which meant that whatever she wanted, he'd have to accept—with the hope that one day there might be more. If she wanted him to move back—as she'd clearly said again and again—he'd move back and watch over her and make her laugh and love her with as much control as he could.

And Wes would know—with certainty now—that it was better than living without her. The weeks at Chad's had taught him that. Living with her was better than anything he'd ever known.

And if she wanted him because she needed a warm body at night—and this would hurt the most, he knew—he would give her what she needed. Holding her and kissing her would mean something else for him than it would for her, but wouldn't this be better, too, than not holding? Not kissing?

Still, the thought of it made his eyes burn. He knew it would be the worst kind of rejection. And if there were any justice or karma in the universe, it was the very kind he deserved. How many times had he accepted a woman's body but rejected her heart? Maybe this was the penance he must pay before he was worthy of her.

Wes combed his fingers through his wet hair and tried to shake off such heavy thoughts. He faced the bathroom door, put his hand on the knob, and steadied his breath.

He found Corinne curled up in her usual corner of the couch. She still wore her robe, her damp hair falling over her shoulders, and she clutched one of the couch's throw pillows in her lap. To his surprise, she looked nervous, even afraid. As if she didn't know that he was hers to command, that she would get whatever she wanted. Nothing more. Nothing less.

It was the look of fear—and his wish to erase it—that gave Wes the courage to cross the room and sit opposite her on the couch. Quite purposefully, he arranged himself as a mirror image of her, grabbing the other throw pillow and hugging it to himself as she did.

And it worked. Corinne smiled. It was shy and unsure, but she didn't look quite so unnerved.

He waited for her to speak because there was no way he could take the lead on this. Wes had to know what she wanted, what he would have to accept. He couldn't be the first to show his cards because he was all in.

Instead, he met her gaze and refused to look away. Corinne's eyes held all of the colors of a summer holiday. Sparklers. Green grass. Sunsets. But the look she gave him was anything but carefree. She was still so hesitant.

Wes let go the breath he was holding and reached across their laps for her hand. If Corinne needed to be reassured, he would reassure her.

As if she understood him, Corinne's hand squeezed back in his own, but her eyes went liquid and her breath stammered, and Wes realized that she was fighting tears.

"I'm so sorry," she said, finally, startling him with the emotion in her voice. He tossed the pillow he still held to the floor and edged closer to her.

"You don't have anything to be sorry about, Corinne," he promised, but she was shaking her head before the words were out.

"I do, Wes. I do," she cleared her throat and seemed to will herself to find composure. "I made a terrible mistake in denying you—in denying what I felt for you, and I've been trying to make up for it ever since."

Everything in the room went still except Wes's heart. That organ threatened to deafen him and drown out the rest of what Corinne was saying.

"—such a fool. I was *such* a fool," she said, gripping his hand with so much force. "I kept ignoring what I felt because if I let myself love again, then I could be hurt again, and the thought of losing you, too—"

"Losing me?!?" Wes blurted in confusion. Had she just said the word *love* in reference to him? Or was this about Michael?

"Yes, you! In a way, I feel like I'm cursed because I've lost the people in my life whom I've loved the most—my mom and Michael—and if I let myself love you, then I might lose you, too," Corinne poured out in a rush, her eyes wide with remembered terror. "And I thought that I couldn't handle taking that chance because if I lost you, I wouldn't survive it—"

"Corinne—" he started, the shock of understanding so great he couldn't keep still.

"No, wait!" she urged him, grabbing both of his hands now in both of hers, looking desperate to finish. "But it wasn't until after I hurt you that I realized that I'd lost you anyway, and nothing made sense anymore."

It was Wes's turn to shake his head.

"Corinne, you haven't lost me," he swore. "I'm completely yours."

Her words had shredded whatever self-restraint he'd managed to maintain around her. In an instant the pillow she'd held was on the floor, and he pulled her onto his lap. His lips claimed hers without warning or permission, just like they had the first time, kissing her on his terms. But this time was better. So much better. Because it was Corinne who opened her mouth and sought his tongue with hers, and it was Corinne whose hands snaked into his hair and grabbed on for dear life.

"I'm yours," he murmured again, against her lips, the whole universe in orbit around their joined mouths. Corinne moaned as his arms tightened around her, cradling her against him.

"Good," she panted, reaching for breath and crushing her breasts against him. "Because I love you, Wes...so much."

The words were like a baptism, purifying and welcoming him at once, allowing him to be part of a race of two. He had never belonged to anyone or anything like this, and Corinne's love was a kind of sacred claiming.

He belonged.

Wes gently pulled her away so he could look into her eyes and claim her right back.

"Corinne, I love you. I've never loved anyone else like this, and I never will. You're the only one."

Corinne reached up and touched his cheek. A mischievous light glinted in her hazel eyes.

"So I'm forgiven?" she asked.

Wes threw his head back with laughter that shook the windows and woke Buck who snoozed by the front door. Corinne giggled, a delightful sound.

"Woman, you were always forgiven. Will you believe me now?" he asked, pressing a quick kiss to her lips.

She looked up at him without answering, wearing an expression that was both daring and timid.

Wes frowned, confused, but when she stood up from his lap and held out her hand to him, he didn't hesitate. The soreness in his feet and legs were all but forgotten as Corinne led him out of the living room.

She stopped in the hall between their two bedrooms and stared up at him, looking beautiful and determined.

"Wes, I want you to move back in, but not as my roommate," Corinne said, clearly, with just the slightest tremor in her voice.

Could she possibly think he would refuse? Even now? The absurdity made him smile.

"I want you...i-in my bed," she said. This time her voice shook even more. He saw that it had taken everything for her to be so brave. To own her fear. To declare her love. To speak her desire. She'd been so bold, and it was fucking sexy, but he wanted to show her that she didn't have to work so hard. Not with him.

Wes grabbed her hands, lifted them above her head, and backed her against the wall outside his bedroom. He heard her suck in a breath when he pressed himself into the softness of her belly.

"I can't do that..." he whispered, his lips grazing over hers as she panted. "Because I want you in *my* bed."

A sigh escaped her throat before her claimed her again with his kiss. Her skin was on fire, and he had to taste every inch of it. Her mouth, her jaw line, the slope of her neck.

"Yes...yours...of course," she whispered between the return of each kiss. His bed. It was where he'd first held her, first slept beside her, but it would be so different now.

Everything was different now.

Wes drew her with him into his room, never letting her leave his embrace. He walked her blindly until the back of her legs reached his bed, and he laid her gently on the mattress, following her down.

"Corinne..." he whispered, overcome by the sight of her beneath him, the press of his body against hers. One of her legs tangled between his, maddening him, and he took his weight on his knees and elbows so he wouldn't crush her.

He wanted too many things at once. He wanted to lose himself in her, and he wanted to take his time. He needed to reassure himself that all of this was real and it wouldn't evaporate with the sunset.

And she had to understand what she meant to him.

"This is really happening, right?" he asked, tracing his thumbs over her cheeks and staring into her eyes as though he could fall into them.

"God, I hope so," Corinne answered, a smile lighting her whole face. "I know I want it to."

He watched as she tamed her smile and studied his eyes.

"And you?" she asked, softly, reaching up and touching his face with a tenderness Wes didn't think he'd ever felt in his life.

He didn't blink, didn't let his gaze falter when he answered.

"I want you now and always," he said, conviction gathering in his chest around his heart, calming him.

Alpha and Omega.

He thought the words, a memory coming with them, and he smiled. He would save those words for later, and his smile grew because there would be a later.

Wes pressed his lips to the base of Corinne's throat and kissed along the neckline of her robe, the damp silk of her hair tickling his nose. She tasted of honeysuckles and warmth. His breath caught when he felt her hands slip under his t-shirt to stroke his abs.

"I've ached to touch you," she whispered into his ear, her fingers tracing against his skin. He went from hard to leaden, her words affecting him as much as her touch, and he stifled a moan.

"If I don't touch you now," he breathed, running his hands along the tie of her robe. "I'll have an aneurysm."

Corinne buried her laugh into his shoulder.

"Well, we don't want that," she said, sliding a hand from under his shirt. She gave him one end of the tie, and locked eyes with him as he pulled.

The knot came undone in his grasp, and Wes settled his hand on the fabric of her robe, the only thing keeping him from the sight of her body. He didn't take his eyes from hers as he pushed the garment aside, fingers brushing over skin, yet unseen.

"I love you, Corinne."

"I love you, W—"

But his name was lost in a gasp. Because he'd found the most perfect breast in his hand and took the nipple in his mouth like it was made for him. She went hard against his tongue, and he could feel the joy of sucking her all the way to his cock. Soft. Hard. Smooth. Puckered. And before he could catalogue all of the other wonders it offered, his left hand found its twin, and he had to worship that one just as well.

Corinne wasn't making it easy for him, either, because she bucked under each squeeze and arched her back with each suckle, panting his name now and trying to yank his shirt over his head.

Whatever rational part of his brain that still worked urged him to help her, so he released the nipple from his mouth long enough to pluck the shirt over his head before claiming her again.

She peeled herself out of her robe so that bare arms wrapped around his neck when her fingers wove into his hair.

And his hands found a new life. Touching Corinne was all that mattered from now on.

He ran his hands along her waist, feeling the taut obliques under impossibly soft skin.

"You feel incredible," he murmured, his lips moving from her breasts to kiss her mouth again.

"You feel like a god," she said, kissing in return. Her hands skated down his back and slipped beneath the band of his shorts. When she grabbed his ass, he thought he'd lose his mind.

"Take these off," Corinne begged, staring up at him with the sexiest look of desire in her eyes. "I want to see all of you."

"I'm yours," he said, jerking down the unwanted shorts and tossing them to the floor. Wes watched Corinne take in his nakedness and his undeniable attraction to her. He was proud of his body, and he worked hard to be in competitive form, but in the long moment that Corinne ran her eyes over his flesh, he felt that none of it mattered if she didn't like what she saw.

She brought her fingertips to his stomach, and his cock jumped.

"Promise me something," she said, a smile lighting her eyes.

"Anything," he breathed, meaning it. Her fingertips stroked an inch lower and ran back up. He closed his eyes.

"I get to paint you one day like this."

It was his turn to laugh, loud and grateful. But when her hand closed around the length of him, his laughter morphed into the pull of a deep, shaking breath.

"Oh, God, C…"

The sensation—the amazing, freaking awesome sensation—was too dangerous, so with one hand, he took her wrist and gently drew it from him and up to his lips. With the other, he found her.

And such a discovery.

Corinne threw back her head and shut her eyes when he touched her, and his fingers were immediately slick with her wetness. He knew to be gentle, but not too gentle. To be slow, but deliberate. To use his thumb on her clit when he let two fingers find their way inside, Corinne's breath quickening at their arrival.

He watched her in awe.

"You're so beautiful, C," he whispered, leaning down to capture her mouth again.

She moved against his hand and panted against his mouth.

"Wes…"

The word was almost a plea. Almost.

"Not yet, love," he told her.

And he watched the frown mark her flushed face as he slid down her body and spread open her legs.

"Oh my God…Oh my God," she cried when his mouth met her pussy.

Wes moaned at the thrill of her scent. She tasted like desire. And love. And sacred vows.

He gave her his fingers as his tongue coaxed her clit. And when he sucked the sweet knot of nerves once, Corinne started coming.

"Oh God, Wes!"

Corinne's heels dug into his back, her hips left the mattress, and her muscles clenched around his fingers, making him damn proud and even harder if it were possible.

As she came down and caught her breath, she reached for him.

"Come here. I want you inside me."

In an instant he was above her, kissing her again, and she reached down between them to take hold of him.

"Condom...condom," he stammered, dragging himself to the edge of the bed and reaching for his nightstand.

He'd always been careful with other women, and he hoped he was clean, but Wes wasn't taking any chances with Corinne until he knew for sure.

Love changes everything.

Wrapped up tight and looking down at Corinne, the thought kept a beat in his head. Wes felt like a virgin. He'd had sex countless times. This was the first time he would make love.

He could feel the difference, and the difference humbled him.

Chapter 35

"Are you sure, Corinne? We can wait if you're not ready for this," Wes said above her, peering into her with such tenderness it made her eyes water.

Corinne brought her hands to his face and brushed her thumbs over his cheeks. He was so, so beautiful. Now that she could look all she wanted, she couldn't get enough.

"I love you, Wes," she reminded him. "I'm so ready for this."

Her words must have eased his doubt because she felt him against her, right against her, and their eyes locked.

"I just want to look at you," Wes whispered, softly, reverently.

She held his gaze until he pushed inside of her, and the feeling broke her down. Dismantled her. One minute she was Corinne, a woman in bed with the man who'd claimed her heart while she wasn't looking, and the next, she was—

Nothing.

And everything.

All at once.

Fusing with Wes, his flesh entering hers, dissolved her boundaries. Self vanished. Because the look of startled ecstasy on his face the instant they came together mirrored exactly what she felt. And the love in his eyes was her love. She didn't know where she ended and he began, and what did it matter anyway?

Until he moved deeper.

"*Holymotherofgod!*" she gasped, clinging to his shoulders and wrapping her legs around the back of his thighs.

"Oh, C," Wes moaned, his eyes going half-closed. He gripped her by the hips and drove them harder, bringing her effortlessly up to meet him again and again.

Corinne felt as though they had been moving slowly toward each other for months, and, finally, the distance between them closed. And being with him was right where she needed to be. Right where she wanted to be.

"At last," she whispered before the second orgasm took her under. And as her universe folded in on itself and narrowed down to the point of their joined bodies and hearts, she watched Wes succumb to his own tortured bliss. His body tightened above her, within her, sending wave after wave of rapture through her core.

Witnessing him arrive was one of the most beautiful sights she'd ever seen. She could think of nothing else as they caught their breath and came back to themselves.

"You're gorgeous," she told him, kissing his face as he rested above her. "Did you know that?"

Wes gave a little shake of his head as he brushed his fingers up and down her arm and dotted her face with kisses.

"All that matters now is that you think so."

This made her laugh.

"Well, I *do* think so." She smiled up at him and brought her fingers to the mussed waves of his hair.

Wes looked down at her with the softest smile as though he couldn't believe what they had just shared. That they were here. Together. Now.

"Don't move. Just stay right here," he said, slipping out of her but planting kisses along her shoulder and down her sternum as though he regretted their separation. When he rose from the bed and walked out of the room, Corinne was granted the sight of his perfect ass, and even though he'd just satisfied her—twice—she doubted she would ever get enough of him.

She heard water running in the bathroom, and then she heard him pad into the kitchen. Would this be what life was like now? A naked Wes stalking through the house in the middle of the afternoon? Corinne decided she could get used to that.

He returned in all his glory, carrying a glass of water, which he handed to her.

"Drink up," he said, climbing in next to her again. "We both need to rehydrate."

Corinne laughed, but she tipped back the glass and drank.

"Wes, you are the biggest surprise of my life," she told him honestly.

He took the glass from her, drained it, and set it on the nightstand before snaking a leg between hers and drawing her against him. Skin on skin, surrounded by his heat, Corinne could not imagine that anything felt more soothing.

"You are the best surprise of mine," he said before placing those perfect lips on hers.

He kissed her until she felt dazed. She half-wondered if he'd be shocked if she attacked him for another round, but when she pulled back to take in his eyes, she saw a hint of shadow in them.

"What is it?" she asked, instantly on alert. She placed her palm against his chest and felt his strong and steady heartbeat.

"I just want you to know…" he started, seeming to grasp for his way. "To know…that I can live with Michael's ghost…that I'd never ask you to stop loving him or to love me more. I'm happy to be second in your heart—just as long as I'm in there."

Corinne's mouth fell open. To be second in her heart? As if she could only love him with just a small piece of herself? Hell, no.

"Wes, you could never be second," she said, shaking her head, and she felt her eyes well. "Love's not like that…at least, not for me."

Wes's frown deepened as he read her distress, and he pulled her tighter against him.

"I'll always love Michael and be grateful for our time together," she plunged on, wanting him to understand. "But Wes, I love you with my whole heart, and I plan to love you for the rest of my life."

She watched Wes's eyes soften before she nailed him with her kiss, locking her hands behind his neck, and she felt his smile against her lips. When they had thoroughly tasted and reassured each other, she drew back again.

"Besides," she said, panting slightly. "Somehow, I think he'd approve."

Wes's eyes widened slightly.

"Why do you say that?" he asked, settling his arms around her waist and cinching her tighter against him.

Corinne gently shook her head, almost dismissing her words as she said them.

"Just a dream I had once," she said, rolling her eyes. "It's silly."

She felt the tiny hairs at the nape of his neck stand at attention and tickle her wrists.

"What dream?" he pressed, looking suddenly intent on hearing about it.

Corinne shrugged, but she kept her eyes on his.

"It was just before the gallery opening—when you were avoiding me," she added with a remorseful dip of her chin. Wes's body responded on its own, his thighs tightening against hers, seeming to remind her that they were past that. She ran her hand down his back, a kind of acceptance that, *yes*, they *were* past that.

"Anyway,...I dreamed that I was showing him the gallery, and he told me that your portrait wasn't finished," she said, watching his reaction. Was it weird for her to tell him all of this?

But Wes just cracked a smile.

"Go on," he said.

"Well, when I argued that it *was* finished, he told me I was stubborn and..."

She paused, her eyes cataloguing his, hesitant to say the rest.

"Tell me," he whispered, dipping down to nip her mouth. "You can say anything to me. About Michael. About anything."

He met her lips again, and Corinne accepted his kiss, its slowness, its openness. It felt like the end of loneliness.

When they broke apart, she drew a long breath before finishing.

"He said that I was stubborn, and that's why he had to give me to you."

Corinne suddenly felt as vulnerable as if she had just been handed to him, as if he might reject her now at this revelation.

But the look on his face said something else entirely.

"Corinne, he did give you to me," Wes said, the conviction in his voice stilling her nerves, even as his words boggled her. "And he gave me to you."

"What do you mean?"

She saw that her question drew up a memory, and the memory drew up pain. The now familiar inking darkened his eyes, and she touched his face on impulse. If it were up to her, he'd never bear his sadness alone again.

"It was in the hospital...the last time we were alone..." Wes said, his voice dropping to almost a whisper. "He asked me to take care of you, Corinne...He knew he wouldn't be able to do it himself, to look after you...and he asked me to do it instead."

The tears in her eyes spilled over. What had she ever done to deserve them both?

Oh, Michael, thank you.

"I didn't know then that I'd fall in love with you," Wes added, quickly, squeezing her in his arms again. "But I've wondered for a while now if he did...Somehow, I think he knew we needed each other."

Laughter bubbled up through the knot in her throat. She'd thought the same thing more than once.

"Yes, that sounds about right," she said, nodding, but she felt she had to confess the truth. "I'm glad to hear that you need me...that it's not just one-sided."

Now Wes laughed. His eyes went wide, but they were lit with joy.

"God, woman, I so need you." Wes brought a finger to her lips and traced her mouth gently, lovingly. "I'm a better person because of you...a better man."

His words touched her, and she hoped that they were true, that he was better off because she was in his life.

"I'm alive because of you," she said, meaning it.

Wes's face darkened in an instant, and he gave a sharp shake of his head.

"Don't say that, C," Wes said with a shudder. Corinne knew he was picturing her OD-ing on ZzzQuil or dead in a dumpster behind City Bar.

She brought a hand to his face to soothe him.

"What I mean is that you brought me back to life," she explained. "Yes, you kept me from going over the edge, but you made me want to live a real life again."

She leaned in to kiss him, her mouth asking his to open. Her tongue seeking his. When she drew back a moment later, she saw that she had managed to chase the shadows from his eyes.

Corinne hoped that she'd always be able to do that.

"You brought me back to life, Wes," she said, again. "And it's a damn good life."

Epilogue

15 Months Later

The sun was just beginning to set, casting an orange glow on all of the white-washed Acadian style houses at Vermilionville. Wes could see as much from his position in front of the altar in the 18th century replica chapel, but he wasn't paying attention to the sunset.

Wes Clarkson watched the church doors, waiting for his Alpha and Omega.

"Relax, man," Chad whispered at his side. "It's only five to 7:00. She's not walking in early. Your guests are still filing in."

Wes let go the breath he was holding. Chad was right. Latecomers were hurrying in, claiming the few empty seats near the back. There wasn't any reason to be nervous.

Not really…

The hour leading up to the rehearsal dinner the night before had been a nightmare. He'd fucked up and squirted toothpaste on Corinne's dress just minutes before they were to head out the door, and he thought that his hair had been singed off the way she'd cursed him out. She had stormed off to their room to find something else to wear, but not two minutes later, Corinne stood in her strapless bra and panties, crying and begging his forgiveness.

And she wouldn't *stop* crying.

Even after he'd held her and promised—truthfully—that he wasn't mad at her. That he still wanted to marry her. That he'd *always* want to.

They'd been ten minutes late to their own rehearsal, but by then, Corinne was glowing, smiling and hugging Chad and Heather who had just flown in from San Diego that afternoon. Later, at the dinner at

Jolie's, she had laughed at speeches and teared up at toasts, but she left her plate of seared scallops and—her favorite—sweet cream corn grits almost untouched.

Wes checked his watch: 6:57.

"Jesus Christ," he muttered.

Chad chuckled beside him.

"I told you early on, dude, you should have gone to Vegas like we did," Chad gloated.

Wes shot his best man a scowl, so tempted to remind him what a pussy he'd been when Heather accepted the San Diego job and left Case's ass in Louisiana. It took Chad two weeks of agony before he figured out that his only choice was to quit his job and chase after her.

A month later, Heather and Chad were married. Wes and Corinne had gotten a drive-thru selfie as an announcement last September.

He snuck a peek at his watch and saw that only one minute had passed since his last look.

Wes sighed. He would have felt better if he'd at least seen Corinne since last night—if she'd woken up with him this morning—but she'd slept at Morgan's instead.

"It's bad luck to see the bride before the wedding, and I've had enough bad luck to last a lifetime," she'd insisted.

Wes could accept that, so after sleeping alone for the first time in months—if sharing a bed with Buck counted as sleeping alone—Wes had called Corinne to wake her that morning.

And she'd sounded...*off*. Like she'd been crying again?

She'd told him she was just tired, but he'd been on edge all day, antsy to see her. Ready to make her his wife.

And what he didn't want to admit to himself—and what he couldn't stop wondering—was if Corinne was having second thoughts.

Wes blew out a deep breath and absently rubbed the back of his neck, which was misted with sweat.

Relax, he told himself, *she wants this.*

He let himself picture her the last Sunday in April—a year, exactly, after he'd moved in—on a walk through the Saint Streets with him and Buck when he'd taken a knee and asked her to marry him.

Corinne had squealed and hugged him. And cried. She'd said yes a dozen times before he could put the ring on her finger.

Even now, nervous as shit and unable to keep still at the altar, the memory of her happiness made him smile.

And just as he did, the music started. *Jesu, Joy of Man's Desiring.* Wes's eyes flew to the door again in search of her, but he saw Mrs. Betsie and Mr. Dan.

Mrs. Betsie's face was wet with tears, but, God love her, she was smiling at him like it was the happiest day of her life. Wes forgot about his nerves because how could he feel nervous when Betsie and Dan—who had always treated him like a son—were here now for him. Mrs. Betsie took her seat as mother of the groom, and Mr. Dan—decked out in a tux and a groomsman's boutonniere, joined him at the altar, clapping him into a fierce hug before going to stand behind Chad.

Wes's decision not to invite his parents had been a point of argument with Corinne for weeks, but he refused to budge. Why give them the opportunity to ruin his wedding the way they ruined everything else? Corinne worried that he would one day regret excluding them, but Wes knew that until they made some radical changes in their lives—and sought to rebuild a relationship with him—being in their presence would only sicken him.

Taking in Mr. Dan by his side and Mrs. Betsie smiling up at him, Wes had no regrets at all. If this was as close as he'd ever get to loving parents, he'd never complain. Having them meant that he knew what a real family looked like, thank God, and it was an example Wes planned to imitate.

Pachelbel's *Canon in D* filled the small chapel, and Wes looked up to see little Clementine standing, wide-eyed in the doorway. In her violet dress and flowered garland, she looked like a cross between a cherub and a fairy, and even though she clutched a little basket of flowers, the toddler didn't look like she was ready to make the long walk down the aisle. Wes couldn't help but smile.

Morgan, in her violet bridesmaid's dress, knelt down beside Clementine and pointed right at Wes. He saw Morgan mouth the words "Uncle Wes," and not a second later, Clementine was tearing down the aisle, petals flying behind her, before she launched herself into his arms.

Clementine seemed surprised by the laughter that erupted in the chapel, and she was only too glad when Wes passed her to Greg, who settled them on the front row on Corinne's side.

Morgan made her way up the aisle, followed by Heather, who smiled at Wes and winked at Chad. They lined up opposite of him, and as the last strains of *Canon* closed in, Wes's heart started pounding in his throat.

The door to the chapel stood empty, and dusk had fallen, leaving everything beyond the chapel's porch in shadow.

Please, God, let her be there.

And then she was.

At the sight of her, Wes caught his breath. She was stunning. Her hair was swept up into a loose halo and a tendril or two artfully framed her serene face. Her eyes locked with his across the chapel, and she didn't smile until she took in Wes's hungry expression. He was leering, but how could he help it?

Her sleeveless pearl gown was sheer just above the bodice. A lace pattern of fern leaves swept down the front of her dress, but above her breasts the airy fabric revealed so much of her lovely form. Her clavicle. Her shoulders. The dress drew in around her waist, showing her slender shape before spilling to the floor in a full skirt.

Wes longed to settle his hands on her hips and draw her toward him, but he couldn't take his eyes off that teasing lace.

He was suddenly very glad that Clement's progress down the aisle was slow and deliberate; it gave him time to drink her in. Corinne walked on her father's right side and held his bad arm as he steadied himself with his quad cane.

By the time Clement placed Corinne's hand in his, Wes was swallowing hard against the lump in his throat, working his jaw.

Thank you, Michael, Wes prayed for the seventy billionth time. *Thank you for trusting me with her.*

As they turned together to face the priest, Wes caught sight of the back of Corinne's dress. Fern lace over skin all the way down her back. Not a bra strap in sight.

"Oh, my," he whispered, dropping one emotion for another.

They stepped together up to Father Duane, an Episcopal friend of the Roushes, and Wes let go a slow sigh. She was here, her hand in his, and they were going to do this.

As Father Duane welcomed all of their guests, Wes let his eyes drift down over Corinne. She looked happy, but the glow she'd worn the night before was a shade or two too light now. He peered closer. Her upper lip was dotted with sweat.

She glanced up at him, and Wes watched a tremor pass over her as if she'd felt a moment of fear.

Ice shot through his heart, and he squeezed her hand.

"What's wrong, C?" he whispered almost inaudibly as Father Duane talked about making families where you find them. "You okay?"

Corinne frowned at the look on his face, one that he was sure spoke of agony and distress, and she bit her bottom lip.

"Mmmhmm," she squeaked, facing forward and nodding almost imperceptibly.

Not good enough, he thought, his stomach plummeting around his ankles. Since the day she'd told him that she loved him, Corinne never gave him a moment's doubt. How could that change in the last 24 hours? Was the wedding too much for her?

He felt his nostrils flare as he tried to pull in enough oxygen to calm himself. If she called it off right now, he'd bawl in front of their 120 guests. No question.

Stop it, he scolded himself. *This is Corinne, the same Corinne who loves you.*

He swallowed and squeezed her hand.

"C, you're killing me here," he whispered, a plea creeping into his hushed voice. "Please tell me what's wrong."

He was dimly aware of Father Duane tripping over his homily in light of such an inattentive bride and groom. Wes couldn't care less. He just needed Corinne to answer him.

Corinne looked up at him, her eyebrows drawn together in confusion, but he saw hesitation in her eyes.

Oh, God, no.

"I took a test today, Wes," she whispered, the look in her eyes so full of worry.

"What?"

What the hell did that have to do with getting married?

"Wes,...I'm *pregnant.*"

Comprehension broke over him like a terracotta pot, and everything else fell away. The priest and the altar. The guests and the flowers. Even the chapel walls. Everything except Corinne and her worried frown.

But the frown didn't stand a chance. Wes let out a whoop that made the priest jump back, and he grabbed Corinne and kissed her with everything he had.

She was pregnant. They were going to have a baby. He, Wes Clarkson, was going to be a daddy!

Happiness now resided in the number three, and he had to keep himself from spinning her around.

Wes didn't stop kissing her until Corinne gently pushed him off after Father Duane cleared his throat.

"We haven't gotten to that part, yet, Wesley," Father Duane intoned, clearly startled by the outburst.

Guests laughed nervously, and behind Corinne, Wes saw Heather and Morgan's bug-eyed confusion.

WTF? They both seemed to be asking.

He looked back down at Corinne, who arched a brow at him. She was fighting a smile, but gone was that haunted look that had turned him inside out. If she'd been worried about how he would take the news—and, knowing Corinne, that had been the issue—she didn't have to worry anymore.

"Sorry, Padre," Wes said, without taking his eyes off her. "First things first. Make it official."

Because that's all it was. A formality to mark the fact that the woman who stood beside him was his family. His future.

His love, first and last.

Acknowledgments

As with *Fall Semester*, I have to begin by thanking my wonderful husband John and our amazing daughter Hannah. Their support for my writing and pride in my accomplishments make me feel continually blessed, and I am so grateful that John is still willing to read and edit every chapter I write. Hannah also deserves some credit on this book for helping me through a few passages and inspiring Corinne's profession and her taste in music.

I'd like to thank Shelly Leblanc for her English goddess assistance with the first few chapters, and I owe the triathletes in my family, Candace Fournet, Amy Leblanc (two-time Ironman) and David Leblanc (three-time Ironman) for making sure that Wes's experience was true to life. Thanks to Byron Daigle for educating me on the wonders of the sweet potato and to Rachel Ledoux for talking paint with me.

I am so grateful to everyone who supported my Kickstarter campaign to publish *Fall Semester* in print, but I give special thanks to Annette Broussard, Ann Kergan, Chad Case, and Heather Lamarche. The unique experience of creating characters for them turned out to be a much greater boon than I expected. I cannot imagine *Legacy* without these characters, and they have become so precious to me. While Betsie Roush has her own name, as my Aunt Netsie wished, the Roush home with its Secret Garden is a warm, welcoming, and very real place. Of course, Ann Kergan had to be someone with style and business savvy, and someone so very helpful to Corinne. Chad Case, true to form, has some of the funniest lines in the novel, and Heather Lamarche—in fiction and in truth—is, and always will be, the dearest of friends.

I'd also like to thank my fans on Facebook, Goodreads, and Amazon.com for their encouraging praise and eager anticipation for my second book. I truly hope you are not disappointed.

Finally, thank you to all of my friends and family who have been so supportive and enthusiastic as I continue to follow this dream. Your words of praise have helped me to remember that it really is worth doing what I love to do—even when the going gets tough.

About the Author

Stephanie Fournet lives in Lafayette, Louisiana—not far from the Saint Streets where her novels are set. She shares her home with her husband John and her daughter Hannah, their needy dogs Gladys and Mabel, and an immortal blue finch named Baby Blue. When she isn't writing romance novels, she is usually helping students get into college, teaching AP English, or running. She loves hearing from fans, so you can follow her on Facebook, message her on Goodreads, or email her at stephaniefournet@icloud.com.

Made in the USA
Charleston, SC
15 October 2016